A WOMAN OF NOBLE WIT

A WOMAN OF
NOBLE WIT

To Sue

Best Wishes

Rosemary

ROSEMARY GRIGGS

Matador
9 Priory Business Park,
Wistow Road, Kibworth Beauchamp,
Leicestershire. LE8 0RX
Tel: 0116 279 2299
Email: books@troubador.co.uk
Web: www.troubador.co.uk/matador
Twitter: @matadorbooks

ISBN 978 1 8004 6459 9

British Library Cataloguing in Publication Data.
A catalogue record for this book is available from the British Library.

Cover artwork by Daphne Patterson

Printed and bound by CPI Group (UK) Ltd, Croydon, CR0 4YY
Typeset in 11pt Minion Pro by Troubador Publishing Ltd, Leicester, UK

Matador is an imprint of Troubador Publishing Ltd

For David

PART ONE
THE MAID

ONE

1527

KATHERINE

"GOD'S BLOOD!" THE GIRL YELLED AS SHE SLAMMED INTO THE wall. He'd done it again; got there first! Only a few seconds ahead of her, but he'd already scrambled up to his favourite lookout point. She leaned against the wall, shoulders heaving, breath coming in jagged gasps. "God's blood, Johnny, I'll beat you one day!" she shrieked, glaring at the unyielding stones as a mocking chuckle drifted down to her.

She stamped her feet in the dirt and beat her fists against her sides, fingers rolled into tight balls of fury. She'd never be able to climb that wall! "Fie upon these accursed skirts. Must they always keep my feet planted so firmly on the ground?" she screamed. "Ooh, ooh, ooh, all right, Johnny! So you think you've got the better of me, do you? We'll see!" Without deigning to look up, she spun on one heel and stalked back down the path between the apple trees. *Swish, swish, swish* went the offending skirts.

But her anger was short-lived. She slowed down, recovered her breath and let her heart calm its furious beating. By the time she reached the gate into the walled garden she was smiling. Everything looked fresh and new, shining in the sunshine. The sweet Devon air held a faint scent of newly cut grass; the gardeners' first cut to clear the path. She stooped to examine the soft spears of chives growing in thick clumps at the edge of the herb bed; fat buds almost ready to burst. A blackbird was reprising his morning music while a wood pigeon kept time. *Ru-hoo, ru, ru, hoo,* he called. *Ru-hoo, ru, ru, hoo.*

She straightened up and brushed the dust from her gown. So be it. Let him enjoy his moment of triumph. Even had she not been hemmed in by her skirts, Johnny would always be two years older than she was. He would always beat her. He was a boy. She was a girl. It was the way of things.

Katherine Champernowne picked up the book she had cast aside when her brother had challenged her to yet another race and skipped back along the path. She flopped down under the spreading branches of an apple tree – the perfect spot; close enough to catch Johnny's words if he decided to share what he could see. Lying back on the springy new grass, she watched the bees busy amongst the pink-tinged blossom.

Her gaze drifted up and she lost herself in the clear, unending sky. *Such a special shade of purest blue – even brighter than Eliza's eyes,* she thought, stifling a pang of envy. A lark rose and she closed her eyes to listen to its fluting song. Surely its little heart must be bursting with the sheer joy of this spring day! At last the long, cold months cooped up inside were over. She could enjoy the warmth of the sun on her face again. If Agnes caught her she'd chide her to have a care for her fine complexion. But Katherine didn't care. Winter was banished at last. Johnny was at home. Best of all, tomorrow they would go to the fair.

She raised her head and squinted into the sun. There he was, up in his eyrie, silhouetted against the sky on top of the wall that used to separate their home from the old Benedictine priory beyond. The French monks had left long before Katherine was born; before the world went mad and the Houses of York and Lancaster fought for the Crown of England. Her brow puckered as she struggled to remember what her father had told her. Ah, yes; he'd said that lots of orchards had gone to ruin after the people who'd survived the great sickness long ago had forgotten how to care for them. It was those French monks who had saved Modbury's apple trees. But she couldn't remember which King had sent the monks away and bestowed the priory lands upon his new school. It was probably one of the Henrys. There had been a lot of them. She did know that the school was many miles away. She could even remember its name: Eton College. Oh, Father would be so pleased with her! He was a stickler for that sort of thing.

Excited voices, laughter, and snatches of song drifted over the wall; an insistent, infectious buzz growing louder by the minute. The people of Modbury were preparing for the annual fair when everyone made merry for St George.

"That's another one, Katherine-Kate," Johnny yelled. "If they take many more holly bushes into the town there'll be none left to deck our hall at Christmastide. It'll be like a forest down there: a holly bush hung outside each house and everyone selling ale at their door. There's another! Oh, Katherine-Kate, you should see them all struggling along under their prickly burdens!" During the fair, anyone could sell liquor without paying any duties if they hung a holly bush by their door.

Katherine watched as Johnny started his descent, and saw him miss his footing and drop the last few feet in an unseemly tumble. She grinned as he landed with a thump and brushed his feet carelessly on a clump of primroses that had found purchase in the dappled shade at the wall's foot. *One of our prettiest flowers*, she thought. Perhaps she'd pick a bunch for her mother before it was time to go inside.

"Looks like tomorrow will be quite a day!" Johnny said, sauntering across the grass to sit beside her.

"Oh, Johnny, I can't wait to see the town decked out with all the banners and flowers," she babbled. "Last year there were stalls all the way up to the church." This would be only the second time in her young life that she'd be allowed to go to the fair. It was simply *the* most exciting time of the year; better even than the twelve days of the Christmas feast. "Do you remember the gingerbread fairings, Johnny?" Her mouth watered, and she licked her lips. "I haven't had the like since Christmas. That cook Father brought back from court made the best feast ever, didn't he?" Her grin grew wider as she remembered the cloying taste of sugared comfits, sticky almonds, pastries flavoured with exotic spices, and marchpane fancies. "Oh, I'm so excited! Tomorrow we'll go to the fair! What fun it'll be!

Mother's sure to give me a few coins to spend. Do you think we'll be allowed to watch the puppet shows and the fire-eaters?"

"Oh yes – at least, I'm sure *I* will, being so much older than you," Johnny chortled with a wicked grin. He must have seen her face fall, for he added, more kindly, "I expect Mother will let you watch the glove-and-flower ceremony to open the fair. There's going to be tumblers and plays and wrestling and music and dancing. Will says that this year there's even going to be bear-baiting. I do so want to see that!"

Will Slade, and his father before him, and his before him, had served the family at the Court House for as long as anyone could remember.

"Well, I hope we *won't* be allowed to see the bear being tormented by all those dogs," cried Katherine. She shuddered and turned to face her brother. "I do hate to see animals treated so."

"That's because you're just a girl, Katherine-Kate," said Johnny, with the unknowing cruelty of a ten-year-old. "Bear-baiting is a man's sport. What can a girl know of such things?"

Katherine sighed. Perhaps he was right. Perhaps she was just a silly, soft-hearted little girl. Kat, their eldest sister, said that the fine gentlemen and even the ladies of the court loved to see such spectacles. She said they placed wagers on which dog would live the longest. But it seemed so cruel. "Well, I think animals should be looked after, Johnny, not teased and tormented. Don't you remember how we visited Dick the shepherd in his hut when it was cold and the grass was all crisp and crunchy under our feet with the frost? Remember how he got that lamb to suck on a linen cloth soaked in milk to get some nourishment into its shrivelled little belly?" Dick had carried the orphaned lamb down from the pasture under his thick cloak, next to his skin. Katherine smiled, remembering how she had crouched beside the hay-lined box near the brazier and marvelled at the lamb's wrinkled skin, several sizes too big for the newborn creature, with its floppy ears and knobbly knees. "*That's* the way to tend beasts, Johnny. I hate to think of that bear shackled to a post or locked in a cage so small it can't even turn its hairy body. It'll be carried around from place to place to be mocked and abused. It'll be set upon by fierce dogs. They'll poke sticks at it! They'll put hot irons to its feet to make it dance!" Her voice had risen to a plaintive shriek and she felt her face go hot. She pursed her lips, drew her brows together and shook her head. "I just don't understand how good men and women can enjoy such a thing, and all for sport or a wager." She closed the book on her lap with a loud snap. The more she read, the more she learned of the world, and the more questions seemed to come to her mind.

"That's just girl's talk; I'm glad I'm a boy," Johnny chuckled. "I'll go a-soldiering as soon as I can. I'll be a knight and serve the King. But you, little sister, I expect you'll just have to stay at home and marry some horrible old man."

"Oh, no! Father would never wed me to an old man. He loves me too much for that," Katherine said with a shudder. "Father's so kind, and he's always giving me new books to read. Do you think he'll have time to read with us today?"

Philip Champernowne sometimes sat beside the fire and read with his children if they had done well with their studies. But lately, since his name had been added to the Sheriff Roll, there hadn't been so many of those cosy fireside reading sessions. Still, he was home today for the fair, so Katherine had high hopes.

"Oh, I do hope he will. Perhaps he'll read from that new one he got from the printer in London; the one with the funny name. Now, what's he called? Blinking at Words, or something like that?" Johnny quipped, collapsing into a quivering heap.

"You mean Wynkyn de Worde," Katherine laughed. "Oh, yes! I hope he'll read from that one. I just love all those stories about King Arthur's court." Her thoughts started to drift away to knights and their ladies adventuring in unknown lands. Then she gave herself a shake and looked down at the book in her lap. Father said that *Aesop's Fables*, translated from the French into English, had been one of the first books to come from Mr Caxton's press. She ran her fingers over the binding, traced the gold-embossed letters, and breathed in the musky leather scent as she turned the precious pages as though they were snowflakes that might melt in her hand. "I do so love the pictures in this one. Especially the fox reaching up as high as he can, but he still can't reach the grapes."

"Oh, yes, I remember that one!" Johnny said. "Sour grapes, indeed! Yes, Katherine-Kate, Father is very keen on learning, and I must say I've more relish for it than Cousin Peter." Johnny was always talking about Peter Carew. "Book learning's all right, but I'd rather be out practising with my sword and riding to the hunt with Father and all the gentlemen. But you, Katherine-Kate," he teased, "must stitch and sew, and play on the lute and the virginals. You must learn from Mother how to manage the household, and all those boring things, so that you can marry some fool with a long white beard."

"Well, that just shows how little you know about anything, clever, clever Johnny! You're supposed to study the classics and rhetoric, and improve your Latin. Ha, ha! Old Smythe, says you're falling behind in that," she retorted, her stomach starting to churn at the thought of an aged husband. "Anyway, you've got it all wrong. Father says that girls should have an education, just like boys. He told me so. So there!" She spat those last words through gritted teeth, as if to expel the very idea of being shackled to some terrifying greybeard. Johnny's taunts had hit home once again. Father saw to it that all his daughters had much more chance to learn than many. She'd heard him boast about meeting the famous scholar Erasmus at the London home of his friend William Blount. If Erasmus was persuaded that women should be well educated, said Father, then that was good enough for him. But deep down, Katherine knew that he would choose a husband for her.

Johnny's next words only reinforced her dread. "Ha, ha! Father might have said that, but we all know that it's the first duty of a well-born girl to learn things that will help her make a good marriage."

Katherine's shoulders slumped. She might be only a child, but she knew her duty all too well. "Well, that doesn't mean I'll have to marry an old man, now, does it?" she insisted. "I wish you'd stop teasing me about it, Johnny. The very thought of it makes my skin crawl. What if I have to marry someone who's hugely fat, like Ralph the carter, with his great wobbling belly and foul-smelling breath? What if I'm to wed someone as stick-thin as Master Rowe the lawyer, with his shiny bald pate and his blotchy skin all stretched over his ugly skull? How could I bear it? It just isn't fair!" Her chin trembled and her throat hurt as she fought to hold back the tears. She could feel them welling up behind her eyes, about to spill down her cheeks. She didn't want Johnny to see her cry.

"What pictures you do paint of your awful suitors!" Johnny giggled. "But cheer up, Katherine-Kate. Perhaps Father will get you a place at court like our sisters and a fine young lord will woo you and wed you. Do you really think our Joan the Elder is going to marry that ass Robert Gamage?"

"He's got a draughty old castle somewhere in Wales, and his sister Margaret serves the Queen with Joan. So I suppose it will be a good match for our family," said Katherine, relieved to be talking about something else. "Lucky Joanie's going to take her place. Do you suppose the Queen will think it strange that she's swapped one maid of honour named Joan Champernowne for another with the same name?"

"I don't suppose so," said Johnny. "It's not that unusual for two girls in the same family to have the same name, is it? After all, you and Kat were baptised with the same name too." Kat was a shadowy, intimidating presence in their lives, held up as a veritable paragon of learning and virtue. "No one would ever get you two mixed up, Kat being so very clever; much cleverer than you!" he continued with an evil grin.

Katherine leaned over and made a grab for him, but he was too quick for her. She smoothed her gown and threw back her shoulders. "You know very well that Kat was named for the Queen because she was born ever so long ago, just after the Queen arrived from Spain to marry Prince Arthur. And you know just as well that I was named for our fine and noble kinswoman Katherine Plantagenet Courtenay. The one who lives at Tiverton," she announced, raising her chin and looking him in the eye.

As soon as she was old enough to say it, Katherine had insisted that everyone use her full name. "I am Katherine, like the Princess at Tiverton, not Katie, Kateryn or Kitty," she would say to all who would listen, stamping her little feet. And so the family had added the diminutive 'Kate' just to tease her, and she had become Katherine-Kate.

Katherine thought that her wealthy relatives, the Courtenays, were probably the most powerful family in all of Devon. She was proud that a Princess was her godmother and had sent gifts when she was baptised. She kept the pretty coral necklace and teething rattle, carefully wrapped, in a carved box in the maidens' chamber. One day she might even go to Tiverton to serve the Princess.

"Our Joanie's joined the household of Henry Courtenay, the Marquess of Exeter, at his fine house in London," Johnny remarked. Henry Courtenay was the son of the grand lady of Tiverton. "It's called the Manor of the Rose."

"Oh, what a romantic name!" cried Katherine. "It sounds like it's come straight from a story. It must be very grand indeed. Father says the King's made Henry Courtenay into Controller of Windsor Castle as well as Marquess of Exeter. I suppose that means he's very important, doesn't it?"

"I suppose it does. The house is at somewhere called St Lawrence Pountney, wherever that may be," said Johnny, sounding rather proud that he'd remembered the name. "Father said it was the home of the Duke of Buckingham until he lost his head." He pulled his hand sharply across his throat and made a face, mimicking the headsman's axe. "Henry Courtenay had better make sure that he doesn't suffer the same fate one day," he added with a ghoulish grin.

"But surely he and Aunt Gertrude are big favourites of King Henry's? And the King would never harm his own cousin!" Katherine interjected, shaking her head.

"I'm not so sure about that," Johnny answered. "The Duke of Buckingham was a relative too."

"It must be so exciting to go to court," said Katherine, drifting off into another daydream.

King Henry's court; the most magnificent, the most glorious in all Christendom. How she longed to see the tournaments, the masques and the plays. She imagined herself watching the joust with some shining knight carrying her favour, and felt a lump come to her throat. Father had selected Joanie for the honour of a place at court. Joanie was truly the beauty of the family and, deep in her heart, Katherine was rather jealous. She couldn't help but notice that there was something about the tilt of Joanie's chin, something in the way she raised her eyes under those exceptionally long lashes, something about the smile that played on her lips, that set Joanie's beauty on another level altogether. Joanie seemed to have everything. She was not only beautiful, but so clever too.

"Joanie's sure to have all the gallants falling in love with her every day," she muttered, poking her chin forward and pouting. Joanie was so lucky! Katherine's shoulders slumped. The truth of it was that no one was suggesting that *she* might go to court or to Tiverton or anywhere else, and Johnny kept teasing her about that old man she'd have to marry. Perhaps he knew something. "Eliza will be the next to wed," she declared. "She wants nothing more than to be fawned on by some fine gentleman. Then I suppose it'll be my turn."

"Eliza's been promised to William Cole for years. Poor old William! He'll need to give her a generous dress allowance!" Johnny chirruped.

"You're right about that. Eliza's always pestering Mother for news of the latest fashions from court." Katherine was more interested in playing with the mannequin dolls that the London tailors sent to Mother to demonstrate fine fabrics and outlandish new styles. She now had two of them, as well as a rather battered Bartholomew baby Father had brought home from the fair in London. She played with her little family as often as she could, whispering secrets to them when she was tucked up at night in the bed she shared with Eliza.

"Well, I've heard enough about marrying for one day," Johnny laughed. "I'm off to find Will." He sprang to his feet and ran off down the path towards the knot garden. Speeding up, he weaved between the lavender hedges and nearly collided with a strapping, tow-haired youth.

Katherine watched them set off towards the stables. Will spent hours with Johnny every day, teaching him how to handle a sword, practising archery at the butts and tilting at the quintain. Everyone knew that King Henry loved the joust and was reckoned to be the best and most fearless of knights. Perhaps when he was older her brother might catch the King's eye. How Katherine wished she could just once try holding a lance and aiming at the target! Her brave little pony, Dapple, wouldn't flinch. She was sure she could do it. But of course, that was not for girls.

Even as the boys disappeared she saw Agnes's short, stout figure waddling up the path. The laces of Will's mother's stained woollen kirtle were straining to keep it closed over her ample bosom. *Surely she gets fatter every day*, thought Katherine with a chuckle. *Why, she must be as wide as she is high!*

"Mistress Katherine-Kate, I be sent to find you. You're to come in now, for 'tis high time you were at your stitching if you're to practise on your lute as well afore dark."

Katherine closed her eyes and let her breath out slowly. Johnny and Will would be out in the sun while she must go inside and sit meekly with the ladies. She would far rather have stayed under the apple blossom with her book. "May I pick some flowers for Mother before I come in?" she asked.

"Yes, but make haste, for your mother wishes you to improve your needlework," the old nurse replied.

She stood by while Katherine picked a handful of pretty blooms, examining each carefully to see which had thrum eyes and which had pin eyes. Agnes had shown her the difference long ago. The flat tops in the centre of some flowers looked just like the dress pins Katherine's mother used to keep the placard in place at the front of her gown. The fuzzy thrums in others looked for all the world like the untidy knots of thread that were left at the loom when the cloth was finished.

"That's enough of your dilly-dallying, young Mistress," Agnes scolded, her dark eyes brimming with mirth. "Come away in, my flower."

As Katherine followed Agnes through the screens passage, Father was crossing the great hall followed by a group of men. The Court Leet had been meeting to make sure that everything was ready for the reading of the town's statutes that would open the fair. The Portreeve, elected from amongst the townspeople every year, held sway over it all, but it was the custom to seek the blessing of the High Lord of Modbury. The Portreeve, puffing as he clutched a long black gown across his rather large belly, held his cap deferentially in his hand as he scuttled after Father.

"May this year's fair prove both profitable and merry for all!" Father declared, clapping the portly little man on the back.

The Portreeve bowed low, drew himself up, threw back his shoulders and swaggered off with the others. Turning towards Katherine, Father rolled his eyes upwards and winked.

She ambled across the hall and climbed the winding stair with dragging feet. In the solar she found Mother examining a pair of completed cuffs. Her face lit with pleasure when Katherine offered her the fragile lemony-yellow blooms.

"Look, Eliza," she said. "These would make a fine design for you to embroider. You've done well with these cuffs. Tomorrow Agnes can find you a piece of fine holland and help you mark it out."

Eliza's face glowed, and she glanced at Katherine to make sure she'd heard Mother's praise.

Katherine shrugged and took her place on the cushions beside six-year-old Frances, whose forehead wrinkled as she concentrated hard on her own simple task. When Katherine looked more closely she saw traces of tears around her swollen, red eyes. "Never mind, Frances," she soothed. "I promise I'll tell you and Arthur all about the fair. Next year you'll be able to go yourself."

Katherine picked up her work-basket without enthusiasm and chose a black silk thread. She started to pick out the pattern, but try as she might she could never get the stitches straight. Soon her mind was wandering, until a hasty thrust of the needle pricked her finger and brought a drop of blood to stain the cloth. She felt her cheeks burning as she saw Mother's lips twitch. But no reprimand came.

"Patience, my child," said Mother. "Tomorrow you may go to the fair. You and Eliza can help me choose yarns and silks for our needlework."

"Will you buy some fine kersey to give to the servants at New Year, Mother?" Katherine asked, glancing at Agnes in her faded, madder-dyed kirtle. Mother nodded, and Agnes's face crinkled up like a year-old apple.

"I have news," Mother announced. "Later today we expect Uncle William to join us."

"Will Cousin Cecily be with him?" asked Eliza, all smiles. "It'll be such fun to talk about the latest fashions with her."

But her face fell when Mother replied, "No, Eliza, Uncle William comes alone this time. Aunt Joan is ill and Cecily and Grandmother Carew must stay at Mohun's Ottery to care for her. Now, girls, look to your stitching. Your father is in need of new shirts, and we must have them all embroidered in the latest blackwork to set him off well when he goes abroad."

In companionable silence, they set to work on the intricate patterns made so fashionable by Queen Catherine.

It was already getting dimpsy when Uncle William blew in, like a gale howling through a forest, scattering a trail of debris in his wake. He flung himself from his horse, dumped his saddlebags in an untidy heap on the flagstones, barked a curt order and threw the reins to the stable boy. His boots sounded loud on the steps as he strode up to the door.

Johnny was the first to greet him, eager for news of his cousin. "Uncle William, is there any news of Peter?" he demanded, without even giving his uncle time to wipe his feet.

Katherine shrank back into the shadows.

Uncle William didn't look at all pleased to be greeted in so peremptory a fashion. "No, young sir," he bellowed, and cuffed Johnny hard about the ears. "I have no news at all of that errant vagabond. I do live in hope that he will return to us more of a gentleman than when he left. It seems to me that you would benefit from some training in gentlemanly behaviour yourself."

Katherine had been about to come forward to greet him, but held back when she heard his angry voice.

"My father awaits you within, sir," said Johnny, looking worried.

"There's no hurry. I'll take a mug of ale first, if you please," William growled. He crossed the hall and sat down heavily on one of the benches, threw his cap onto the floor behind him and glared at Johnny. "Fetch my bag, boy. I need something warm on my feet in this great barn of a place. I can feel the draught already."

Johnny hesitated, starting first towards the kitchens and then turning to head for the door to retrieve the bag. Bessie, Agnes's niece, solved his dilemma by appearing with a flagon. Tentatively, she approached Uncle William and offered him the pewter cup with hands trembling so much it was lucky none was spilt. The white-faced serving girl then made to withdraw, but Uncle William threw back the first mug in no time and beckoned her for a refill. You could see why Bessie was so afraid. Sprawled across the bench, William

Carew was a terrifying sight; a huge bear of a man, with his bristling beard and unkempt hair. The beaming, benevolent uncle Katherine remembered had been replaced by an impatient, beetle-browed stranger. Uncle William ran his fingers through his mop of grizzled hair and took another long draught of ale.

Father must have heard the commotion. He hailed his brother-in-law with a cheery greeting. "Stay seated and rest awhile, William. It's good to see you here at last."

Uncle William scowled, drained the cup and called for another. "Whatever's wrong with boys these days, Philip?" he grumbled.

Johnny – who, having retrieved the bags, was trying to help William off with his boots – blushed and rummaged frantically in the pack, searching for the necessary footwear. Parchments spilled across the rush-strewn floor.

"Young people," William growled. "No manners; good for nothing, the whole pack of 'em! Thomas was no better: all that fuss and bother when he ran off with the Courtenay girl when we were living over at Bickleigh. Worse still, the girl was in my care!" He sighed, and took another quaff of ale. "Ah, that's better – you always brew good ale at Modbury."

"Your brother redeemed himself with his exploits for the King in Scotland," Father offered.

Uncle William drummed his fingers on the board beside his cup and gave Father a hard stare. "Must all the Carew boys inherit a taste for reckless deeds, do you think?" he exploded. "Must they all set off a-soldiering? Perhaps if my father, good old Sir Edmund, hadn't been quite so hot to serve his King in France we might all be in better case. I'm sorry, but I find it hard to think of my father with the deference and kindness a dutiful son should bear the man who sired him. All those debts he racked up to finance his warlike ways hang round my neck like a noose."

"Now then, William, you're tired," said Father soothingly. "I'm sure you'll feel better after a good night's rest. Can we get you some food?"

But Uncle William seemed to be in no mood for eating. He drained another cup. "Look at my boys, Philip – what do you see?" he asked, giving no time for a reply. "My second boy; named him for you. Gone off to fight the Turk. Last heard of in Malta. No one knows if he be alive or dead." He shook his head from side to side before continuing. "Then there's George! At least there was some hope that my eldest would buckle down and do the right thing. After all, he's had his duty drummed into him ever since he was born. But oh, no! He must set off on that mad escapade of his; sailing from Dartmouth in what you can only think was dubious company, without the King's permission. Ha! George thought to make a big noise of himself in France! Thanks be the King's pardoned him, though the servant who went with him's still held in Calais. I'm sure you know we're still paying for his keep. It's costing a fortune." He wiped his mouth on his sleeve and cocked his head to one side. "It's to be hoped that George has learned his lesson. It'll fall to him to carry our branch of the Carews forward when I go to meet my Maker. And that'll be sooner than it should be, with all this on my shoulders!"

Father tried to interrupt, but the ale was having its effect. Uncle William was not going to be diverted.

"And now here's another one: my sister's boy, getting so excited about that miscreant, Peter. Like to follow him on that illusory path to empty dreams of glory, eh?" He studied Johnny's bent head as though he thought he would find devil's horns under the thick brown curls.

"Well, of course Johnny's always idolised the boy," said Father. "It's only natural. There's but four years between them, William."

Johnny's relief was written all over his face.

"Peter. That disgraceful brat! Might as well throw my coin down the midden as pay to send that one to school. Always going missing from his studies in Exeter and roaming about the streets. It was the last straw that day they called me from my hearth to sort him out. Had to come all the way from Mohun's Ottery. There was Peter, sat up there on the city wall, cocky as could be, chest puffed out like a peacock. Refused to budge!"

Johnny's head shot up when a bitter laugh burst from Uncle William, who at last had his feet properly shod.

"Remember how I tied the young devil like a dog on a line and made him run beside my horse through the city streets?" he barked. "Made him run all the way back home. Eh, eh?"

Katherine could see that Johnny was struggling to keep a straight face.

"Harrumph!" Uncle William exclaimed, pulling his fingers through his hair once more. "What are you staring at, boy? What do you think you're sniggering at?"

Johnny blushed again and studied the floor. He didn't dare meet Father's eye, and hovered uncertainly, waiting for some sign that Uncle William was ready to dismiss him.

It didn't seem so. William drained the pewter cup again. "Ha! You went to school in Exeter with Peter for a time, didn't you, boy?" he roared, prodding a finger in Johnny's direction. "Lodged in that same house with Master Hunt? Hunt's a decent fellow but he couldn't deal with Peter. Nothing for it but to take that jackanapes up to London. Thought I'd send him to St Paul's School; Colet's got a fine name for schooling. I thought, *If he can't instil some love of learning in my good-for-nothing son, no one can.* But Colet did no better. Told me to my face that Peter was more interested in liberty than learning. Said to me..." – Katherine had to suppress a giggle when he put on a funny, high-pitched, wheedling voice – "said to me, 'In no wise can I frame this Peter to even look at a book, or to like any schooling.' What do you think of that?"

By now Father had given up trying to stop the flow of complaints.

"Well, at least Colet came straight out with it," moaned William. "Good thing I met that chap strolling by St Paul's. Took Peter to France with him as his page; said some training at the glittering French court would at last make a gentleman of the young tearaway. Harrumph!" He paused. "Goodness only knows what he's up to now. Joan's worried about him, of course."

Uncle William took another long look at Johnny. "This boy looks healthy enough to me, Philip. My sister made too much fuss when he took that chill after I took Peter away. I suppose she thought some sickness was raging through Exeter. Brought him home, and here he is still." He drained the cup yet again and hauled himself to his feet. "Look to it, boy. Help me up the stair," he demanded. "I've got much to discuss with your father."

Katherine watched as he staggered off, supported on one side by Johnny and on the other by Father. She was shocked to see her uncle so changed. *Perhaps a few days' rest will bring him ease*, she thought, as she crept from her hiding place.

But rest would not come soon for Uncle William. Katherine could still hear the faint but insistent hum of his voice when she was tucked up beside Eliza in the maiden's chamber. She wondered vaguely what he and her father could be talking about, but soon she was dreaming of the fair.

TWO
1527
KATHERINE

KATHERINE SLIPPED FROM THE BED AND, HEEDLESS OF THE CHILL nipping at her bare feet, rushed to the narrow window, screwed up her eyes and knelt to offer up a prayer. "Please don't let the sky be dark. Don't let there be any clouds at all," she murmured.

When at last she dared peep out she couldn't suppress a cry of joy, which provoked a grumpy protest from Eliza. The soft rose-gold early morning light had barely kissed the stones below her lookout. But there was not a single cloud in the brightening sky. The sun would shine on the fair!

Katherine splashed water on her face and hands, left her shift on the bed for the laundress to take, and put on a clean one of finest linen. She rummaged in the coffer at the foot of the bed, breathing in the aroma of lavender and rosemary that wafted from the folded clothes, and selected her best kirtle and the red gown passed on from Joanie last year. "Agnes? Agnes? Are you there?" she whispered, running her hands over the soft fabric. Best not provoke her sleepy sister any further.

Agnes's truckle bed lay just beyond the door to their chamber, and soon she came stumbling in, yawning and bleary-eyed. "God's greetings on this fair morning, Mistress Katherine-Kate," she murmured sleepily.

Katherine was hopping from foot to foot with her arms full of clothes.

"Ah, so you wish to don your finery for the fair today, sweeting?"

"Oh yes, Agnes, this is my very favourite gown for such a day as this. Do you think we'll be allowed to see the Portreeve set things going?"

"Mayhap you will," said Agnes, smiling as she tightened Katherine's laces, then pinned on her new sleeves: Mother's New Year gift. This was the first time she'd worn them and, bubbling with excitement, Katherine turned her hands about, this way and that, to set the long points dancing.

"There now," said Agnes as she placed a linen coif over the dark plaits coiled around her charge's head. "There will be none more lovely than you at the fair today. But first you must look to your prayers, young Mistress. Then you may break your fast."

Nothing could disturb the morning routine. Wash, dress and pray. Then – only for the children – a light breakfast. After that they usually went to their lessons with Master Smythe until the family met at midday for their main meal. But there would be no lessons today. A wide grin spread across Katherine's face till it reached nearly from one ear to the other. She started to dance around the room, giddy with excitement, until Agnes put on her stern face and signalled to her to be still. Heart still beating fast, Katherine knelt by the bed and began a rather hasty recitation of the Lord's Prayer, prompting more anguished groans from the bed. Eliza had turned fourteen and she was never at her best in the mornings.

Johnny was waiting outside with a grin that matched Katherine's own. Eliza appeared, trying studiously to appear unconcerned. Katherine bounced up and down on her toes and waved her arms, wondering what was taking her parents so long. They emerged at last and Father took off his feather-trimmed cap and ruffled his slightly thinning hair before offering his arm to Mother. His short gown fell open at the front to reveal a rich velvet doublet slashed in the latest style. He frowned as he turned to Uncle William, who had tidied himself up considerably since the previous evening, though he still had a face as long as a fiddle.

"Well, William, this doublet cost a pretty penny when I ordered it from the tailor in London. Money I can ill afford. But what can I do? King Henry wants to be known as the best-dressed monarch in Europe, and a magnificent ruler must have resplendent courtiers. I value my place, so I must keep up appearances as befits my rank. More's the pity I'm not one of the lucky ones who get all their clothes provided from the Great Wardrobe. It's all a heavy burden on my purse. Not to mention dressing the girls too. Then there's Joan's dowry to find."

Uncle William studied the cobblestones without answering.

Father turned to Mother, who was waiting beside him in a black silk gown that showed off her still-trim figure to perfection. "I see you're wearing the necklace I gave you last year. It becomes you well and matches the sparkle in your eyes."

Katherine tittered when she heard Father's loving tone, but Mother seemed to like it, and smiled up at him.

"Is that a new headdress?" he continued. "I rather like it. It shows off your lovely auburn hair. It still glints like gold in the sun, for all that we've been together all these happy years."

Katherine caught Johnny's eye. Behind Father's back, he screwed up his face in a grimace and pretended to retch. Parents were such an embarrassment sometimes.

Mother's new headdress, in the latest style from France, was certainly a flattering fashion; much nicer than those heavy gable hoods. Eliza said it was King Henry's sister Mary, the one who had been married to the King of France, who'd brought that style to England when she returned with her new husband, Charles Brandon. But Katherine had heard Agnes whispering to the other maids that there was another woman at court who loved to wear the French hood; someone they called Nan Bullen. She'd heard them muttering that it was she who set the fashion these days, even more than the Queen. Whenever Katherine tried to listen to their talk they clammed up immediately, so there must be something odd or shocking about this Nan Bullen. Something she wasn't supposed to know.

Six tall serving men wearing the Champernowne livery – bright red tunics emblazoned with the cross of blue vair on white – escorted them down the hill and into the town. Katherine found she was stepping in time with the music as it grew louder and louder as they neared the market cross. The Portreeve heaved his well-padded frame into position, almost tripping over his old-fashioned gown in his struggle to climb up onto the platform. The crowds were thick but, standing on tiptoe, Katherine could see the leather glove held aloft. The Portreeve wiped the sweat from his brow and started to recite the town's ancient charter, and the crowd fell silent as his voice rang out clear and strong. A girl came forward with a garland of spring flowers to place around the glove, and a cheer went up as it was hoisted high above the Portreeve's head and fixed in place. It would stay there, proclaiming that everyone had the right of free trade within the town, until the fair started to wind down and all the stalls were cleared away in nine days' time.

After the proclamation there was some scrambling for position before they climbed back up the hill to the church. The heady, resinous scent of incense hung like a trail in the open doorway, beckoning them in. Once inside, it took a few moments for Katherine's eyes to adjust to the cool, musty gloom. She stared at the tomb with its carved effigy of a knight in armour with a collar of roses. *That must be Great-Grandfather William*, she thought. She was sure he was the one who had supported the white rose of York alongside an uncle. A Bonville uncle, perhaps? Well, whoever he was, he'd perished after the Battle of Somewhere. Oh dear! Father wouldn't be pleased that she'd forgotten her family history, but it all seemed so very long ago.

"I hope this won't take long," Johnny whispered. "I don't want to miss a minute."

Released at last, blinking in the sunlight, they ran back into town to enjoy the fair. Katherine turned her head this way and that. Stalls groaned under the weight of all manner of cloth and trimmings, tools and implements, all laid out alongside a confusion of eggs, cheese, butter, and loaves of fresh crusty bread. Sweetmeats, toys, purses, singing birds, and puppies all jostled for her attention. Her ears rang with the alarming, maddening noise of it all; a deafening clamour of laughter, shouts, songs, fiddles, drums and rattles. With Agnes at her side, she pushed her way through the throng and soon saw a booth piled high with pies and gingerbread fairings. That was where she'd spend her penny. But nearby was another with a display of wooden toys. She wanted to find something for Arthur; perhaps a cup and ball, or a carved animal. She was trying to decide between a little horse and an ugly-looking lion with horrible, ragged teeth when she saw the very thing. A wooden sword, just like a real one. Oh, how his face would light up at that! Arthur already thought himself a fine soldier.

"Do I have enough for this, Agnes?" she asked, taking some coins from the leather pouch that hung from her girdle. "Oh, please can I buy it for Arthur?"

"Yes, of course you can, sweeting. 'Tis a kindly thought, and that young blade will love to march to war with such a fine sword. You're a good girl to think of your brother before you buy for yourself," said Agnes, casting a disapproving glance at Eliza, who already had her hands full of coloured silks for her latest fancy project. "I'll make sure you have enough coin, young Mistress Katherine-Kate." The corners of Agnes's eyes creased as she returned the coins to the pouch, surreptitiously adding a few more she'd had concealed in her sleeve.

Katherine bought the toy sword, a bunch of pretty ribbons, and a line of peg dolls for Frances, and still had enough left over for a gingerbread fairing. It was her favourite treat: a dainty morsel of breadcrumbs soaked in honey mixed with precious ginger. She popped it into her mouth and the sharp, aromatic spice set her tongue a-tingling.

A group of musicians struck up a tune and young men brought out their partners for an early dance. Katherine would have loved to join in, but it wouldn't be seemly for the daughter of the Lord of Modbury to cavort in the streets like a peasant girl, so she contented herself with tapping her foot in time with the beat of the drum. Across the street a tall youth approached a pretty girl with a garland of flowers in her hair. He offered her a nosegay of spring blooms and they seemed frozen for a moment, gazing into each other's eyes, lost in wonder. With a smile, the girl accepted the flowers, took his arm, and they strolled off together to enjoy the fair. Katherine would, in that moment, have traded all the advantages of her birth for the freedom of that young couple with their joy in each other. She'd happily have given up all the Christmas sweetmeats, her lovely Dapple, even her beloved books, to be free to choose her own sweetheart. She remembered Johnny's hurtful teasing about the old man she would be required to wed, and tapped her foot again, this time in annoyance. It was all right for Johnny. He'd already gone off with Will in search of the bear-baiting.

She wandered down to the bottom of the steep street, searching for her brother in the crowd. Near the cattle pens, the stench of all the animals, combined with another distinctly unpleasant smell of unwashed bodies, was overpowering. She didn't really want to find the bear anyway. Agnes, shuffling along a few steps behind, looked relieved when Katherine turned back to join the crowd watching the puppet show. Eliza was already there, laughing and glancing towards a group of finely-dressed young men across the street. Amongst them Katherine recognised some of their neighbours, the Fortescues and Hills, and one of the Prideaux boys from Orcheton. Eliza was making eyes at one of the Fortescue lads, while William Cole of Cornwood stood shyly behind the others. Johnny had said that he was the one intended for Eliza, but the boy was trying to hide as if he were afraid of his own shadow. *Oh dear*, thought Katherine, *what a silly girl my sister is.* She turned her attention back to the show, laughing as the whale appeared, ready to swallow up poor Jonah.

Much later, as she made her way home, she caught sight of the young couple amongst the dancers, whirling around, so radiantly happy together, for all that, by his dress, the young man was no more than a shepherd. Katherine felt another sharp stab of envy.

A deafening noise, wailing, and a fearful crashing and banging greeted her in the hall. She bounded up the winding stair and found Arthur in the nursery with his cheeks on fire, stamping his feet and shouting at the top of his voice.

"Don't want to pray! I want to go to the fair!" he yelled as Agnes caught up with Katherine, panting and holding her sides.

The nursemaid tried to calm her noisy charge, but Arthur was having none of it. With his plump little belly sticking out and his lower lip looking like a fat caterpillar, he continued to stomp and shout.

"What's to do, young sir?" asked Katherine, putting on her most grown-up voice. "I thought the whole house was under attack! I'm come to give thanks that Father left so fine a knight as you to protect us all."

Arthur looked up at her questioningly, and the noise came down a notch.

"Ah, but I know what a fine knight needs. Now, close your eyes, hold out your hands, and see what I've found for you at the fair."

Arthur, quiet at last, obediently screwed up his eyes and held out his arms to receive the toy sword.

"Open your eyes now, dearest," said Katherine, and Arthur did.

The brightest of smiles creased his round, rosy face. Frances peeped out from behind the arras, where Arthur's noise had driven her.

"And I didn't forget you, Frances. Now it's your turn." Katherine offered the gifts, which the six-year-old turned over and over in her hands.

Agnes shook her head and sighed. "'Twas well done, young Mistress Katherine-Kate," she said, turning away to hide a tear. "You always have such a way with the little ones."

"Now, Sir Knight and Fair Damsel," Katherine called to the two children, "let us pray together in thanks for the magnificent victories you will surely see, Arthur, and the fine knights who will come a-courting you, Frances. And then 'twill be time for your beds."

Without a murmur, Arthur joined the girls in prayer. Later, Katherine looked in on her way to bed, and there was Arthur, curled up in his cot, with the little wooden sword hugged tightly to his chest.

Uncle William and Father had been closeted together while the fair ran its merry course in the town. Father usually talked to Katherine and Johnny about the books they were reading, or rode out with them down towards the river or along the ridgeway track. His fine voice often rang through the house as he went about his business. But now he had no time for them, and there was no singing. Mother's face was set and strained, her lips pursed tight as if she were keeping some bleak secret. All the joy of the morning when the fair had opened seemed long spent.

Every day, when their lessons were done, Katherine crept away with Johnny to their favourite spot in the orchard, where he tried to cheer her up with his jests and silly tales. Johnny loved to play tricks on people, like when he'd put a spider in Agnes's cot and sent her shrieking through the house in her shift. His cheeky grin let him get away with it every time. Even their tutor, the rather dour Master Smythe, had at times been known to hide a smile. Johnny's latest jape had been to hide away the ribbons Eliza had bought at the fair. She'd made such a din and bother about it, as if those silly ribbons meant more to her than life itself. When Johnny had emerged from the stable with them trailing from the headpiece of old Dobbin's bridle, how Eliza had screamed at him! But now all his jokes fell flat.

On the last day of the fair, after the midday meal, with a face as dark and dismal as a wet Sunday, Mother said, "Now, children, Father asks that we join him and Uncle William."

Katherine shot an inquiring look at Johnny, but he just shrugged his shoulders. To be called together like this was beyond unusual.

"Well, now, my dear children," said Mother. "Listen well, for Father has much to tell us."

And so it all came out. How Grandfather Carew had borrowed so much money when he was serving the King's father. How, when young King Henry was set to fight the French, Sir Edmund had borrowed even more. Although it had all happened years before she was born, Katherine had heard that story many times. She felt rather cheated. Surely Father hadn't called them in for this conflab on a lovely sunny afternoon just to tell them that old story again? She could recite it herself. Sir Edmund Carew had served the young King. He'd been in charge of all the ordnance for the army in France in the year 1513. The King's councillors met in Lord Herbert's tent during a long siege at a place called Thérouanne. A stray cannonball flew from the town, and Grandfather Carew was killed outright and buried far from home. Katherine had heard it all before. With an effort, she drew her thoughts back into the parlour and tried to concentrate on what Mother was saying.

"Your father stood surety with Uncle William for some of the loans my father took out before he left for France. They've worked so hard to sort it out; even the money owed to the King himself. But some debts are still outstanding. Many of the Carew manors have been sold off. My dears, more creditors are pressing for payment."

Father gave a slight nod of his head, and took up the tale. "I have to keep up appearances. The King expects nothing less. So, once again I've had to borrow from Henry Courtenay." He kept shifting in his seat and fiddling with his sleeves. He glanced at William, but no flicker of sympathy crossed that stony face. "Perhaps I shouldn't have paid that cook to come down at Christmas, but that added only a little."

Mother fingered the jewelled necklace at her throat.

"It was just one small extravagance. But now, my dear children, I must tell you that we've run through much of your Grandfather Champernowne's wealth. Our coffers are running very low," said Father.

Next he confirmed what Katherine and Johnny had suspected. Joan the Elder was to marry Robert Gamage of Coity, and that would mean more expense. "We'll have to put on a splendid wedding since Joan's served in the Queen's chambers. And there's the dowry to be found," moaned Father. "And, on top of that, our singers and musicians have been playing for the King at Windsor, and I've had to pay for their livery and the upkeep of all their instruments. I can tell you, lute strings don't come cheap. Then there's lodging at court and food at the King's table. And I've not had so much as a single silver penny from the King."

Katherine remembered interrupting hastily stifled gossip in the kitchens. Anne Boleyn, the one they called Nan Bullen, liked the Champernowne musicians' playing very well. She supposed that meant that King Henry was loath to let them go.

"I expected the King to repay me for the loan of my players," Father grumbled. "Now he's said I can bring them home soon, but I've still had no allowance for their keep. When I was last at court I talked to William Blount, I talked to Henry Courtenay – I even talked to Thomas Cromwell. You've heard of him? Kat says he's an up-and-coming man. He serves the Cardinal. But none of them had any advice to offer. They all know the vagaries of the King's mind. There's nothing I can do but wait." He glanced again at Uncle William, who seemed to find the back of his hand rather fascinating. "I'm at my wits' end with this matter of the musicians. It's added another heavy weight to all those debts." Father rocked in his seat and bit his lip.

To Katherine's surprise, he then launched into a diatribe so unlike him that she became quite frightened. "I've served the King for many years. I worked my way up to secure a place as Squire of the Body. I suppose you could say I've been well rewarded. He did at least make me keeper of the park at Curry Mallet. Lately he's been asking me to be much more active nearer to home. He relies on people like me and William to keep the peace and collect his taxes in far-flung parts of his kingdom. Well, being appointed one of the Devon collectors for the Lay Subsidy might have been an honour. But being a tax collector hasn't always made me very popular with our landowning neighbours. And now I'm forever up in Exeter. Oh, I'm proud to have been pricked for Sheriff of the County. But it does add to my costs, and I've got everyone plaguing me. Now, here's your Uncle William with another tale of woe: creditors pressing hard for their dues and nothing left to settle." He gave them a bleak stare and scratched his head. Katherine had never seen him so distressed.

"But, Father," Johnny said, "if you're Sheriff and don't have to attend the King so often, you won't need to spend so much on keeping your clothes up to date, will you?"

"Harrumph! Well, that might be true, my boy. But I'm afraid it won't be enough to ease our money worries," Father replied, shaking his head vigorously.

All the time, Uncle William sat silent as the tomb.

Katherine had been flattered at first to be included in the family council. It was a sure sign that her parents thought that she was no longer a child. But all this talk of money and debts was really boring. She didn't like to see Father so upset, and wished she was under the apple tree with a book. She studied the dust motes dancing in the afternoon sun streaming in through the parlour window. Her gaze followed the sunbeams' slanting path to the floor, where the mullioned windows were casting a chessboard of shadows on the stones. Her thoughts drifted away to an imaginary place far across the ocean where the sun always shone and the trees grew gold coins as big as apples. Suddenly, her head came up. What was that Father had just said? He could no longer afford to keep Aston Rohant?

"I will speak to Henry Courtenay to see if he'll take it against some of my debts," Father was saying.

Aston Rohant was where Katherine's parents had lived when they were first married. In Oxfordshire, convenient for the court, it had been Grandfather John Champernowne's favourite of his many manors. Katherine had only been there once, but she still held treasured memories of that magical visit. Sometimes, when she woke from a dream, the dark corners of her chamber would turn into strange and frightening beasts, and she'd call out in terror for Agnes. Her beloved nurse would sit on her bed, take her hand and say, "There is nothing here for you to fear. Now, young Mistress, take out your memory box and find a happy time. Think only of that, and you'll soon be sleeping soundly again." The memory of that golden autumn visit to Aston Rohant had often been the one she had selected to soothe her back to sleep.

Shifting on the hard bench, she closed her eyes. She could almost see the majestic old house, with its turrets and towers, furnished far more lavishly than their home at Modbury, with candles, not just rushlights, twinkling in every room. She remembered running through the gardens with the tall trees towering up to the sky above; running towards the sound of laughter as Father and Johnny struggled with the oars of a boat they'd taken out onto the lake just for the fun of it. There were two lakes, not just one, with lots and lots of pretty little ducks and swans swimming on them. Too many for her to count. She remembered how Mother had caught her hand and pulled her back from the water's edge. She remembered watching the ripples moving over the shimmering colours reflected in the lake's surface. Those autumn days had been a gilded time of long, lazy days spent with the people she loved best. She couldn't believe it. Surely Father couldn't really have said that they must give it all up: the house, the gardens, and those beautiful lakes?

But it was true.

"It's a hard decision, but your uncle has made me see that there's no other way," Father said.

Katherine stared at him as he wriggled in his seat and studied his fingernails.

"But, Father, I just can't believe it," Johnny interrupted. "Aston Rohant's been in the family for such a long time. I remember what you taught us: that it's more than a hundred years since one of our ancestors married that heiress, Eleanor de Rohant. Grandfather John died at Aston Rohant. You really can't—"

Uncle William cut him off mid-sentence. "Quiet, you insolent pup. I don't know why your father thought he had to go to the trouble of telling you children like this. The decision's made and there's no more to be said. Selling Aston Rohant might go some way towards clearing some of those loans we took out to stand over your Grandfather Carew's spendthrift ways. It'll help with the cost of keeping the musicians at court. It might even cover your father's tailor bills." He shot an unforgiving look at Father, who was slumped in his chair.

Katherine's tears wouldn't wait any longer; rivers of grief for that lovely lost time of her childhood. She didn't really hear what Uncle William said next – something about someone called John Gilbert and the Carew lands on the River Dart. That couldn't concern her. But she pricked up her ears when he spoke again.

"It's time for this boy to make his way in the world," he said, looking pointedly at Johnny. "I'll take him to London; find a place for him at court or in some other noble house. In the unlikely event that he finds favour, who knows, it may ease our burdens in time. First he can go to St Paul's School to sharpen up his learning. The master still holds fees I paid for Peter. As you know, that boy didn't last long there. I expect Colet will take this one in his stead." Turning to Mother, Uncle William continued. "The boy's in good health now, and it's high time you ceased your mollycoddling. He's far surpassed what Smythe can teach him. He must move on and up in the world. I'll take him up to London in three days' time."

Katherine's heart fell to her shoes and suddenly she felt numb all over. She'd got so used to having Johnny there: sharing her studies, riding together, playing bowls on the green at the top of the gardens, sitting under the apple trees, talking and dreaming. Sometimes his teasing hurt her more than he knew, but she forgave him in light of all the other, fun-filled times. She'd be lost without him, with only simpering Eliza for company. It was too much. A heavy sob burst out and her shoulders shook.

But there was Mother, calm as a millpond, telling her that it was a woman's lot in life to bear such things well and patiently. "Now then, Katherine," she said. "It is the way of families like ours to send our young people off to some other noble house. I'm sure Johnny will do well and bring honour to our name." She pushed back her shoulders and raised her chin. "It's high time you and Eliza learnt how we women must remain calm and patient and, with a smiling face, accept that our menfolk know what will bring the best fortune for us all."

Katherine's chin trembled again but, catching her mother's eye, she raised her own head and bit back the tears. She was a Champernowne. She must never forget the long line of those who had gone before her; as far back, as Richard called King of the Romans. Johnny would go off to seek his fortune. Little Arthur would do the same one day. She and Eliza, and even Frances in the nursery, must all play their part to secure the family fortune through marriages arranged for them. It was the way of things.

Katherine stood on the mounting block, fiddling with her gloves, impatient for Will to lead Dapple alongside. She swung her leg across the grey mare's back. No side-saddle for her. She wanted to ride like the wind. "Oh, hurry up, Johnny," she called. "Let's make the most of this last day."

At last he too was in the saddle. They skirted the church, walking the horses in the earthy shade of a massive yew tree, and went on down the lane and over the bridge. Beside the Aylestone Brook the buttercup-bright meadow stretched invitingly before them, sparkling in the spring sunshine as though some unseen hand had sprinkled yellow stardust over the lush grass. Johnny pressed his mount to a reluctant canter and they were off. Dapple soon caught up with Johnny's lumbering bay and matched him stride for stride. Katherine surrendered to the sheer exhilaration of the race beside the babbling brook. The rushing wind stung her cheeks and snatched tendrils of hair from beneath her hood as she pressed Dapple on. For those few minutes, all her sorrows were blotted out.

After Uncle William announced that he was snatching Johnny away, time had seemed to slow down, each moment a long agony of despair. Agnes had asked Katherine what ailed her.

"Oh, I'm just tired, Agnes," she'd replied. "All is well." But all was most certainly not well. Johnny was leaving, but she must remain, weighed down by her skirts just as surely as if the hem were filled with stones.

Up on Dapple for those few moments, she felt alive again. Her little pony edged ahead of Johnny's stocky mount. Whooping with triumph, she reached the fence well ahead of him. "Who's the loser this time, then, Johnny?" she crowed, as his sweating horse came alongside.

"Well ridden, Katherine-Kate. Dapple showed us a clean set of hooves that time," he laughed, gathering up the reins. "Let's see how far we can get before we need to turn for home."

They waited for Will to catch up on his sturdy cob and then walked the horses through a closely planted orchard, then woods of ash and holly with a scattering of tall elm trees. The sun filtered through the leafy canopy to reveal a sea of nodding bluebells that stretched as far as Katherine could see. The birds were singing, a clump of cowslips lit up a sunny spot by the riverbank, and, far away, a cuckoo was trying his voice. Usually that springtime song would have brought a smile to her face, but not on this day. The countryside had put on its best to greet them, but to Katherine, it might have been pitch-dark midwinter; the trees bare, the riverbanks devoid of flowers, and the joyous birds silent. The elation of the chase had faded and she felt the black veil of her sadness creeping over her again.

She glanced at Johnny. His wide grin and sparkling eyes showed how excited he was. He couldn't hide it from her. She wished he'd find something to say. Even one of his silly jokes would do.

"You will write, Johnny, won't you, and tell me all about the court and all the fine ladies you meet?" she said, turning to look full into his face.

"Nay, sister; I'll tell only of jousts and cockfights and bear-baitings," he replied, with just a hint of his usual humour.

"But I want to hear about the plays and the masques, and the King's music, and the Queen and all her ladies," said Katherine.

"Nay again, but I'll tell all about Nan Bullen," Johnny replied with a mischievous wink.

"Pray do, brother," said she, "for I really don't understand why everyone's talking about her."

"I'm sure to find out when I get there, though Father says I must keep well away from gossip." Perhaps he did understand how she felt, for, with an edge of real concern in his voice, he went on, "You'll be all right, Katherine-Kate. When King Henry takes a shine to me I'll send for you and the King will find you a fine husband."

They were both silent as they continued their ride past Oldaport, stopping for a desultory look at how the building work there was progressing. All too soon it was time to turn for home. Their last day together was done.

The next morning, Katherine stood dry-eyed with her chin held high as she watched him ride away. None should see that she had cried herself to sleep last night. Johnny turned in his saddle and waved as he and Will followed Uncle William. Then they were gone.

THREE
1527–1528
KATHERINE

THE WEATHER TURNED COLD AND WET, AS IF JOHNNY HAD TAKEN the sun with him. Each dull, dim, dismal afternoon, Katherine picked at her lute, though its strings seemed to have lost all power to soothe the rage growing inside her. To be left behind with the womenfolk while Johnny was gone to London where everything was so exciting! It wasn't fair! She ground her teeth. She fumed. She slammed doors. She snapped at Agnes. She sat, tense and rigid, at the hated sewing, stabbing the cloth with her needle until Mother made her undo the ragged stitches and work it all again.

After a week, Mother spoke. "I know well the cause of all this simmering anger, Katherine. It simply will not do. It is ungrateful of you, a girl who has so much, to be so jealous of your brother's chance to go out into the world. I miss him too, you know. I've already seen three of my girls leave home, and now Johnny. But, Katherine, our duty is to put on a brave face and accept our fate with good grace. We each have our part to play, and yours is to stay here and attend to your studies. You must accept it. I've seen quite enough of your silly behaviour, young lady. Now, go to the priest and make your confession."

Katherine groaned, muttered a grudging apology, and flounced off. Mother insisted that she speak with Mr Hunte, but he seemed at a loss to know what penance to set the belligerent girl who knelt before him. He muttered about the sins of anger and jealousy, about acceptance of God's will for her as the favoured daughter of such a noble lord, about true contrition coming through prayer. But Katherine shut out his words.

Suddenly, he thrust out his puny chest and raised his bushy eyebrows. "Mistress Katherine, God has shown me the way. Your penance is to master well the feminine art of needlework," he announced, and a self-satisfied smile spread across his beady countenance. "Each day you must apply yourself well to it and pray that God will help you learn humility. You must show your mother and God that you can do as well as your sister Eliza; indeed, as well as any other woman."

Now those last words were a master stroke. Katherine's head flew up and she looked hard at the priest. There was a challenge in this. She'd show them all. She wouldn't let Eliza best her.

Once she set her mind to the task she worked hard at it every day, concentrating to make her stitches small and regular. It blotted out the misery, and passed the time well enough. After a while she realised that she actually found those afternoons in the solar quite soothing now that she no longer resented time lost from adventures with Johnny. There came a day when Katherine felt a real surge of pride when Mother praised her neat work and set her to a more complicated pattern.

The rain continued as day followed gloomy day. No one could till the land, the crops seemed like to wash away, and everyone was sure that the harvest would be a poor one. One wet and stormy afternoon towards the end of August, Katherine heard the servants talking in the kitchen.

"'Tis that Nan Bullen that's to blame. Her and old Wolsey, that puffed-up Cardinal, with all his rich palaces," the cook declared as he brought down a flashing meat cleaver on a joint of beef. "It's God's punishment on them. That's what's brought us to this. It'll be the worst harvest in years. But it's us ordinary folks that'll bear the pain of it, not them!"

"Aye, that Nan Bullen! She's a wrong one, right enough. Leading our King astray all this time! He's taken up with her for sure," replied Adam the gardener, his sopping cloak dripping onto the flagstones. Adam didn't seem in a good temper. Katherine had seen him struggling to keep his feet as he gathered a few green apples; early victims of the strong winds roaring through the orchard like a rampant bull. As he faced the prospect that all his best efforts in Mistress Champernowne's gardens would this season come to nothing, it was no surprise that he wanted to blame someone. "We'll all suffer because our King wants a warm body in his bed."

"But what about Queen Catherine?" Agnes asked in shocked tones. "Oh, I do remember that lady when she first came to marry Prince Arthur. I saw her in Plymouth. Such a beautiful girl, she was, with that lovely hair."

"My mother told me how she stood at the roadside and waved to our Queen as she passed by," added the laundry maid. "What's to become of her now?"

"More to the point, what's to become of us with little enough to feed ourselves this winter?" snarled the cook.

His tone so frightened Katherine that she crept away before she was discovered. The Modbury servants were usually a jolly crew and she was shocked to hear them all so fired up with anger. She still didn't understand who exactly this Nan Bullen was or what she had to do with the King or the Queen, but one thing was clear: the servants didn't like her at all.

She still attended lessons with Master Smythe, kept on as secretary and scribe to her mother until Arthur started his studies. In their straitened circumstances, it was fortunate that Thomas Smythe valued his living in the Court House and expected little in the way of payment. He had gone up to Oxford, thinking to enter the Church or take up law; either must have seemed a sensible path for a bright young man, likely to open doors to advancement. But a riding accident had left him with a crooked leg and a pronounced limp. His ability to serve any master who needed him to travel was therefore limited. He seemed well pleased to continue his employment at Modbury.

When one day Smythe complimented her on her translation of

a tricky text, Katherine felt her confidence grow. As she let go of her anger, she returned to her beloved reading. Every spare minute of that dreary autumn would find her curled up in some nook with her nose in a book.

Only once did she have a short note from Johnny. It came wrapped up with his dutiful missive to Mother, but was addressed to Katherine alone. As promised, he wrote about cockfights and his fencing lessons. He said he was to attend St Paul's School until the year's end to improve his Latin. The books held his interest well. The other boys were good fellows. The hours were long and the food not enough. At Christmas he would go to Henry Courtenay's house. He was sure to be noticed at court. There was no news of Cousin Peter. Johnny hoped that Katherine did well enough, and remembered her in his prayers. That was all. It made her feel even more lonely.

Autumn winds explored every cranny and stripped all the leaves from the trees early. The rivers and streams ran high, brown and furious. Michaelmas came; the traditional time for cattle to be slaughtered. The terrified squeals of pigs being killed down in the town made Katherine shudder when she walked in the gardens. But stores must be filled against the coming winter, and it wasn't beneath Eliza or Katherine to join Mother in checking that enough pork was salted down and all was in order. Nothing must be wasted, or some might go hungry before the next spring. Fallen apples were collected up in baskets and taken to the cider press. Soon barrels were filling with the tart juice that would ferment to make a potent drink; a process handed down from the French monks.

Agnes looked on approvingly. She was very partial to a draught of cider. "Too much ale might take the head and senses," she advised, her apple cheeks glowing, "but too much of Devon's zider takes first the legs. There's many a man will stumble on his way home after filling his belly with our good apple zider."

All Hallowtide passed with the children of the town out and about singing rhymes for soul cakes. The days grew colder. Katherine could see her breath as she set out across the courtyard on frosty mornings. In the elm trees behind the church the rooks set up a dreadful din, their mournful cries echoing long into the darkening evenings. Of all the birds, Katherine hated most those black, ugly creatures with their long beaks and horrible, raucous calls. In the spring the village boys plundered young birds from their nests for the cooks to make rook pies. But in November, they were of no use to man nor beast. She wondered why God, in all his wisdom, had created them. She must, of course, confess that thought the next time she sat with the priest. Who was she to question the all-powerful God?

The musicians and singers returned from King Henry's court, all dressed in their splendid red gowns. Katherine felt her heart lift when their voices rang out in the chapel, or when they played from the gallery as the family sat at board. But even they seemed subdued, perhaps worn out after all that time at court. They seemed to play none but the most plaintive tunes.

On a still, cold afternoon in late November, Katherine tiptoed past Father's chamber on her way to the solar. He seemed bone-weary and she didn't want to disturb him. The women huddled over their sewing, trying to keep warm by the brazier. Then hooves clattering in the courtyard had the girls rushing to the window. They craned their necks to see who the rider might be, while Agnes, who had moved almost as quickly, stood at Eliza's shoulder, wheezing and gasping. *She must be hungry for news of Will*, thought Katherine.

But they were all disappointed. The messenger wore the livery of Katherine Plantagenet Courtenay, and there was a black band on his arm. So that was it. Princess Katherine, Countess of Devon, daughter, sister and aunt of Kings, had given up her grip on life. Father came down from his chamber and beckoned the messenger in.

"I am sent to summon you to Tiverton to join the ceremonies that will mark the passing of My Lady," he said, bowing low.

Father set off early the next morning, taking their best choristers with him. Three weeks later he was back. As soon as he had changed out of his muddy riding clothes he called them together. The whole family pressed close around him in the great hall; even Arthur and Frances. The children's eyes grew round to hear of the part he had played in the lavish funeral; surely the most splendid Devon had ever seen.

"On the second day of December," Father proclaimed, "the coffin, covered with a rich pall of cloth of gold, was carried from the castle to the Church of St Peter. Oh, you should have seen it; decorated with a silver tissue cross and coats of arms. It fell to me, your Uncle William, Sir Thomas Denys and Sir John Basset to support six tall yeoman, all of the same height, who carried the coffin. Like all the mourners, we wore black hoods and gowns. What a procession! I was right at the front of all the local dignitaries. My children, it was a great honour for our family to be placed so; to be at the head of such a noble company. Why, every gentleman in the county and some from far beyond turned out."

Katherine thought that he looked a new man, so proud to have been given such a prominent place in the proceedings.

"I've never seen such a gathering, at least not outside King Henry's court," he went on. "And then, dear children, such a meal as we had, back at the castle while the coffin remained at the church, attended all through that long night! Your Aunt Joan, Lady Carew, led the mourners at the Requiem Mass, and Cousin George carried one of the banners. Our own singers joined the choristers of Exeter and those from Montacute in the Mass."

Katherine smiled. She could see it meant a lot to him.

"I should think they received more than five hundred at the castle afterwards for another splendid meal. Many left with a sore head," Father remarked.

"Oh, how wonderful it must have been to see all the knights and gentlemen, and the ladies in their finest gowns!" Eliza burst out, as always focusing on clothes.

"Well, maid," said Father, "the gowns were certainly of the finest quality, and black's such an expensive colour. It must have cost a King's ransom to clothe all the attendants so." He pulled in a deep breath. "Now the noble lady is laid to rest, and poor people of the town will be paid tuppence apiece to pray for her soul every day."

She didn't want to spoil his moment, but Katherine thought she'd ask him later if all those prayers would really ease the passage of the Countess's soul through Purgatory. Perhaps she should remember her godmother in her own prayers, just in case.

"Was she a real Princess, Father?" lisped Frances.

"Oh yes indeed," said Father. "She was the youngest daughter of King Edward of the House of York. She was aunt to our King."

"To think that she was also related to us," said Katherine softly. She didn't want to break the spell. But then it dawned on her that now she would definitely not be going to Tiverton Castle to learn a lady's ways.

Later that day, Katherine heard her parents talking.

"'Tis all settled, my dear," Father said. "The Marquess will take Aston Rohant. I'm so sorry it's come to this. It was part of your jointure lands and I do hate to ask you to part with it. But it'll buy us a breathing space from our most pressing creditors. There remains the question of how to manage John Gilbert, and we must settle matters for Eliza's marriage soon."

Katherine did not catch all of her mother's reply.

Next she heard Father say, a little louder, "There was much talk at Tiverton of the King's Great Matter. Since he appeared before the Cardinal to confess his sin of living with Catherine as his wife, King Henry's even more convinced. He truly believes that his marriage was against Leviticus, which forbids a man to marry his brother's widow. Wolsey is pressing his case with the Pope, but no one knows how it'll come out."

"'Tis so very sad for the Queen, to call it sin," Mother replied. "Oh, Philip! Remember how we danced at her first wedding, when she came from Spain to marry Prince Arthur? She was such a lovely girl and we were all in wonder at her strange costumes and Spanish ways. What a time that was, with all London so gay to welcome our new Princess! Do you remember the tournaments, and the feasting, and the dancing? In those days you and I could trip and twirl a measure with the best of them, husband! Do you remember the King? Well, Prince Henry as he was then. He must have been only nine years old, about our Katherine's age. He cut such a figure in the dance with his sister Mary. Remember how he threw off his doublet and danced in his shirt?"

"Yes," said Father, laughing with her, "and his face was bright red, and everyone clapped and cheered him!"

"And do you remember how he went about dressed so fine all in white, bedecked with jewels? All eyes turned to him."

Katherine had heard about this many times over. How Grandfather John had rushed to Plymouth to welcome the Spanish

Princess when her ship unexpectedly came in there instead of at Southampton. How her parents had travelled from Aston Rohant to see him honoured with a knighthood at the tournament that marked that splendid wedding. Father always said that on that one occasion the old King, usually known for his miserly ways, had spared no expense to show off his magnificent court to the whole world. Katherine closed her eyes and tried to imagine it. The streets decorated with bunting and banners, the Tudor rose, the dragon and all those royal emblems displayed for all to see, and the fountains running with wine.

"How he enjoyed all the attention," Father laughed. "When he became King he couldn't wait to wed Catherine. It did seem a match made in Heaven in those early years. Remember the tourney after the birth of Prince Henry of Cornwall; that babe that lived but a few weeks? You know, the one your Aunt Elizabeth Poyntz nursed? Remember the King as Sir Loyal Heart? Now he'll put aside that kindly lady who is so loved by the people." Katherine could hear the sadness in her father's voice. "The King has changed. I suppose his love for Queen Catherine is worn away in the face of all those lost babies. They've but one girl to show for nigh on twenty years of marriage! We're well blessed to have such a bevy of daughters, and now two fine sons as well."

Her mother's muttered reply was too low to reach Katherine's ears, but she clearly heard her father say, "I think he fears his youth be spent. No heir to keep the House of Tudor on the throne of England. But we must have a care how we speak of this. The Lady grows in power. King Henry is a learned man and has studied the laws of the Church. He's persuaded that his marriage to Catherine was against those laws. It is not for us to wonder otherwise. Who knows who may overhear us?"

Katherine jumped back, confused and worried by what she had heard. It seemed strange that any man, even a King, could put aside his wife, and she didn't know who exactly the Lady might be. She crept away quietly and went to bed with a heavy heart. The ways of the world were strange.

Advent was always a dreary time of fasting, but at last Christmas Day arrived and the Court House came to life to celebrate the season. The servants carried holly boughs, ivy and all manner of greenery into the great hall, where the fire burned brightly. The cook excelled himself with a sumptuous feast. The singers lifted their voices. At New Year they exchanged gifts as usual. Katherine was pleased with her new kirtle and her warm cloak trimmed with rabbit fur. But the magic was gone. There were too many poignant reminders of last year, when Johnny had held them all in mirth on Twelfth Night as Prince of the Pea.

Biting cold continued through the long, dark days of January and February. Icicles dangled from the roofs and water froze in pails left for the horses in the stables. Agnes said there were places where the sea froze over.

March blew in. Father came and went about his business across Devon. The ladies sewed in the solar. Katherine studied with Smythe. She could read fluently in English and French, and even make a good try at Latin, though she struggled to master the art of writing. Johnny's one letter, written by that young man himself, bore testimony to his struggle in the many blots and crossings-out which decorated the page before his well-practised signature appeared at the bottom of the parchment sheet.

Day followed day, until, one April morning, everything changed.

FOUR

1528

KATHERINE

"As you know, you can't go to Tiverton to serve the Countess, as we hoped. But, Katherine, you are nine years old," Mother said. "It's time for you to learn more of how a lady must order her affairs."

"Am I to go to London and the court, then, Mother?" Katherine gasped.

"No, child," Mother replied. "It is all arranged. You will go to Uncle William's at Mohun's Ottery as companion to Grandmother Carew."

Katherine had little time to decide if she was disappointed, pleased or fearful. Only a few days later the whole household rose early to bid her farewell. Seeing them all there on the steps set her heart aflutter.

Eliza presented a sweet-bag she had embroidered, filled with dried lavender. "'Tis for your journey," she said with an exaggerated yawn. "Put it under your pillow to help you sleep at night."

Arthur, still in his nightshirt, and Frances, growing so fast her shift hardly covered her knees, stood shivering beside Agnes, who wrapped cloaks around their shoulders to ward off the morning chill. The laughter lines on Agnes's round face looked strangely misplaced on the sombre countenance she presented that morning, and a lump came to Katherine's throat as she tried to smile. She knew that Agnes would have loved to go with her favourite charge. But that task had fallen to her niece, Bessie.

"Cheer up, Agnes," called Katherine from Dapple's back, where she sat trying to keep the butterflies in her stomach from escaping. "'Tis not so very far, and I'll send word as often as I can. Arthur, I shall look for news of my brave soldier. Frances, you must go to the fair this year in my stead and find some treasure for this fine young man."

Father had business to conduct in Exeter later that week, and after leaving Katherine in her grandmother's care he was required to head for London to deliver a full account of his proceedings as Sheriff of the County. Mother stood beside his black gelding as he bent from the saddle to brush her hand with a farewell kiss.

Flanked by livery-clad servants, Father led the little cavalcade off into the brightening morning. Following Katherine came a white-faced Bessie, perched precariously behind a dark-haired serving man. More servants led packhorses carrying clothes and provisions for the journey. The cart bearing the coffer with Katherine's few possessions stowed safely inside brought up the rear. It would make its slow and laborious progress through the leafy Devon lanes in its own time.

Katherine turned for a last look at her home and her family waving from the steps. She swallowed hard and brushed away a tear as she raised a hand in what she hoped looked like a cheerful salute. Squaring her shoulders, she guided Dapple through the gate and down the steep hill into town. The pony was skittish at first and pretended to start as a cat crossed their path, but Katherine soon had her in hand. People bowed their heads, touched their caps or called greetings to Father, and a woman pressed a bunch of late-flowering Devon violets into Katherine's hand.

"To bring thee luck, Mistress," she called.

Katherine accepted the flowers with a smile, and tucked them carefully into the front of her gown beneath her cloak. It was a happy omen for the start of her new life. Everyone knew that violets warded off all manner of evil and brought good fortune.

They soon left Modbury and its townspeople behind. They joined the King's Highway, only a little wider than and just as muddy as the lanes, and met a steady stream of people. Men and women, old and young were making their way between the ports of Plymouth and Exeter, and the towns and villages that lay between them. Women weighed down by heavy baskets held their skirts hitched high above the mud, from which their wooden pattens gave scant protection. Men trudged along carrying bundles of firewood. Some struggled with heavy packs strapped to their backs or tied to long staves. Others had a yoke across their shoulders to balance the load. Twice they had to steer the horses past men driving cattle, chivvying the beasts along with loud calls and sticks when the animals paused to graze on patches of grass on the steep banks beside the track. Once, a cart loaded with sacks of grain blocked their way, its wheels sunk deep into the mud, and Father's servants lent their weight to free it. A priest in long, dark robes, seated on a moth-eaten donkey, raised his hand in blessing as they overtook him. Later they passed a chapman with a bulging pack. Katherine thought of how Eliza would have wanted to stop and see if he had any fine ribbons or silks for sale, and felt a twinge in her chest. She might even miss her sister, just a little.

A light wind soon chased away the showers, and fluffy white clouds scudded across the azure sky. They paused in a clearing on the edge of some woods to drink from flasks of small ale and eat bread and cheese, while the horses cropped the grass and drank their fill from the stream. In places branches touched overhead as they rode between steep banks, making Katherine feel like she was in a dimly lit green tunnel. She was so tired she found it hard to concentrate on Father's lesson when, late in the afternoon, they followed the narrow street down the hill into Ashburton.

"This town's growing fast," he explained. "It's become quite the centre for Dartmoor's tin mining. They weigh the tin, check it for quality, and the merchants haggle over prices. Then it goes to Totnes or Dartmouth to be traded far across the sea. Cloth's still big business here too, of course."

Signs painted with teasels hung over doorways, marking the cloth workers dwellings. They passed frames with cloth hanging out to dry on tenterhooks. Just as in Modbury, girls and women sat at spinning wheels in doorways.

They made for the inn in the centre of town; a three-storeyed building with a gaily painted mermaid sign high on the grey stone wall. Passing through an arch, they entered a cobbled courtyard surrounded by high galleries. Katherine's legs felt quite wobbly as boys rushed to take the horses and an ostler took their bags. They were greeted by a jovial innkeeper, and everyone who served them put on their best face in the hope of a tip from such a fine lord.

In the inn's finest room a girl in a dark kirtle served them pottage from a steaming cauldron. Katherine ate heartily of the simple fare and a welcome warmth spread slowly through her aching limbs. She sat by the fireside, feeling as limp as the linen the maids spread on the bushes to dry while Father finished eating. He didn't seem to notice that Katherine was near asleep in her seat. At last Bessie bustled in and hurried her into the adjoining room.

Father must have greeted the worthies of the town that night, but on the other side of the thin partition wall, Katherine was only dimly aware of the hum of their voices. She pushed Eliza's gift under the pillow and fell into a dreamless, lavender-scented sleep.

They set off early the next morning, skirting the high wasteland of Dartmoor as a light mist swirled in the cool air. She strained her eyes to see the dark and distant heights of the rugged moor. Strange outcrops of rocks, the Tors, brooded menacingly over the windswept slopes. When Katherine was younger, Agnes had told stories of those led to their deaths when they lost their way as the mists rolled down from those high tops. "Pixie-led, they were," she used to say. Katherine shuddered, and was glad that their route lay some way below the moor and was well marked.

Squally showers and a driving wind soon had her gloved hands feeling cold and numb on the reins, and her feet chilled to the bone, despite her thick woollen hose and leather overboots. Later the wind subsided and the sun glinted through the trees lining their route, casting patterns of dappled shade on the muddied path. After crossing the River Teign just outside Chudleigh they stopped to rest in a newly built inn named for Bishop Lacey, who Father said had held the See of Exeter years ago. Soon they were following the Exeter Road again through thick woodlands of oak and ash. They dismounted to ease the burden on the horses in the steepest parts as they climbed Haldon Hill. Near the top, Katherine grabbed Father's arm and her breath caught in her throat. The ground dropped away and a break in the trees revealed a breathtaking view.

"It's as if a whole world has opened up before my eyes! Is that the sea, Father?" she cried.

"Look, over there," he said, as his gloved hand traced an arc across the landscape. "See where the River Exe winds up from the coast. There – can you see the cathedral towers and the City of Exeter?"

"Is the whole city afire, Father?" she asked, screwing up her eyes to peer at the haze hanging over the distant roofs and steeples.

"No, child," he replied with a chuckle, "'tis but the smoke from all the chimneys. Now, make haste. Our destination is in sight."

The way down was steep and rough, so they walked their horses carefully until they reached better ground at the bottom, then remounted and spurred on. Katherine's legs were aching by the time they rode across the Exe Bridge. It was by far the longest ride she had ever undertaken. Only once before had she been any distance from home – when they all went to Aston Rohant – and then she'd slept most of the way, snuggled up to Agnes in the litter. Now she struggled to sit straight in the saddle as they made their way to the house of a wealthy merchant where they were to lodge that night.

She barely acknowledged Mistress Hurst's kind welcome, hauled her stiff limbs up the stairs, and was asleep as soon as she clambered into bed.

But Eliza's sweet-bag with its lavender perfume did not bring a good night's rest. She dreamt she was wandering the moors, being led from her path by strange little people as the thick, swirling mists closed in.

Still held in that frightening dream, she started up, pulse racing. Once fully awake, she realised that the echoing cacophony of noise was just bells – church bells, but oh, so many of them, all ringing out for Matins. Bessie had laid out her clean shift to warm by the fire. No wonder the city looked afire if every house in Exeter was built like this, with a fireplace in every room.

Father had already gone about his business. He knew the Hursts well and had been pleased to take up their offer of accommodation for Katherine rather than place her in the lodging house at one of the priories, or crave a room from his Courtenay relations. William Hurst's family came from Modbury and were wealthy merchants in the thriving city of Exeter. Father said that Master Hurst had been Mayor of the city a few years before, and was like to sit in the King's Parliament one day.

Mistress Hurst and her daughter, Joan, were waiting to show her something of the city.

"Why, you could fit our streets of Modbury many times over into this city!" Katherine declared. Everywhere she looked, new houses – two, three or even four storeys high – were being squeezed in. Her nostrils wrinkled as she sniffed the pungent, acrid smell of woodsmoke, hazy trails lingering in the street as if afraid they'd be caught up by the breeze and blown clean away. "Do all the houses have fireplaces in every room?"

Joan, who Katherine guessed was only a year or so older than she was, looked at her and giggled. "Lots do, just like ours. It's the new fashion. Everyone wants to be rid of the draughty old places that stood here before to build anew. And they all want to outdo their neighbours." She blushed prettily, and Katherine warmed to her new friend.

She thought she would rather not identify the other odours competing with the woodsmoke, and held the sprig of dried lavender Joan had pressed into her hand to her nose. Oh, how welcome was the smell of fresh bread as they passed a baker's! The hammers and the workers' calls vied with the street vendors seeking the attention of passing citizens; people called out greetings, dogs barked, and groaning carts bumped and rattled over the uneven street. It was a lot for a country girl to take in. Seeing Katherine's confusion, Joan took her hand and led her across the busy street in the wake of Mistress Hurst, who swept before them like a magnificent ship under full sail.

"Why, how many churches there are," Katherine murmured. There seemed to be one, built of red stone, on every corner.

"Yes, indeed," Joan replied. "The people of this city have many places where they may worship. Each is named for a different saint and has its own little parish. Further down there, behind St Olave's, you can see the Priory of St Nicholas. As well as churches, we also have monasteries, convents and priories to spare."

There were shops, taverns and market stalls all along the main street, which was covered with a layer of gravel so that everyone could walk freely. Turning back the way they had come, a narrow street led past another inn. Set amongst houses on the right, Katherine saw a sprawling church with a solid square tower.

"This is the Church of St Mary Major," said Joan. "It was here long before the cathedral was built. See the spire and weathervane atop that disturbed Princess Catherine's sleep?"

Katherine knew that tale well. While the Princess's party was resting in Exeter before going on to London, there had been a terrible storm. The creaking, groaning weathervane woke the Princess at the Dean's house and had to be taken down. Looking up at the high tower, more like a castle than a church, and the spire above it, Katherine wondered how the man sent out to remove the offending vane that night had managed to avoid being blown away himself.

The dark bulk of the cathedral rose up before them, towers stretching to the sky. She stopped on the threshold, took a deep breath, and stared. She took a faltering step forward, tipped her head back and gazed, unblinking, at the soaring columns and the vaulted ceiling with its gaily painted bosses. Goosebumps slid down her neck and along her arms as she slowly released her breath. It was like being in a stone forest, with branches entwining high above. Near dazzled by the light from so many windows, she was in a new world full of gaudy colour and light. She felt like a tiny, insignificant speck as the vast cathedral cast its spell over her, and sank to her knees on the cold stone floor.

Far away, near the altar, a minor priest was celebrating the Mass, while ordinary people milled around in the great space of the nave. Katherine could just see the priest raising the chalice aloft. She, like everyone else, accepted that he, with his vows of chastity setting him apart from other men, must take centre stage in the performance with the wine and the wafers. It was easy to believe that some miracle was taking place; something she could only watch and wonder at.

After the Mass ended, the obsequious priest recognised Mistress Hurst as someone of importance in the city, and oiled his way towards her. But before he reached his quarry, an elderly woman came limping up. Her back was so bent and crooked that Katherine towered over her. She was dressed in rags, and wisps of white hair straggled from beneath a soiled knitted cap pulled down over a wizened face. The old woman stretched out clawlike hands, mottled skin taut over grotesquely swollen joints. Katherine had often seen poor people in Modbury so afflicted. Mother said it was because of Devon's damp climate. The crone reached towards the priest, whose sumptuous robes strained across his generous belly. He brushed her hands away with no more attention than if he were swatting a fly, signalled to two men to carry her away, and turned his oleaginous smile on Mistress Hurst. Katherine's hostess dismissed him with a nod, before hurrying off to instruct her own serving man to find the woman and inquire as to how they might assist her. William Hurst was well known for his support of those less fortunate, and his wife had much more time for the old woman than for that puffed-up priest.

Katherine was appalled. If God had set priests so far apart in the miracle of the Mass, then surely he would also equip them with humility and a desire to care for others and lead them to God? She knew enough of the Scriptures to know that Jesus himself had always taken pains to help the poor and the hungry. She had thought it was a priest's place to do likewise. She was so troubled by the incident that she returned to the Hursts' house in silence, no longer noticing the vivid scenes of city life all around her.

After they had eaten she recovered herself sufficiently to enjoy the afternoon with Joan and her sister, Margaret, working at their needlework and swapping stories.

On the second day they worshipped at St Petrock's Church, as was the Hursts' usual habit. The girls then showed Katherine more of the city: the ancient city walls, the Guildhall where the important Aldermen met, and the wide River Exe she had crossed when coming into the city. She was astonished to learn that years earlier the ever-present Courtenay clan had put a weir into that mighty river so that ships could no longer bring their cargoes into the city, and instead had to disgorge them at Topsham.

"They collect tolls from any merchants who want to bring goods into the city," declared Margaret.

Katherine was surprised to hear the note of censure for her wealthy kin.

"My father doesn't think that's right at all," Margaret went on. "He thinks one day a new river can be made to bypass the weir and reinstate Exeter as a true port."

Katherine's mouth dropped open and she gave a loud snort of laughter. "Fie, Margaret, no man can change the course of a river made by God, nor yet build a new one! What a strange place this city is if you can make such jest of these things. You're just teasing me."

The Hurst girls exchanged amused glances.

The next morning, the girls embraced with promises to meet again one day, and soon Katherine, Father and their attendants were on their way. Bessie, hoisted up again behind the same serving man, seemed much more cheerful.

"That's old King Henry, though why he's clad in a Roman toga I don't know. But see, Katherine, how he holds a globe and sceptre?" said Father, pointing to a statue as they went through the East Gate. He clearly didn't want to miss any opportunity to broaden her education. "They restored the gate after the supporters of Perkin Warbeck attacked the city. You remember that, don't you? Both of your grandfathers were there, helping to defend Exeter. Well, the King was so pleased that he visited the city and presented Exeter with a hat and a sword."

"Yes, Father, I saw them on display at the Guildhall yesterday," Katherine replied wearily. He did go on so!

She kicked Dapple on, past the Church of St Sidwell, and soon they were in open countryside, heading for Clyst Honiton, the best crossing place in the low-lying morass of wetland that formed the broad valley of the River Clyst.

"That village over there was always called Clyst Champernowne, you know," said Father, waving his arm. "They call it Clyst St George now, because of the church. But everyone knows that our family held all the land here generations ago."

Katherine smiled. He was so proud of his ancestors, and never missed a chance to impress upon her just how splendid they all had been.

"So how did you like the city of Exeter, Katherine-Kate?" Father asked.

"Oh, Father, I was frightened at first by all the noise and bustle of the place; so different from home. But there is always something interesting going on," she babbled. "I think I might in time grow to like it." She thought for a moment and her brow furrowed. "But there are things I've heard and seen that confuse me much, dear Father." She told him about the incident at the cathedral, when the priest had turned away the old woman. "It did surprise me. Are we not taught that we should give alms to those in need? And surely the men of the church should be first to do so?"

"Indeed, daughter, there are many in this land would agree with you. A lot of people think that priests and such have grown too rich; especially those in the abbeys and monasteries. Some think they've forgotten the humility of their calling and prefer to live off the fat of the land. 'Tis best that you do not speak of these matters," he cautioned. He put on his severe face and took refuge in mild chastisement. "Look to your own deeds, rather than criticise those of others."

They went on in silence, through the market town of Honiton with its wide street, before branching north along narrow lanes. Near the tiny hamlet of Beacon, huddled at the foot of a long, low hill, they made another turn, and Katherine bit her lip as a shiver of apprehension passed through her. They were leaving the sparkling River Otter behind, and would soon reach Mohun's Ottery.

FIVE

1528

KATHERINE

THE EMPTY FEELING IN THE PIT OF HER STOMACH WAS BACK, AND her mouth felt dry. She was about to start a new and very different life, far away from Mother and Father and Agnes and everyone at home.

Nestling amongst meadows, Mohun's Ottery stood all by itself behind a battered wall. Beyond a dilapidated gatehouse was a substantial grey stone building with neither battlements nor towers, surrounded by a jumble of outbuildings. The whole rambling place sat within a large park scattered with spreading oak trees.

"That's Hartridge Hill over there," said Father, waving his arm vaguely, "and down there is the River Otter. See how the land rises up again on the other side? It's good hunting country. I'm looking forward to taking the greyhounds out before I'm on my way to London."

That was a relief. Father would be staying for a day or two to see her settled in.

She took a deep breath as they clattered under the arch. There was Uncle William, looking much less harried and angry. There was Aunt Joan, smiling, and Cousin Cecily, somehow grown into a young woman near seventeen. And there was Grandmother Carew.

After her husband died in France, Katherine Huddesfield Carew had worn nothing but severe black. With her white hair hidden under an old-fashioned gable hood, she stood poker-straight and forbidding. But when Katherine came closer it was as if a ray of sunshine lit up that stern countenance. There was the grandmother she loved, dimpled cheeks wreathed in smiles, blue eyes sparkling. Katherine's eyes flew straight to her grandmother's girdle. There it was, hanging by a gold chain entwined with a richly embroidered ribbon: the well-remembered book of hours that had so entranced her when last they were together.

"Ah yes, child," Grandmother Carew volunteered, nodding her head. "Yes, I have it still. We'll be sure to read from my book of hours every day."

Oh, the time they'd spent poring over that wonderful little book when the old lady had come to Modbury when Frances was born, and again when Arthur joined the nursery! Katherine would never forget those days with Grandmother Carew, who had told her stories about her sister: the one who had written an inscription on one of the pages; the one who had married Anthony Poyntz and nursed the short-lived Prince Arthur, the first of King Henry's ill-fated babes. The book had been started long ago for a Carew ancestor, and Grandmother said that ever so many monks had worked for hours and hours to decorate its pages with wonderful pictures. Katherine loved best the page with the elephant and the unicorn. As she climbed the steps, a warm feeling spread through her. Everything was going to be all right.

After a few days' hunting, Father left for London with Uncle William, but Katherine had little time to miss him or to feel homesick. Grandmother Carew took her role as teacher and mentor very seriously, and Katherine was soon swept up in a whirlwind of activity.

"If you are to supervise servants about their duties," said Grandmother Carew, "you must first do the work yourself. How else will you know if each task is rightly performed?"

So every morning Katherine laboured long in the malthouse, the brewhouse, the bakehouse, the still room, the dairy and the kitchens. Some of the work was familiar, but now she was required to put her own hand to kneading the dough, to picking the herbs and hanging them to dry, or to turning the churn and listening to the steady *slip-slop, slip-slap* as it went round and round, until that sudden, magical moment when the butter came. All of this Grandmother Carew deemed necessary for her to fully understand how a noble household worked. So Katherine rose early and spent the first few hours of each day at this learning.

There was not much time for the books carefully packed in her coffer. Father had slipped in a new volume, Geoffrey de la Tour's book of advice to his daughter, *The Book of the Knight of the Tower*. She was allowed to read from this worthy tome as the womenfolk were at their needlework in the afternoons. She vowed to try her hardest to live by its advice about the behaviour and demeanour required of a well-born girl. But she doubted that she would always be able to display such retiring manners and respectful obedience to her menfolk. Her wider reading had opened her mind to new ideas. She was still struggling to accept her lot in life.

Most days they spent a pleasant hour before bedtime when Katherine would practise on her lute and Grandmother Carew would question her gently about all she had learnt.

"Oh, Grandmother," she said one evening, setting the instrument aside, "I hadn't realised there was so much to learn. How will I ever remember it all?"

"You don't need to know it all at once, my dear." The old lady's blue eyes twinkled. It was easy to see how Eliza came by her bright eyes. "Your parents will arrange a match for you when you are quite young, and you'll likely live in your husband's household. But at first you won't have to take charge of everything. No, you silly goose. You'll grow into managing a household, just as you have mastered your precious books, or even your needlework. Now, you didn't always find that easy, did you? But you've worked hard and practised, and now your sewing is just as good as Cecily's."

"Um… er…" Katherine muttered with downcast eyes as she fiddled with the laces of her gown. "I suppose so. But, Grandmother, there is so much I don't understand. Mother often has to take Father's place when he's away. Aunt Joan does the same for Uncle William. They have to settle all sorts of disputes about land and rents and goodness knows what. I don't know anything about those things at all."

"You will in time. A marriage is a partnership, child," said Grandmother Carew with a knowing smile. "A good wife does have to stand in her husband's stead at times. But where there is trust and respect betwixt man and wife, it's a task easily accomplished. When the time comes, you'll know your husband's wishes and it will be easy to carry them out when he's away."

"Er… er…yes," Katherine murmured, still not convinced, "must I always be obedient to my husband? And what about love?"

"Ah, now, my dear, the Church does teach that a wife must obey her husband, but that shouldn't mean that you can have no will of your own. Rather that you will care for his interests as your own, and give your obedient duty and gentleness to serve his concerns in every way. You have the best of examples in your dear parents. Time will make it all seem as natural as could be. As to love, all I can tell you is that I came to love your grandfather as dearly as life itself, though I hardly knew him when first we were wed. Don't rush to answer all these questions too soon, Katherine-Kate. Give yourself time to learn and grow."

They usually worshipped in the chapel beside the mansion house, but on saints' days and special occasions they went to the Church of St Mary in the village of Luppitt. The first time Katherine stepped up to the door she was startled by two carved heads, a man and a woman, peering at her from the stonework.

"They're supposed to be our ancestors John Carew and his wife," Cecily explained as they stood in the doorway. "His tomb's inside."

"I don't like those heads much," confided Katherine. "The way they stare so, as if they want to see into my soul."

She was even more shocked by the strange carvings of men and improbable and terrifying beasts that wound around the ancient stone font. On one side a man was driving a huge nail right through the head of another, and on each corner a mask-like face seemed set in the throes of terrible agony. She shuddered, but couldn't take her eyes off the gruesome images. That font was supposed to welcome innocent babies into the family of God's Church. Surely it was not the place for the Devil's own work? Those carvings returned again and again to torment her dreams.

As well as visits to church, sometimes Katherine was allowed to take Dapple out for exercise. One May morning she rode out with Cecily to explore the woods and meadows surrounding the manor. Cecily was a rather timid rider, so Katherine slowed Dapple to an ambling walk. The accompanying serving man kept at a discreet distance as she turned to her cousin.

"Now, tell me true, Cecily. Are you afraid, now that you're betrothed? Mr Kirkham's been married before, and he already has children. Will he be forever comparing you with his first wife?"

"It's all part and parcel of a woman's lot, you know, Katherine," Cecily replied evenly. "I've only met Thomas once but he seems a fine man."

"At least he's not so very old. Oh, Cecily, I am so afraid that I will have to marry an old man," Katherine whimpered. "Johnny used to tease me about it all the time. Uncle William says he's doing ever so well and has a place as a page at the court. How lucky for him!"

Cecily raised her eyebrows, but said nothing. She pointed upwards and Katherine saw a heron, wings wider than a man's height, swept back in the shape of a huge 'M' as he carved a lazy arc across the sky.

"Ooh, just look at him!" Katherine cried, catching her breath. "He's making for his roost in that stand of oak trees. No doubt Uncle William's falconers would relish the challenge of bringing him down."

"Yes, I'm sure," Cecily replied. "Heron is a favourite dish at many a feast."

"Well, he looks magnificent. I hope they don't catch him," said Katherine, pulling a face.

"Trust you to think that. You're such a soft-hearted creature. Well, perhaps he will escape," laughed Cecily. "There's an even bigger heronry down towards Honiton."

They halted for a moment to enjoy the cool shade under the oaks, where the rich, damp, earthy scent brought back sharp memories of other rides with Johnny. Katherine pushed down the sinking feeling that threatened to overwhelm her whenever she thought of times past. It was such a fine morning, and the ride was a welcome break in her daily routine. Looking up through the leafy canopy, she said brightly, "Better not tarry here too long, Cecily. Look at those sprawling, untidy nests the herons have built up there. They're not good housekeepers, are they? Tangles of twigs and branches just heaped up together! They look as though the merest puff of wind might bring them crashing down onto our heads."

They turned back toward the willow-lined riverbank. The sparkling water was so clear Katherine could see speckled fish shimmering silver as they darted in the dappled sunlight.

"Brown trout. Good for eating," said Cecily. "Eels from the river also make their way to our table, Katherine-Kate. The cook has an excellent recipe for eel pie, with currants and dates and lots of cinnamon and ginger. You should have it noted down."

Again, Katherine pulled a face. She knew she must learn of all these things so that she could manage her household well, but today she just wanted to enjoy the ride.

They continued along the riverbank until they came upon a family of otters splashing and playing.

"Look, Cecily," Katherine whispered, as the otters dived and snaked under the water in search of fish. "See, they've made their home amongst the roots of that ash tree. They look so free and merry."

All too soon Cecily reminded her that they must turn back. Grandmother Carew would be looking for them.

As the month of May wore on, a change in the weather put a stop to the girls' pleasant excursions. The sun hid under dark, lowering clouds, and day after day heavy rain fell. The usually benign, lazy river rushed and tumbled, its clear waters turned to angry brown torrents. The ground became heavy and waterlogged, and the little brook nearby overflowed. Nonetheless, at the start of June, Grandmother Carew announced that she wished to go on a progress.

"I have a fancy to visit the church at Shillingford and see the new rector I have put forward for the living there. I want to see him properly installed," the old lady insisted. "And I would visit my father's grave, and see again the church where one day I will rest beside my parents."

Grandmother Carew would soon approach her seventieth year – a fair tally for a woman who had borne eight children and seen them grow – and her thoughts had lately seemed melancholy. Katherine often caught her staring out of the window with a sad face, and she talked a lot about Sir Edmund, buried far away. Unable to lie with her dear husband, she had decided she wished to be laid to rest at Shillingford.

"I would speak with George if he's at home. He's a good boy at heart." Grandmother Carew seemed very fond of Cousin George, and didn't appear to share Uncle William's exasperation at his youthful exploits.

"Oh, Grandmother, why, oh why must those boys all get into such trouble?" exclaimed Katherine, thinking of how Johnny idolised George's younger brother, the rascally Peter.

"It's their way, my dear," Grandmother replied mildly. "After Shillingford, we'll go on and visit your Uncle Thomas over at Bickleigh. It's long enough since I saw him."

Uncle William would certainly have forbidden the foolhardy journey, had he been at home. But nothing would gainsay Katherine's grandmother this trip. Neither Aunt Joan nor Cecily, who declared that they would remain at home, could persuade Grandmother Carew of the folly of her intention. Katherine was bound to accompany her. At more than twenty-seven miles, it would be a long and exhausting ride for an elderly lady and a young girl.

They left on the first day of June, wrapped in thick woollen cloaks, Katherine shivering on the ever-willing Dapple, her grandmother on a dark-legged pony with a coat that shone like a bright hazelnut. A smiling Bessie was up behind the same young serving man, and two more rode alongside to keep them safe from robbers and serve their needs on the journey.

At first they made reasonable progress through light drizzle that did not trouble them overmuch. But soon the rain pelted down, stinging Katherine's cheeks even though she pulled her hood close. As they passed to the north of the town of Ottery St Mary, glancing up at the sky again, she said, "Grandmother, would it not be wise to turn off and seek shelter until tomorrow?" But her grandmother's mind was made up. She would not turn aside.

The roads quickly became a quagmire, the horses' hooves slipped and slithered dangerously, and soon they were drenched to the very bone. Katherine asked how much further it was to their destination.

"Why, Shillingford be more than fifteen miles further, Mistress. And how we shall fare on the low ground near the River Clyst, I really don't know," the serving man grunted. "If we must go on then we'd best make for the Bishop's Palace. That be less than ten miles. We might manage that afore dark."

"Grandmother," Katherine implored, "we cannot reach Shillingford this day. Let us seek shelter with the Bishop of Exeter."

At first Grandmother Carew insisted that they should go on, but as time passed even she could see that their progress was too slow.

It was very late in the evening, the daylight almost gone, when their man thumped his fist on the carved oak door. After a good deal of grumbling, the bolts were drawn back and the door swung wide. Bishop Veysey was not in residence, but they were met by his steward, a tall man who introduced himself as Thomas Yarde. Katherine hardly noticed the lofty hall and the fine buildings ranged around that huge courtyard. She was just glad to find a cosy chamber with a fire to dry out their clothes. Grandmother Carew stood shivering and pale as Bessie offered a bowl of warming gruel sent from the palace kitchen.

"'Tis best that the mistress be warm in her bed now, or I'm feared she may take a chill," said Bessie, standing with one arm clasping her other elbow, her plain, round face white as a linen bedsheet.

Grandmother insisted on rising early the next day, and Mistress Yarde greeted them, rather condescendingly, in a most elegant gown. Master Yarde seemed much friendlier. Grandmother asked him whether the roads would be passable to continue their journey.

He frowned and shook his head. "You must pass low, marshy places liable to flood; the worst the bridge and causeway you must cross to leave the palace behind. I'll send a man out to see what state the roads are in."

Katherine could see that he thought it a fool's errand for an old woman and a girl to be out in such conditions. The answer returned. If they would go, then best go soon, before the waters could rise further. Thomas Yarde stood by as they prepared to leave, twisting a large ring round and round on his finger.

"You seem worried, Master Yarde," Katherine said, eyes brimming with sympathy and kindly concern.

"That I am, young Mistress. It's my responsibility to see my master's barns well filled against the winter. We can't stand another bad harvest. There's many couldn't even keep back enough seed corn for sowing this spring," he said, his voice dropping lower. "God willing, this season won't be quite so bad. If it is I don't know how the crops will be garnered in, nor how the poor folk will manage. They'll have little enough to pay their tithes to the Church, that's for sure. All this wet weather brings diseases to the sheep and cattle, the meadows are already under water, and there's no hope of a decent hay crop. Last year's yield of grain was very low, with much left rotting in the fields. Prices are rising, and they'll go even higher." He rubbed his hand across his face and shuffled his feet.

"I'm sure you'll do what's best, Master Yarde," she replied. "It's to your credit that you think of the people at this time."

Thomas's eyebrows shot up. He nodded and repeated his advice. "Best that you leave now, if go you must; the waters will rise quickly as the day passes."

Katherine's cloak, not completely dry after the previous day, felt like a lead weight on her shoulders as they crossed the rising river. The meadows on either side of the causeway were already under water. Trees poked up from a new-formed sea and cast eerie reflections on the water's surface. Ducks and coot had adopted the watery expanse as a new pond, and a mournful heron watched from the twisted branches of an oak, probably hoping that fish would soon migrate to the new waters.

After a long, wet ride they approached the manor house at Shillingford at a snail's pace, horses and riders all bone-weary. George Carew rushed out to greet them and was soon bellowing out orders, sending servants scurrying in all directions. Katherine almost fell asleep before the roaring blaze kindled in the hall, but Grandmother Carew would go straight to the church.

William Huddesfield's impressive stone tomb stood close by the wall in the Church of St George. Katherine knelt with her grandmother through a long service led by the new vicar; a lanky, bald-headed man called George Sherard. The old lady had got her way and seemed none the worse for their adventure, but Katherine's teeth were chattering and her head ached. She shifted her position, and wished the hammers inside her skull would cease their pounding. As she rose the walls seemed to sway and her legs gave way under her. She sank onto the cold stones, shaking uncontrollably as Cousin George towered over her. She felt his strong arms sweep her up to carry her from the church.

For two days she lay in the huge bed in the turret room, her sleep disturbed by strange dreams. On the third day she woke with a clearer head, though her whole body ached and her throat felt as if it were filled with shards of glass. It was an effort to raise herself even to swallow a sip or two of the spiced wine Bessie offered. Several more days passed before she could take more than a mouthful of bread and a spoon or two of pottage. She felt weak and shaky as a newborn lamb, and when Bessie held the glass for her she saw dull, sunken eyes looking back from a haggard face, all skin and bone. Katherine had never been ill before. It was not an experience she wanted to repeat. It was galling that she was the one who had taken a chill, while, most of the time, Grandmother Carew seemed none the worse for the drenching. But now and then Katherine noticed that the old lady winced and clutched her chest as she sat at her bedside reading from the book of hours.

June was almost over when a racket and commotion had Katherine rushing to the window. She peeped out and let out a delighted yelp. Father was dismounting from his horse with a tall youth beside him. She stumbled down to greet him and he soon had her wrapped tight in his arms.

"We stopped at Mohun's Ottery and heard what had befallen," Father said, standing back to look at her as he brushed a tear from his cheek. "Thank God to see you recovering, daughter. But 'tis no thanks to your foolishness in taking such a journey in weather like this," he added, turning an angry face on his mother-in-law.

Father fussed around, demanding that wine be brought and ordering everything for Katherine's comfort. All the time the tall youth stood in the shadows, watching.

"Well, daughter," said Father, "I've brought you a rare tonic to heal your ills. Come, boy."

The youth stepped forward. There was something familiar about him. Why, the set of his shoulders reminded Katherine of Johnny. But he was much too tall. As the young man threw back his cloak, she gasped. It was indeed her beloved brother, grown so much she'd never have known him but for his dark curly hair and cheeky grin.

"My Lady Katherine-Kate," he said, sweeping a well-practised courtly bow. "His Majesty has allowed that I may visit my sister, though how His Grace can begin to manage without me, his most loyal henchman, I fail to see."

Katherine quite forgot about her aches and pains as he took her hand. Johnny was the very best medicine. The long months of separation fell away and they were soon best friends again as he regaled her with stories of his life at court. Most of them she suspected were rather tall tales, although it really did seem that the King had taken a liking to Johnny. According to Father, King Henry always met him with a beaming smile. Perhaps Johnny reminded him of his own younger days.

"I keep such company at court, Katherine-Kate," Johnny boasted, and proceeded with some shameless name-dropping. "Uncle Gawen is a close friend of My Lord of Suffolk. You know him? Charles Brandon! He married the King's sister that was Queen of France. Oh, he's so close to the King. 'Tis said that the Duchess of Suffolk has little liking for the Lady Anne, so how that toil will unravel is anyone's guess. Aye, and I wouldn't be surprised if Uncle Gawen wed Suffolk's sister, had she not a husband already! My Lady Gertrude, the Marchioness of Exeter, has already suffered of the sweat but, thanks be, has made a good recovery. Ah, 'tis a relief to be away from the court at this time, for that disease stalks around us there. King Henry's ordered most of his courtiers and attendants away. Everyone knows that sickness spreads fastest in the cities where the people cram together, cheek by jowl. The Lady Anne's been dispatched to Hever Castle, the King in mortal fear. He's sent his best doctors to care for his new love."

Johnny grinned mischievously. Perhaps he was embellishing his position just a little, but he must hear quite a lot of the court gossip. Who could blame him for playing up his role to impress? But his talk of the sweat made Katherine wonder fearfully if she too had suffered from that illness. If so, she had been lucky to survive. But no one else around her had been ill, so perhaps it was just the soaking on that long ride to Shillingford that had laid her so low.

Father left Johnny at Shillingford and headed for Modbury a few days later, promising to bring Mother and Eliza with him when he returned. A week later, true to his word, he was back.

Mother couldn't wait to tell all the news. "We're off to London to see Joan married, though how we'll get there with the roads so bad, I really don't know. Perhaps we should delay awhile until fear of the sweat has passed," she gabbled. "And we've all but reached agreement upon Eliza's betrothal. Oh, and Frances is growing into such a comely girl. And what about this? Arthur has insisted that he'll no longer wear gowns, but must be breeched. He's only five, but he's had his way, of course. You should see him. Goes about with a rare swagger, just like a small copy of your father. Agnes sends you much love and an embroidered shift she's been stitching."

The thought of Agnes brought a thick lump to Katherine's throat. How she would have loved to cuddle up to her nurse when the illness was upon her! But she brightened up thinking of Arthur strutting around in his new grown-up clothes.

It was so very good to see her family. She even gave her sister a hug. Eliza's lovely face was flushed and glowing with excitement.

"I'm so looking forward to seeing the court while I have the chance, Katherine-Kate," she trilled. "As soon as Joan's wedding's done, everything will be set in hand for mine. Then I'll have to settle down."

Katherine's mouth turned down. William Cole was a nice-looking boy. There would be no ancient bridegroom for lucky Eliza.

Mother said that the transfer of Aston Rohant to Henry Courtenay was complete. "Your dear father will be glad that he no longer has to bear the cost of that sprawling old place." So it was goodbye to those shimmering lakes and all the ducks and swans. What must be, must be! "I am looking forward to seeing my friend Gertrude. I do so want to talk to her," Mother added, unable to keep the excitement from her voice.

Katherine sucked in her breath and clenched her teeth for a moment. They were all going up to London to see Joan married, but she was still too weak to make the journey.

Although Devon was several days' ride from London, news travelled surprisingly quickly. The problem was that you were never quite sure what to believe out of all the stories circulating amongst the messengers and merchants who travelled the highways or passed through Devon's ports. Everyone was agog to see what would happen with the King's Great Matter. Wolsey, the King's right-hand man for years, was still trying to secure papal agreement for the annulment of the King's marriage to Queen Catherine. But Johnny said that people were whispering that the Cardinal's power was waning fast.

"They say he's so desperate he might give his palace at Hampton Court to the King," he announced.

"That's as may be," Mother replied. "Gertrude will have no time for this talk of an annulment. Most women in England – and, if truth be known, many men too – think it cruel shame to treat so kind and loving a lady in such a fashion. She has borne all those pregnancies with fortitude, and suffered the loss of all those babies." Mother became shrill in her indignation. "She even led the King's armies against the Scots while he was in France. Never forget that she was a valiant regent, and sent her husband the Scots King's bloodied coat. The Queen is well beloved of all the people, and it's shame to treat her so."

Father was frowning. "Best not speak of such things," he cautioned.

But Mother went on as if he wasn't there. "Thanks be that I have a kind and loving husband," she said, crossing her arms across her chest. "Whatever this will mean for our girls at court, I don't know. I suppose we must watch events very carefully. If the King has his way the girls might have a new mistress to serve, whether I like it or no. Men like your father must always have a care to see which way the dice will fall."

Katherine found all this talk confusing. Later, as they walked together, choosing the driest paths in Shillingford's garden, Johnny told what he knew.

"Yes, Anne Boleyn is often with the King. And yes, I have seen her," he confirmed.

"She must be very beautiful," said Katherine.

"Well, that's the strange thing," he replied. "She's not at all pretty in the usual way. Not a bit like her sister Mary, who used to be the

King's mistress. Some say Mary bore him a son, but Anne's keeping him on tenterhooks. I'll tell you this, though, Katherine-Kate: even a page like me can see how men might fall under the spell of the Lady Anne's striking dark eyes."

"So will Wolsey succeed?" she asked. "Will he get the King's divorce?"

"I'm not sure of that, but if he fails, odds on he'll be done for. A lot of people won't be sorry. They think he puts the Pope before his country. Oh yes, there's plenty of whispering about old Wolsey. How he's grown rich and fat, and feathered his own nest."

Katherine remembered the way the priest on the steps of the cathedral in Exeter had treated the poor woman, and thought she understood.

"I really don't know what will happen," Johnny breezed, "and I don't much care either. I don't give a jot, so long as I can serve the King, practise for the joust, and go hunting with my friends at court."

She sighed. All this talk of divorce was worrying. "Johnny, Father says the King's convinced that it says in the Bible that a man may not marry his brother's widow. But you told me that the King has actually fathered a child on the sister of this Anne Boleyn. Should that not also be an obstacle?" she asked, shaking her head. "I know he wants a son. But aren't such things in the hands of God? And I heard talk in the kitchens that he already has a son: Bessie Blount's boy. Now, what's his name?"

"By Our Lady! It's no use asking me about all that stuff," said Johnny, blushing to the roots of his hair. "But you're right that he's acknowledged Henry Fitzroy, Duke of Richmond. Father says it's best not to think of such things.

"Did you hear about Cousin Peter?" he asked, changing the subject with a chortle. "A kinsman of Uncle William's found him in France, but he wasn't serving as a page. What do you think? He was looking after the mules in the stables, and bedding down with them too!" At this, Johnny laughed as if his sides would split. He obviously thought Peter's exploits wonderful beyond words, but Katherine didn't share his opinion of their cousin.

"Well, that's just typical of Peter," she snapped with a smirk. "He's in good company with those mules!"

"He's really gone off somewhere now; nobody knows where. I bet he's in the service of some mighty lord," Johnny continued, ignoring her comment, though he must have heard the disapproval in her voice. "He's sure to acquit himself famously in some battle or other before he comes home to roost."

"As to that, time alone will tell," Katherine retorted. "Grandmother Carew says he's got too much of the Carew recklessness in his character."

It was an effort to get onto Dapple's back, but she was determined to go. They all gathered in the courtyard, where Cousin George waited to wave them off.

"Best mend your ways, my boy," Father admonished. "The King may have pardoned you for your silly adventures in France two years ago, but your father isn't convinced that you're ready to take a more mature and purposeful course. It looks as though Philip may have perished fighting the Turks, God rest him. Peter's whereabouts remain a riddle. William's depending on you to uphold the good name of the family. By God, George, it would be such a relief for your father if you would just settle down and marry."

"Uncle, I will see what I can do to convince him that I can be trusted again. I really will," George stuttered, avoiding Father's eye.

Water still stood in the fields and meadows, but the roads were passable with care, and they made steady progress under dismal grey skies. Katherine was shocked by how soon she became exhausted. When they reached Mohun's Ottery she slipped from the saddle and allowed Bessie to put her straight to bed with a hot drink infused with camomile. She fell into a troubled sleep and dreamed of a dark lady feeding mules with Cousin Peter.

Back at Mohun's Ottery, her strength slowly returned. The London party stayed for a while and soon she was well enough for short rides with Johnny, and they spent hours reading together in the orchard behind the house. This did not escape Grandmother Carew's notice.

"Your duty, Katherine, is to serve me, and you're well enough to do so. You still have much to learn if you are to make a good wife," she admonished. "It's not for you to waste time on wild tales of the court and soldiers, and who knows what else, with your brother."

But Katherine would treasure those times with Johnny through the long months that followed. After he left, she missed his cheery smile and teasing jests more than ever. Oh, how she envied him the chance to have such an exciting life, while she must accept her fate! It was all so unfair.

SIX

1528–1529

KATHERINE

AUTUMN BROUGHT NO RESPITE FROM THE DISMAL WEATHER. Heavy black storm clouds rolled in over the Blackdown Hills, sheets of rain obscured the meadows like a living veil, and raging winds teased tiles from roofs and brought down branches. There was no news of the London party.

"Now, child, 'tis time to put away that sad face," Grandmother Carew said as they sat at their stitching one gloomy afternoon. "Oh, I understand how you miss Johnny. But it won't do at all to envy him his life of adventure. Oh yes, I know well, Katherine-Kate, how you fret and fume that you can't live as he does."

Katherine blushed and stammered and tried to reassure her grandmother that she knew her duty very well.

"Knowing is not the same as accepting in your heart of hearts, my lovely girl. You cannot live your brother's life. Your role is just as important – nay, more so. Ask yourself this. Without us women, what can men ever achieve?" the old lady continued, with a soft, secret smile.

Katherine looked into her grandmother's face and saw the path of her long life etched there in every wrinkle; a study in pride and contentment. Life's work well done.

"I'm so very proud of my own brood of fine sons, my dear. William's so straightforward and true. He's shouldered a heavy burden as head of the family these many years, and done it well. Then there's Thomas. Dear Thomas, such a brave soldier. Remember Flodden Field."

Katherine smiled. Grandmother had omitted to say that Thomas had only volunteered to fight in Scotland to escape his family's wrath after the scandal with the Courtenay girl.

"Gawen, such a fine young man at court these days," Grandmother went on. "And George, studying in Oxford and set for a splendid career in the Church. It is the greatest comfort of my days to see my boys rise well in the world. One day, you too will know the pride that comes from being a mother of fine sons. I'm proud of my girls too, of course; your mother and Dorothy wedded to such fine men, while Ann and Isobel are brides of Christ. But I freely confess to you, it's my boys that give me the most joy." She took Katherine's hand in hers and held it tightly. "Katherine-Kate, you must accept this. We cannot live as men do. But we women bring honour to our families through the sons we bear. And 'tis through us that the land passes from one generation to another. We are not without our own power."

"I will try to accept all of this, Grandmother," said Katherine, biting her lip. "But what of my husband? How shall I serve him well when my parents will choose him and I don't know who he may be? What if he's an old man and cruel to me?"

"Ah," said Grandmother Carew, squeezing Katherine's slim fingers in a bony grip. "Perhaps now we reach the nub of it. Have no fear, girl. Your father is the best of men and will choose wisely for you when the time comes. That you must accept. It is the way of things."

The London party, now without Johnny, arrived late in November when frost had firmed the rutted lanes. They stayed a week, full of their time in the city, Joan's splendid marriage, her fine gown and the feast that followed. Father grumbled about the cost of it all. Mother seemed to have thoroughly enjoyed her stay with Gertrude Courtenay, who had told her of strange rumours about a girl who saw visions.

"The Holy Maid of Kent, they're calling her," said Mother.

"Elizabeth Barton's an untutored girl, but she's seeking an audience with Cardinal Wolsey himself! Says his future has been revealed to her. She even dares to speak of the King." She dropped her voice low and whispered in Katherine's ear. "She's been heard to say that if he casts his wife aside, then God will see to it that he's no longer King!"

Katherine glanced at Father, whose eyebrows drew a stark black line above his flaming cheeks.

"Hush now, wife; I'll hear no more of that," he said, speaking much more sharply than was usual. "I have told you before. Steer clear of this sort of nonsense and have a care."

"But, Philip," Mother interrupted, not reading the danger signals, "Gertrude's quite persuaded that the Maid speaks true, and I'm intrigued."

Katherine could see the muscle in his jaw working, but he quickly changed the subject. "Gawen's doing well in the King's service. George came down from Oxford."

All this time Eliza sat listless and wan, her eyes cast down. Katherine had expected her to babble on about the splendours she'd seen at court. But she just sat there, subdued, quiet and dreamy. Not a bit like the sister she knew.

"Do tell all about the wedding and the court, Eliza," begged Katherine. "It must have been so exciting."

"The wedding was well enough," was Eliza's dismissive reply.

"But what about all the lovely gowns and the fine ladies?" Katherine persisted.

"Sumptuous indeed," Eliza muttered.

Searching for some topic that would elicit a more enthusiastic response, Katherine asked, "Did you see Kat and Joanie? What news of them?"

"Kat's as bossy as ever, and Joanie grows more lovely by the day. Oh, will you stop your pestering? I'll be glad to return to peace and quiet and the green fields of home."

This was strange indeed. With her marriage to William Cole soon approaching, Eliza should be bubbling over, chattering on about the latest fashions and what style of gown she would choose. But instead she sat quietly with her sewing still in her lap. Try as she might, Katherine could not discover what had happened in London to bring about such a change.

The family left in the first week of December, leaving Katherine even lonelier than before. That Christmas season was a quiet one at Mohun's Ottery. Another New Year came. She tried hard to remember her grandmother's words; to put aside her dreams and let go her envy. Helping Aunt Joan, watching carefully how she managed the household and received important visitors, was not so bad. She sat with Grandmother Carew and found contentment in reading, as the months sped by.

While little of note was happening in rural Devon that summer, shocking events were unfolding in London. At midsummer, Father called on his way home from Curry Mallet. "The King and Queen Catherine both had to attend a special legations court at Blackfriars," he said, rubbing his hand across his brow and shaking his head. "Can you imagine that? All to examine the case for the King's marriage. Well, the Queen gave such an impassioned speech right in front of the King, and then she swept out of the chamber! All the lords were quite astonished."

What a brave lady Queen Catherine must be, thought Katherine.

"So the case is adjourned, the final decision to be left to the Pope himself. The King won't stand for that, and I think Wolsey's done for," Father went on with a wry smile. "I heard Will Sommers chanting a rhyme – *A halter, a rope for him that would be Pope, Without all right or reason*. Ha! The King's fool often knows more than most, and gets away with saying it, too."

Another autumn with leaden skies and roads barely passable; another dreadfully wet year, the third in a row. Katherine spared a thought for Thomas Yarde, whose worries must have grown since they spoke.

Uncle William said the King seemed determined to divorce his wife, whether the Pope agreed or not. "As your father predicted," he said, looking straight at Katherine from beneath his bristling brows, "Wolsey's fate's sealed. He stands accused of putting the Pope before the King, to whom he owes his true allegiance. He's been stripped of office and most of his property, including that grand house at York Place."

Katherine heard about these shocking events as if they were echoes from some other land far away, unlikely to have any impact on her life at all.

On a dark October morning she rose as usual and, after a hasty prayer, made her way to her grandmother's chamber. She found the old lady slumped beside the bed, unable to catch her breath or speak. A doctor was sent for, but by the time he reached Mohun's Ottery, Grandmother Carew was dead.

Katherine couldn't take it in. There was a tightness in her chest that just would not loosen; a thumping pain in her head that would not go away. She felt as if she'd suddenly lost her way home. How she missed the touch of those gnarled hands with their blue veins that stood out so clearly; how she longed to be enfolded in those arms one more time! She searched in vain for the familiar scent – essence of violets – that wafted around those swishing black skirts, and struggled to pray as she should for the repose of Grandmother Carew's soul. She thought of all the knowledge in that old head, all the memories and stories, all the kindly deeds and valiant acts, all lost forever. All for nothing! She couldn't even cry. After despair came red-hot anger that God should have allowed it to happen.

No one had time for her. The family gathered for the funeral at Shillingford, the coffin carried there in slow stages on a wagon covered with black cloth embroidered with the arms of Huddesfield and Carew. Oh, Grandmother Carew would have been so proud to see the Carew lions and the ugly boars of Huddesfield on all the banners. She was laid to rest with all due pomp, as she had wished, near her father in the Church of St George.

To Katherine's eternal distress, Grandmother had ordered that the book of hours should be returned to the Poyntz family; to the children of her dear sister whose dedication in that treasured book had meant so much. She and Katherine had read that inscription together so often. Katherine knew how keenly Grandmother Carew had missed her sister. She understood why it was given back to her great-aunt's family. But, oh, to think that she would never hold that dear little book again or gaze at those wondrous pictures! She had other mementos left to her – a silver thimble, an embroidered coif – but nothing could replace that wonderful book.

After the funeral they all returned to Modbury. Once home, Katherine sank into a deep and troubling depression, lying listless in bed of a morning, reluctant to stir, while at bedtime she tossed and turned. She picked at her food, pushed it round the bowl, but ate little. Her books lay closed, pages unturned, stories confined. Her needle was still, her lute untouched. One of life's certainties was no more. It was as if the sun no longer rose each day. Even her faithful Agnes, who had taken over Bessie's duties again, could not prise her out of it. A sad Christmastide approached, and even the exciting news Father brought from court could not cheer her. It was news of some moment for the family.

"I am at last rewarded for all my faithful service to the King. You see before you Sir Philip Champernowne," he declared, his face lit by a dazzling smile.

"Oh, you have so long deserved it, husband," cried Mother, looking like a girl of sixteen again, all flushed cheeks and sparkling eyes. "Think of it, girls! I shall be on the same level as Aunt Joan! I'll be set above our neighbours' wives. Gertrude will be so pleased! Oh, it'll be good for Johnny and the girls at court."

But Katherine couldn't share Mother's joy. The news fell like a millstone into the deep pool of her grief, causing only a momentary ripple in her misery.

In the end it was Arthur who made her smile. He had the portion of the Twelfth Night cake which held the dried pea. What a time that little boy had as Prince of the Pea; his mirth so infectious that even Eliza, who seemed almost as sad as Katherine, had to laugh. Arthur was nearly six years old, but thought himself already a man. How he revelled in his powers, giving out ever more audacious commands. He ordered Father to sit on the floor amongst the dogs, Mother to dance on the table, and the girls to wear their headdresses backwards. The minstrels played, Arthur strutted around, and the waves of uncontrollable laughter that engulfed them all seemed to release a spring in Katherine. She started to emerge from her despair like a moth carefully shedding its dark pupa and gingerly spreading its wings.

As she sat in the orchard with her book one sunlit April morning, Agnes came puffing along the path, calling her to come inside quickly and put on her best gown. Katherine had heard a horse in the courtyard earlier but thought nothing of it. Father often had visitors.

"What's all the fuss about, Agnes?" she asked as she followed the wobbling figure. Agnes had not lost any weight.

"I know not, young Mistress," said Agnes with a worried frown, "but make haste, do."

So Katherine changed as fast as she could and, suitably attired, went down to the great hall, where she found a truly ancient man.

"Come, Katherine," said Father. "Make your curtsy to Master Gilbert, who has come here this day on your account."

She felt the blood drain from her cheeks and her hand flew to her throat. The man seemed to her as old as time itself; just a dried-out husk of the man he might once have been. She watched, aghast, as he gripped the arms of the chair, hauled his skinny frame upright and turned to look at her. It was all she could do not to flinch away.

She swallowed hard and forced herself to study the menacing face that loomed in front of her. A sparse fringe of powder-white hair protruded from a linen coif topped by a dark cap, below which bushy white eyebrows nearly met. A wintry spade-shaped beard, neatly trimmed, concealed only a little of a map of wrinkles spread across a wizened face. Eyes of the most striking blue, as bright as a jackdaw's, were set deep in sunken sockets from which a veritable cobweb of lines spread right up to the edge of his coif. Those eyes now turned their cold, penetrating gaze on her. She looked down and saw his knotty, misshapen fingers gripping a silver-topped cane as he made to bow to her, managing no more than a slight dip of his head. His wasted body was enveloped in a long black gown in the old style, but she could see that it was of the finest wool, the cloth dyed a true high-status black. The heavy fabric only served to emphasise the wiry shape beneath. His gown fell open at the front to reveal a fine doublet, but without the slashing that was the latest fashion. Those blue eyes never wavered. Katherine felt as if they saw into her very soul. Her heart was beating so furiously that she thought the old man must see it thumping in her chest; that he must hear its frantic drumming. With eyes dutifully lowered and a forced, watery smile, she sank into a deep curtsey. Rising, she stammered out a greeting as she had been schooled.

"Master Gilbert has come to me with a proposal I shall need to consider most carefully," Father was saying with a fixed smile on his face. At those words she was overtaken by panic, though she must somehow stand politely and hear the old man's greeting. The horrible old fool had come a-courting!

"Young Mistress Katherine, it does my old eyes good to behold you at last, for the beauty, wit and grace of Sir Philip's daughter are known to all in these parts."

It was a pleasant, courtly greeting, but to Katherine the words only intensified her terror. Next he was asking questions. Did she play the lute? Did she enjoy the hunt? Something like that. Later, she could never recall what he'd asked or how she'd answered, nor how that dreadful interview had ended. At last she was given permission to withdraw and stumbled up the stairs, nearly tripping on the hem of her fine russet gown.

In her room she fell, trembling, upon the bed. Johnny's jest had come true. Father was even now discussing her marriage to that terrifying cadaver. Her dear, kind father, who encouraged her so in her studies, who had given her Dapple for her very own, and had always treated her with such courtesy and consideration! He would wed her to that odious creature! They were talking about her as if she were a prize cow to be sacrificed, though she'd not yet seen her twelfth birthday; the date at which she could in law be wed. She lay there sobbing and beating her arms on the pillow, and there Agnes found her, much later that afternoon.

"What's amiss, young Mistress?" she asked with her kindly smile.

"Oh, Agnes, I cannot bear it," Katherine wailed, leaping to her feet. "Father means to marry me to that horrible old man. I shall be like the King's sister, who had to go to France and leave all her family and marry the King of France, who was ever so much older than her. But it's worse, for Master Gilbert is quite the most frightening man I have ever, ever seen." She sat back down on the bed with a bump, head drooping, as the tears began to fall again.

Agnes just stood there, smiling. "Well," she said, drawing in her breath, "'tis true enough, the Princess Mary did marry the King of

France. But he didn't live long and then she married her true love. Though whether that match did truly bring that fair lady joy, none may know." But then she took pity on Katherine. She drew her forward until her head was cushioned against her well-padded breast, and wrapped her arms around her. "Silly maid, you have this all on its head," Agnes said, her voice like a soothing balm. "It's not for himself Master Gilbert wants you; 'tis for his nephew and heir, Otho. The lad's not many summers beyond your own age. How could you really think your father would sacrifice his lovely lamb so? Wipe your eyes now, child, and make yourself presentable. Come down to hear what your parents have to say."

They were seated in the hall when, still dazed and confused, she stumbled in.

"Well now, Katherine-Kate. What think you of a match with the Gilbert boy?" Father asked brightly.

At last the light dawned. He had said, 'the Gilbert *boy*'! So John Gilbert really was after her for his nephew, not for himself. She fell to her knees, kissing Father's hand over and over, as floods of tears ran down her cheeks. "Thank you, thank you, Father," she wailed.

"Why, daughter," said he in mock horror, as Mother tittered, "I didn't know you were so keen to be married and leave us. You are young yet to be wed."

"It's not that, Father," she ventured. "It's that it is not Master Gilbert himself that I must consider, but his nephew. Oh, that is an enormous relief to me."

Father burst out laughing. "In all probability you will be betrothed to Otho Gilbert, Katherine-Kate. So long as we can sort out the details. He's from a good family. The Gilberts have been men of consequence in Devon for a long time."

To her surprise, he went on to say that this would not be the first time the Champernownes had been linked with the Gilberts.

"Generations ago, William Gilbert married Elizabeth, one of our family line. She was heiress to the Valletort fortune," he said, with pride in his voice. "Now, let me see what I can remember of the Gilberts and their history. Ah yes, well, they've held Compton, over by Marldon, for a long time; since at least the time of the third King Edward, if I remember aright. Now John Gilbert, who was here today, he's been head of the family since his father died; must have been a few years after Bosworth. He was another Otho. Served as Sheriff of Devon, and Grandfather John spoke well of him." His brow puckered. "I remember now. That Otho Gilbert served the House of York, and he was at the very top of the list of those called to be knighted at the coronation of the boy who was to be Edward V of England. You know, daughter; the one who was never crowned."

Katherine knew the sad story of those two boys, last seen in the Tower of London.

"So Otho Gilbert never received his knighthood," Father continued. "Like many another, his allegiance shifted and the family thrived. John Gilbert has served with me often as a Justice of the Peace. As Escheator of Devon he used to convene all the Inquisitions after anybody of note died, so the old boy had early knowledge of any land deals in the offing. Knew who had fallen on hard times, and all that. Oh, yes, John Gilbert got his hands on acres and acres of land. There's no doubt he's now a very wealthy man. This young Otho will be able to keep you in good estate."

Somehow, although she was enormously relieved that she would not be marrying the aged monster she had met that afternoon, Katherine didn't feel particularly enthused by how rich Otho might become. She'd much rather not be married at all.

"Gilbert got so wealthy that he began to lend money to others. I'm afraid your Grandfather Edmund borrowed a very large sum from him before he went to fight in France, my dear," Father continued.

Katherine remembered all the talk of debts that had made them sell Aston Rohant. It was all starting to make sense.

"There's still a running sore between the Gilberts and your Carew relatives, Katherine-Kate. You know how Uncle William has been saddled with debts throughout his life. It's wearing him down. Perhaps it's money worries that send his sons gallivanting off a-soldiering."

More likely it's just that they are a bunch of hot-headed fools looking for glory and fame in some world of their dreams, she thought, but she didn't say so.

"Anyway," Father went on, "Uncle William is still making payments on all those debts, and I must do all I can to help him.

Don't you see, Katherine-Kate? A match with the Gilbert boy, the heir, can only help."

"I suppose I can understand all that," she said. "I can see that you must consider this most seriously. But, Father, why may it not be Eliza that weds this Otho? She's much older than I."

"Now, Katherine-Kate," said Father. "Eliza was promised to William Cole long ago, even before you were born. I'll not go back on my agreement with the Cole boy's grandfather. No, my dear, Otho is for you."

The wedding would happen at some time far in the future, so for the moment, she could put it all to the back of her mind and enjoy life. Spring came early, and the sun beat down on St George's Fair. The snowy-white blossom of hawthorn and blackthorn – the Blackthorn Winter, some called it – was long past. Dog roses and pink valerian replaced bluebells and primroses in the garland that adorned the glove. Father had given way to Arthur's pleading. Though he was only six, he went to the fair, and what a time he had.

Katherine watched the dancers wistfully. As couples exchanged loving glances, she wondered about Otho Gilbert. Would he prove to be her own true love? In her imagination he was a tall, strong and handsome fellow. He would share her love of books, write poems to her beauty, and wear her favours in the joust. She would, of course, fall instantly in love with this paragon. But the realist in her knew that she must accept Otho Gilbert whatever he was like. There really was no point in wasting time wondering how it would be to follow her own heart. She did envy the village couples dancing at the fair, but she tried to remember Grandmother Carew's wise counsel. Those silly, romantic dreams were not for a girl like her.

As it turned out, the negotiations with John Gilbert were not easy. Long years of amassing his fortune had taught him how to drive a hard bargain. With his legal adviser, John Rowe, Serjeant-at-Law, he went over the marriage settlement with a fine-toothed comb. Eventually the dowry and the lands that would be earmarked as Katherine's jointure, should Otho die, were thrashed out and agreed. Just a few loose ends needed tying up and a date could be set.

From her corner in the parlour, Katherine could hear the annoyance in the old man's voice.

"Now then, Champernowne. I'll level with you. It's been more than thirty years since I inherited the Gilbert lands. I was granted no children in my own marriage to my dear Elizabeth." An unexpectedly wistful expression softened his craggy features. "Daughter to John Croker of Lyneham, you know. Our marriage was a wise move, but though I came to love her dearly, God did not favour us. I've known the miss of her all this time. After she died I just couldn't bring myself to think of taking another wife." He paused and, to Katherine's amazement, blinked away a tear. "I had brothers, you see, all younger than me, and my father's will was clear. If I had no heirs then next in line would be Thomas; failing him, *his* heirs. Thomas is gone now; dead the year before last, worn out by that termagant wife of his, I expect." At this, he gave a mirthless laugh. "Thomas's son Otho is only seventeen. But he's the heir to all our lands now." He leaned forward and thumped his fist on the tabletop. "Look here, man. I feel the weight of my years keenly. I want above all things to see the succession settled safely according to my father's wishes, before I too must leave this earthly coil. I first approached you for your girl more than a year ago when we both served as Justices of the Peace; just before you were raised to the knighthood. Can we set a date now and have done with it?"

Well, that was news to Katherine. Father had known about this much longer than she'd thought.

"I do understand all that full well," Father snapped. "But I worry that you'll have that boy fill the nursery with babes before my girl's grown. I won't have her harmed."

John Gilbert's face contorted. Father had struck a nerve. "Let me be clear," the old man snapped. "I give you my word. She'll come to no harm. They can have a year or two to grow to like each other before they need be bedded."

Father sounded unconvinced. "She's a well-educated girl. I hadn't thought to marry her off so soon. Oh, I know it's still not that unusual in families like ours for a girl to wed when young. But I would prefer that Katherine, like my other girls, wait until she's grown. What say you that they live here at Modbury first? I can give Otho many advantages."

"The boy needs to be with me to learn our business. I've given my word, Champernowne. She shall not be harmed under my roof," John Gilbert growled, as his colour rose and his face set into stern lines. He sat back in his chair and studied the backs of his hands as though looking at a map of long-lost treasure. The awkward silence grew longer. At last he spoke again. Leaning forward until his face was closer to Father's than looked comfortable, he said in an icy voice, "There is the matter of the Carew debt."

Slowly, Father shook his head from side to side, then turned to look at Mother, who sat beside Katherine in the corner. Mother took a deep breath and nodded. With a voice choked with emotion, Father replied, "Very well, Gilbert. Shall we set a date, then? If you give your word that they shall not lie together for a further two years after, let them be wed a year from September. I have your agreement as to dowry? Her jointure is secure as we have discussed? Then have Rowe draw up the agreement and I'll sign."

A smug smile crept across John Gilbert's features and he took his leave. Father sat with his chin on his chest.

"Now, Katherine," said Mother, "as you have heard, we have come to an agreement with Mr Gilbert. You will be wed next September, a year after Eliza."

"Thank you, Mother; thank you, Father," Katherine said with a grin. She'd half expected it might be sooner. "I was sore afraid I would be an old maid before you reached any agreement."

Her little joke brought a flicker of a smile to Father's lips. "Oh, Katherine-Kate," he said, his voice dropping low, "I was loath to agree that you be wed so soon. You'll be well past twelve, of course, but I'd have put it off longer if I could. I'm sorry, my dear. You know all about the money business."

"Yes, Father," she replied, as he gave her a fond look.

"I just can't afford to send any more of my girls to court. Joanie, she's our best hope of a marriage into the higher echelons now. She'll probably be more than twenty before she's wed. I wish I could delay matters longer for you too, but it'll be a good match, you'll see. There's no shame in marrying into the Devon gentry."

"Have no fear, Katherine-Kate," said Mother. "I wasn't much beyond your age when I married your father, and look how well that turned out."

Her husband nodded and the corners of his mouth turned up.

"Eliza is older, and her wedding must come first," Mother continued. "Now that we have agreed to a formal betrothal, John Gilbert will bring his nephew here to the Court House and you will meet him for the first time."

SEVEN
1530–1531
KATHERINE

On a glorious, sun-filled summer's day, the Gilberts came to Modbury.

"Tell me, Agnes, how does it suit me?" Katherine asked, jiggling from side to side as she peered into the glass.

"Well, young Mistress, I'm in no ways familiar with this French headgear," Agnes replied, looking disapprovingly at the new headdress. "It does show quite a lot of your lovely glossy hair in front. More than's seemly, if you ask me! But I'll own it does set off those beautiful dark eyes of yours very well. Lovely eyes, they are, my flower, with all the colours of the sun glinting on an autumn wood. Now, don't you worry. You look a real picture. That Gilbert boy has fallen right on his feet to claim you as his bride."

She felt as though her insides were vibrating as Agnes gave her a reassuring hug before she went tripping down the stair. The deep tones of the old man echoed through the hall as she paused, frozen to the spot, and stared. The boy was a good few inches shorter than Father, but a head taller than his uncle, who seemed even more stooped and shrunken than she remembered. Otho's shoulders were not quite wide enough to proclaim him a strong man, and a pair of rather spindly legs emerged from a short doublet of green cloth. Katherine waited with her heart in her mouth.

OTHO

He ran a finger round his shirt collar. The hall was stiflingly hot, and his new doublet was much too tight. He could feel his eyes begin to prickle. He looked down. New rushes on the floor; meadowsweet, or some such. That was sure to set his eyes streaming. It always did. He wanted to run the back of his hand across his brow, to wipe away the sweat beads gathering there. But that would not be mannerly. No need to steal a glance at his uncle. He could imagine the disdainful look, the shake of the head that told everyone what a disappointment his nephew was.

What could be taking so long? It seemed an age since they'd sent the fat serving woman to fetch the girl. And what was he supposed to do when she did make an appearance? Uncle John had said that he must talk nicely to her, but he had no idea how to speak to a girl. Otho only knew two women: his mother, and his sister Joan. He couldn't think of any conversation he'd ever had with his mother. She had no time for him at all; far too grand and hoity-toity, always on about her friend Honor, Lady Basset. And Joan was more interested in feeding her fat face than talking to him. What on earth could he say to her?

He wished the floor would open up and swallow him when he felt, rather than heard, her come in. He took off his cap and pulled his fingers through his hair. He felt a bit dizzy as he turned. There she was, much taller and more elegant than he'd expected. Uncle John had said she was a child, but she seemed so composed, looking down that fine, straight nose at him. He felt the flush creeping up his cheeks; felt his ears burning. She could probably see his knees shaking. He looked down at his boots, scuffing them about amongst the rushes, and stirred up more of the heady almond scent that set his eyes streaming. She'd think him a fool. What was he supposed to do now?

KATHERINE

Katherine dipped a shaky curtsey before raising her eyes to look for the first time into the face of her husband-to-be. He had removed his cap, and raised a hand to tug at his untidy, mousy-brown hair as he turned toward her. He had his uncle's startling blue eyes, the best feature in a rather narrow face, though they looked very red and rheumy, as if he'd been crying. His cheeks were flaming, making their sprinkling of unsightly scars stand out as livid white blotches. He must have survived the smallpox as a child and was clearly trying to grow his beard to cover the pockmarks. A sparse growth of reddish-brown whiskers sprouted on his top lip and chin. She swallowed hard. No! This was not the man of her dreams. This was not the shining knight who would rescue her, the fair damsel, and sweep her off to live in a rose-scented bower. But at least he was young. Things could have been far worse.

John Gilbert turned cold eyes on her fine new headdress, leaving her in no doubt that he did not hold with the new French fashions. Katherine frowned and her hand flew to the back of her neck. She bit her lip and her eyes darted anxiously back and forth between Father and the old man.

Father suggested that she might show Otho the gardens. She took his awkwardly proffered arm and they stepped out into the sunshine. Otho's face was as red as Agnes's flannel petticoat. They both stuttered, not knowing what to say. After a few false starts they found themselves discussing the fair in Modbury. Katherine was first to find her voice, and was soon listing the delights she'd found on the stalls and telling him how much she and her sisters had enjoyed the plays.

"Bu... b-b-b-b-but did you see the b-b-b-bull-baiting, Mistress Katherine?" Otho stammered. His voice was hesitant and croaky as he tried desperately to get his stammer under control.

"No indeed, sir, I did not," she replied, more tartly than she'd intended. "I hate to see those dogs hurt so, not to mention the bull driven mad by their snapping teeth."

"W-w-well, p-p-p-perhaps 'tis man's sport, and of course, you are a child still," he said, raising his head in a vain attempt at a condescending air. "F-f-for I do delight in such things."

A faint bell of alarm sounded in Katherine's head. Perhaps it was simply bravado; an attempt to sound more grown-up and manly. But could there be a hint of a cruel and brutal nature?

She hastily pushed the thought aside and spoke of her love of riding and of the books she had read. He told her of his uncle's ships and how he would one day oversee the Gilberts' seagoing enterprises as well as all their lands. Otho was doing all he could to impress her. Weighing her words more carefully, she steered the conversation toward him. She refrained to mention her family's connections to the court, all the lands her father held, or his recent knighthood. She saw immediately that John Gilbert had high hopes for this nervous boy, but allowed him few opportunities to shine. As they returned to the house she realised with a jolt that, though he was older than she, Otho would need her help to become a strong and confident man.

All in all, the meeting was disquieting. She had felt no instant uplifting of her spirit when first she saw him. Her heart had not been set all aflutter. Rather, she felt something closer to pity for the lad who seemed to be trying so hard to live up to his uncle's expectations. But the die was cast and, as she kept reminding herself, it could have been so much worse. So the betrothal went ahead and the date was set for her wedding. The Gilberts rode away, leaving Katherine to enjoy one of the best summers the country had ever seen.

A wonderful high summer of glorious, hazy days, long, balmy evenings, and gentle rain that fell only at night. The family took to picnicking out in the gardens, enjoying the last rays of the warm evening sun. They followed the fashion set by the Duchess of Suffolk, who delighted in eating out of doors. As they sat in the orchard in late July, Father told them about the bonfires of forbidden books in London. "Just like they did nine years ago at St Paul's. This time a merchant, Sommers by name, and others were paraded to Cheapside and made to throw their forbidden books into the flames. He tried to save his translation of the New Testament into English. I don't know if he succeeded," he said, shaking his head.

"To burn books! That's dreadful!" cried Katherine. "And anyway, what's so wrong with bringing the Word of God to more Christian souls in English?"

"Don't even think such thoughts," Father advised. "These are dangerous times, particularly for men like me who embrace all learning. Thomas More, the new Chancellor, is hot to persecute any he deems heretics."

Katherine had always thought Thomas More was a learned man too. It was all most confusing for a girl growing up in rural Devon.

"There's more trouble at court. The Duke of Suffolk told the King that the Lady Anne had a dalliance with Thomas Wyatt," Father went on. "All was denied, but Brandon's been sent away, even though he's been the King's friend for so long. No matter what befalls, it seems the King is set to divorce his wife. The Queen's been separated from Princess Mary since last year."

"Poor lady," said Mother. "What's to become of her? Anne will be Queen in her place, even though she's kept him dangling so. Gertrude's up in arms about it, as you can guess."

"It seems to me," said Father, giving Mother a stern look, "that the best course for sensible people is to steer well clear and keep busy at home. We have much to do with two weddings to arrange. Don't get too close to Gertrude Courtenay. She's over-strong in her support of the Queen. I wouldn't trust her not to speak out of turn and get into a lot of trouble."

Katherine and Eliza exchanged glances. It wasn't often that Father spoke sharply to Mother.

September came: time to prepare for Eliza's wedding. Katherine tugged at her laces. The gown was really uncomfortable where it strained against her small, high breasts. She stamped her foot and threw her headdress aside.

"Katherine-Kate, I declare, your moods go up and down like the weather. It's your age. You're no longer a child, but not quite a woman," Agnes mused as she stooped to retrieve the discarded hood. "I'll see if I can let that gown out a bit. Now try the one you'll wear for your sister's wedding day. You'll look a picture in that, and it fits you well."

"It won't be so pretty as Eliza's, will it?" Katherine said with a pout. Kat had brought Eliza a new gown from London; a blue damask that matched her eyes. Eliza was a summertime beauty, glowing and golden, with her cornflower eyes, cheeks touched with a blush like eglantine, and hair the colour of sun-drenched wheat fields.

"Now then, push aside the green-eyed monster, if you will. This is Eliza's day of days. Your turn will come," Agnes chided. "Now then, all the family are here and 'tis a holiday for us all. This red velvet suits you."

Agnes was right about one thing: Katherine's moods *did* seem to change all the time. One minute she felt hopeless, in the depths of despair; the next she was singing like a lark. She wriggled into the velvet gown and, turning, saw her reflection in the glass. All her black thoughts evaporated. She strutted round the chamber, preening like a Princess, until Agnes collapsed in laughter at her antics.

The next day, Katherine stood behind Eliza at the church door as the couple exchanged their vows: Eliza quiet and deliberate; William over-loud and very excited. At the wedding breakfast, there was much talk of affairs at court.

"Now that the Lady Anne has risen so high, who knows what may befall?" Joanie said, as they watched the newly-weds step out for a dance. "I don't know which mistress I'll be serving. If she gets to be Queen, I'm afraid the Lady will be very demanding. She has such a temper."

"But you're still so lucky to be at court, Joanie," Katherine replied. She puffed out her bottom lip and muttered under her breath. "And you don't have to get married next year like me!"

On her other side, Kat brought out a beautifully decorated velvet purse the Cardinal had given her. "We thought Wolsey might yet return, but now he's reduced to a mere Archbishop, and banished to York. I doubt we'll see much more of him," she said between mouthfuls. "There's a man called Thomas Cromwell who's served Wolsey for years. Mark me well, for I do believe he's the coming man."

"Well, I neither know nor care about him," Katherine declared. The affairs of the court seemed so far away. What would it matter to her? She would always be stuck in Devon.

"But, oh, it's nice to be out of London for a space," Kat said, tucking into another helping of roast beef.

So Eliza was married and went off to her new home; a fine house called The Slade, near Cornwood. Things settled back into their usual pattern soon after the family and guests left, and everyone rejoiced at an abundant harvest.

The last year of Katherine's childhood sped by. Matters in London also moved on apace. Wolsey was gone; dead in November on his way back to London to stand trial for treason. Katherine cared little for that. She hardly noticed the news that Queen Catherine had had to sit through the Twelfth Night revels with the Lady Anne in full command. Her thoughts were elsewhere. In a few months she would be a wife; the wife of Otho Gilbert. The women stitched away the days, embroidering fine linen against her wedding day. Kat sent bolts of cloth and two tailors to join the household and make up new clothes for them all. Katherine wondered how Father could afford it. Perhaps Kat had some secret income.

A cold snap in February had her shivering behind the bed-hangings when she woke to a grey and cheerless dawn. A stomach ache had grown into a griping pain and she wondered if she'd eaten too much salt fish. As she got out of bed she found the bloodstain on her night shift. So that was it. She'd shared a chamber with Eliza long enough to know that it would happen one day. She shouted for Agnes.

"So you be truly a woman now, little Mistress Katherine-Kate," said her faithful Agnes with a glowing smile. Patiently, with many reassurances, she showed Katherine how to fix the bulky bundle of linen clouts to a girdle around her waist. Acutely conscious of her new burden, Katherine's sensitive nose twitched at the faintly metallic smell she thought she could detect. Agnes explained how she must leave the soiled clouts in a basket for the laundry maid to take. No wonder laundresses were the first to know of a woman's intimate business.

"Here you are, my flower," said Agnes as she offered Katherine a bunch of sweet-smelling herbs in a silk pouch to tie around her neck under her shift. "Now don't you fret. None shall guess your woman's secret."

But Katherine still preferred to remain in her chamber through those first anxious days. She knew that she must, like all women, bear this burden every month. She should be proud. It was a symbol of her passage from childhood into the world of adults. But still she wept and fumed. Agnes brought comforting camomile drinks infused with feverfew, yarrow and lady's mantle. Sometimes she even added some costly ginger. Agnes could have prepared another draught for pain relief made from willow bark steeped in boiling water.

"We won't do that, my lamb," she explained. "The Church's teaching is clear. The courses are part and parcel of God's punishment of women for the sins of Eve. All women must suffer and bear it."

"Well, I think God is wrong to punish all good women so. It's not fair!" Katherine railed.

Agnes raised her eyebrows and put a finger to her lips. "Now then, my flower, you know full well that you must follow the teachings of the Church without question. But I'll not tell your mother, nor the priest, what you said; 'tis just the shock speaking. You'll get used to it."

Katherine sobbed in Agnes's arms, leaving a spreading wet patch on the front of her nurse's kirtle.

"Now here's a surprise for you," Father announced when he returned from Mohun's Ottery later in the year. "You know William's become very melancholy of late? Well, I think we'll see him much more cheerful now. He told me he was sat by the fire with Aunt Joan one afternoon when a finely dressed young man marched in and made a perfect bow. In most educated tones, the stranger said he was Peter returned from Europe with a letter of recommendation from a Princess! What do you think of that? Well, at first William challenged him. You see, he just couldn't believe it was that ne'er do well son of his."

"I'm not surprised," Katherine interrupted, narrowing her eyes. "Last time they heard of Peter he was bedding down with the mules."

Father laughed. "Well, the stranger said he'd already had an audience with King Henry and his letters of commendation were well received. Said he'd fought in the Siege of Florence where Prince Philibert of Orange perished; seen foreign cities and learned much of the ways of the world. Then your Aunt Joan looked carefully into the stranger's face and saw it really was their boy, transformed into this perfect gentleman. Who'd have thought it? When I got there they were having such a celebration. They thought that boy had gone from the world. Would you credit it? Peter's gone back to court. He's joined the ranks of King Henry's henchmen."

Ah, thought Katherine, *how happy Johnny will be to have his idol restored to him.*

Katherine sat quietly beside Mother when John Gilbert came again. There were only a few details to settle. Father was pressing for Agnes or Bessie to go with her to her new life.

The old man puffed and fumed. "I've got serving women aplenty, Champernowne. I've no need of more," he blustered.

Katherine could see that he wouldn't be moved, and in the end Father had to give way. So she'd have no friendly face in her new, uncertain world. Worse still, her books were another bone of contention.

"She'll need no books," Gilbert snarled.

Katherine felt her jaw clench. She wasn't going to sit by and let the old curmudgeon deny her that one comfort! She stood up, made her curtsey and looked John Gilbert straight in the eye. "Good Uncle, books will be a boon to me when I introduce Otho's fine sons to the world of learning," she said in a firm voice, as Mother's mouth dropped open. "My dearest wish is to see those sons grow to be well-educated men who will bring honour to the Gilbert name. Books will help me give them a fine start."

Father smiled. The old man muttered and glared. Perhaps he thought it a pert speech from one so young. She waited, heart in mouth, for his answer.

"Very well, Mistress. You may have your books," he growled. "Though I'll remove them should I see you neglecting your duties and frittering away your time reading."

"Well done, Katherine-Kate," said Father after he'd gone. "You spoke with rare courage and sense. In his twilight years he yearns to see a nursery full of sons. Striking that note with Master Gilbert will always touch the spot."

She felt as though she had grown several inches, and her chest almost burst with pride.

On a bright September morn, Johnny rode up to the Court House door with Peter. The Carew contingent followed: Cousin George,

Uncle William (remarkably recovered after Peter's return), Aunt Joan, and a host of other Carew relations. The family was gathering for Katherine's wedding.

William Cole looked sullen when he arrived with Eliza; there was no sign that a Cole baby might be expected any time soon. Katherine wished all her sisters could be there, but neither Kat nor Joanie could get leave of absence this time. Joan the Elder was in Wales with her ailing child. But Katherine had Johnny. The sun beat down on apple boughs bent nearly to the ground with ripening fruit which filled the air with a pleasant, sweet aroma.

"Well, Katherine-Kate, the King's declared himself Supreme Head of the English Church, and Parliament's confirmed it," Johnny said, as they sat together in their favourite spot.

"How can that be? I thought the Pope was Head of all the Church everywhere?" She drew her brows together and then gave a throaty chuckle. "Does it mean the King can now annul his own marriage? How very convenient!"

"That's sharp of you, Katherine-Kate!" Johnny said when his own laugher had subsided a bit. "King Henry's been a-visiting Queen Catherine, begging her to accept it. He wants everyone to think he's putting the Queen aside against the dictates of his heart. Ha, ha! I doubt if Emperor Charles will fall for that. After all, he is the Queen's nephew. Nor do I think the Queen will budge. She insists that her marriage to Prince Arthur was never consummated; that she's the King's true and loyal wife. And she certainly won't accept that King Henry could set himself up above the Pope."

Katherine swallowed and shook her head, acutely conscious that she was about to embark on matrimony herself. Surely nothing like this could ever happen to her?

"When I went with the royal progress in July we had to make do with the Lady Anne instead of Queen Catherine. You'd have thought that would make the King happy, wouldn't you? Not so!" said Johnny mischievously. "You can see he's tired of all the fits of temper she throws at him. I can't say I blame him, either. But, if you ask me, the Lady will not rest happy until the Queen's banished forever and she set up in her stead. But what care I? I have my place at court. Peter's there too; it's a fine life so long as you steer clear of intrigues."

"Oh, Johnny! You're so lucky. I've just got to accept that I must marry Otho. I don't know him at all. I don't feel ready to be a wife," Katherine wailed. She'd seen Otho only once since that first unsatisfactory meeting. Again he'd seemed nervous and tense, stammering and stuttering, especially under his uncle's piercing gaze.

"Well, at least he's young. I'm sure he'll do. Father says old Gilbert's done up a fine house for you to live in. You'll have every comfort in the land. Imagine – soon you'll be lording it over all the servants there and living in the lap of luxury. A grand lady indeed!" Johnny tried to console her as he gave her a hug. "Don't worry, Katherine-Kate, you'll be all right."

The bridegroom and his supporters arrived. Isabel Gilbert, Otho's mother, was a haughty woman with fine features and a high forehead. Thomas Gilbert must have been nearly fifty when he married Isabel Reynward, widow of a Cornish gentlemen named Penkervell, and daughter of another well-off Cornishman. It was easy to see what had attracted him. She was still an outstanding beauty, although her looks were marred by the pinched and sour set of her mouth. Otho's sister Joan, a plump dumpling of a girl who shared her brother's mousy colouring, stood pouting beside Isabel. Joan's features, which otherwise might have been pretty, were lost in a moonlike face. Her greeting was grudging, as if she resented all the attention showered on Otho's bride.

"My girl will have her work cut out to manage these women," Katherine heard Mother whisper behind her hand to Agnes. "I must find excuse to visit often and give her what help I may."

The Court House seemed full of unfamiliar sounds as the guests slowly retired to bed, feet echoing on the stairs, voices and laughter slowly dying away. All night long the sound of pots and pans banging and rattling drifted in through the open window as, in the kitchens, the cook set everyone to work on the wedding feast. But it was not the unusual nocturnal activity that kept Katherine awake. It was her struggle with the demons of the morrow that held her rigid into the small hours, sent her eyes flitting toward the still-dark window, and kept her mind in a turmoil of possibilities and fears. The linen sheet felt itchy against her skin. Her mouth felt dry. Her heart thumped in her chest. She turned this way and that and listened enviously to Frances's steady breathing. She tried to take deep breaths herself, but the air felt like a lump of ice stuck in her throat.

She must have drifted off, for she dreamt she was aboard a ship on a cold, dark, storm-tossed sea with no land in sight. Waking with a start, she saw that dawn's light had outlined the faint grey shape of her window. But Katherine did not rush to welcome the joyful day. Instead she lay huddled in the bed she shared with Frances. This was the last night she would spend there. After today, all would be changed. The sun was rising, just as it did on any other day. It would set again that night, as it always did. Tomorrow the party would be over and life would continue just as before at the Court House. It was she, Katherine, who would be changed.

As the contours of the chamber emerged from the shadows of night, she knelt beside the bed in prayer. The Church taught that the rosary could be used to say special prayers. But Katherine had always addressed God more directly. She hoped that it would not put her immortal soul in jeopardy when she chanted, "Help me to be a good wife to Otho. Help me get through this day to the credit of my family. Please, please, dear God, let Otho be a kind and loving husband to me, and please, when the time comes, bless us with fine sons and beautiful daughters."

A beaming Frances bounced out of bed with an excited squeal and joined her at the bedside, and Agnes swept in with her arms full of clothes, Eliza trailing in her wake. At Agnes's instruction, Adam the gardener had made an early morning raid on the gardens and brought in armfuls of gillyflowers, late-blooming honeysuckle and roses. Frances sat on the floor, chattering away, weaving the flowers into a bright garland, but Katherine was so lost in her own thoughts that she had no idea what her sister was saying.

Katherine took a deep breath and stood up. It was time to prepare for her day of days.

First they washed her hair in rainwater infused with rose petals. She gave herself up to the unusual, sensuous pleasure of the perfumed water trickling over her scalp before it splish-sploshed into the waiting bowl. As she sat before the fire to dry her luxuriant hair, her heart started skipping again.

Next they rubbed her body with scented linen cloths until it glowed. She washed her hands and face and slipped on a new shift, admiring the embroidery. Katherine, the erstwhile reluctant needlewoman, was proud of her handiwork. It was a fitting symbol of her acceptance of her lot in life.

"Keep still, Katherine-Kate. You're all of a fidget. Eager to meet your husband, is it?" Eliza quipped as she fastened the ties of a thickly padded underskirt.

Katherine felt her lips tremble as she looked into Eliza's cornflower eyes. "Oh, Eliza, I'm so afraid. 'Tis such a big step to change from maid to wife. I'm not sure I can do it, but I know I must. Were you fearful when you married William?" Her stomach was churning and she just couldn't keep still. She rocked back and forth on her heels.

Eliza turned away, and Agnes gave a tiny shake of her head.

"All brides feel like this," Eliza said briskly. "There is nothing to fear. Now, let's get that fine kirtle."

Katherine ran her hands down the soft, shining fabric, luxuriating in the slippery feel of it; Italian silk of the brightest red imaginable. What a pity it would be hidden under the heavily embroidered front-part Agnes was tying in place. Last of all came a gown of green damask, with separate sleeves in the latest style, pulled back to reveal the embroidered cuffs of her shift. She would wear no headdress, just Frances's pretty garland of flowers. The gardeners, with the help of a giggling laundry maid, had been busy tying ribbon-festooned bunches of rosemary for her, Otho and all the guests to wear. Eliza pinned one to the front of her gown, and the pungent, piny fragrance hung in the air.

Agnes stood back with tears in her eyes as the garland found its place atop Katherine's flowing brown locks. "There now, just look at you, my flower. Be sure to hold rosemary in your posy, too, for it stands for love and for loyalty." She wiped her eyes on her apron as she added a few sprigs to the pretty blooms. "'Twill bring you luck on your wedding day."

The house was already astir, all noise and bustle, servants rushing around as the wedding guests waited for their first sight of the bride.

Katherine felt as though her heart would jump right out of her chest as she made her stately progress down the stairs. Father was waiting, love and pride written all over his face. He squeezed her hand encouragingly.

"Why, you look so fine, I hardly recognised you, Katherine-Kate," he said. He was fiddling with the ring on his finger as he looked into her eyes. "You look so grown-up, so serene. You'd put any of the fine ladies at court in the shade today, my dear. I am so very proud of you."

She felt anything but serene as she stepped out into the bright morning. Her legs were trembling as she took Father's arm and they set off at a slow pace down the familiar path towards the church. She felt strange; light as a feather tossed in the breeze that lifted her unbound hair and set it streaming behind her like a banner. Everything became a hazy blur: a sea of faces, indistinguishable shades, all gathered at the church door. With an effort, she focused her eyes. There was Otho, his cheeks flushed red, making as fine a show as he could beside his uncle, whose self-satisfied grin sat oddly on his craggy face. Otho's mother held her nose high in the air as if to avoid some offending smell, and smoothed out the folds of a rather old-fashioned gown. Joan would have been better advised not to team such a striking shade of yellow with black sleeves and trimmings; she resembled nothing so much as a fat bumblebee. And there were Johnny and all of Katherine's Carew relations, beaming their support. She found a smile for Frances, who skipped along beside Eliza and William Cole, then almost laughed out loud at Arthur, swaggering behind Peter Carew, copying his every move like a proper little gentleman. Buoyed up on the tide of her family's good wishes, she took her place beside her bridegroom at the church door.

Mr Hunte looked pompous as he intoned the words that would change her from maid to wife. Taking a deep breath, she spoke her vows with confidence, and stole a shy glance at Otho as he did likewise with a slight tremor in his voice, trying hard not to stammer. Poor Otho! They went into the church as man and wife and knelt amongst the tombs of long-gone Champernownes.

After a cup of wine they all walked back to the Court House for the wedding breakfast, stopping to plant a branch of rosemary in the hope that it would take root and grow. If it did, it was supposed to be a good omen for their future life together. Katherine sat on Otho's left in pride of place. With flaming cheeks, he brushed her cheek under the kissing knot. Everyone clapped and cheered. The traditional kiss was supposed to be a reminder of romance and another promise of a long and faithful marriage. Emboldened by the cheering crowd, Otho ventured a second kiss, this time on her lips, and it was Katherine's turn to blush. She tried to hide an involuntary shudder as he placed his wet, sloppy mouth onto hers. It was the first time he had kissed her like that and she wasn't sure she liked it at all.

The nocturnal activities of the cook and his helpers had produced a wonderful array of delicacies, but she could eat only a little. Even her favourite confections, marchpane fancies and tarts sweetened with honey, failed to tempt her. Beside her, John Gilbert sat, silent and smug. She looked past Otho to Mother, who was laying down the law, ramming home the message that he must love, protect and, above all, respect her daughter. Father was having a hard time of his conversation with Isabel, to judge from his pained expression, and Johnny and Peter Carew were making sport at the expense of Otho's plump sister Joan.

The minstrels struck up and all eyes turned to the young couple. But Otho was busy downing another glass of wine and didn't seem to notice the waiting well-wishers. Putting her hand carefully on his arm, Katherine rose. "Come, husband, everyone is waiting for us to start the dance."

Otho blundered ungraciously to his feet, offered her his arm, and they stepped out into the centre of the hall. He was not a natural dancer, she thought, as she steered his stumbling steps through the familiar patterns with a forced smile.

Much too soon, the time came for them to be escorted to bed. They would lie in the best chamber where clean sheets of the finest linen had been scattered with rose petals and rosemary. Katherine would for evermore associate the pungent scent of rosemary with that day.

In the tiny dressing space, a weeping Agnes helped her from her clothes and into another new shift. Everyone crowded into the bedchamber, and the priest said a prayer and blessed the bed. Johnny and Peter made rude jests, pointing at the huge bolster Father had insisted be placed in the centre of the bed. Katherine's cheeks glowed fiery red.

All of a sudden, they were alone. Otho peered over the top of the bolster and looked full at her, making her blush again to be seen so, in nothing but her shift. "Why, you are but a child," he said. "I can find my pleasure better in any of the stews in Dartmouth than here with you." And with those cruel words, he turned over and the effects of the wine he had sampled in some quantity took over.

She could hear him snoring long into the night, while her tears seeped into Mother's finest feather pillow. When she woke, she was alone.

PART TWO

THE WIFE

EIGHT
1531
KATHERINE

The Gilbert party assembled on horseback in the shadow of the imposing crenellated walls. Katherine's few treasures and her precious books were crammed into a coffer, mixed up in a jumble of gowns, winter sleeves and headdresses. A gaily coloured scrap of fabric bundled together Johnny's letters, Katherine Plantagenet Courtenay's christening gifts, and, most special of all, Katherine's family of dolls. She was far too grown-up to play with the little figures now, but they had been a treasured part of her carefree childhood days. It was comforting to know that they would follow in the baggage wagon.

She leaned forward in the saddle to pat Dapple's neck. At least she would have one friend in her new life. Thank goodness Master Gilbert, whom she supposed she must now think of as Uncle John, had allowed her to take her own pony with her. She gulped and tried valiantly to hold back stinging tears as she raised her hand in farewell to her family and home. A cloud crossed the sun as she followed Otho's retreating back through the gate and into her new world.

In view of his advancing years, John Gilbert sat his mount well, leading them down the lanes at a fair pace. Katherine tried to strike up a conversation with Otho, but he was nursing a sore head after his wedding-day excesses, and remained sullen and withdrawn. She offered a comment on the weather to Isabel, but her new mother-in-law turned rudely aside to speak with Joan. Rebuffed, Katherine let Dapple fall behind. It was all she could do to fight against the thick feeling rising in her throat and resist the urge to turn back and ride for home. Only pride kept her head held high.

The track, too narrow to glory in the name of 'road' or 'highway', wove between high banks that obscured all but a band of vivid blue high above. Katherine's eyes were blind to the few ragged butterflies flitting amongst the late blackberries that tumbled down the steep banks. Most of the swallows had already gone, and even the birds searching for seeds amongst the brambles seemed to have lost their voices. The gloomy silence was broken only by the steady *clink, clack, clatter* of the horses' hooves as they struck the stony ground, or the *thump, thunder, thrum* when they pounded over a hard, dusty patch. She spent most of that dreary journey wondering how she could possibly bear the new life drawing ever nearer with each lonely mile.

Sometime after noon they reached the little village of Dittisham set on a sweeping bend in the River Dart, which narrowed to a thin neck just downstream. She could see a quay clinging to the opposite bank, and a cottage with a thin trail of smoke curling from the chimney. There was no bridge.

John Gilbert gave a loud halloo and waved his arm. Following the direction of his outstretched arm, Katherine saw a flat-bottomed boat propelled by very long oars advancing slowly towards them.

"That's our ferryboat: we Gilberts have run the ferry here for generations. It saves a good deal of time on many a journey. Otherwise, it's a long ride all through the town of Totnes five miles away. Of course, all must pay a fat fee to use it. It brings in quite an income," Otho said, puffing out his chest. He always adopted a bragging tone about the Gilberts' wealth.

"So will horses and all have to get aboard that creaking boat?" she asked.

Rather than reply, Otho motioned her to dismount and give the reins to a serving man. With rough, heavy hands the man made to lead Dapple onto the rocking ferryboat, but the little mare threw up her head and, with a high-pitched whinny, dug in her hooves. Katherine pursed her lips and took the bridle from the open-mouthed churl.

She whispered quietly into Dapple's ear, stroked her velvety nose with calm, reassuring hands, and, after a few moments, the pony set her hooves gingerly onto the boards of the bobbing craft. The timbers groaned as the ferry started to edge slowly across the water, and soon they were in the middle of the flowing river.

"This ferry doesn't just transport men and horses, you know. It takes cattle across too. Bound for market in Galmpton, our nearest village over on the other side of the river. From there the drovers take them to other markets far away," Otho lectured, waving his gloved hand. "Our mansion house lies beyond those tall trees over yonder."

The ferry pulled into a sloping ramp and Katherine stepped out nimbly. Back in the saddle, she squared her shoulders. They were almost there.

They emerged from the trees, where a strong, earthy scent lingered, into the afternoon sun. She caught her breath. Spread before her was quite simply the most beautiful setting for a house she had ever seen. The broad, lazy river, winding its slow and stately path towards the sea between tree-clothed banks, formed a truly breathtaking backdrop. She raised her hand to her mouth and stared. Uncle John had replaced a tumbledown dwelling that had stood on the promontory high above the Dart with a stunning mansion in the latest style. With its myriad windows glinting like jewels, it exuded wealth and status. It stood behind a low wall within its own bright emerald courtyard, calm grey walls topped by a slated roof and chimneys reaching up to the sky. John Gilbert's mansion had every appearance of a grand country seat; a place for a wealthy man to live at ease in the countryside and display his riches to all.

They dismounted and started to walk slowly towards the house.

"We call it Greenway Court," Otho announced with a knowing grin. "Named for an ancient track, the Greynway, that runs all the way from Dartmoor down through Totnes and onwards to the coast. It must be the most magnificent house for miles around! But this fine house isn't all Uncle John's built these last years. He's added a new chapel to our church in Marldon, too." He stuck his thumbs into the front of his doublet, and Katherine could swear that his chest puffed out even more. Oh, he was so proud of his uncle's wealth-driven deeds.

"'Twill be my pleasure to visit the church with you soon, husband," she said, using the unfamiliar term carefully, as though saying it out loud might make it all seem real.

Otho continued, barely acknowledging that she had spoken. "And even that's not the end of Uncle John's building works. I don't suppose you know anything about this," he continued with a cold, contemptuous smile, "but when King Henry was at war with the King of France years ago, well, everyone thought, being close to the coast, Compton might be vulnerable. So Uncle John had high walls raised, and now there are five towers and all sorts of defences as well as a gatehouse. We could withstand any attack there."

No high walls surrounded Greenway Court, although Katherine had noticed the well-armed men standing guard down at the quay.

"Near the quay there's a sheltered haven. That's Galmpton Pool," Otho went on, and again she heard the pride in his voice. "There's at least five fathoms of water at low tide. It's a safe anchorage in times of war; attackers would have to pass the defences of Dartmouth as well as others at Brixham and Churston to get here."

His words tumbled out so very fast it was hard to keep up with them, especially when he started to talk about all the forts and bastions that would repel any attack. She listened carefully, hoping that he would now speak to her more often and more kindly. But her hopes were soon dashed.

"But what would a girl like you care about such things?" Otho snickered, and marched off through the green court towards the door.

Katherine swallowed hard before she stepped over the threshold for the first time. She followed Otho up a magnificent carved-oak staircase into a well-proportioned room with huge windows overlooking the river. Sweeping past the servants without a glance, Isabel sailed in as though she owned the space, Joan rolling along behind her, to be greeted by a swarthy little man. His bow completed, he turned to fold Otho in a bear hug, with much backslapping and guffaws of laughter.

If it was possible to fall instantly in love with someone, then perhaps it was also possible to fall instantly into hatred. There was something in that man's eyes that made Katherine's flesh crawl as he turned to appraise her from top to toe. Her cheeks coloured at his unwanted scrutiny. It felt as though the horrid man could see right through her clothes. She waited to be presented, for it was clear from his dress that this man was no servant. Otho seemed to have forgotten her completely, so it was left to Isabel to introduce her dear son, Philip Penkervell.

"Delighted to make your acquaintance, Mistress Gilbert." He leered as he swept her a mocking bow and raked her again with those impertinent eyes.

As she rose from her curtsey, she was pleased to note that she stood equally as tall as this Penkervell fellow. She could meet his gaze eye to eye, and did so with unwavering coldness. "I am sure the pleasure and surprise are all mine, Master Penkervell," she said, unable to keep the venom from her voice. "I had not learned until this instant that Otho had such a brother."

The horrid man returned her gaze for a moment longer and then shrugged his shoulders. He was soon laughing with Otho, turning occasionally to gesture in her direction.

She escaped to a pretty chamber with views over the river. To her relief, she discovered that the room was for her alone; Otho would presumably sleep elsewhere. A sallow, sharp-featured waiting woman introduced herself as Jane.

"Master John has placed me to act as your maid, Mistress," she said with barely concealed contempt.

How Katherine wished that Agnes was not so far away. But, tired after the journey, she allowed Jane to help her to bed.

On waking, she called for Jane. After some delay the woman shuffled in, bearing water for Katherine to wash her face and hands. After saying her prayers she dressed with the help of the surly maid, whose pinched face made her look as though she had just taken a sip of vinegar.

Seeing that her coffers had been brought in, Katherine announced, "I shall wear my French hood, Jane."

"Nay, Mistress, I see no such here," replied the servant, with a malicious smile. "But here be a fine English hood you may have."

Katherine had seen Uncle John eyeing her hood months ago. He must have ordered that, as Otho's wife, she would no longer wear such fripperies. She bit her lip. The serving woman was waiting expectantly, perhaps hoping that her new mistress would rail at the restriction. She wouldn't give her that satisfaction. Better to wait and fight on bigger matters. So Jane's eyebrows shot up and her mouth turned down even more when Katherine smiled sweetly.

"Ah, my thanks, Jane. 'Tis indeed a fine hood," she said, and set it on her head without demur, carefully concealing her lustrous hair.

She was up just in time to say farewell to Uncle John, who had determined to return to Compton. She looked into the great parlour, thinking how fine it was to have two parlours, one much bigger than the other. It was empty. The voices must be coming from the little parlour. There she found John in conversation with Otho's mother, who didn't sound happy with the outcome.

"A fool and her money are easily parted, Isabel. All the world knows that Honor Grenville, or Lady Basset, or Lady Lisle or whatever name she now goes by, never pays her debts. To advance money to her was plain folly," the old man growled. "Did you think that if you called on kinship she'd find a place for your daughter? She's only interested in getting her own Basset girls a place at court."

"Well, I have made my case to you again. The girl will never make a good match with the meagre portion you have allotted. The world will laugh to see a Gilbert girl so poorly dowered! On your head be it, then, John Gilbert!" Isabel marched from the room in a crackling flurry of black silk.

"Harrumph!" he exploded, glowering at her back. "'Tis pity my brother ever married you! Well, if you think I'm going to stump up any more to swell a dowry for that fat dolt of a daughter of yours, you've got another think coming! You'll have to find another way to entice some fool to take Joan on."

He sat down heavily and only then noticed Katherine hesitating in the shadows. He motioned to her to sit, eying her modest headdress, and she assumed her most demure pose, eyes dutifully downcast. It seemed an age before he spoke.

"Well, girl. You're young, but you show promise," he growled. "I gave my word that you'd have the company of women. Isabel and Joan are all that's available."

She raised her head, found him peering at her slender frame, and shifted uncomfortably under his probing eyes. She didn't like the way he was looking at her, weighing her up like a prize milker in the byre. But Mother had stressed that she must act the dutiful wife before him, so she must endure it.

"I give you good morning, Mistress Gilbert," he barked, emphasising the name. Then, to her astonishment, he rose from his chair and stalked off. A few moments later she heard his horse's hooves clatter out of the courtyard at the back of the house.

She saw little of Otho in those first days and weeks at Greenway Court. Isabel held sway within the house, with fat Joan her willing acolyte. How Katherine hated those autumn afternoons in the bright parlour! Otho's mother was forever finding trivial errands for her to run, or setting her to the most tedious stitching. She and Joan shut Katherine out of their conversation, which centred mainly on Joan's marriage prospects, so she watched the cog boats making headway on the Dart. In one of his more communicative moments Otho had mentioned that much larger carracks and hulks, like those Uncle John owned, now voyaged out to sea. But smaller craft with clinker-built hulls of dark oak still worked the river route between the town of Totnes and the port of Dartmouth. She loved to see them bobbing along bearing cargoes of salt, spices, wine and cloth. Her needle still, she daydreamed about the exotic places those cargoes might have come from, and escaped into an imaginary world.

Whenever she could get away from Isabel's nagging and Joan's disdainful looks, she explored the gardens clustered round the house. She went often down to the quay to see if any of the Gilbert ships were tied up to load bales of wool, cloth, or casks of wine. Sometimes she saw carts weighed down with limestone hewn from the nearby hillside, or sand dredged from the river rumbling over the cobbles to await the next barge; cargoes to be sold at profit for building in Dartmouth. Once in a while, Otho joined her. They were still very awkward with each other, their exchanges stilted and short.

On one of these rare occasions, searching for a safe subject for conversation, Katherine asked, "Otho, why does Uncle John bring all his ships right up to the wharf here at Greenway Court? Why doesn't he unload in Dartmouth and trade his goods there?"

Otho seemed surprised by the question. "Why, yes, of course everyone knows cargoes must be assessed in Dartmouth for customs dues. But Uncle John prefers to bring his ships safely to his own wharf." His voice was so patronising she itched to punch him on the nose. "More than a hundred years ago we had licence to convey pilgrims to Santiago de Compostella in Spain. Uncle John says William Gilbert was in partnership with someone from your family. Ha, I bet you didn't know that, did you?"

"Well, Father did tell me that one of your ancestors was married to an heiress from our family," she retorted, then clamped her lips together, wishing she could take the words back. It wasn't a good idea to draw attention to the superior wealth of the Champernownes.

Predictably, Otho bristled. "It was William Gilbert's ship the *Charity* that used to take on a full load of those pilgrims, each one paying a fat fee. Filled the hold with bales of English cloth to trade, and brought back wine from Gascony. Since then we've built up a fleet of ships," he boasted. "But Uncle John says the bottom's gone right out of the pilgrim trade. The *Charity's* still seaworthy, though she's had a few refits. Uncle John says she's creaking a bit, so mostly he charters her out to fishermen these days." He turned and looked down his nose at her. "But I don't suppose you care about any of that." His preachy, condescending voice set her hackles rising. "I'm off to meet Penkervell." And he bounded up the path, leaving her fuming on the quay.

Katherine soon learned to recognise the *Hope of Greenway* and the *George*, and John Gilbert's pride and joy the *Trinity*, a model of modern shipbuilding. She longed to step aboard and sail away, but her life was clearly mapped out, and it didn't involve embarking on any voyage of discovery.

Being a God-fearing man, Uncle John insisted that the household worship regularly at St Mary's in the nearby village of Churston Ferrers, as well as receiving the ministrations of the priest from Compton at home. The Sunday excursion was a welcome diversion, and Katherine's only chance to see something of the countryside around her new home.

The tiny hamlet of Galmpton, ramshackle hovels all squashed

in higgledy-piggledy beside the road, housed men who smelted limestone in the kilns, quarrymen who cut stone for Uncle John's building work, and carpenters who worked on the Gilbert fleet. Katherine was shocked at the squalid conditions they must endure; the Gilbert cattle were better housed. She vowed that when she had the running of the household she would try to improve the lot of the children who ran in the lane in their bare feet, gawking at her as she passed.

St Mary's had once been the chapel for the manor house, Churston Court, held by the Yardes of Bradley. They were rarely in residence, preferring their manor in Newton Bushell. So it was a pleasant surprise to see Thomas Yarde in the congregation one October morning.

"Why, good day to thee, Mistress Gilbert," he said with a well-practised bow. "You are well met here at Churston Ferrers. I'm here upon my father's business." And then, dropping his voice to a sympathetic murmur, "I was sorry to hear of your grandmother's passing."

"It was a shock to us all," she replied. "She was ever grateful for your kindness to us. I trust your father is in health?"

"May God be praised that he is, Mistress Gilbert," replied Thomas.

But there the conversation was cut short. Otho gave Thomas a curt nod and hustled Katherine to the waiting horses. As soon as they were out of earshot he berated her sternly for speaking to the man.

"I meant no offence, husband," she snapped, her eyes flashing. "'Tis a strange world indeed where the wife of so fine a man as Otho Gilbert may not greet someone who once offered her shelter in a time of need."

Otho calmed down a bit when she told him how Thomas had taken them in on that nightmare journey. But they rode home in frosty silence, Katherine so furious that she hardly noticed that Longwood was aflame with autumn colour, stunningly beautiful in the watery October sun. Perhaps he wanted a wife who never spoke to anyone; a wife kept shut away, kept only for the purpose of breeding heirs.

NINE
1531-1532
KATHERINE

UNCLE JOHN HAD DECREED THAT THEY WOULD CELEBRATE Christmastide at Compton, so on Christmas Eve she approached the Gilberts' strongly fortified home for the first time. The manor house, with its soaring walls, battlements, high towers and turrets, stood dark and forbidding beyond a squat gatehouse. A jumble of farm buildings stood away to the right, and behind them, large fish ponds bordered a stream. Katherine slipped lightly from the saddle and, dusting down her skirts, followed Otho into an old-fashioned hall where banners bearing the arms of the Gilberts and the de Comptons fluttered in the acrid, smoky air. While the hall was clearly still used, as in times past, for feasts, estate business and meetings, it was not set for a meal that day. Instead they sat down to a meagre supper, since the Advent fast would not be broken until the next day, in a comfortable parlour. Afterwards Katherine joined the prayers in the chapel, and then retired thankfully to bed, to have her sleep disturbed by Joan's loud snores. She didn't relish the prospect of sharing the chilly little chamber with Joan for the whole twelve nights.

She could make no complaint of the Christmas Day feast. Great swathes of greenery decked the hall and the tables looked fit to collapse under the weight of so many tasty dishes. Enormous cuts of beef and pork vied for space with salads of vegetables, and pies with raised pastry crusts. Ducks and geese, woodcock, larks and quails were all roasted to perfection. Fresh fish from the Compton ponds eked out the catch of Brixham's fishermen, amongst an array of tempting sweetmeats.

One of the serving men gave a rousing rendition of the 'Boar's Head Carol' as the traditional dish, dressed with rosemary and bay, was borne into the hall on a large platter. Katherine hated to see the pig's head so displayed, but she was learning that Uncle John liked to keep up all the long established customs. A solitary lute player was soon joined by an enthusiastic, if not well-practised, boy with a fife. Katherine smiled to see fat Joan trying to keep pace in the dance with Edward Gilbert, Otho's broad-shouldered cousin. She looked across at her husband laughing uproariously with Penkervell and downing quantities of John Gilbert's Christmas ale. No one offered to be her partner.

She felt his eyes on her, and blushed. Otho's uncle was staring at the front of her gown where she'd had to let it out again to accommodate her developing figure. The old curmudgeon got regular reports from the laundry maids and sour-faced Jane, and Katherine knew only too well why he took such an interest in the state of her laundry. No doubt he was thinking that she'd soon be grown enough to bear a Gilbert heir. Well, if Otho didn't start to pay her a bit more attention, there didn't seem much chance of that! He seemed much happier quaffing ale and roistering with that repugnant oaf Penkervell than stealing a kiss under the kissing bough.

On New Year's Day, after presenting her with a pretty jewelled collar that had belonged to his grandmother, Otho surprised her by inviting her to tour the house. He was at his best when talking about military topics, and launched into an excited explanation of Compton's defences. His stutter seemed to have disappeared as he gabbled through the list of weapons at their disposal and invited her to look upwards at the strange gaps high in the walls. "They're for pouring boiling oil or water, or for throwing down stones onto the heads of any who would attack us."

Katherine dutifully craned her neck and peered at them.

"Not that any will ever get so close as that. We can cut them off before they get anywhere near the walls." He led her back inside and showed her a squint window tucked into the corner on the right of the screened archway. "See how it lines up perfectly with another in the courtyard wall, giving us a clear view all the way to the gatehouse?" Otho explained. "We'd see anyone coming that way. The portcullis can be down in an instant."

He proceeded to lead her all over the building, showing her the towers that projected to ensure that every angle was covered, the high battlements where armed men could patrol, the thickness of the walls, and the second portcullis that protected the inner court. She wasn't really interested, but she went along willingly, happy to seize any scrap of attention. It didn't even matter that it was probably old John who had prompted the unexpected guided tour. Likely he'd insisted Otho get to know her better, and this was the best entertainment the boy could think of. Penkervell's cold, cackling laughter hung in the air as she hurtled along after her husband.

The next day, the weather being fine but cold, Otho suggested they explore the Gilbert lands around Compton. What a joy it was to be out on Dapple and to breathe the fresh air as they rode down through the village, past the church where his ancestors lay! Katherine was careful to let him speak, so learned more than she cared to about gunpowder and arquebuses, about cannons and the new handguns that fascinated him so. The masculine obsession with warfare seemed to her an abomination that only got young men into trouble. But she couldn't change the world of men, and at least Otho was talking to her. It was a start.

To Katherine's surprise, after they returned to Greenway Court, Otho was keen that they continue their rides together while the weather held. Her father had given her his treasured copy of the tales of King Arthur and his knights as a wedding gift. When the weather turned too wet and cold for riding she took *Le Morte d'Arthur,* from her coffer and suggested they read it together. So started an almost daily ritual in which they nestled into one of the broad window seats in the great parlour and read together. When the ground was again thawed they let the horses have their heads on Warborough Common.

"I never knew a girl could ride so well," said Otho one windy morning as he watched her bring Dapple to a skilful halt.

She shielded her eyes and looked out over the wide expanse of Torbay, glistening in the wintry sun. "I love to see the sea like this," she said with a smile. "I wish I could take ship to see what lies across the ocean. Don't you long for adventure, Otho?"

Otho's eyebrows shot up and his mouth gaped. "You say the strangest things, wife," he said with a nervous laugh.

So the days passed, and, as matters improved with Otho, Isabel and Joan's hostility stung a little less.

"Can that self-possessed, elegant lady before the fire really be our daughter, Katherine-Kate?" Father whispered, not realising how his words carried.

Mother's eyes flew to the keeper of added cloth at the hem of Katherine's gown. Isabel Gilbert loomed in the doorway and ushered them into the room, her face a mask of haughty disapproval.

With more assurance than she felt, Katherine stepped forward. "I give you thanks, Mother Isabel, for showing my parents where I am," she said. "I'm sure they bring much trivial news of my family. Perhaps we may join you later?"

It was a bold dismissal. Isabel's mouth fell open and she stepped back. "Well… well… oh, yes, I will leave you, of course, if that is what you all wish," she answered, her voice cracking. She turned on her heel and swished out of the room.

Katherine had gambled that Isabel wouldn't really be interested in the Champernownes, who weren't likely to be much use in her quest for a husband for Joan. She had guessed right. As soon as Isabel was out of the way, Katherine darted forward and buried her face in the front of Mother's gown.

"Now, what's to do?" Father asked, with a face like thunder. "Do they not treat you well here?"

"Oh, Father! No one treats me ill at all," she wailed, dabbing ineffectually at her eyes with the linen kerchief Mother had drawn from her girdle. "But I've been so very lonely, and I do miss everyone at Modbury so much. It is just seeing you here that has made me weep like the silly little maid I am."

Father shook his head and studied her face. "Harrumph. Well, so long as you're sure? I hope Otho hasn't breached the bounds of our agreement? I'd never have allowed the marriage had Gilbert not agreed to keep you young people apart until you're grown."

"Dear Father, Otho does treat me with proper respect, as you would wish. We're starting to become friends, I think," she said, trying to smile. "Now, sit here in the window seat and tell me: what news is there from Johnny?"

Father looked at her uncertainly, then at his wife.

"There, there, child, it's no wonder you've felt starved of news from home," Mother said. "Tell her the latest from our boy, Philip."

"He does well enough at court with your cousin Peter, who has impressed the King with his impeccable French and courtly manners. 'Tis to be hoped that Johnny can learn something from him. They were both at court for Christmas. For the first time Anne Boleyn was there in Queen Catherine's place. What do you think of that? I really don't know what it will mean for Kat and Joanie." He scratched his head, flopped into the window seat and was soon engrossed in the manoeuvres of a cog boat making its way downriver.

"Now, Philip, why don't you rest there while I speak with Katherine, mother to daughter?" said Mother, taking her hand. "My dear, your mother-in-law has invited us to stay for a day or two before we travel on to Mohun's Ottery. I'm going on to London to visit Aunt Gertrude. She's sure to know what's going on."

Father closed his eyes and was soon dozing.

"All of this turmoil at court keeps your father awake at nights. But Johnny's doing ever so well."

Katherine thought it sounded as though her brother spent too much time with Cousin Peter, but let her mother run on. Father stirred, refilled his mug from the flagon, glanced towards them, saw they were deep in conversation, rested his head on his arms and closed his eyes again.

The next afternoon, leaving Mother with Isabel, Katherine walked in the gardens with Father. "Mother's all aflutter about visiting Aunt Gertrude," she remarked.

"Aye, more's the pity. I'm not sure Aunt Gertrude is such a good influence."

"How so? Surely she's well placed as the wife to our kinsman Henry Courtenay?"

"Ah… um. You'd think so, daughter. But the King trusts no one, least of all those with Yorkist blood. Those stories that came out of Cornwall a year or so ago damaged Courtenay, and Gertrude's known as a staunch supporter of her former mistress. She should keep a guard on her tongue. The King's made up his mind and Parliament's sitting. There'll be new laws to restrict the power of the Church and to curtail our allegiance to Rome. It's no use to swim against the tide."

"Now, Father," Katherine said, "I really don't understand this at all. Will everything really change?"

Settling himself on the stone wall by the wharf, Father looked worried. "I don't rightly know about Rome," he said. "You're a good listener, Katherine-Kate. Let me tell you what I *do* think. I don't like the look of the factions that are shaping up with Wolsey gone. It's a dog-eat-dog world at court. Norfolk is forever discrediting his rivals for the King's ear. Take Nicholas Carew – he's a distant relative of William's. Sometimes he's in favour; next thing you know, he's out. Then there's that lawyer, Thomas Cromwell; used to serve Wolsey, and now he's close adviser to the King. If he can get the divorce then we'll all do well to keep in Cromwell's good books. He's strong for reform and hot to seize monastic lands and the abbeys' wealth."

"Uncle John did speak of this man Cromwell," she remarked. "I don't think he likes him much. Though I do remember that Kat said that he's a man of some import."

"Should Cromwell succeed where Wolsey failed, he'll be the power in the land," said Father.

They chatted on about this and that. Father's eye's nearly came out of his head when Katherine asked if he would find her a book about firearms, the mysteries of gunpowder, or its use in warfare.

"If there are none such at Modbury, could Mother seek one at the printers in London?" she suggested.

"Why, daughter, this is a strange request," he said, smiling. "I didn't know of your interest in such matters."

When she explained that it was not for her, but for her husband, his smile broadened.

"So you and Otho are getting along a bit better, are you?" he asked.

"I'm trying to get to know him, Father. He has such interest in all these new weapons. I thought it might give him pleasure to learn more," she murmured, blushing furiously.

"I couldn't help noticing you two in the window seat, heads together over a book, this morning," he laughed. "You've grown to be a lovely young woman, Katherine-Kate. But don't go getting too fond of your husband yet. I know old man Gilbert wants an heir in the nursery, but you're over-young for that." Katherine felt her neck and ears grow hot. There was really nothing like that between her and Otho. She was lonely and wanted a friend. That was all.

It took a lot of patient questioning before she pieced Otho's history together. Born at Thomas Gilbert's manor at Broadwoodkelly, he'd spent most of his rather lonely childhood at Compton under his uncle's watchful eye. When Thomas died and Otho became the heir, John Gilbert's expectations of him had grown. He didn't hesitate to make it clear when he thought her husband was not coming up to scratch, undermining the boy's fragile confidence. Otho looked up to Penkervell as to a god. But Katherine saw how that odious man belittled his achievements and laughed at his blossoming friendship with her. There was a marked change in her husband after a day spent with the ghastly little man.

A bright spring gave way to a warm summer and, to Katherine's relief, the Penkervells left for their Cornish lands. With them gone, she seized the chance to spend more time with Otho. Mother sent an Italian treatise on gunpowder and Katherine spent hours with him, poring over the text. Sometimes she thought he really was beginning to enjoy her company.

When Father next called at Greenway Court she saw at once that he was very upset. "Have you heard the news?" he demanded, throwing himself down into the seat by the window. "That woman Elizabeth Barton! That one will cause untold damage with her talk of visions and voices. There's pamphlets circulating, probably produced by that stupid monk... Edward Bocking, that's his name. He's the one who encouraged the silly girl, and caused a lot of trouble by it. Pamphlets full of dreadful prophecies against the King! Tell Otho to be sure to burn them if any come your way." He fell silent as the maid filled his cup. "Mark me well: it won't be long before Barton and her friends are arrested," he continued as soon as the coast was clear, "as should be any who compass the King's death. A man came to me in Plymouth with papers that mentioned Gertrude Courtenay, among others. Said she had knowledge of this so-called 'Nun of Kent'."

Katherine gasped. Aunt Gertrude was Mother's friend.

Father took a long draught of beer, set the cup down carefully and took her hand. "I can trust you with all this, can't I? You won't mention what I say to anyone, will you? But I need to tell someone or it'll drive me mad!"

She nodded.

"The thing is, I wouldn't put it past Gertrude Courtenay to be involved in this Nun business. And your mother is still a-visiting with her! So when that man came to me with his story, I sent a messenger to your cousin George post-haste with those papers, and a strong warning. I urged him to take them to his employer, Henry Courtenay. Gertrude's husband needs to know. I'm much afeared, Katherine-Kate. I just hope I've done the right thing."

"Cousin George will know what to do in this, Father," she said, "and surely Mother has had no contact with the Maid?"

"I wish I could be sure about that," he murmured, "but what more can I do? The messenger will reach George far more swiftly than I could."

Katherine urged him to rest awhile.

"You're a good girl, you know," he said. "And this house has a happy feel to it now that you're in it. I don't know why, but I always feel better for sitting here in this window and watching the river for a while. Calms me down, I suppose."

"Yes, Father," she replied. "It's my favourite spot too."

He continued his journey later that day, leaving Katherine perplexed. It seemed strange that Father, whom she'd always looked up to so much, now came to her for comfort in his troubles. But more than that, she was afraid for Mother. That night she offered a prayer that Cousin George would put things to rights.

Katherine said nothing when Otho and his uncle returned the next day with the lawyer John Rowe, and Cowyke, John Gilbert's proctor. There were always legal disputes to be dealt with, and this time it was a long-running case in the Admiralty Court concerning the *Charity*; something about money advanced against a catch of hake not repaid. The Mayor of Dartmouth was involved and there were fines due, or paid. She'd ask Father to explain it next time she saw him.

The men went on to talk of other matters. Lawyer Rowe was holding forth on the King's Great Matter. "All this talk of the King as Head of the Church in England and making us separate from Rome! I really do not hold with it at all."

"I tend to agree with you there, Rowe," said Uncle John. "The Church of Rome was good enough for my father and grandfather, so it's good enough for me. The reformers will have the whip hand, and where will that lead us? Some of them even question Purgatory. I've laid out a tidy sum on a chapel in Marldon church. I pay two poor men eight pence apiece to pray daily for my dear departed. I even founded a chantry school for the children of Marldon for good measure. Why, the first Geoffrey Gilbert of Compton built a chantry chapel in Totnes and they still pray for him there to this day. So don't tell me there's no Purgatory. That's the right way of things; not all this change, and all on account of that strumpet the King wants in his bed!"

Katherine sunk back into the shadows, hoping they wouldn't accuse her of eavesdropping. She wasn't sorry she'd been listening in. It had been quite revealing.

Katherine and Otho were sitting in the window seat surrounded by books and pamphlets when a horse galloped into the green court. Leaving the sweating beast unattended, the rider ran up the steps and burst through the parlour door.

"Begging pardon, Master, but Master John has taken a fall from his horse," the messenger panted. "He's been knocked senseless. We've carried him back to Compton but, Master, you must make haste to see how he does."

Otho was gone in no time. The day's heat had been replaced by a gentle, cooling breeze, and darkness was falling by the time he got back.

"How does your uncle?" Katherine asked, searching his face when she met him at the door.

"Well enough, though his temper has certainly not improved! He's back in his senses and giving all the servants an even harder time than usual. He'll be abed for at least a week, I should think, but he'll mend."

A week later a summons came with all the force of a royal command. Otho and Katherine must hurry to Compton to wait on the head of the family.

Katherine was bubbling with the joy of an outing on so fine a day. They chatted amiably as they left Galmpton behind and enjoyed a canter across Warborough Common. An occasional trail of briny air wafted across on a gentle breeze, and the summer sun felt warm on her back. The haymakers had long since scythed the flower-filled meadows. Amongst the lush regrowth a few late-cut strips shimmered in the heat haze, pale and dry as a new scrubbed table. Katherine grinned. It was high summer and all was well in her world. As they crossed the road to Totnes, she turned in her saddle. "Over yonder is Blagdon Manor House," she chirped. "On our way home, perhaps we can see if Cousin Cecily is at home? It's been long enough since I saw her; she's been so busy filling the cradle for Thomas Kirkham."

"Well, that depends on what my uncle has to say," Otho responded, blushing and biting his lip. He cast an anxious glance upwards to gauge the sun's position. "We must press on, and find out why we are so summoned."

The shadows cast by Compton's high walls were short by the time they arrived. They found Uncle John ashen-faced, propped up on a pile of pillows in his bed.

"So you're come at last!" he barked. "Took you long enough."

"Good Uncle," said Katherine tentatively. "I trust you are well recovered."

"I'll see a few more dawns, if that's what you're wondering," the old man grumbled. "But such a fall brings home to a man the weight of his advancing years. And still no Gilbert heir in the cradle. How old are you now, girl?"

"I'm past fourteen, as you know," she replied as the first inkling of what was to come dropped like a sliver of ice into her mind.

"Hmm," he muttered. "Nearer fifteen by the look of you, and healthy, from what I hear."

Her cheeks flamed, thinking of the laundry maids who reported on her linen.

"Now then," he went on, groaning as he shifted his skinny body on the mattress. "Our King's own grandmother was a mere girl when she bore his father. Now, she was a wise and learned lady who lived to a very great age, so it did her no harm, did it? Perhaps there's more to be feared for a lad. Might endanger his health if he indulges too much in the pleasures of the marriage bed at too young an age!"

Katherine darted a glance at Otho, who was biting his nails and staring at the floor.

"Wasn't that what they said about Prince Arthur?" Otho's uncle demanded, before he drilled Otho with another steely stare. "Well, you're of an age now for it to cause no concern!"

Otho shuffled his feet. The very tips of his ears were flaming.

A bilious flush spread across the old man's face as he cackled and jabbed a finger in Otho's direction. "Pity you haven't filled out a bit more. Pity you're not cut from the same cloth as your cousin Edward. Geoffrey's boy's a fine, strong lad, he commands the loyalty of all who serve under him on my ships, and he's got a sound head for business," he barked, raking Otho with a withering glare.

Katherine shot another sympathetic look to Otho, who shrank visibly in the face of his uncle's tirade.

"Well, you are as you are, boy. My father's wishes were clear and I'll see them carried out to the letter. As God didn't see fit to bless my Elizabeth and me with sons of our own, you're next in line. Son of my brother Thomas, may God give him rest. There's no changing that. So get to it. I would see you get a few lusty boys on this Champernowne girl before I go to my Maker."

"B-b-b-but, Uncle, her father insisted she must not bear children yet," Otho stammered. And then, his voice barely audible, "Y-you… you agreed to it, sir."

"Do you think I haven't thought of that, boy?" stormed Uncle John, as raddled colour crept up his cheeks. "Champernowne might be a knight, but he's not yet paid the money for the girl's dowry. And that family's closeness to the Courtenays is a mixed blessing in these times. I've heard the Marquess is out of favour. Champernowne might cause a fuss, I suppose, but what can he really do? Eh? Eh?" he growled, glaring at Katherine, who took a step backwards and put a hand to her mouth. "Don't forget I still stand over a parcel of debts for him and his Carew relations. So your duty is clear? Get to it in the bedchamber while that interfering woman Isabel's away in Cornwall. Now be gone, the both of you."

They crept from the room, leaving him bellowing for his servants. A loud thump followed as something hit the chamber door.

They rode home in silence, all thoughts of an excursion to visit Cecily given up as they tried to take in what was being asked of them. Katherine knew that Otho went in fear of his uncle. There was no question that he would seek to defy him. But she could see from his white face and rigid features that he was quite terrified. He stared, unseeing, at the road ahead, unable to meet her eye. *Ha!* she thought. *He may have boasted of his exploits in the stews of Dartmouth, but perhaps in reality he's much less experienced than he pretended. Well, somehow or other the deed must be done.*

"We are tired after the journey, husband," she said with as much assurance as she could find. "Come to me tomorrow night." It would give her one more day.

TEN
1532-1533
KATHERINE

She knew her duty. Mother and Grandmother Carew had coached her well. Her role in life was to provide healthy babies for her husband and, with good luck, she might continue to do so well into her thirties. If she must now make a start, so be it. This turn of events was really no surprise. It was bound to come sometime, though it would have been more pleasant had it been her husband's lust for her rather than a command from that stick-like monster that finally brought them to bed.

She had Jane lay out her best night shift and bring wine. When Otho came to her chamber she tried to set him at his ease with light talk. But the boy just stood trembling by the door.

OTHO

All his brave talk of adventures with the whores of Dartmouth had come back to haunt him. The truth of it was that there had been but two such occasions. Unfortunately, it was the first that flashed to Otho's mind as he stood hesitating on the threshold of Katherine's chamber.

Two years had passed since that awful night when Penkervell had taken him to Dartmouth to 'make a man' of him. Standing shivering in his nightshirt as Katherine chattered on, he remembered how his steps had dragged as he followed his half-brother along the Undercliffe; how he'd looked in fascinated horror at the tiny hovels where the ragged ladies of the night displayed their wares for all to see; how, in a moment of absolute panic, he'd thought that Penkervell meant for him to take one, there and then, from the street. He remembered his short-lived relief when they went on to the inn that stood up the hill beyond Hawley's Hoe.

He tried to blot out those thoughts as he reached behind himself and felt the smooth, polished wood of the door to his wife's chamber at his back. He hung his head and studied the knotty floorboards beneath his feet. His fingers pulled at the hem of his linen shirt, his face aflame, his whole body shaking. How could he face her? They were becoming friends. She was the only one who'd ever shown him kindness. This night's work would surely put an end to all hope of that.

The ugly memory of that other time would not be dismissed; the time he stood hesitating, just like this, by the door of another room; the room Penkervell had secured. He remembered the woman sat on the bed with her knees bent up and her legs spread apart; he felt again his revulsion when he'd realised that she wore nothing but a shift, hitched up high to reveal the tops of her skinny thighs. She had raised a hand to undo the cord that held the shift across her bosom, and he'd seen that under the crude paint her narrow face was lined; seen that the bedraggled hair hanging in rats' tails over her shoulders was peppered with grey. She had smiled, showing her blackened teeth, and let the shift fall open. In his mind he saw again those dangling, ugly breasts as the woman beckoned to him to come closer. He remembered how he'd stood transfixed; how his eyes would not move from those drooping breasts; how he'd staggered backwards, felt for the handle, and been out of the door as if all the hounds of Hell were after him; how he'd raced down to the quay; how Penkervell had found him an hour later, still shaking and sobbing. His brother's words came to him again: "Well, your uncle won't be pleased. What a waste of good coin that was, boy."

Uncle John would know if he failed again. He must think of something else; recall the other time when the exercise was repeated with more success. That woman had been younger, and Penkervell had paid extra to be sure that the slender girl was clean and wholesome and had combed out her dark hair. When Otho went through the door that time he'd found her fully clothed. She had shown him much kindness – as, no doubt, she had been instructed – taking time to set him at ease before, with expert hands, she guided him through the mysteries that would make him a man.

Now, in the bedchamber at Greenway Court, he tried in vain to banish the image of the first ancient whore and summon the younger one, of whom he had much fonder memories. Try as he might, he found he could feel no desire for the clever, high-born girl he'd begun to think of as his friend. At first he'd thought of her simply as a bright, over-educated child. But, starved of love and affection all his life, he'd come to like her and enjoy the time they spent reading together. If he must now force himself upon her, he would lose that fragile friendship. He groaned and stood by the door in an agony of indecision, trying to resist the temptation to feel for the handle and bolt for cover again.

KATHERINE

When Katherine reached out and wrapped her unhappy husband in her arms she was certainly not stirred by lust. Rather, by intense pity for the boy who stood shivering by the door, incongruously clad in his nightshirt. It was all she could do not to laugh on seeing his skinny bare legs. That would not do. It would only make him feel more inadequate. Together, somehow, they must accomplish this deed that bound man and wife together. She held out her hand and led him gently to the bed.

With Otho's limited experience and her own shyness, it was a fumbling, unsatisfactory night for both of them. When she woke, the bed beside her was empty, and she lay wondering what all the fuss had been about. It had seemed of much less consequence than she'd expected; not particularly pleasant, but bearable. It was just something that must be endured.

A spot of blood on the sheet, which no doubt Jane would report, confirmed that she was now a wife indeed. When at last Otho had groped his way into her, she had felt but a fleeting stab of pain. She smiled. It was done. When Isabel returned Katherine would insist that she, the true wife of the Gilbert heir, would have much more involvement in the running of things.

They were sitting in the great parlour when she came in with her basket of herbs. Otho was haranguing his uncle about a ship that had come into Dartmouth with a Flemish soldier on board; a man who knew how to use a new, improved form of the arquebus. Katherine sighed and set the basket down. Otho's interest in new weapons had not diminished, and he was always trying to convince Uncle John that they should add a gunner to the number of armed men who watched over the Gilbert ships. It seemed he'd persuaded him that they should interview the man in Dartmouth.

"May I join the party then, husband, for I've never yet seen Dartmouth town?" she wheedled. A trip to the town at the mouth of the River Dart would be fun.

But Uncle John would have none of it. "The docks are no place for a young wife. Full of infections and the sort of folks you should not see. No, you must bide here at Greenway Court and look to your duties," he said, as she saw his eyes dwelling on her belly. He was always staring at her like that, trying to see if she had an heir on board yet.

She shook her head and slowly turned away to hide her disappointment.

A few days later, Otho strutted into the little parlour where she sat with her sewing. "Oh, Katherine, he had so much to tell us. I really think the future lies in these handheld weapons!" he babbled and, taking her by both arms, he lifted her right out of her seat. "In these times we need to have all our vessels well armed against attack. Pirates are a real problem on our normal trading routes to Brittany, Gascony and Spain. Our ships use those routes all the time. We need to defend our ships well when they lie at anchor off the Greenway Quay as well. And don't forget we must stand ready if called to fight for the King in times of war. Well, you know that some of our ships, the *Trinity* and the *Hope*, already have gun ports, and we've got them well furnished with small cannons and a few culverins." He was speaking nineteen to the dozen as he always did on his favourite subject, giving her far more information than she needed to satisfy her limited interest. "Uncle John told me he saw the King's finest ship, the *Mary Rose*, at close quarters when she was at anchor off Dartmouth years ago. It was when we were fighting the French; 1522, I think it was. That's where he got the idea for the gun ports on the *Trinity*. They've taken the *Mary Rose* out of commission now. She's to have a refit; even more of those gun ports so she can carry even more cannons. Oh, I would so love to see her!" he continued with eyes shining.

"Husband, do be seated as you tell me all," she said. It was difficult to take in everything he said while he was buzzing around like a bluebottle on the midden.

"The man we met told us all about the new handguns, Katherine. They're not so common in England yet, but the Flemish have been using them for a while. The Spanish have muskets far more powerful than a bow at close range, but they're long and heavy. There's a new device; it uses some sort of wheel to ignite the powder. It's lighter and you can reload faster. Oh, Katherine, I do so hope to have one of the new firing pieces, if I can only persuade Uncle John."

He grinned at her, and she was pleased to see him so relaxed and happy, although she would never share his enthusiasm for killing machines. She also doubted that John Gilbert would be persuaded to part with much of his precious store of wealth in pursuit of Otho's dreams.

Isabel's haughty features froze in disbelief when she learned of the nightly visits Otho now paid to his wife's chamber. Shock was quickly replaced by anger, and her cold eyes bulged and flashed. Katherine thought those eyes looked just like the hard flints the maids used to kindle the kitchen fire. But she stood her ground.

"Good Mother," she said, using her most reasonable tone of voice, "I am grown enough now to take on this and other duties in this household."

"Well, *child*," said Isabel, emphasising the word with a grimace, "whatever will your father have to say? It would not have happened so had I been in residence." With that she flounced off, a smirking Joan waddling along behind her. The suggestion that Katherine would take on the household management clearly rankled. But she was truly Otho's wife now. There was nothing Isabel could do to change it.

Isabel must have given the matter some calm consideration, for the next day she said, with a condescending smile, as though the whole idea was her own, "I have decided that it will be of benefit if you help with the household management." Turning to Joan, she went on, "I will then be free to work on John Gilbert about your dowry, and to petition Lady Lisle for repayment of her debt to me. It's high time we found a match for you."

So a grudging truce was agreed. While Isabel was distracted by her money worries and the abortive search for a man to take on her unappealing daughter, Katherine took her first tentative steps as a housewife. She felt happier than she had at any time since her wedding day. It was almost worth putting up with Otho's fumbling every night.

As dawn broke one September morning, she lay cocooned in her warm bed, listening to the familiar sounds of the house waking. A dog barked down by the stables, a cock repeated his morning crow, and the servants called to each other as they went about their tasks. Suddenly, Katherine rushed to the garderobe and was violently sick. Thinking it some food that had turned her stomach, she kept to her chamber that day. A day's rest would surely set her to rights. But the next morning the same thing happened. It was so unusual that she consulted her mother-in-law in some alarm.

"Why, 'tis clear what ails thee, child," Isabel exclaimed, rather kindlier than was usual. "Mayhap Uncle John shall see his heir next year."

When her courses failed to appear at the usual time the next month, Katherine was forced to accept that she might indeed be pregnant. Such a mixture of emotions coursed through her: disbelief, elation, wonder, and raw fear. A string of unanswered questions rattled around inside her head. What exactly must happen once the baby had made her belly swell? How would it come out? She'd seen lambs born in the fields but it was hard to connect that process to her own body. Grandmother Carew had kept her well away from the birthing chamber when Arthur was born. The muffled sounds she remembered hearing as she'd waited at the foot of the spiralling stairs only added to her panic. Everyone knew that a lot of women died in childbirth.

Otho came in as she sat listlessly watching the river.

"Please, please can we send for Agnes to come?" she cried, jumping from her seat and clawing at his doublet. "I've only got your stuck-up mother and your ghastly sister for company, along with that spy, that misery guts, Jane. Oh, Otho, I am so afraid."

How she longed to be wrapped in Agnes's plump arms; how she longed for Mother. But Mother was far away, sent to Coity to visit Joan the Elder, well out of the way until the furore about Elizabeth Barton had died down. Katherine's eyes were stinging and she felt so very tired. She despaired that there would never again be a morning when she did not bring back everything she'd eaten the night before. She sobbed and stamped her feet as she drummed her fists against Otho's skinny chest.

OTHO

Perhaps at last he'd done something right. Uncle John went about with a most unlikely smile on his wrinkled face, convinced that the heir was on the way. Well, it was more of a smirk than a smile, really. The old man had even spoken more kindly to him lately. And at least it meant he had an excuse to desist from those awkward night-time visits to Katherine for a while. Somehow he'd managed it and now everything could go back to normal.

But no one had warned him she'd be like this: weeping and wailing, and drooping about the place. She should be full of pride to be carrying the Gilbert heir; happy and contented, not moaning on that she couldn't go out riding, and bursting into tears all the time. He hardly recognised his clever young wife in the stranger whose emotional outbursts were driving him mad. For the past few weeks he'd tiptoed around her and treated her as though she were made of brittle glass. Now here she was wailing and crying and beating her hands on his chest. Perhaps if he talked about something else she'd be distracted.

"I've been down to Dartmouth, Katherine. They say the King went off on his summer progress with Anne Boleyn, but he had to give it up because everyone hates her so."

"That's no surprise, is it?" she snapped. "The people still love Queen Catherine, and they don't like Anne. I overheard the kitchen maid call her a goggle-eyed whore."

"But everyone says the King will have her," he went on, wondering if his ploy was working. She seemed angry now, but perhaps that was better than being so miserable. "It's beyond belief! He's made her Marchioness of Pembroke! No woman has ever been so ennobled before. The King's showered properties and wealth on her to boot, so they say. Uncle John thinks it's all madness."

"What should I care about that stupid woman?" Katherine yelled. "I just want Agnes."

"Katherine, you know very well that Uncle John has expressly forbidden you to send any message to your parents until the child has quickened."

"I suppose he's worried about how Father will react, since he was supposed to protect me until I'm older," she muttered. "Who's going to look after me, Otho?"

"Now then, Uncle John has everything arranged. He's said you're to have the best cuts of meat for your table. He's ordered that on fast days you're to be served possets of eggs and milk to keep up your strength. You're even to get small portions of meat and fish on those days, which is more than I get!" Otho's voice had become an angry rant.

"He treats me like one of his best ewes," she spat back. "Sheep raised on the richest pastures bear the strongest lambs. So I must be served the best of everything while carrying the Gilbert heir!"

"I give up," he shouted, throwing his hands up into the air. "There's no pleasing you at all these days. I'm off to find Penkervell." He stalked out of the room, slamming the door behind him.

KATHERINE

A messenger arrived early in November with a rare treat: a package enclosing a short letter from Johnny, clearly composed with care lest it fall into other hands, and several weeks out of date. Though it was splashed with the usual scattering of inkblots and somewhat crumpled, she treasured it, and read it over and over.

To Mistress Katherine Gilbert.

My very good and loving sister,
I send yow this token, a rare and precious jewel, that yow may hold me in remembrance. I am in health and like to set sail for Calais this very week, where goes our Sovereign Lord King Henry, the Marchioness of Pembroke, and the right High and Noble Prince Henry, Duke of Richmond and Somerset. My well-esteemed friend Master Peter Carew is like to be in the fore of the company that serve the King. Our good sister Joanie has the great good fortune to serve My Lady the Marquess. Kat doth send thee greeting and bides in health in the service of Master Cromwell.
In haste from the court, this fifth day of October,
Your assured and loving brother.

At the foot of the letter he had set his name with a rare flourish. As she unfolded it, a leather lace fell into her lap. It had a single rusty nail attached. How she laughed at this typical Johnny jest, and felt her spirits lifting! She felt stronger now that the sickness had passed, and it would soon be Christmas.

For the King to take Anne and Henry Fitzroy, his baseborn son, with him on his visit to the French King must have felt like a kick in the teeth for Queen Catherine. Whatever next?!

After much discussion it was agreed that Katherine could travel the short distance to Compton for the Christmas festivities. As she rested in the chamber above the solar, she felt the strangest fluttering sensation. It was as if a tiny bird were trapped inside her and was flitting about, seeking escape. The child must have quickened in her womb. As the days passed, the movements became stronger, and she held Otho's hand on her belly so that he too could feel the first movements of his son. No one had any doubt that this child would be a boy. *And a boisterous one at that*, thought Katherine, as she felt the kicking and wriggling within her.

She enjoyed the Christmas feast far more than she had a year earlier when she was a lonely bride. Otho was at her side, attending to her every need, and Uncle John beamed his joy on everyone. Isabel seemed a little less haughty, and even Penkervell accorded Katherine a modicum of respect. No doubt his nose was out of joint, but he knew he must be civil. Only the petulant Joan maintained her hostile attitude.

The weather became icy and Katherine had fur underlinings stitched into her gown and bands of fur added to the sleeves. The lanes were covered in snow for two long weeks. Uncle John insisted that she remain at Compton until her confinement. The Gilbert heir must be born in the ancient manor house built by his ancestors.

The midwife, a Marldon woman whose family had seen Gilberts come into the world for centuries, was already standing ready. But Katherine's gossips, the women who would cheer and support her, and would aid the midwife, had yet to be summoned. One cold February morning she went to John with a request.

"Good Uncle," she said, holding her hand pointedly across her expanding belly, "would you allow that my mother and my old nurse Agnes attend me when I enter my confinement to await the arrival of this lusty heir?" She was banking on him being willing to agree to anything that might secure a safe delivery.

She had judged him well. After some musing and posturing, he agreed that as soon as a thaw came a messenger would be sent to invite the two women to Compton. He even asked Katherine who else she would like to have with her, and Eliza was added the party. Messages were exchanged, and towards the end of March, Mother and Agnes arrived on the same day as Eliza, who was still slender and fair. It seemed strange that she had been married so much longer than Katherine but had no child to show for it.

Agnes clasped Katherine to her breast, which seemed even softer than she remembered. "Mistress Katherine-Kate, yoon a gurt big belly on 'ee!" she exclaimed at the top of her voice, with its thick accent that would always remind Katherine of Devon's moors, rivers and green hills.

They all started to laugh, and suddenly Katherine just couldn't stop as all the tension of the past weeks overflowed. Such a fit of giggling is always infectious, and before long even Mother was holding her sides, until sour-faced Jane appeared in the doorway declaring, "Master Gilbert be below and he do say ye must all stop that cackling. He do say you sound like so many hens in a coop. He won't have it!" which only set them off again.

Later, Katherine asked how Father had taken the news.

"Well, of course he was beside himself at first," said Mother. "But he has much on his mind in these strange times. He'll come round and accept that things are as they are. All his prayers are that God will grant you a safe delivery."

"I trust 'tis not me that has angered him, and I hope he won't blame Otho. But how did you enjoy your time in Wales, Mother? How does my sister there?" asked Katherine.

"She does well enough and the babies thrive, though I'd not trade Modbury for that bleak castle she lives in. Now, let us see if we can make this chamber more comfortable for you."

So Katherine relaxed in the company of her womenfolk, and felt like a queen bee with all the workers buzzing around to look after her.

The chamber above the solar had become a snug if rather oppressive bower, warmed by a constantly smouldering brazier. Katherine hated the dark, stuffy atmosphere and the smothering tapestries and cloths, but custom dictated that it must be so.

She could hear the sheep bleating. Some would already have lambs at foot in the pastures that rose steeply behind the walls on the north side of the manor house. She could hear the song of the small birds busy building their nests among the trees and bushes that grew in profusion beside the kitchen. At dawn their notes flowed like a bubbling brook of sweet melody, eddying and tumbling as each songster added its own distinctive notes to the chorus.

Early each morning she slipped from her bed to peep out. A pair of enterprising blue tits flitted around one of the putlog holes left by the scaffolders. It amused Katherine to wonder if it was the female bird that flitted so busily to and fro, bearing feathers and twigs to line her nest. Perhaps the one that followed, twittering importantly but carrying nothing, was the male. In the herb beds, a more attentive male robin scuttled and hopped in search of titbits to take to his mate. A blackbird chattered in alarm whenever the castle cats came too close. Overhead, the jackdaws gave out raucous calls as they carried twigs in through an opening in the watchtower above the kitchen. But soon Agnes appeared to draw her back from her lookout.

"What's a woman to believe or cling to when her time is come?" asked Agnes as they sat stitching. "In times past you could bring relics from the church; a girdle of the Virgin Mary, or perhaps saints' bones. That would ease thy pain, good Mistress."

"Shush, Agnes. Belief in the power of such things doesn't find favour with the religious reformers, who say that lots of them aren't even true bones of the saints at all. Your father would likely not wish us to use such, Katherine, though perhaps Master Gilbert would," Mother cautioned. "Your grandmother brought her own book of hours for my lying-in. Reading those prayers was a great comfort. Shall I read to you now, daughter?"

Tears filled Katherine's eyes as she remembered the bright scenes in that lovely little book, and those treasured times with Grandmother Carew. She took comfort from the well-remembered pictures as her mother read softly from her own, less decorated, book of hours.

The women talked about the strange turn of events whereby a King might put aside his wife for another.

"Kat says the Lady has much wit and learning, but her temper is terrible," said Mother. "She has all her ladies in fear and trembling of her rages. Kat says it's whispered that she likes to have men around her!" She tittered like a girl.

"The King's new love is clever and she's confident. She's a strong supporter of religious reform, you know. Do you suppose she's encouraging him in the new ways?" asked Eliza.

"Hmm! That I don't know," Mother answered with a little frown. "I suppose it may all gather pace if we are truly separate from Rome."

"William came back from Dartmouth just before I came here

with all sorts of tales. After the King returned from France with Anne on his arm, it seems that Nun, that Elizabeth Barton, predicted the most dire consequences should he take Anne to wife. Don't you think it odd, Mother, that no action's been taken against the Barton woman?"

Mother busied herself tidying up the dishes from their latest meal, and her cheeks coloured. "I don't know anything about it, I'm sure. But word is that the King and Anne Boleyn are married indeed. It's supposed to be a secret but nothing travels as fast as a tasty morsel of news. I did hear that Anne has a craving to eat apples."

"So, Mother, think you that she's in like case to me?" asked Katherine with a chuckle. "I've such a fancy for gooseberry pie!"

"Do you think she'll give him an heir?" asked Eliza.

"I think it'll go ill for her if she doesn't," said Mother, and Katherine felt a shadow flicker across her face for a split second. The unwelcome thought was instantly banished when the boy she carried landed a kick that set her gown jumping.

"I'm so relieved that your father can spend more time in Devon," said Mother. "The court's a dangerous place in these times. Your father thinks Cromwell's got his eye on filling the King's coffers with all the wealth of the monasteries. If he can succeed in that then the King will likely be well pleased. But I do declare that the King's treated Queen Catherine very badly. It might come to war if her nephew, the Holy Roman Emperor, takes up her cause."

Katherine grew bigger and bigger and felt like a lazy, fat slug. She was tired of all the fuss and bother about religion! So what if the King called himself Head of the Church?! She needed God on her side. She prayed daily for a safe delivery when her time came, speaking directly and privately to her God, as she had always done.

"Grant that I may be delivered of a fine son to bring credit to his family. Give me the strength to bear what I must endure. And please, please, God, allow me to live through this, that I may bring up my son and see him grow to be a man."

One April morning, as she rose from her bed thinking to open the window a crack and drink in some fresh air, Katherine felt a rush of wetness down her legs, and a pain that started in her back and came in waves across her belly. But it was quite bearable. Perhaps childbirth was not so terrible.

A few hours later she'd have laughed at that thought, had she had any strength left to do so. Waves of agony shot through her like hundreds of sharp knives. The midwife would have her sit in the birthing chair. What a horrid contraption! She would not cooperate with the dreadful woman. She was angry with everyone, burning with a furious, boiling rage. She blamed Mother for not telling her what dreadful pain she must bear. She shouted at the midwife with all her ordering about. She cursed John Gilbert for wanting her to produce this heir that was intent on splitting her body in two. She even turned her fury on Otho, who had put her in this plight. The midwife smiled. It would not be long now.

At last she knew she must push, push, push! She accepted the support of the hated birthing chair and her knuckles grew white as she gripped its wooden arms. "But 'tis a baby!" she cried.

"Why, whatever did yer expect, Mistress Katherine-Kate?" Agnes chuckled.

"You have a fine babe, Mistress Gilbert," the midwife announced.

Katherine heard a mewling cry grow to a full, lusty howl as the child took a first breath of the warm, festering air. While the women fussed over the baby, the midwife helped Katherine back to bed. It seemed she had more labour to endure, but she expelled the afterbirth with no fuss. It was over. She had done it!

They placed the tightly wrapped bundle in her arms. Strange how quickly all that searing pain was forgotten in that moment when she first looked into the steady eyes of her baby. John, she thought; her own little John. Let them think him named for the old curmudgeon. She would always know that he was really named for Johnny; the best friend of her childhood, her companion in all those days of blissful freedom to which, as a mother, she could never return. She placed her hand close to the tiny, clenched fist and the fingers opened and closed around hers. *This dear boy already has a strong grip on life*, she thought. *God willing, he'll grow to be a fine man.*

Agnes appeared at her side, smiling at the happy scene of mother and child. "Mistress Katherine-Kate, how like thee this fine little maid of thine?"

Katherine stared at her. That was a cruel joke indeed; unworthy of her kindly nurse. To say that her boy be not a boy, but a daughter! Then she looked into Agnes's face and saw that it was no jest. "Show me, Agnes," she whispered.

Agnes undid the swaddling bands and revealed that her baby really was a girl.

ELEVEN

1533-1534

KATHERINE

LET THEM SEE TO IT ALL: ALL THE SWADDLING AND THE ROCKING; all the washing and the changing; the cooing and the doing; the singing and the sighing over that little maid. Let Otho and his uncle look to the baptism. Let them choose a name. A girl, a girl, a girl! She had borne a girl, not a Gilbert son and heir. A girl! She had been so certain it would be a boy! Katherine clenched her hands into fists and sobbed until the down-filled pillow was quite soaked.

The room was dark by the time sheer exhaustion took hold and, resting quietly at last, she drifted off to sleep. When she woke it was as if she saw the world through a veil of grey mist. She barely looked at the red-faced creature when the nurse brought her in, but turned her head aside. She overheard Agnes consulting the midwife, but their words fell like hard pebbles into the vast, echoing space of her failure.

"Aye, I've seen the like afore now," said the midwife, nodding. "She's strong in body, but weak in mind. 'Twill afflict a young mother so, as when a ewe don't take to her lamb. Oftentimes that do happen so with ewe hoggets in their first season. The shepherd's cure is to pen her till she'll stand for the lamb to suck. Best bring babe to breast. If Mistress do feed the babe herself, she'll like as not bond wi' the little mite, e'en now."

Agnes shook her head. The midwife's remedy could not be tried. John Gilbert's orders were clear. A woman from the village was to serve as wet nurse, and the mistress was to hasten her recovery and return to her husband's bed. Katherine's duty was clear. She must regain her strength quickly and fall pregnant again as soon as possible. Breastfeeding her baby might delay when she could conceive again. So Katherine remained distant from the child, staring blankly forward.

No one had warned her how painful her breasts would be as they swelled till they felt fit to split open and burst. No one had warned her that there would be no escape from that milky smell, nor that stains would linger stubbornly on her shift as all the sustenance her body was working so hard to provide went to waste. Agnes said that the milk would dry up and she would soon be able to take up her duties again. But first she must spend another month in that stifling room, her breasts aching and bound. All fear of childbed fever or other infection must be well past before she could emerge again into the light.

She hardly noticed that they named the child Katherine. Mother and Agnes fussed around and tried to tempt her from her melancholy with morsels of her favourite delicacies. She pushed the food around the bowl before casting it aside hardly touched. Eliza sang and played on her lute. Mother read from the book of hours. They chattered about this and that. But Katherine remained silent. Her dark eyes, fathomless pits of despair, showed no flicker of interest.

After a week they got her out of bed and sat her by the window. The bright springtime seemed faded and flat; the blossoming garden dismal and dull; the birdsong muted and mournful. A constant refrain echoed in her head, blotting out all other senses. *A girl, a girl, a girl!* This was not how things should have turned out. She had failed. She was an imposter. Not a fine and capable lady at all; she was just a silly little maid.

So Katherine shrank back inside herself, unable to focus on the news that Anne Boleyn was like to be crowned in June, nor to rejoice that the new Queen might be delivered of a Tudor heir late in the summer. Well, the best of luck to her. She may be Queen of England, but they probably wouldn't let her feed her child. She'd be back in the King's bed as soon as may be. And woe betide Anne if she had a girl!

In the eyes of the Church, a new mother was unclean, so Katherine was required to kneel at the church door to be cleansed. No use to fuss and fume about it, though she had but done God's will in bringing forth a new life; an innocent and perfect tiny being, even if she was only a girl. She must go through the charade. Four weeks after the baby took her first breath, it was deemed that Katherine was sufficiently recovered for her churching.

The ride through the rutted lanes to Marldon did not cheer her, but passed in a blur; one more thing to be endured. Beyond the church house she set her feet firmly on the slippery steps. She inhaled deeply, bracing herself for the last few yards, and stepped out around the corner towards the priest waiting at the church door. With her head covered as required, she knelt in the porch, secretly praying for forgiveness for her failure to give Otho a son.

Back at Compton, she could not shake off the heavy feeling of disappointment, shame and guilt.

Po-faced Jane, ever the harbinger of bad news, brought them the request from John Gilbert a couple of days after Katherine's churching. "Mistress Champernowne," she simpered, ignoring Katherine completely, "Master Gilbert did ask that I tell you he deems it wise that My Lady Katherine should now return to her duties at Greenway Court, and you to Modbury. He says you may visit her again in due time."

Eliza and Mother exchanged concerned looks. "Very well," Mother said through gritted teeth. "We will be away as soon as our belongings may be packed and a suitable escort engaged. But I would have speech with Master Gilbert before we go."

Katherine sat wilting in the window seat with her needlework idle in her lap.

"I will ask if Agnes may remain," said Mother, after letting out a loud breath. She placed her hands on her hips and looked into Katherine's face. "If Master Gilbert will allow it, she may stay. But, Katherine, you must put this behind you and look forward to other babes. It's our duty as wives. And you must show more interest in that little maid. 'Tis hardly her fault. Come now. You've always been a sensible girl. The babe's well looked after in the nursery, but it's not natural for a mother to be so uncaring for her first child. I hate to say it, but perhaps your father was right. Perhaps you are too young to shoulder the responsibilities of motherhood."

Katherine's head went up for the first time since her daughter's birth. There was a challenge in Mother's words. She would try to rouse herself. She would show them all that she could do it.

Mother's request that Agnes might stay fell on deaf ears. So the women went their ways. Katherine and the baby returned to Greenway Court in early June, with Jane in attendance. Baby Katherine, whom they called Katie, was as well served as any royal babe in her own nursery staffed by local girls. Otho took no more interest in the child than Katherine did. The old man never visited.

At the end of July, Katherine's courses returned, and with them Otho's nightly visits to her chamber. She turned her back as soon as his floundering efforts were spent. Their friendship did not rekindle. They did not pore over books together or ride out for the sheer pleasure in each other's company. Otho was away with Penkervell, while Katherine threw herself into managing the household. Slowly, through small achievements – planting a new herb bed, harvesting an abundant crop of cherries – she began to recover some of her lost confidence. But she still spent little time with her daughter.

Jane smirked as, one afternoon late in August, she announced that Father was waiting in the parlour. Katherine walked in with short, jerky steps, feeling quite sick.

"Now, daughter," he said as he watched the red sail of a boat take the breeze as it wound its way down toward Dartmouth, "I won't pretend I'm happy about it, but what's done is done. The important thing is that you are well, and so is the little maid."

"Father, I am much restored, and it is so good to see you," she gasped, trying to stop herself from trembling.

He shifted uncomfortably in his seat and changed the subject abruptly. "Gertrude Courtenay was reluctant to go to Queen Anne's coronation. Like a red rag to a bull, that was. The King was beside himself. Gertrude's a foolish woman; I've insisted your mother steers clear of her. Elizabeth Barton's been brought to book. Confessed it was all a hoax! All those prophecies were pure fabrication. Bad business! I'm still worried that Gertrude might bring us down into the mire. We need to make a show of loyalty, just in case. So I'm off to collect your mother from Modbury so that we can be on hand when the royal baby comes. I'll bring her to see you on our way back."

"I hope for Anne's sake that she bears a boy." Katherine saw her father's face fall. Perhaps he had realised too late that talking of the Queen's situation might strike the wrong chord.

He wrinkled his brow and searched around for another subject. "Kat says King Henry's gardener has brought new varieties of apple from France. The King thinks we all need to restock our orchards. Your cousin Peter's sent a big consignment of trees down to Uncle William at Mohun's Ottery. I see you've been busy in the gardens here at Greenway Court. How would it be if I brought some trees down for you to increase your orchards here? Kat will know how to secure them."

"That would give me the greatest pleasure," she replied, already plotting in her head where she would plant them.

At the end of September, as promised, Father returned with Mother. Katherine hurried, rosy-cheeked, from the kitchens, wiping her hands on her apron. She had set the maids to preserve wardens; small cooking pears that yielded a bounty of fruit too hard to eat without cooking.

"Father, I have set aside a space for the apple trees you promised. Shall we have them by the spring?" she asked in a bubbly tone.

"Indeed we shall," he replied. "We'll get some sweet pears too. You look so much better, my dear."

"Oh, Katherine-Kate," Mother gushed, without waiting to be offered refreshments. "You should have seen the christening. It was on the tenth day of September at the church of the Observant Friars in Greenwich, the babe just three days old. What a shame all the tournaments and festivities had to be cancelled."

Katherine saw Father place his booted foot firmly on Mother's square-toed shoe as he jumped in. "I made sure your mother stood right next to Gertrude Courtenay. Of course the King insisted that Gertrude stand godmother. Kat carried the train of the christening robe. It was right for us to show our loyalty to the King. Now, look here. However much you women might feel sorry for his first wife, there's no point in standing out against the new one. That way leads to danger. Let's hope the King forgets about Gertrude's involvement in the Elizabeth Barton affair." He gave his wife a warning look.

"More likely he would if Anne had given him a son," said Katherine bleakly. "Now, Father, there's no point in tiptoeing around this. I know you mean well, but we may as well own it. She suffered the same fate as I: had her hopes dashed by a daughter, just as I did."

"Are you sure you don't mind to speak of it?" asked Mother.

"As you've told me many a time, I must move on. I must look forward," Katherine snapped. "I must say I'm surprised to find myself in so much sympathy with Anne Boleyn. I doubt the King's happy. After he chased after her so long she's done no better than Queen Catherine before her. Queen Anne may be a talented, accomplished and well educated woman but, at the end of the day, she'll be judged on whether she bears a male heir."

"You're right in that," said Father. "He's got a well-formed, red-haired girl with as strong a pair of lungs as I've ever heard on a child. But the King is still in want of an heir."

"Well, I hate to think how much pressure that will place on the new Queen," said Katherine, screwing up her face.

"Now here's a cruel twist indeed," said Mother. "The child will have her own household, and Princess Mary's to be declared illegitimate! She'll be known simply as the Lady Mary, and the King's forcing her to serve as maid of honour to this baby, Elizabeth."

"Welladay," said Katherine. "What times we do live in! Now, what's the news of Johnny?"

The trees by the riverbank were bare when, on a frosty December morning, Father next rode into the green court with a face as dark as a winter storm. He stood warming himself by the fire, but was soon pacing up and down, sloshing mulled ale all over the floor.

"Do be still, Father," Katherine said. "Let me pull up a bench here near the fire. Now, tell me what has set you in such a state."

"That stupid Barton girl's been sent to the Tower. There's a long list sent out: all those who knew about her revelations. Gertrude's on it, but worse still, Katherine-Kate, so are your mother and your cousin George! I can't think why Henry Courtenay can't keep his wife in check. There's no doubt that Gertrude went in disguise from her house at Kew to visit the woman. It's just plain stupid to take such risks," he bawled. Then, dropping his voice a notch, "Who knows what might follow? Oh, Katherine-Kate, did I do wrong to send those papers to George?"

"Oh, Father," she said, smiling weakly as she dropped her own voice to a soothing tone, hoping that none of the servants were within earshot. "For sure the King will think that Gertrude is just a silly, foolish woman led astray by others. He knows that her husband is loyal, and he knows you and Mother are too."

"Well, I don't know how sure he is of Courtenay. The Marquess is worried. He's advised his wife to make a full apology and to use just the excuse you've suggested. She'll decry that Barton piece as an unworthy, subtle and deceitful woman, and grovel before the King. God willing, it will be enough. We must bide in Devon and keep our heads down."

"Then come to Greenway Court this Yuletide – oh, please do!" she cried. "It would cheer me so much. I'm sure Uncle John will allow it. He's said he has a mind to invite half the county this year. He wants to show off his fine mansion house, though he'd have been even happier with an heir to parade before them. I'm sure Otho won't mind at all, and it would be such a help to me."

John Gilbert was at first reluctant to have the Champernownes visit at Christmas, but Otho plucked up his courage for once and spoke for his wife's parents. In the end, the old man relented, and, along with Johnny, they joined the party that gathered at Greenway Court. Father had persuaded Johnny to forsake the court festivities until the Barton affair was completely forgotten.

"What's that long face for?" Johnny cried when Katherine met him under the green boughs strung across the passageway. "You and Otho have plenty of time to fill the nursery with fine sons." He made a rather rude gesture. "Don't forget, Katherine-Kate, it's your job to make sure that Otho enjoys his bedchamber. A long, miserable face won't be any aid in that purpose."

"Oh, Johnny," she murmured, blushing. "It's just that I don't want to go through all that again and have the same result."

"Well, that's the way of it, and it's no use you railing against it. Look at Queen Anne," he advised. "High-and-mighty woman with all the education under the sun, but she has no choice. She's already pregnant again. She's shown she can bear a healthy child, just like you, and this time she hopes for a boy. Ha! But what about this for a bit of news? The King's eye's already wandering! Queen Anne really does need to give him an heir before he gets fed up with her. Now, take me to meet my niece, if you please."

Katie took to Johnny instantly as she had to no one else. Katherine laughed to see the plump little girl sitting on his knee, looking up into his face, smiling and giggling as she tried to pull his beard. How she wished she could find it in herself to love her daughter. After all the guests had gone and the Christmas wreaths were taken down, she resolved to use the quiet winter months to put things to rights. But the damage was done. Katie cried, turned away and looked about for her nurse whenever her mother came near.

At the end of March the wind lifted choppy waves on the normally tranquil river and rain pelted hard against the expensive glass in the windows. John Gilbert sat in the little parlour at Greenway Court, deep in conversation with John Rowe, while Otho stood by, twiddling a knife idly between his hands. Katherine busied herself bringing a platter of seed biscuits and cups of spiced wine before she took a seat in the corner.

"That Barton woman's been found guilty at last," announced the lawyer. "Not before time, if you ask me. She'll go to Tyburn within the month."

"Aye, but will any go with her?" queried Uncle John, his blue eyes flashing. "Courtenay's wife's in the business up to her neck." He turned towards Katherine. "Your father would be well advised to put some distance between himself and his fancy kin."

Katherine said nothing. According to Kat, Thomas Cromwell, the King's Secretary, was protecting Gertrude Courtenay in the hope that she might prove useful. Cousin George and Mother seemed safe from further censure. But she wasn't going to let Otho's uncle or the pinch-nosed lawyer know that. It wouldn't be easy for Father to cut loose from Henry Courtenay. He still owed him a tidy sum, and often deputised for him at the Stannary Courts.

She pulled her head up sharply when John Gilbert observed, "There's a big row coming about this Act of Supremacy and the oath to swear to uphold the succession of the children of King Henry and Anne Boleyn. They'll make it treason not to sign, so it can't be worth refusing."

"Did you hear, sir?" John Rowe asked. "More and Fisher are standing against it and are already in the Tower. Queen Catherine's been banished to Kimbolton and won't sign. Nor will her daughter Mary."

"We're not supposed to call her Queen any more, Master Rowe," chirped Otho, and received a withering glance in reply.

"We must steer a course 'twixt our strongest beliefs and what's in our best interests, I'm afraid, Rowe. We'll all sign. Lately it's been a hard task to balance conscience with our allegiance to our King. But down here in the West Country that allegiance counts heavily. Oh, we might be a good way from the centre of the King's court, but our coasts are the first to be exposed when there's threat of invasion. We need the King and the State to protect us. So, I'll sign."

"You're right, sir," Rowe agreed. "Best keep a lookout for Cromwell's men, too. 'Tis said they're out and about looking at the wealth of churches and monasteries. Cromwell's got a network of spies everywhere."

"Sits at the centre of his web of intrigue like a fat spider," John Gilbert barked. "In these times you can never be sure whom you can trust."

Katherine flushed as she felt his eyes on her. Surely the old fool didn't suspect her of being a spy? She must be careful to show that her allegiance now lay with her husband's family first and foremost.

"All this talk of reform," John Gilbert complained. "Such matters weigh heavily on a man's mind."

TWELVE

1534-1535

KATHERINE

On a sultry June day, John Gilbert stomped into the little parlour at Greenway Court. About his business with the Exeter merchants, he had heard a man called Hugh Latimer preach.

"There was such a crowd clamouring to hear him that they took the glass from St Mary Major's windows so those outside could hear. It was his second time a-preaching his heresies in Exeter," he fumed, his words loaded with poison. "Ha! The first time it rained till he was soaked to the skin and blood poured from his nose. Some said that was vengeance for the words that godless knave dared speak. But still he preached again. This time I heard him." Uncle John paused for breath and turned his flinty eyes on Katherine. "'Tis a good thing that your kinsman Thomas Carew spoke up well. He had a lot of support when he called that man out as a heretic and threatened to pull him from the pulpit."

Katherine bit her lip. Not all of her kin were on the same page as Thomas Carew. A memory of the man Benet, burnt in Exeter for his Lutheran views, flashed into her mind. Her brow furrowed and she bit her lip, and then could contain her thoughts no longer. "'Tis indeed a strange thing that this man Latimer may speak such things openly, when 'tis but two years since a man was sent to his death in nigh that same place for espousing similar ideas." She had been truly horrified to hear about Benet. That same Thomas Carew had been one of those who called on him to recant, to call on the Blessed Virgin Mary and all the saints. But Benet had insisted that he would call on God for help, and God alone, and perished in the flames at Livery Dole. "But I cannot be so very proud of Thomas Carew for inciting violence against Latimer," she declared. "Would that all men had more tolerance of the views of others, and could debate these matters more peaceably!"

As the words flew from her mouth she saw John Gilbert's face go puce. His eyes widened. "Hush your mouth, girl," he yelled. "This is what happens when women are encouraged to read. No good will come of it. Keep your place and look to provide more babes in the nursery."

She felt a hot flush creeping up her cheeks right up to the roots of her hair.

"There's no doubt that you manage the household well enough," he said, more kindly. "Mayhap I should lay the blame for the tardy appearance of an heir on your shoulders, not hers. Eh?" And he jabbed a bony finger in Otho's direction.

In November she had a rare letter from Johnny. He had represented Father at William Blount, Lord Mountjoy's funeral in Derbyshire, and wrote that Mountjoy's daughter Catherine, the younger sister of Gertrude Courtenay, was most comely and fair. He hoped they might one day be wed. Katherine clapped her hands. Johnny to be married! Well, Lord Mountjoy was one of the wealthiest men in the land. It would be a fine match. But agreeing a settlement would not be easy. Mountjoy's son Charles was still a minor and sure to be a royal ward. It wasn't even clear who'd have the rights of marriage for the girl. The King himself might have to be involved.

Katherine's life continued serenely in Devon as another year turned. But matters didn't seem to be progressing so well for Queen Anne. The child she had said she was carrying soon after the red-haired Princess's birth never made an appearance into the world. Some said she had miscarried. Others whispered that in truth she had never been pregnant at all, but had pretended to keep the King at her side. Katherine overheard the cook saying that Anne's hold over the King had weakened.

"Ah," he declared. "Now the thrill of all the chase be done, he's soon tired of his new Queen. Mayhap the apple was not so sweet when he did taste it!" The man's bawdy guffaws rang across the courtyard to where Katherine stood clutching a bunch of early primroses. As she turned away, the servants' mocking laughter trailed behind her.

On a fine June day, Katherine was gathering gillyflowers and trying to encourage Katie to add some to the basket instead of stamping them underfoot. She had enough sugar put by to preserve some of the petals in syrup. They would add a bright pink colour to drinks or a salad. She smiled and held a bunch to her nose, enjoying the exotic clove scent. She was thinking that they must next gather rose petals when she heard a horse approaching; a messenger with a letter from Eliza, who asked that Katherine stand ready to attend her lying-in in September. Humming a merry tune, Katherine skipped into the house, where she found Otho and his uncle discussing estate matters with Penkervell.

The old man looked up from the map they were studying, and she saw his fist clench. "What is the meaning of this?" he barked.

She babbled out her news.

"Of course you should go. There's no need to interrupt us. You have my permission."

Katherine whirled round to send the messenger back on his way with a basket of preserves and her answer.

A scant two weeks later, as a sudden downpour soaked the cobbles in the back court, another messenger came from Cornwood. This time he bore sad tidings. Eliza had gone into labour far before her time and lost the child; a son too tiny to survive. There had been no time to summon her gossips.

"My sister has need of me, husband," Katherine said. "At times like this, we women must aid each other."

"Provided Uncle John agrees, of course you must go to her," Otho replied, although his downturned mouth told a different story. It might not be the friendship they had had before, the one that had shattered after Katie's birth, but Katherine acknowledged that things were improving just a little. But Cornwood was only a day's ride away and she wouldn't be gone for long.

She found Eliza in a sorry state, huddled under an embroidered coverlet in a pretty chamber above the buttery. William Cole had certainly spared no expense in furnishing The Slade to receive his bride. The hangings of green tynsell and tawny damask on the carved bed must have cost a pretty penny, thought Katherine as she sat on a rosewood stool and took her sister's hand.

"Be of good cheer, Eliza. It is our lot in life to bear these things. You and William are young. More babes will come in time." Katherine thought how often those same platitudes had been rehearsed to her when she had been low. The words hadn't touched her then, but now she acknowledged the truth in them.

She had to bend close to catch Eliza's reply. "'Tis God's punishment on me, dear Katherine-Kate. 'Tis all due to me!" she whispered.

Katherine lay down beside her, placed her dark head next to Eliza's fair one, held her so close that their cheeks touched, and tasted the salty tears that spilled from Eliza's cornflower eyes. Gradually her sobbing subsided, but Eliza said no more. She just stared at the carvings above her head for hours at a time.

Waiting below, William Cole paced up and down, his unlined face white and drawn. "Dear sister, I pray you will help my wife," he wailed. "She's refused all but the merest crumb of food, and I fear she's sorely weakened."

"Ah," said Katherine. "That's likely addled her wits." She ordered nourishing pottages laced with wine and spices, but at first Eliza refused to touch them. It took two more days to coax her to swallow a few tiny mouthfuls, but gradually the nourishment began its work.

Soon she encouraged Eliza to walk in the sunlit gardens, and later to try a short ride. Eliza had never been a keen horsewoman, but acquiesced without demur. On a bright morning they set off, past fish ponds, a warren, and a pretty stream, the Yealm, teeming with trout. Katherine yearned to ride up to the high moors, where Penn Beacon reached towards the blue summer sky, but Eliza was not yet ready for such exertion. Instead they turned to the south, where, only two miles distant, lay Fardel Manor; another slate-roofed manor built of local granite.

"Who are your neighbours at Fardel?" asked Katherine as they passed the gate.

"It's the Raleighs' home; an ancient family, it seems now fallen on hard times," Eliza replied. "The heir married a daughter of Drake of Exmouth and the manor is rented out, while he lives somewhere over that way. I know little of them, but for some gossip that he be something of a rogue."

"Do tell more," said Katherine, thinking how nice it was to see the smile hovering near Eliza's lips as she contemplated this juicy morsel.

"Well, his wife died, leaving him with two sons. The story is that in no time at all he got another woman with child and had to marry her in haste," said Eliza with another arch smile. "No doubt 'tis idle talk and we shame ourselves to dwell on it, Katherine-Kate. There's an ancient saying about the place, too. Something about a great stone in the courtyard. Now, let me think…" She furrowed her brow for a few moments, and then announced, with a triumphant air, "Ah, I know. 'Between this stone and Fardel Hall lies as much money as the Devil can haul.'"

"Whatever can that mean? Lost treasure?" asked Katherine.

They laughed together, and Katherine soon forgot all about Fardel and Master Raleigh in her pleasure at seeing Eliza smile. She never did press her to explain what had prompted her dark thoughts and strange words in the early days of her illness.

William felt confident enough of his wife's improving health to leave them for a couple of days while he went to Plymouth about some business. He returned with all the latest talk. "Queen Anne's miscarried of another child, but she recovered well enough to accompany the King on progress," he told them, shaking his head. "They didn't spare a thought for Sir Thomas More, who followed Bishop Fisher to the block the very day after they set off."

"To treat More, his former friend, so!" Katherine scolded. "To send a man as long in years as Fisher to the block! It seems our King can turn his back on any erstwhile friend and loyal servant."

With her sister on the mend, towards the end of July, Katherine returned home and got a thorough soaking on the way. She rode with more care than usual; in the New Year another baby would join the Greenway Court nursery.

She worked hard into the autumn, building stores to see them through what promised to be a hard winter. Food prices rose and the servants muttered. They laid the blame for a bad harvest at the King's door; punishment for his marriage to Queen Anne, and for the execution of Bishops. People said that the loss of another royal baby that June was surely God's revenge on the King and that woman.

Although her waistline was already expanding, Katherine ran to meet Father on a crisp October day. His visit was a welcome distraction in such dreary times. He took his usual place in the window, and smiled.

"So another Gilbert babe is on the way, then, daughter. I trust you're in good health. I expect you're hungry for news? Well, Johnny was full of the progress when I saw him," he said with a laugh. "Said they all went to Wulfhall. I've never been there myself – it's in Wiltshire; the Seymours' place. Johnny couldn't wait to tell me that the King has his eye firmly fixed on Jane Seymour. She's a lady-in-waiting to Queen Anne. Joanie knows her. Johnny says she's as plain as a pikestaff and goes about looking like the perfect dutiful little woman. As if butter wouldn't melt in her mouth, he says. Ha, ha! Not much like the current Queen, then. Ha, ha!"

"Welladay! Whatever will become of Queen Anne and her daughter, then? Surely the King can't find reason for *another* divorce?" said Katherine incredulously.

Katie was now of an age to delight in all the greenery brought into the hall as they gathered at Compton to celebrate the Christmas season. The little maid pushed sweetmeats determinedly into her overflowing mouth, but a surfeit of sugary delights did not sweeten her nature. Compton's hall rang with her tantrums and squeals until John Gilbert banished her to the furthest tower chamber.

Katherine, too big and ponderous to make the effort to climb up and down the winding stair, yielded herself to that same oppressive room above the solar. This time, when she peeped out, the garden presented a bleak winter face for her inspection. Stark against grey stone walls, gnarled and naked branches stretched up towards the dove-grey sky like an old man's hands reaching for Heaven. Although the sun had been up for hours, frost lingered on the grass and no birds sang. She closed the curtain swiftly and wondered where the robin and the blackbird went to shelter from the winter's cold.

Agnes and Bessie came from Modbury with Mother, and Cousin Cecily added her support. After five years of marriage she had a daughter and a son and, if appearances were anything to go by, the Kirkham cradle was like to be filled again before the spring was over.

On the thirteenth day of January, Katherine's pains began. It was not a long labour, and this time there was no disappointment. She really did have her own son; her own little John. Happy, triumphant tears spilled down her shining cheeks as she cradled her boy. It was all the women could do to keep her from leaping from the bed and dancing a jig all around the chamber. She had really done it this time!

With unusual determination, Otho came up the stair and hovered by the door. The midwife carried the child to him and Katherine saw him tremble as, slack-jawed, he gazed uncertainly at his son.

OTHO

As soon as he heard the baby cry he was up the stairs. He had to know if he'd failed again. A slow smile spread across his thin face as he heard the news. What a relief! This time it was a boy, and a strong one too by the sound it.

He stood in the doorway, beaming and shaking his head. "Oh, oh, oh," he repeated, reaching out a shaking hand as the midwife pulled back the coverings to show him his son. "'Tis hard to believe he's real. He's so small and wrinkled, and see, these tiny, tiny fingers!" He glanced toward his wife, but remained by the door, awestruck and afraid to approach the woman who had achieved so much. "Uncle John decreed that the Gilbert heir must be born at the family's ancestral home, and now he has his wish. He'll arrange the baptism for a few days' time."

Uncle John would surely host a splendid feast and celebration, inviting all his friends and neighbours to share in his good fortune. Otho was glad that he wouldn't have to go to the baptism. He was sure he'd stutter in front of all those people.

Katherine glanced his way, and he actually thought he saw a spark of fondness in her eyes. But he didn't go into the room.

KATHERINE

"There is news from the court, my dears," Mother said with tears in her eyes. "Queen Catherine died just after the end of the Christmas feast."

Cecily's hand wavered in front of her, as if in warning.

"Oh, I know, Cecily, we're supposed to refer to her as the Dowager Queen. But I will always remember her as our Queen; that lovely girl who came so far to marry a Prince. 'Tis hard to credit, but the King and Queen Anne seem to have received the news most joyfully! They could at least show some decorum and mourn that gracious lady properly."

"I suppose this means that Queen Anne's place is secure, since she's pregnant again," Katherine remarked. "Johnny thought she was losing her appeal, but perhaps an heir will save her. It is a strange thing how the King blows hot and cold for the woman he pursued for so long."

But Katherine was so secure in her new status as the mother of the Gilbert heir that she spared few thoughts for Queen Anne. She wanted to go home to Greenway Court. She wanted to take charge.

THIRTEEN
1536
KATHERINE

IT WAS SO DIFFERENT THIS TIME. SHE HAD A SON, A LUSTY BOY, sleeping happily in the cradle. Uncle John, cock-a-hoop, would deny her nothing now. At last she could dispense with sour-faced Jane. He agreed readily that Bessie could replace her.

Bessie had enjoyed only a few years of happiness with the serving man she had sat behind on the road to Mohun's Ottery before he drowned in the River Dart in a shocking accident. "*River Dart, oh, River Dart, Every year thou claimest a heart*, so the saying goes," she said. "I'll be closer to him at Greenway Court, Mistress, and it'll be my pleasure to serve you again."

They were still at Compton when Bessie rushed up the stairs one morning. "Mistress Katherine, young Master's just come back from Exeter, where he heard that the King took a fall from his horse in the joust," Bessie gasped. "They all thought him dead and gone! Imagine what would have happened then? But praise be to God, he was just knocked senseless, though he's injured his leg. But that's not all! A few days after, the Queen miscarried again. So there's no Prince on the way."

"Oh dear! I do feel for Anne. To have her hopes dashed again. I suppose the King will blame her? Well, I give thanks that my dear boy seems hale and healthy. Now, Bessie, can you see to the coffer? We can be on the road for home tomorrow," Katherine answered as she hugged her baby tight.

There was a spring in Otho's step, and he went about as happy as a hound with two tails. Uncle John was allowing him more leeway in business matters, and he was often in Dartmouth, where he picked up the latest gossip. Everyone was waiting to see what the King's next move would be.

"Is that Nicholas Carew related to you in some way, wife?" he asked when he looked into the little parlour where Katherine was looking over the household accounts. Kat said that the Countess of Devon had kept great books of accounts to record her spending, and Mother had a simpler set of records at Modbury. Katherine was determined to establish a foolproof system now she was Queen of her own demesne.

"He's a very distant connection of my Carew relations, yes. He's been in and out of favour more times than you've had hot dinners, husband. We've never had much to do with him," she answered.

"Seems he's back in favour and in cahoots with the Seymours," Otho continued. "Rumour has it that Jane Seymour's gone to his house at Beddington. The King visits her there in secret."

"How shocking! Do you think the King means to put Anne aside? How on earth will he manage that?"

"That I don't know," said Otho. "Perhaps Cromwell will pull it off for him. Now, how's that boy of ours doing? I swear he smiled at me yesterday when I hung over the crib."

"Most likely it was wind, Otho," she laughed, thinking that it was good to see him taking such delight in his son.

Their peaceful moment was disturbed by a loud scream from the nursery.

"That will be your daughter," Katherine murmured, shaking her head. "She think's John's a rare cuckoo come to push her from the nest. I don't know what to do with her at all."

"Harrumph! I've got no time for her screeching and her wild ways," Otho replied with a shrug as he moved towards the door. "I have to see the steward on important business. Can you see that the nursery maids put a stop to that caterwauling?"

But Katherine was at a loss to know what to do with Katie.

May Day came. Katherine no longer went out early to wash her face in the morning dew as she had as a girl at Modbury. But Bessie had picked armfuls of spring flowers, and they were trying to encourage Katie to help weave them into garlands with hawthorn and woodbine.

"When you're older, Katie, I'll take you to the May fair at Modbury," Katherine said with a bright smile.

But Katie was not to be won over with promises. She soon wandered off, to be found later pulling the heads off the primroses in the orchard.

Unbeknown to them all, unbelievably shocking events were unfolding at the court while they went a-Maying. Toward the end of the month, John Gilbert rode over from Compton to pay yet another visit to the nursery. Katherine set down a pitcher of hippocras beside him and had just picked up the cup ready to pour when Otho burst through the door.

"The King has cut off Queen Anne's head!" he shouted from the doorway.

Katherine sat down hard on the bench beside the old man, letting the empty cup fall from her hands to roll across the floor with a clatter.

"Surely not, lad," said Uncle John. "It'll be some tall tale, grown taller in the telling."

"No, 'tis true as I do stand here," was the reply. Otho threw back his head and thrust out his chest. "I had it from Master Richard Prideaux, the Mayor of Dartmouth, and from Master Rowe the lawyer. It's not just idle chatter on the docks. What a story! It all seems to have happened so fast. One minute Queen Anne was watching the May Day tournament, all decked out in her best, cheering on her brother George and Henry Norris, the King's close friend. You know? He's the one that served in the privy chamber. Well, the next minute the King had gone from his place and those two gentlemen, and some others as well, were all arrested there and then! Then Queen Anne was taken to the Tower. There's not many go in there and come out with their head still on their shoulders!"

Katherine shuddered and gripped the bench hard.

"Go on then, boy," said the old man, shaking his head from side to side. "You'd best spit out the whole sorry tale."

"Well, 'tis shocking indeed. She was charged with adultery with no fewer than five men, including some lowly musician and even her own brother. Two others are held under suspicion: Thomas Wyatt and Richard Page. Those two are still in the Tower, but not so the others, and not so Queen Anne. All found guilty in hastily arranged trials. The Duke of Norfolk was one who sat in judgement on his own nephew and niece. *He* sent them to their deaths."

"Do you mean to say that the King has actually signed his wife's death warrant? Is she actually dead, then?" John Gilbert thundered. "What on earth is the world coming to? He was hot enough for her not so long since. I had little time for her, I'll own. But to send his own wife to the block! Norfolk, you say? Harrumph! He was happy enough to profit from her elevation, but I'm guessing he showed no remorse at her downfall. He'd be callous enough to condemn his whole family to death if he thought it would save his own skin and make him rich."

"How can the King be so cruel? Could he not have sent her to a nunnery, or put her aside as he did his first wife? I can't believe it," whimpered Katherine, rubbing her eyes. "Did they all have to die?"

"Now this is odd. He *could* have set her aside," said Otho, sitting down beside her and taking her hand. "Apparently Archbishop Cranmer obligingly gave his view that the marriage had never been lawful on account of King Henry's earlier affair with Mary Boleyn. Master Rowe told me that Cranmer tried to defend the Queen. She'd been a strong ally to the Archbishop in the religious reforms that he holds so close to his heart. Master Rowe's pleased to see her gone, of course. He says Cranmer must have seen that the King's mind was set against his former lover, so he delivered the result that was demanded. But it did not save her. The King showed some mercy and ordered a swordsman from France to strike off the Queen's head with a single blow. And then he went to have dinner with Jane Seymour the very same day!"

"That's a very small measure of mercy if you ask me!" Katherine exclaimed, holding her hands around her own slim neck. "Can there be any truth in those dreadful allegations? Surely not! She seemed such a clever woman. Would she really risk all, just for a few moments' pleasure with those men? To think they even accused her, a woman of refinement and education, of the dreadful sin of incest..." She bent to retrieve the cup and, with shaking hands, began to fill it, sloshing more than a little of the spiced wine onto the floor. The spreading puddle of red made her think of Queen Anne's blood. She felt her legs turn to jelly, and sat down again with a bump.

"Rowe said that her brother put up a spirited defence to the most shocking allegations. But no one dared listen. His own wife, Jane Parker, was the one that betrayed him."

"I smell Master Cromwell's hand in this," growled Uncle John. "I wonder how he managed to get those confessions and enough evidence to condemn them all?"

"It does seem strange that none of these men are close friends of Master Cromwell," said Katherine, putting into words what had been in all their minds. "Wyatt and Page are both associates of the King's Chief Minister and they live still, from what you say. There's surely no coincidence in that."

"Hold your peace, girl. 'Tis not for the likes of you to speak so," John snapped. "Can you not curb your wife's tongue, boy? It'll get us all into trouble one day." He flashed a cold, thin-lipped smile in Katherine's direction. "Women should know their place."

"Yes, Uncle John," said Otho, though he must have felt Katherine's scathing stare like a knife between his shoulder blades. "But listen. The King's already married again to Jane Seymour, and the red-haired child is no longer a Princess, but must now be called the Lady Elizabeth. She's gone to Hatfield in the charge of Mistress Margaret Bryan."

"Hmm! This will strengthen Cromwell's hand," the old man grumbled. "He'll be hot for reform, and he'll come after the wealth of the monasteries with a vengeance. No good will come of it."

But some benefit did come of Anne Boleyn's demise. Kat was appointed to serve the Lady Elizabeth.

John Gilbert strode past Katherine, who had paused with her foot on the stair on her way to the nursery, and stormed into the parlour, waving his arms wildly as his face turned puce.

Otho and Penkervell, waiting there to discuss some business, stared him.

"Outrageous! What a commotion!" John spluttered, eyes bulging. "What an uproar! Bad enough that they sent workmen to take down the rood loft in Exeter's priory church. Set upon, they were! Ha – 'twas women who beat about 'em! Can you credit that?"

Katherine tried to steer him to a seat, fearing that this purple-faced excitement might provoke an apoplexy, but he pushed her aside.

"Women! Took up shovels and brooms and pikes and whatever they could lay hands on, and went for those Breton carpenters like a pack of she-wolves! Those heretic workmen made to throw down the crucifix! Well, that poured oil upon the flames, sure enough. The women hurled stones at them, and they climbed up high, until one fell. Ha, ha, ha! That John Blackaller – Alderman Blackaller – tried to pacify them and put an end to the riot. They turned on him and attacked him as well!" The old man let out an evil chuckle. "Serve him right. Got the better of me in a business deal years ago. Ha, ha, ha! Well, he met his match in those women! Had to send for the Mayor to bring a force and restore order!"

He thumped down on the bench, shaking his head. A broad grin spread across Katherine's face. To think that women would dare to take matters into their own hands in such a way! But then she thought again. It was rather frightening to hear of such strong resistance, in Exeter of all places, in the Priory Church of St Nicholas.

Uncle William had been ill for some time, and when the meadows around Mohun's Ottery were ripe for cutting, he slipped quietly away. Katherine's parents joined Aunt Joan at the church at Luppitt to see him laid to rest. One of Uncle George's long list of Church appointments was as rector of the free chapel at Mohun's Ottery. Katherine thought it must have been a comfort to William to have his brother beside him as he laid down his cares at last.

All the Carew family's hopes now rested squarely on Cousin George's broad shoulders, and it was high time he took a wife. So a happier family gathering followed later that summer when George married Thomasine Pollard at King's Nympton in North Devon.

Katherine was brimming with excitement as she and Otho travelled through the lush green countryside to join the wedding party. The high moors had their best colours on show and it was a rare chance to spend a happy time in her husband's company.

"My, oh, my! This wedding is indeed a family affair," she exclaimed as they rode through the lanes. "What tangled knots do twine the Carews with the Pollards." Seeing his puzzled look, she went on. "Mother's sister, my Aunt Dorothy, is married to Thomasine's elder brother Lewis. They've a daughter, another Dorothy, who'll carry a posy at the wedding."

Otho hung his head, and Katherine regretted drawing attention to her high-flown relations.

An outbreak of plague in London meant the lavish celebrations for Jane Seymour's coronation were postponed, so it was easy for Johnny and Peter to get leave of absence for the wedding. Katherine sat with Johnny, enjoying the summer sun.

"Did you hear? Bessie Blount's boy, Henry Fitzroy, is dead. It wasn't the plague that took him. Some wasting sickness; had it for some time, by all accounts. Everyone thought the King might name him his heir one day."

"I wouldn't trade places with Jane Seymour for all the gold in Christendom! She'll be under such pressure to produce a son," Katherine observed. Then she flashed Johnny a grin as she asked, "How go the negotiations for you to claim the hand of William Blount's daughter?"

Johnny's cheeks flushed.

"Oh, oh! So you really are truly smitten," she teased.

"I'll own I am. She's the fairest maid I ever did see, and I do hope that within the next year we'll all be celebrating my wedding."

"How on earth can you tell who's who amongst all our Devon families? All those marriages that bind us all together," Katherine whispered to Otho as she looked around the glittering throng of well-wishers. In the excitement, she'd forgotten how prickly he could be. She waved a hand towards Thomasine Pollard, who stood stately and solemn beside the groom. "Now, let me think. Her father, Lewis, he was Serjeant-at-Law to the old King and Justice of the Common

Pleas. Her mother, Agnes, came from a family of wealthy Devon landowners, so I suppose Cousin George has made a sensible match."

"Uncle John mentioned another Pollard. Richard, I think he said," Otho replied under his breath, as he shuffled his feet and nodded towards another tall, well-dressed man. "There he is, over there. Uncle John says he serves Cromwell and is in the thick of sharing out lands from the priories. People will want to sidle up to him now, trying to get their piece of the pie. It's not only St Nicholas's that's fallen into Cromwell's greedy hands; six other small priories in Devon have already been swept away."

"Cousin George has the lease on Frithelstock. Isn't there some sort of dispute about that with Lord Lisle?" she whispered. "Does Honor, Lady Lisle, still owe money to your mother?"

"She won't speak to me of that," came the hissing reply. "I think Richard Pollard's representing Lisle, so that'll complicate matters."

Later, as Katherine sat watching the men, she thought that everyone must be sure to be on the right side of someone to get a slice of the pie. She suddenly realised that Uncle John wasn't lining up to take advantage. Either he was allowing his religious convictions to override his avaricious instincts, or he hadn't got close enough to the right people. She turned to ask Otho, but was pleased to see him deep in conversation with Johnny, so put the thought aside.

What a rare chance to see so many young men, she thought, with a wicked grin. How alike the Pollard men were! All so tall and handsome, and none more so than the second son, John, in his dark clerical robes. *Rather a waste of those dark good looks and those smouldering eyes*, she thought idly, the effects of the wedding ale making her drowsy.

The men enjoyed a few days hunting in the deer park Thomasine's long-dead father had enclosed around his manor. The women gossiped about the latest news and fashions. None were very happy that the new Queen, determined to show she was quite the opposite of Anne, favoured the old-fashioned English gable hood. Katherine groaned. She hoped Uncle John wouldn't hear that Queen Jane insisted on such ugly headgear.

After the wedding, Katherine was swept up in a whirl of domesticity,

diligently overseeing the Greenway Court household as they prepared
for another winter. Her life was as much ruled by the routine of the
seasons as any. Ploughing, sowing, harvesting, lambing, shearing,
spinning, weaving, and fulling cloth all came in their season. Changes
in the way of worship had affected her no more than they affected
the ordinary people of Devon. Most in the West Country just got
on with their lives, but elsewhere it seemed that resistance to reform
was growing.

Later that year, Father sat in his usual chair by the window in
Katherine's little parlour and smiled. "Kat's right glad to be serving
that young maid Elizabeth. Did I tell you she's been leasing a house
in Greyfriars, to keep a place near court? Your Uncle George, he's
now at the Chapel Royal, and he's been helping her. She can rent
the tenement out when she's no need of it, and that brings her in an
income. Just like our Kat: a single woman leasing a home of her own!
Whatever next?"

"No doubt she has her reasons, Father," Katherine replied, still in
awe of her formidable elder sister.

"I don't think she'll need the Greyfriars place now. Cromwell
recommended her for her new post. Gawen may have had a hand
in it too," said Father, showing his even white teeth in the broadest
of smiles. "Do you know, Katherine-Kate, our Kat actually wrote
to Cromwell and asked for a stipend! Oh, she spelt it out to the
great man that her father couldn't afford to support her in her new
position. She said I had enough to do with my own little living as
any man she knew! Ha, ha, ha! Joanie's serving another new Queen,"
he went on, his smile replaced by a frown. "At least she knows her
new mistress quite well. They were both ladies-in-waiting to the one
that went before. Joanie says she thinks Jane will be more kindly.
Everyone else is keeping well out of the way until the dust settles."

"At least Kat's position seems secure, Father," Katherine replied,
with a concerned glance at his furrowed brow.

"Goodness knows how it'll come out," he said, then shook
his head and let out his breath slowly. "Between you, me and the
gatepost, Katherine-Kate, I find it hard to believe that the bright,
clever, athletic youth I used to serve as a Squire of the Body can have
turned into this seeming monster; a man who would even cut off the

head of the woman for whom he so recently professed undying love! Everyone needs to watch their step."

"Best be on the right side of the Seymours, I suppose," she observed. "What about Cromwell? Is he still the coming man?"

"Oh yes, Cromwell's strong! All the empty places in the privy chamber have been filled by his supporters. Looks like religious reform will pick up apace, though I think it'll bring trouble soon enough."

She let him continue his musing, thinking that it would do him good.

"There's someone Joanie speaks of, Anthony Denny. Haven't met him yet. Sounds like he's from the same stable as Cromwell himself – well, perhaps not quite so low-born. Anyway, he's well educated, and sharp as a needle. Oh, Katherine-Kate, it does seem odd to see men like that favoured above the scions of noble houses who always used to be closest to the King. Whatever would your Grandfather John think? Some of our friends and neighbours in Devon feel very threatened. Well, lots of 'em are in dire financial straits, anyway. The old order does seem to be turning on its head; rich merchants and lawyers buying up land and estates everywhere!"

"Well, Father, what do *you* think of it all?" she asked, wondering what all this might mean for her son's future.

"Oh, I have huge respect for men of ability and learning. I hope some of the reforms stick," he replied. "Best form alliances with the new men wherever we can. Something might come our way in time; abbey lands will be in the offing. Now the Marquess of Exeter says he's concerned about our West Country communities. But it's pointless to try to stand in the way of this. Henry Courtenay might not be the best friend to have at court in future. If Cromwell pushes too hard we'll see rebellion, and then he'll have to choose his side."

"Oh, Father," she cried, wringing her hands before her. "I don't think Uncle John's keen on all this change. If you hadn't called and told me I'd have remained in ignorance, I'm sure. He doesn't think women should bother their heads about anything but making babies."

FOURTEEN
1536–1537
KATHERINE

FATHER WAS RIGHT. THE CHANGES TO RELIGION DID LEAD TO trouble. It started far from Devon when, early in October, commissioners sent to assess and sequester the wealth of local abbeys in Lincolnshire were attacked. Father and Cousin George answered the King's call and took their men to Ampthill. Seventy-seven nobles were so called, but John Gilbert's name did not appear on the list. Fortunate, perhaps, thought Katherine. The old man probably had a good deal of sympathy with the rebels. But Otho fumed and complained.

"Why have I not been called to fight for the King, wife? Your father's gone, but we've had no summons to muster our men. I can fight as well as any other. Our men are well harnessed. They have weapons: billhooks, pikes and even an arquebus! But we are not so called."

She gave a curt nod as he paced up and down. Otho's resentment was easily rekindled.

After waiting at Ampthill for a while the King's forces were stood down. Father called on his way home.

"What a relief! I really thought I'd have to march north. But it cost far too much to feed all those men and keep us standing ready," he told Katherine. "The King thinks that if the mighty Duke of Suffolk descends on them with his army, and Norfolk too, it'll soon be over. Anthony Harvey mustered a force at Bradninch and Courtenay's leading them up to Doncaster. The King wants to test his loyalty. I'm glad to be sent home. I've no relish to go a-soldiering at my age. I'm not so young as I was, you know," he declared with a boyish grin as he tried to tidy his tousled, greying locks. "I won't see fifty again, though I'm sure that's hard to believe."

Katherine giggled.

"You might well laugh, but the ride to Ampthill alone was enough for me. I'm happy to join your menfolk in keeping watch for any seditious persons or vagabonds who might be scattered abroad."

"Father, tell me more of this, for I don't rightly understand what has set so many men against the King. Is it just the changes in our ways of worship?" she asked in a low voice. She looked around furtively to make sure no one could overhear them and dropped her voice even further to a mere whisper. "Uncle John is against these changes. He clings to his familiar relics and images, and I think he resents that he can't make money from pilgrims like his ancestors did."

"You must be careful, daughter. You know where your allegiance must now lie." Father studied her earnest face and seemed to come to a decision. "It's not just the ways of worship. No, Katherine-Kate, it's more complicated. Resentment has been festering against Cromwell's agents for a while. Seeing them strip away the church plate, jewels, gold crosses and bells is the last straw for some. It's personal. When it was one of your family that donated a silver cup or a jewel-encrusted cross, you don't take kindly to seeing those precious things snatched away to swell the royal coffers. A meagre harvest, rising prices, and simmering anger about land enclosures... put it all together, add in religion, and you've got a volatile mix. Feelings run deep and times are hard. I doubt we've seen the last of the troubles."

"Well, I pray that they won't touch us here in Devon," she said, nodding her head. "Now, Father, when you have finished your drink, I will call for your grandson to entertain you."

Temperatures dropped so low that the River Thames froze, and even the lanes of Devon saw their share of snow. Little John slept soundly through it all, snug and warm in the nursery at the top of the house. A month before his first birthday, Katherine laughed at his first attempts to stand, hauling himself up on tables, benches and chairs. With his solemn face and his earnest striving, he soon had a special place in everyone's heart. How she doted on her boy!

She wasn't the only one to spoil the baby. Uncle John came nearly every day, and his visits to his namesake wrought a miracle in the curmudgeonly old man. Smiles etched new lines on the map of his stern features, and Katherine had even heard him humming a little tune as he stepped briskly up the stairs. He often lingered for a mug of ale in the parlour with her, keen to celebrate every small milestone.

As she felt a warming of relations with Otho's uncle, had she stopped to consider it, Katherine might have detected a distinct chill growing between her and her husband. At first he'd been thrilled to share in his son's progress, and had spoiled the boy as much as anyone. Katherine and her husband had been easy in each other's company at George's wedding, and Otho had seemed more comfortable in his own skin. But as the months wore on he became preoccupied and distant. Had she troubled to look, she would have seen the black looks he often directed towards her. But Katherine barely noticed.

One dark November day, Katherine opened the coffer at the foot of her bed to renew her acquaintance with those little figures, her childhood companions, that had lain there untouched since her marriage. She hoped Katie might learn to love them as she had herself. But the next day Bessie came to her with a troubled face, and one of the nursery maids hovering behind.

"Now, Mary, Mistress won't bite," said Bessie, as she pushed the frightened girl forward. "Tell Mistress what you told me."

Katherine gasped and pressed her hand against her breast. Mary was clutching the disjointed remains of one of the tailors' figures; the one with a fine blue gown and yellow hair. The head had been wrenched away; the dress cut to ribbons.

"Mistress," whimpered the red-eyed girl. "She was a-chanting, 'Chip-chop, chip-chop, chip-chop, off with your head.' Then she said, 'That's what happens to the wife of a King', and then 'That's what happens to all bad wives. Chip-chop.' And then I saw what she had done. She must have taken shears from a sewing basket, or I know not how she did it. I am so sorry, Mistress. 'Tis my fault. I should have kept a better watch. But never in all my days did I think she would do such a thing."

"No, Mary, the fault is not yours," Katherine said, controlling her tone with an effort. She stretched out her hand to raise the trembling girl from her knees and took the doll from her. She turned the dismembered remains in her hands and bit her lip. To see her old friend so destroyed cut her to the quick, but she took a deep breath. "Mary, I know you to be both diligent and careful in your duties. You watch Katie as you would any other child. But she is not as other children. What anger must there be in her heart to do such a thing? Let us see what she has to say."

But when they discovered Katie hiding in the storeroom, she simply refused to speak.

Christmas came and went and another year turned. A slight thaw in February brought Father calling again with more news of the rebels.

"They might be calling it the Pilgrimage of Grace but it won't succeed. That man Aske who leads them; he's a lawyer and a man of reason, but he's a fool if he's taken in by all that bonhomie at the court over Christmas. There's been another uprising. The King might have put on a show of listening to their concerns, he might have entertained their leader at Christmastide, but if you ask me we'll hear soon enough that Norfolk's got them all in chains. It'll end badly." He looked at Katherine with a whimsical smile. "I'm come from Exeter where I sat with Sir Thomas Denys, and John Blackaller, the Mayor of Exeter, to consider the case of those involved in the St Nicholas Priory riots last summer. Henry Courtenay heard reports that some were men disguised as women!"

"Ha! So he thinks mere women incapable of such independent action, does he?" Katherine quipped.

"Well, if he did, he was proved wrong. There was clear evidence that both men and women were involved," Father chortled. "Arundel looked at all the evidence as well as us. We've concluded that they only intended to stay the hands of those Breton carpenters. Their actions were without traitorous intent."

"So the fierce women of Exeter are vindicated, dear Father," she said with a saucy wink.

"Aye, indeed they are. Devon has its share of formidable women, it seems," was his teasing reply, before he lost himself in a prolonged study of his boots. "It was just another duty for me, my dear. I have to make some difficult and uncomfortable judgements in these times. I'm charged to root out any who might have what are now deemed traitorous intentions."

"At least you weren't chosen as Sheriff again," she said. "It is an honour for you to be on the Roll again, but I know it adds a load of burdens."

He took her hand and held it in his. "You're an understanding girl, Katherine-Kate. It does me good to visit you here, even if it does mean a slight detour from the highway. I can speak freely knowing that I can trust you never to betray my confidence. I'm proud as could be to see how well you're managing the household here."

Katherine glowed as she waved him off, and burst into a chorus of 'Pastime with Good Company' as she climbed the stairs.

Father was kept busy over the next few months. "I said it would end badly," he said when he next came a-calling. He smoothed his crumpled doublet as she offered him wine. "Robert Aske; convicted of high treason. He's dead; hanged in chains at Clifford's Tower in York. Ha! The Duke of Norfolk brought all his brutal forces to bear to restore order to the North. There aren't many stauncher in the old ways than old Norfolk, but he had to show his loyalty. Tell your husband to keep on his guard. The uprisings have got rid of some troublesome lords of the North, and that's consolidated Norfolk's power base. That wily fox is Cromwell's arch rival for power. No good will come while those two vie to be top dog. I just hope that Johnny and the girls have the sense to navigate their way safely through the choppy waters of royal favour."

"What news is there of our kinsman, Henry Courtenay, Father?" Katherine asked.

"He might have done just enough to get by this time, but I don't think the King really trusts him after the Nun of Kent business."

"I don't suppose Aunt Gertrude was very happy about his role in putting down the rebellion," Katherine observed.

"Best say no more of that," said Father, shaking his head as John Gilbert stepped briskly into the parlour to join them, a broad smile on his face.

"Been to see that young tyke in the nursery, Champernowne," he said, for all the world as happy as a cat that has just upset the cream jug. "Good to see you here again. Pray tell me, what's the news, sir?"

Katherine turned away to hide a grin as she saw Father's eyebrows shoot up at this unusually charming greeting. My, my, how the old man was changing.

"Well, the rebellion's put down for now and it seems Queen Jane's with child, Master Gilbert. All reports suggest that she fares well. But I fear the plague has reached London. The court's gone to Windsor to avoid infection."

"Well, I do pray for the Queen's safe deliverance and hope that we see none of the plague in these parts," said John. "I hear the King's strengthening his fleet?"

"That he is. He's ever fearful of invasion. My nephew Sir George, he's at sea with John Dudley. There are some reports, unconfirmed as yet; skirmishes with the French off St Michael's Mount. Best keep a watch on your ships and stand ready to defend our shores."

"Oh, Father," cried Katherine in alarm. "It won't come to war, will it?"

"'Tis to be hoped not, daughter," he said. "But Dartmouth's well defended so you're safe here."

"You'll come to Compton should there be any threat, child," said John firmly. "And bring the boy with you, too. We could withstand any siege there. Now, what price is wool fetching?"

Katherine left them deep in conversation, thinking of George Carew; another young man hot to go a-fighting for his King.

All this time, baby John, a solemn and biddable child, grew and thrived, blithely unaware of the upheavals across the country. It was as if his comfortable little life rested on a milking stool with three solid, well-placed legs. The first was the warm, cosy lap of Annie, his wet nurse, where he could snuggle up, breathing in her milky scent, and be asleep in moments. But Katherine, his mother, was surely just as important: a tall figure who crouched down to meet him eye to eye; who ruffled his hair and rained showers of kisses on his head; who stroked his dimpled cheeks, smooth as a ripe plum. How his little face lit up when she praised him for some small achievement and produced a treat from the folds of her skirts! But the third leg of John's stability was not Otho, who drifted in and out of his world like a shadow. No, the third prop that kept his world to rights was his Great-Uncle John. Katherine's boy sat enraptured as the old man talked, telling him who knew what, but giving his attention freely.

On one particular September afternoon, a heavy shower had cut short their usual walk. John Gilbert and his great-nephew had rushed up to the nursery, and excited laughter was drifting down the stairs in waves. They'd be happily occupied there for a while, so Katherine had plenty of time to do her rounds of the dairy and the still room undisturbed.

OTHO

He climbed the winding stair with slow, deliberate steps, carrying the cup and ball hidden beneath his cloak. Droplets of water fell from his soaked clothes and spattered the steps. The rain must have kept the boy inside.

As he climbed higher he heard voices and delighted squeals of laughter. He hesitated in the nursery doorway, amazed at what he saw. His stern and overbearing uncle was on his hands and knees while little John capered round him, whooping with delight.

They were so wrapped up in their game that they didn't see Otho standing there, dripping wet and scowling, turning the toy over and over in his hands. He pursed his lips and watched for a few more moments. Then, with an oath, he swung on his heel and stomped back down the stair, leaving the gift he'd brought from Exeter outside the door for the startled nursery maid to find.

His wife was nowhere in evidence. She never was when he was around. Why, he hardly knew her, she'd become such an accomplished young matron, always too busy for him. But he'd seen her sitting drinking wine with the old man. Oh, yes! She could find time for Uncle John.

Otho paused in the hallway and kicked at a stool. His jaw hurt from clenching his teeth so tightly together as his anger smouldered. The old man showered attention on the boy, but he'd never given any to Otho. His own son hardly looked at him. Nor did his wife.

He'd find Penkervell. They could go down to Dartmouth, hear the latest news, take a draught of ale. He'd heard that the King's agents were in town, surveying the defences. It'd be good to learn whether they were planning just to strengthen the gun tower at the castle, or if they had other ideas better suited for the most modern warfare. He'd like to talk about guns and cannons and the threat of the French. Otho clumped off towards the stables, cursing and shouting for Penkervell.

KATHERINE

She heard him calling out, and caught a glimpse of his retreating figure as she came in from the dairy. She stamped her foot. Typical! Off with Penkervell again. What was wrong with him? She and Otho still shared a bed whenever he chose to be at home. He could make no complaint that she failed to fulfil her wifely duty; oh, no! But he was so rarely at home these days, while she was working so hard to run his household and care for his son. He seemed to find more and more excuses to be away with Penkervell, hanging around the taverns of Exeter and Dartmouth.

In the autumn they heard that Cousin George was back in Mohun's Ottery, serving as Sheriff of the County. That was a feather in his cap, he being so young. Otho, of course, viewed any success of Katherine's 'fancy relatives', as he called them, with suspicion. There was no sign that he would ever be asked to serve, even in a minor capacity, amongst Devon's great and good. Well, that wasn't her fault, was it?

Plague had reached Exeter, and the autumn assizes moved to Kingsbridge under the oversight of one of Cousin George's undersheriffs. Fearing contagion, John Gilbert remained at Compton and little John missed his friend dreadfully. Father stayed at Modbury as much as he could. Otho stomped around like a caged bear, growling at the servants, and generally making everyone's life harder than it need be. Katherine kept her children close and exhorted everyone to wash their linen, pots, pans, mugs and cups regularly. Everyone knew that the plague ran rife through cities where masses of people lived close together, often in filthy conditions. Whatever it was that caused the sickness, cleanliness could do no harm.

All faces brightened when church bells across the country rang out the glad news that, on the twelfth day of October, Queen Jane had been delivered of a boy. But they soon heard that the Queen hadn't lived long enough to enjoy her son. Twelve days after, she was dead.

Not until late November did Father venture out again. Katherine had missed him, and was overjoyed to see him looking so well.

"No cases of the plague for a few weeks, so it's probably passed us by this time, God be thanked," he said as he flopped back into his usual seat. "Joanie's sent word that the King's distraught at the loss of the woman he says was his one true love. The funeral was a couple of weeks ago at Windsor, with the Princess Mary as chief mourner. Joanie says she's somewhat reconciled with the King."

"So, Father, what will the birth of a Prince and the Queen's death mean for my sisters at court?" Katherine asked.

"Good question. I think Joanie will go to Gawen's house to await events. He's done well for himself at court, largely through his marriage. Ha! Johnny guessed what was in the wind there, didn't he? He always said Gawen would marry Anne Brandon, sister of the King's friend, the Duke of Suffolk. Shocking! Married her before her first husband was cold. John Shilston was a sound man; keeper of Dartington Manor for a time. Harrumph! Marriage seems to have settled Gawen down a bit. Hot-headed in his youth, as are most of the Carews. Got into trouble along with one of his servants in some brawl, as I remember it. His brother-in-law's pulled a few strings for him so Gawen's profited well from licences to import wine and timber. It won't do any harm at all for Joanie to stay with him in Southwark. She's a clever girl, our Joanie. I've got high hopes that we might make a match for her soon. Anthony Denny's a good sort."

"Oh, I do hope Joanie likes him, then," said Katherine.

"He's from a family of royal servants, all able administrators," Father answered, shifting in his chair to watch a boat make its way downriver. "He's close to Thomas Cromwell and seems to be a friend of Archbishop Cranmer. He'll do for our Joanie, I think. He's been Yeoman of the Wardrobe for more than two years, and now he's keeper of the Palace of Westminster as well. He'll keep Joanie in fine estate, but what's more, I like the man, Katherine-Kate. He's well educated; went to St Paul's and to St John's College."

"So where does he stand on reform, Father?" Katherine asked quietly, thinking that she knew the answer if Denny was friends with Cromwell and Cranmer.

"Well, he does seem to be leaning towards reform, but he's careful not to upset the King. Sensible chap. Might encourage our Joanie to be a bit less outspoken," Father replied.

"Is he much older than Joanie, then?" asked Katherine,

remembering her own fear of marriage to a man in his dotage.

"Only ten years or so, I should think; that's not so great a difference."

"What about Kat?"

"Ah, that's the best news of all," he said with a proud gleam in his eye. "Margaret Bryan's been sent to take over the new Prince's household. Kat now has full charge of the Lady Elizabeth."

"That'll suit my bossy sister well," laughed Katherine.

Frances visited Greenway Court and stayed all through the summer months. Katherine's sister had become a beautiful young woman. How they laughed about Frances's intended groom, Roger Budockside from St Budeaux near Plymouth! His name, in its different forms, was one to conjure with. They spoke of marriage and a woman's lot, but Katherine spared her sister too much detail of the pains of childbirth she would certainly endure. And she spoke with as much fondness as she could about her husband, omitting to complain that he spent too much time in the alehouse.

When Father came to escort Frances back to Modbury, to Katherine's delight he brought Arthur with him. Her brother was now a stocky youth of thirteen, with even a hint of whiskers on his still-rounded cheeks. He had been away at school; then with Uncle Gawen in London. Back in Modbury he would learn about his home county so that he could one day take his place among the gentry who kept the wheels of power running smoothly for the King.

"I'd far rather go a-soldiering," confided the young man, swishing a stick through the air to demonstrate his sword strokes. "Or stay with Johnny at court, where the action is. But if Father says I'm to learn about Devon affairs for a bit, so be it. Perhaps I'll be able to visit my big sister sometimes."

"I wonder if I did wrong to put such ideas in your head when I bought that sword for you at the fair, little brother," she answered with a chuckle. "I hope you'll stay out of harm's way and not do anything reckless. I'll be glad to see you whenever Father says you may visit."

FIFTEEN

1538

KATHERINE

What a year it would be for weddings! The first would be that of Joanie and Anthony Denny.

"Think of it, Otho. To be there in London. The King and Queen will be there, and lots of important people of the court. Even Cromwell and the Archbishop. Oh, I wish I could go!" Katherine closed her eyes and tried to picture the scene.

Otho stared at her and drew his lips into a cold smile. "There can be no question of you going to London in the midst of winter. Your children have need of you."

"Nonetheless, I shall ask," she declared. "Uncle John will be here soon. He's always prepared to brave the cold weather to see his favourite boy."

Otho turned his back on her and marched out of the room without another word.

John Gilbert arrived an hour later. Katherine stopped him at the foot of the stair to tell him about the wedding.

"I do so wish I could go and see my sister wed to such an important man," she said. "But Otho says I may not, and my parents are gone already."

"Can't do any harm to have someone close to the King in the

family, eh, girl?" said the old man gruffly. "Might be of use to us poor folks in Devon. For once I've got to agree with your husband, though. The roads are rough and the weather over-cold for you to set out on such a journey now. We need you here. No doubt your parents will call again and tell you of all that passes."

Katherine lowered her head and her shoulders slumped. She enjoyed being mistress of the household and teaching the children, even though Katie tested her patience. But, oh, she would have so liked to go somewhere else for a change!

"Now then," Uncle John continued, unexpectedly benevolent. "Don't look so downcast. Bring me a draught of your finest ale and sit with me awhile. You can tell me what that young imp up the stair has been getting up to. How is he progressing with his hornbook?"

March came in like a lion, with high winds threatening to bring down trees, and brooks overflowing. But the weather was calmer by the time Katherine's parents called on their way home.

Mother's eyes were sparkling and she spoke rapidly, even before they were through the door. "What do you think, Katherine-Kate? We went to London for Joanie's wedding, but when we arrived, we discovered that Johnny was already wed!"

Katherine shuffled back a step or two and gasped. This was a real surprise. "What? How so? I had high hopes that I might go to his wedding later in the year. Father, tell me all," she exclaimed, not sure whether to be delighted or cross.

"Well, it's simple enough. Do I need to spell it out?" said Father, his voice gravelly and rough. "As you know, the negotiations for Johnny's marriage to my old friend William's daughter have dragged on for a long time. It seems your brother could wait no longer. Nor could his bride. Pre-empted the marriage vows; Catherine Blount's already with child. By all accounts, the wedding was a quiet, hastily arranged affair with your cousin Peter standing witness."

Katherine blushed.

Father seemed more concerned about the financial implications than anything else. "The King's Chief Minister, Cromwell himself, is trying get me the dowry payment," he complained. "He's written to the Marquess of Exeter seeking payment of a thousand pounds in lieu of lands, plate and jewels William Blount set aside for the girl's marriage portion. I'm not best pleased about this." He flexed his fingers, and Katherine winced as she heard the knuckles crack. "Mountjoy's widow delivered those valuables to Gertrude. After all the support I've given him over the years, you'd think Henry Courtenay could be a bit more helpful. But no, he's denied all knowledge! Says he knows nothing about any jewels and plate, or lands either! Looks as if it'll be some time before I see the dowry. But I'll tell you this: Henry Courtenay needs to watch his step with Cromwell."

"I'm sure it'll all be sorted out in time," Mother murmured, placing a soothing hand on Father's. She turned to Katherine with a beaming smile. "A Champernowne heir's on the way! Johnny's promised to bring his Catherine to Modbury Court for the birth later in the year. Now, Katherine-Kate, no doubt you want to know about Joanie's wedding too?"

So Katherine heard how Joanie and Anthony had been married by licence on the fourth day of February, and how the King had shown his favour to the pair by granting them the dissolved Priory of St Mary near the Denny estates in Hertfordshire, amongst other lands. That would significantly increase Anthony's already considerable income.

"Lucky Joanie," replied Katherine with a sad smile. "She'll be able to live in style and indulge her passion for jewellery!"

If Katherine was sad to have missed those two weddings, she was much less concerned about missing the third. Otho's sister Joan had finally snared a husband. Despite all her wheedling over the years, Isabel Gilbert never had persuaded her brother-in-law to stump up a more generous marriage portion. She had to fill that need from her own rather depleted purse. How bitterly she must have regretted those loans made in a time of plenty but still not repaid! At long last she found a likely suitor in Richard Prideaux, a younger son of Humphrey Prideaux of Theuborough, in the parish of Sutcombe in North Devon. A rising family, the Prideauxes were extending their land holdings into Cornwall. A branch of the family were also at Orcherton, near Modbury. Isabel took her daughter to the Prideauxes' London home to pursue the bargain. Katherine sniggered to think of Joan kitted out in grand gowns and displayed before her prospective in-laws at the expensive dinners Isabel provided. Joan was a girl of ample proportions, so the gowns alone must have cost a small fortune. Prideaux drove a hard bargain. On top of the cost of all those trips to London, Isabel also had to cough up a hundred marks before the match was finally agreed. Joan was married in London with only her mother in attendance.

When she returned to Greenway Court, Isabel was uncharacteristically downcast. "Just at the crucial time, Lady Lisle's payments dried up completely," she complained, as Katherine fussed around her.

Otho listened with a thin veneer of politeness.

"She's been sending money in dribs and drabs over the years, but there's still a goodly sum outstanding. How I shall manage, I simply don't know," wailed Isabel. "It doesn't help to know that I'm not the only one waiting for Honor to pay up. Oh, yes, she's now the famous Lady Lisle! Wed to Arthur Plantagenet, who serves his nephew King Henry as Deputy of Calais! She and that husband of hers are a pair of spendthrifts! She doesn't even pay her servants. Of course, she's determined to find places at court for her Basset daughters, and she can spend ever so much on gifts and costumes. But she can't repay me, for all we're related."

Otho's patience broke. "Well, dear Mother," he said in cutting tones, "sounds as though you're at the back of a long queue. But take heart. Perhaps my uncle will remember you in his will. Ha, ha!"

They all knew that wasn't likely, and Isabel's head drooped. Katherine found it hard to muster much sympathy. It came as sweet relief that her mother-in-law and Joan would now rarely grace the Gilberts' Devon properties. No, she didn't mind missing that wedding at all. The last to be wed that year would be Frances, who would marry Roger Budockside in the summer. Katherine was determined to be there.

OTHO

"Of course, I'll be able to go to that wedding," she announced in her disdainful, preening way, as he pulled on his boots in readiness for a ride to Exeter. "Surely he will allow that?"

"That I don't know, wife," Otho mumbled with a shrug.

Katherine was always talking about her grand relations: the ones up in London, serving the King; and the ones at that mausoleum of a place at Modbury, with all the coats of arms and tombs of her ancestors in the church. Ha, ha! No doubt she'd love to visit them and be away from him. He looked around at the fine hangings, the carved furnishings, the fireplaces and the tall windows. Greenway Court was one of the finest mansion houses in all the county, yet she'd still rather go to her high-and-mighty relations. All smiles whenever her father visited, but all Otho got from her was impatience and a sour look. She didn't want him at all; just like Uncle John. After all these years he still favoured Cousin Edward over him. Even the boy in the nursery would rather spend his time with that old fool.

He left the room without giving her another glance. He'd go and find Penkervell; spend the afternoon at the tavern. He shuffled off down the path, taking a few desultory kicks at stray pebbles on the way.

KATHERINE

As Katherine watched him go, her fingers curled tightly around the bunch of keys at her girdle. She saw him duck behind the stables just as old John Gilbert breezed up the path and hailed her with a cheery halloo.

"Where's he off to in such a hurry, then?" he asked, flashing her a beaming smile.

"The nearest alehouse, if I'm not mistaken," she said bleakly, and then wished she could call back the hastily spoken words.

"How's the boy? Sturdy and strong? That's good to hear. Needs a brother in the nursery, though. That husband of yours should spend more of his time at home! Can't think what's wrong with Otho; pretty wife like you to come home to."

Katherine's cheeks coloured. "I do my duty, sir, as you well know."

"I do know the way of it, right well," said he, before he was nearly knocked from his feet when the excited boy wriggled from Annie's grasp and hurtled over the stones towards his best friend.

As soon as he could walk, little John would take the old man's hand and they would wander down to the quay beside the Dart, where he'd sit, spellbound, listening to tales of ships and cargoes. Katherine often found them on the bench in the garden, side by side, with a pile of coins Uncle John had taken from his purse for the boy to count.

"My boy, this is the most important lesson of all," he would say. "Always know how much money you have, how to keep it safe, and how you can make your pile of coins grow bigger."

One April morning, as the song of small birds filled the air, the two John Gilberts, old and young, were back in the kitchen garden after admiring the *Trinity*. John the elder sat on a wooden bench, watching the boy gleefully poking sticks into newly turned soil in search of worms. The gardeners were preparing the ground to plant salads or onions, leeks or cabbages. Annie, young John's nurse, bustled along and tucked the boy's baby skirts up high to keep them from the mud.

"Let him be, woman," cried old John. "Boys will be boys. They like to be in the mud. He'll wash."

Katherine paused at the gate and surveyed the neatly kept herb beds, the strawberry patch and the gooseberry bushes. The cherry trees beside the wall were in full blossom, a shower of petals already fallen in a snowy drift along the path. In the orchard, her newly planted apples and pears were doing well. She looked back the way she had come. At the front of the house, formal knot gardens were placed to delight anyone who glanced out of the sparkling windows. All looked neat and in good order.

Katherine stood, hand on hip, congratulating herself on all she had achieved. A smiling maidservant came out with a mug of ale and took it over to the old man without his having to ask. The laundry maid arrayed linen on the bushes to dry in the warm spring sunshine, humming a lilting tune as she went about her work. The excited boy let out a squeal and held up a handful of soil as another wriggling worm tickled his palm.

Uncle John noticed her hovering in the gateway and beckoned her to join him. "'Tis a fine morning," he said with a twinkle. "We've been down to the quay. That young rascal likes to see the ships loading there. The *Trinity's* in; ready to load wool for London. Edward will take her in a day or two. Might be tin as well, or perhaps lime to carry down to Dartmouth. I leave the ordering of such things to Edward these days. Pity that husband of yours lacks Edward's head on his shoulders, eh? Pity he lacks Edward's shoulders too. Ha, ha!"

Katherine made to protest, but he laughed again.

"Well, Otho's still much too slender for my liking." He spluttered into the mug, gulped down a long mouthful of ale, and looked round the garden. "You've wrought a near miracle in the ordering of my nephew's household, young Mistress Katherine. When Isabel ruled here it was grudging service at best, and surly looks. Oh yes, girl, everyone went in fear of her sharp tongue. It does you credit, though I do wish you'd keep a curb on your own tongue sometimes. You know I'll never really approve of women getting above their station through too much learning." He actually chuckled as he said this.

Katherine smiled at his good-natured teasing.

"You do your duty well as a wife. I congratulate you. Now, why do you put on such a sad face these last days?"

"I'm well, Uncle," she said. "I have no complaint."

"Harrumph! Think I'm blind, do ye?" he exploded with a snort. "I have eyes to see, young woman. That husband of yours spends too much time away; too much time thinking of those newfangled handguns. I'd be better pleased if he practised archery more often to develop his muscles, or he could usefully study contracts and law. But better still, he could leave the alehouse and give better attendance to his pretty wife. Then he might get another baby in the cradle."

She blushed and shook her head. Neither spoke again for several minutes.

Then old John's eyes lit up. "How would you like to go with the *Trinity*?"

Katherine's mouth fell open. She blinked several times and stared at him.

He grinned. "It's spring, girl. It's unlikely there will be an outbreak of plague in the city. The weather looks set fair. You can be there in three days by the *Trinity*, rather than the five or six it would take to ride. Otho can go with Edward to learn how to deal well with those roguish merchants in the port of London. You can go and visit your relations. A holiday together will do you both good. The *Trinity* might be going on to the Netherlands from London, but you and Otho can return by the roads. In May they'll be fair and passable. What do you say?"

SIXTEEN

1538

KATHERINE

A week later, Katherine set her foot upon the well-scrubbed deck of the three-masted vessel. She felt light-headed, dizzy with delight, her legs suddenly weak as water. She really was on board the *Trinity*! Messengers were speeding to Uncle Gawen, to her sisters and to Johnny. What a family reunion it would be, and, oh, the thrill of it! She would see London for the first time. Perhaps they'd even see the King!

She had dressed with care, selecting a blue-green gown that was more comfortable than fashionable. At the last moment she donned a bead-trimmed headdress. It would not do for the good mistresses of Dartmouth to see her pass by looking like a serving woman. A coffer containing her London wardrobe was hauled on board and stowed in the tiny cabin she would share with Bessie, who was clutching the handrail as tight as she could.

Cousin Edward had charge of the voyage, but deferred generously to Otho, who seemed as excited as Katherine was. The ship's master, a short man with piercing, far-seeing eyes, bowed and turned to give an order to his crew. The sailors – only a dozen of them – nodded their heads in greeting and were soon manoeuvring the *Trinity* from the wharf. The carrack's oak timbers, brown and welcoming as hearth and home, creaked and groaned as they began to move out onto the confident river. Tall trees clothed the banks and reached up towards the sky. Sunlight filtered between their leaves, shedding bright reflections onto the rippling water, and reminding Katherine of the light that spilled into the vast cathedral in Exeter. The whole world seemed confined between the riverbanks; a ribbon of water snaking along under a clear blue sky, as the Dart made its timeless way toward the sea.

She turned and caught a last glimpse of her home standing proud on its promontory, the windows sparkling like so many eyes watching her go. Perhaps John and Katie were at the top window, watching the ship make its stately progress amongst the flotilla of other craft already on the water. The green wooded slopes of the Dart were soon rushing by as the tide carried them towards Dartmouth. The river had been the backdrop to Katherine's life for years; constant, flowing steadily on, just beyond her windows. She had crossed the narrow neck that separated Dittisham from Greenway Quay, and felt the flimsy ferryboat rocking beneath her feet. But never before had she felt the river's strength like this. Able to hold the weight of the heavily laden *Trinity* bobbing above its depths. Able to contain the mighty tide between its banks. Her pulse calmed as she filled her lungs with the spring-scented air, with its musty hints of damp leaves and cool, cool water.

All was quiet save for the shifting and straining of the carrack's wooden walls as they eased and settled, welcoming the burden of their latest cargo. Then, as they glided past inlets, shipwrights' hammers clanged and tapped. Snatches of other sounds drifted in on the light breeze that stirred the topmost leaves: a dog yapped, urgent and demanding, until cut off in a frantic, high-pitched yelp; the monotonous, mournful lowing of a cow grown hoarse from calling for a missing calf carried plaintively across the water; a loud, insistent *rat-a-tat-tat, rat-a-tat-tat* echoed behind them as a woodpecker drummed out his territory or searched for insects in some unseen hollow tree. Katherine caught a whiff of woodsmoke as a thin trail drifted across their path from some homestead hidden deep in the woods.

They drew near to Dartmouth, where a huddle of grey slate-roofed buildings clung tenaciously to the river's edge, while dilapidated thatched hovels climbed higher up the steep slope. Katherine wrinkled her nose as the briny, fishy smell mingled with smoke from the town's chimneys. Fishing boats, larger three-masted carracks, and the smaller cog boats she was used to watching as they plied their trade past Greenway Court jostled for space on the crowded wharf. All was hustle and bustle as cargoes were disgorged or taken on.

"There's the *Charity*," yelled Otho, pointing to an aged barque. "Uncle John's chartered her out to the fishermen again. Let's hope Cowick and Master Rowe have sorted out a binding contract this time. Of course, you wouldn't understand how the law of the Admiralty Court touches the common law of the land."

He'd crossed the deck and stood with his arms folded over his chest, and spoke slowly, as if to emphasise the hurt he intended. Katherine pressed her lips together and kept silent. Better not antagonise him by telling him how well she understood that difficult case with Barker over the rightful share from a haul of fish. She'd been hoping they might get on better away from home. Perhaps he would relax when they got to London.

She studied the thriving port with interest. Dartmouth was second only to the harbours around Plymouth as a centre for West Country trade, and the local merchants were thriving. Fine timber-framed town houses lined the street that bounded the wharf and spread along the Butterwalk.

The *Trinity* found berth in front of a cavernous warehouse with the name John Hawley written in huge painted letters on the doors. Katherine remembered reading Master Chaucer's tale of the Shipman of Dartmouth. Father said it was based on the Mayor of the town, that same John Hawley whom the poet had met… oh, it must be so very long ago. Seeing the direction of her gaze, one of the sailors, a brawny, bow-legged little man with a face as brown as a walnut, broke into song. His companions soon picked up the chorus: *Blow the wind high, blow the wind low, It always blows fair to Hawley's Hoe.*

The *Trinity* was at the quayside only long enough for Edward to make sure all was in order with the port authorities; then the sailors cast off and they were on their way again. A crowded ferry headed for the opposite bank, where a few dwellings clustered around a squat church with a square tower. Katherine wondered why so many would wish to make their way across.

"The church at Kingswear is named for St Thomas of Canterbury," Edward answered. "The Abbots of Torre have the ferry tithes, though perhaps not for much longer. They used to make a penny or two from pilgrims that came over the sea to go all the way to Canterbury. At least, that's what they say. See, the ferry will put into Kittery Point. The passengers look more like serving women or sailors' goodwives to me."

She smiled her thanks as they passed a new fortification on the Dartmouth bank. The stone walls gleamed brightly in the sun, not yet weathered by the salty breeze that told her the ocean was close. In a rush of excitement she realised she could see the open sea. Beyond the river mouth, past the castle, a glittering, shimmering expanse of water stretched all the way to the horizon.

Otho was in his element, talking so fast about guns and garrisons and cannons and black powder that she couldn't make sense of what he said. "That's Bayard's Cove Fort we've just passed. King Henry ordered it built as a last line of defence against any enemy ships that might squeeze past the defences of Dartmouth Castle. See, over there on the other bank, that's Kingswear Castle. The enemy won't get past those gun ports," he babbled, waving his arms. "Oh yes! See how formidable they are! Can you see it, wife? The chain that keeps us safe from harm up river? They can sling it across the river to keep the enemy out. I heard in the tavern that the King's sent men to map the coastline and all our defences. He's always afeared that the French will attack us. Can you see the places where our cannons sit? And above them, the gun loops for the new handheld arquebuses?"

Yes, she could indeed see the castle with its gun tower hugging the rocky shoreline, the church half hidden behind, and, across the river, another tower built of the same stone. Yes, she could see why Otho was so sure that whichever way attackers tried to advance, they would easily be cut down. But she'd heard quite enough about war and cannons and guns. They were leaving the river mouth!

Katherine nearly lost her balance when the deck lurched as waves began to lap against the hull. Soon they were out into open water and barefoot sailors were climbing to dizzying heights on the rigging to loose the sails. Others on deck hauled on the halyards and the sails were hoisted high. Released from their bondage, they hung limply, like a wet linen shift newly raised from the washtub, but then the breeze caught them and they billowed overhead, dove-grey clouds against the perfect blue sky. The canvas sheets filled, the ropes chafed and the timbers groaned as they set their course.

Katherine clutched the gunwale and caught her breath. She gazed far out across the water. Oh, to think that they could harness the wind! And oh, the vastness of that shimmering sea! There was Berry Head, towering out to protect the sheltered waters of Torbay. As they rounded the headland she noticed Bessie, her face as white as snow, staggering towards the cabin's dark entrance. Like her mistress, the plump serving maid had never been on a ship before. But where Bessie was terrified, Katherine exulted in the power of the sea.

As they began to cross the wide waters far out from the bay, the fuzzy shoreline receded. Katherine screwed up her eyes and tried to focus. She couldn't make out Paignton's buildings, unless they were that smoky blur against the green woods. The distant heights of Dartmoor sketched a thin blue line next the sky. Even the solid bulk of Torre Abbey was reduced to a tiny speck. Strange to think that not far inland lay Compton, where her children had been born. Fishing boats crossed their path, heading for Brixham with their catch, though the village was hidden from view under the headland. One little boat with red sails caught her eye, a cloud of seagulls trailing behind it. Their squabbling calls rose on the breeze, which whipped up white froth atop the waves. She was reminded of Katie hitching up her red dress to run like the wind through the daisy-strewn meadow.

The *Trinity* had by now taken them far from land. Edward tried to point out where the mighty Exe crept into the sea. But it was much too far away. All Katherine's landlocked cares were forgotten as the *Trinity* made steady progress over the waves. She turned and reached out for Otho, and gave his hand an affectionate squeeze. With tears in her eyes she begged him to hand her up to the prow. She wanted to see how the ship cut its path through the water, ploughing its own furrow and pushing up new waves on each side. She wanted to feel the power of it.

OTHO

How long was it since she'd taken his hand like that? It felt rather good, almost as if she cared about him. Perhaps things would be better away from home, away from her household and her children. She looked different already; younger and happier. She'd seemed to listen when he'd told her about the Dartmouth defences. She hadn't given him that disdainful look that made him feel such a fool. But would she spare any time for him when they were in London with all her high-and-mighty relations? He wasn't really looking forward to being with all those snooty toffs. They'd probably look down their noble noses at him, just as she usually did.

What on earth was she doing? It really wasn't seemly at all that she should climb about like that. But if he didn't agree she'd only stamp her feet and make a scene in front of Edward and all the sailors. He gave a snag-toothed ruffian a hard stare as he caught him ogling Katherine's trim figure, and the man turned away with a grin. A good thing Uncle John couldn't see her clambering about like a chimney boy! Otho hoped she'd have the sense not to topple overboard.

He turned away and looked around for the gunner. He'd like to hear all the man knew about the latest weapons.

KATHERINE

Katherine leaned forward, gripped the rail, and drank in satisfying breaths of bracing air. She felt the wind stinging her cheeks as it whipped strands of hair free from her headdress. Running her tongue lightly around her lips, she tasted the salt as she looked down at the foaming water. Why, this was even better than galloping Dapple across the moorland! Giving herself up to the rhythmic rolling of the waves, she closed her eyes and imagined all her thoughts and dreams flying high above her head to join the wheeling gulls and be blown clean away.

A few tresses of hair became enmeshed in the beaded billament of her hood and started to tug. *Ouch! That hurt!* She tensed, irritated at the interruption of her joyful moment, and furrowed her brows as she tried to loose her tangled locks. But her furious yanking only made the knots tighter. There was nothing for it. She must remove it: the hood, the linen coif and all. At last she teased the strands of hair from the beaded trim and set the hood down by her feet with the coif inside. On an impulse she reached up and untied the ribbon that kept her long braids anchored. She combed her fingers through the luxuriant waterfall until, after a final defiant shake of her head, it streamed out behind her like a flag in the wind.

She hadn't heard the sailors' shouts, nor the master's call to heave to. Their voices were snatched away on the wind as the *Trinity* turned and the second vessel came alongside. Only when she nearly lost her footing did she turn and see him, standing amidships, hands on hips, with the unassailable confidence of one used to command. Tall and well built, dressed in plain sailor's garb, his only claim to rank was a feather-trimmed cap tipped rakishly over one eye. As a compass needle finds true north, her eyes found his. In an instant, even over the distance that separated them, she felt herself drowning in the depths of those sparkling eyes. Locked together in that moment of wonder and discovery, neither was aware of the men around them, the tossing ships, or the watery expanse of the sea. They were transported to some other place, where all the world was theirs and theirs alone.

What was it she felt in that instant, that seemed to her to span all time? A deep and welcome recognition, as if coming home after a long, long absence to well-remembered comforts. But more, a new, fluttering excitement that started somewhere below her belly and spread through her whole being until she was near quivering with its thrill. Her knees felt strangely weak and her heart thundered so loudly she thought they all must hear it. Never before had she felt thus as she'd looked at a man!

Of a sudden, she remembered herself and took her headdress in hand. Otho was looking at her pointedly. She felt the heat in her cheeks as she blushed furiously. She fumbled, trying to braid her errant locks so that she could secure them under the hood. But, without Bessie's assistance, her hair proved stubborn and she ended up with half her mane still rippling down her back. But the headdress was in place, albeit at an angle, as Otho handed her down and they approached the rail where the man had come aboard the *Trinity*. Removing his cap with a flourish, he smiled. He even dared to laugh gently at her confusion, revealing teeth of a startling white that shone against his sun-burnished skin. His laughter, warm and lyrical as a brook burbling happily over pebbles, set her senses throbbing.

"Katherine, my dear," said Otho, making a show of placing his arm about her waist, "may I present Master Raleigh? Master Raleigh, my wife."

Katherine looked up and found again those smiling eyes set in a face she felt she had known forever.

Some conversation must have followed. Raleigh presented two lads, barefooted and wearing only open shirts over ragged breeches such as the serving men were wont to wear; these were his sons. Some talk of the sea, of fishing, of trade and business and, knowing Otho, of gun ports and warfare. Perhaps they spoke of affairs at court, or of the chance of war as fragile and shifting alliances were forged and broken. Katherine had no recollection at all. She only knew that, too soon for her, Master Raleigh took her hand and brushed it, oh so gently, with his lips. His warm breath on her skin, the touch of his hand, started a delicious shiver that tingled down her spine and spread through her whole body. Taking his cap in hand, he favoured her with a sweeping bow. Did he keep his grip on her fingers just a little longer than was really necessary? As he bent over her hand, she noticed his overlong, somewhat unkempt hair. Dark with a few grey strands, it sprang up in curls, as if it had life all its own. Then his eyes locked with hers for one last moment in which all was known and all was lost. And then he was gone.

The ship sailed on but the waves no longer had power to enthral her. Much later, she found excuse to retire to the tiny cabin where Bessie was trying vainly to sleep. She sat on the rough mattress and searched her mind. Where had she heard that name before? It came to her at last. *Oh no! He must be that rogue, Raleigh of Fardel, from Eliza's tale!* Shaken and confused she knelt in prayer, seeking forgiveness that she, a respectable married woman, should have felt such things at the sight of such a man.

"Dear God," she prayed, "how have you allowed this to happen to me, of all women? I am so fortunate to have an honest and true husband, two fair babes at home, and to have set forth on this journey, such as I never thought to travel."

That night, she dreamed she was in the bow of a magnificent ship, sailing towards a sunset of the brightest, shimmering gold. In her dream, a man stood close beside her, but the hand that rested lightly on her shoulder was not her husband's.

WALTER

As the *Lion* came alongside he saw her, perched high at the prow, her banner of dark hair flying in the breeze. At first he'd thought Gilbert had adorned the carrack with some painted figurehead. He'd intended to make a jest of it when he hailed the *Trinity*. But as the two ships drew closer he could see that this was no wooden image, but a living, breathing woman. And what a woman! Walter stood transfixed as he took in the trim figure, clad in a sea-green gown, silhouetted against the clear blue sky. Never, in all his days on the seas, had he seen such a vision of loveliness. It was as though Amphitrite herself, great Goddess of the Sea, had materialised before his eyes. A jolt rocked him and shot through his body, almost as though he had been hit in the stomach. In an instant he was felled by a new pain, sharp and raw. But what exquisite pain!

The *Trinity* hove to. The boys soon had the grappling hooks secure, but still Walter stood stock-still, clenching his hands and then releasing them. He felt the two boys staring at him, and was across the deck in two strides to swing his leg easily over the gunwale. Only then did he tear his eyes from her face to greet Edward Gilbert. The other boy had gone to her. He saw her start and hurriedly try to put herself to rights as the Gilbert boy helped her down. With his arm about her slender waist, the boy led her forward. She had managed to get the headdress back over that glorious hair, though it was somewhat awry and a gleaming shower of beauty still tumbled down her back. She approached, head held high, and he could not suppress the laughter that welled up from somewhere deep in his soul. Oh, what joy he felt just at the sight of her! Sweeping his hat off, he looked away from her face just long enough to give her his bow, as politeness required. She smiled, and he was lost again in the gentle curve of her lips, the rounded dimples of her cheeks, the warm brown eyes set in that perfect oval face.

There was some talk; he knew not what was said. He'd have spun it out longer if he could, but Gilbert was clearly eager to be away. She offered her hand. Dare he take it? Wild horses could not have prevented him! He bent to brush that soft, warm skin with the briefest kiss, and a thrill passed through him like a bolt of lightning. But he must take his leave, be over the side and back on board the *Lion*.

As the *Trinity* moved slowly away, Walter sank down onto a pile of ropes coiled at the masthead. That Cupid's dart could have found its mark on him now of all times! He was in his late thirties, had been twice widowed, and, as well as the two lads watching him, mouths agape, had a little maid back at home. He glanced at his sons going about their tasks, sure-footed and strong. Joan Drake, their mother, Walter's first wife, had been a good woman. Though the match had not been of their choosing, they had fared well enough together, though Joan had been firmly wedded to the old ways and the Church of Rome, while Walter held the cause of reform close to his heart. Although they had differing ideas about religion their union had been founded on mutual respect, and he still missed their lively debates. He had been truly sad and sorry when she died and they laid her to rest in the church of East Budleigh, close by the farm of Poer Hayes where they had made their home. A pity the mason had transposed the writing on the inscription on her gravestone. No matter; Walter couldn't afford to spend more coin on changing it. No, there Joan must lie. He knew that some men of the village said that he'd had that stone carved backwards deliberately to mark the difference in their beliefs, and to show that he cared not for hers. Let them think what they liked; it was his business alone.

His second wife, not so long departed, had been a different matter altogether. Isabella, the comely daughter of a London merchant, had set her cap at him quite blatantly, and what man on God's earth could resist those charms, so freely offered? He'd wondered afterward if her father had put her up to seducing him. He had been vulnerable, of course; newly a widower, and no doubt seen as quite a catch. The result had been inevitable, and he had wed her as soon as she'd told him of the babe she carried. For, whatever men might say, Walter retained a strong sense of honour, and in any case, an alliance with that wealthy Londoner could do him no real harm. Through Joan's family, the Drakes, he was already shipping goods to and from London and beyond. He also farmed the land around Budleigh and Woodbury. It gave him a reasonable income. But Isabella's money might allow him to build a ship of his own.

Sadly, her stunning blonde beauty was soon revealed to be but skin deep, and he tired of her senseless chatter which didn't offer much in the way of true companionship. The changes rocking the country and setting its government and ways of worship upon their heads seemed not to register in that empty brain of hers. He'd found himself missing his former sparring partner Joan more and more. There was little to miss after Isabella's death when the babe, a fair-haired maid they named Mary, came. Isabella never recovered after the birth, and followed Walter's first wife to the grave. In his deepest heart he acknowledged a hint of relief at her passing.

His friends had pressed him to take another wife. A well-negotiated alliance could bring many benefits. But for some reason he had felt reluctant to do so. What cruel fate, he thought, sitting there by the masthead, that he should now yearn for one who could never be his. He stared down at his feet, then focused once more on the retreating *Trinity*. He heaved a mighty sigh, causing the boys to look at him askance. *Might as well cast my eyes upon the Moon Goddess, Cynthia. What a woman, though!* He judged her young, perhaps less than twenty, but he had seen the assurance in her after she'd replaced her hood; had noted in that instant the proud lift of her chin, bearing in it a challenge to any who would criticise. To think she was tied in marriage to that shambling Gilbert boy, who'd seemed but a shadow of his cousin as they'd stood together on the deck!

Walter groaned, and the boys exchanged smirks. Better that he had never thought to hail Edward Gilbert and come alongside the *Trinity* on a whim. He knew Edward was well liked by the sailors of Dartmouth. He'd only thought to hear the latest news in their chance meeting as he sailed home from France with his cargo of salt, and he'd thought it would be good for the boys to practise coming alongside a friendly vessel, using the iron grappling hooks to lash them to her side, and climbing aboard.

They might have need of such manoeuvres in more hostile times, for Walter was training his boys for a life at sea. How could he have foreseen that the *Trinity* carried such a cargo?

Heaving himself up from the ropes, he found he was straining his eyes for one last glimpse of that retreating figure in the sea-green gown. Only when *the Trinity* had faded to the merest dot on the horizon did he give himself a shake and stumble across the deck. Best put her from his thoughts and set about his business. Glancing around uneasily, he ordered a course for their home port.

SEVENTEEN
1538
KATHERINE

THE REMAINDER OF THE VOYAGE MIGHT HAVE HELD MANY wonders, but it passed in a blur. Katherine's mind was in torment. As she tried to bury the feelings stirred by that chance meeting, she couldn't rekindle the elation of start of their adventure. After a dream-filled night she woke to find that they were passing the Isle of Wight. Edward pointed out the sheltered harbour of Portsmouth, but it hardly registered in her mind that King Henry's finest ships were anchored there. They sailed on. Even the towering White Cliffs around Dover had no power to move her.

Otho seemed quite unaware of the change in her. He pointed out the coast of France, a shimmering line in the far, far distance; another country. Would she ever travel to such places? Perhaps only in her tormented dreams. A desperate groan forced its way up from the depths of her soul. Otho stared at her, and she gave herself a shake. This would not do. It must be enough that she was going to London at last.

Near dark on the third day, they sailed up the Thames through a flat and featureless landscape. Bessie poked her head out of the cabin door. "'Tis a relief to see us bounded by land on either side again, Mistress," she said, clutching the rail. "But this don't no way look like our Devon hills."

Soon they passed King Henry's dockyards and his palace at Greenwich. After they rounded two sweeping bends, the fortress of the Tower of London loomed grim and menacing. That dreadful place did have power to move Katherine. She shuddered, thinking of all those who had been held there and sent to their death beneath the headsman's axe.

The *Trinity* found a space at the wharves close to London Bridge, which seemed like a small city all in itself, with all the tall houses piled upon it. The ship secured, Bessie tottered down the gangplank behind Katherine and planted her foot firmly on the cobbles. "My, but that feels better to be back on solid ground again!" she exclaimed, looking around at the sailors and porters hoping to catch a penny or two by carrying cargo and bags, or hailing a lighter. Dressed in motley rags, some carried cutlasses or knives; some were fair and tall; some were short, stooped and bald; and some had skin as black as soot. One leaned at a perilous angle, supported by a wooden leg, while another had dangling gold hoops in his ears. "So this be what Londoners do look like, then!" Bessie declared, her broad Devon brogue carrying so far that heads turned.

Katherine laughed out loud.

They left Edward to look to the ship and took a barge to Uncle Gawen's house. Warmly welcomed, Katherine went soon to bed to toss and turn another night away. Those troubling dreams would not abate. She had prayed and prayed; had asked over and over that God might guide her. The only bleak answer she had found, from deep within her own heart, was that she must forget Master Raleigh and redouble her efforts to be a truly good wife. So, throughout their holiday, Katherine danced attendance on her husband. She flattered and praised him before all her relatives, as she tried to push Walter to the very bottom of her mind. She would have no truck with fanciful ideas of romance! By day she succeeded and played the dutiful wife. But, try as she might, those dreams still came each and every night, leaving her empty and bereft.

A few days after they arrived, more of Katherine's family gathered. She was exchanging news with Kat and Joanie when she noticed a tall priest. Was it Uncle George Carew? No; he was studying in Paris.

But there was something familiar about the handsome figure bearing down on her, his dark robe swishing over the floorboards.

He held his hands together, fingertips touching, and hailed her. "Why, Mistress Gilbert, is it not? How do you like to be away from the green pastures of Devon?" he asked. His grey eyes searched hers more than seemed necessary for such an ordinary greeting. "What do you think of our city?"

After a few moments there came a long pause in their conversation. He stared out of the window behind her, turning the crucifix hanging from his waist over and over in his hands. Katherine was taken off guard by the far-off look in his steady grey eyes when he dropped his voice to a wistful whisper.

"Do commend me to your sister, Mistress Cole. I trust she does well."

"So far as I know, Eliza is in good health," she replied, rather louder than she had intended.

He hesitated, took a deep breath, and spoke again. "Pray tell her when next you see her that John Pollard remembers her daily in his prayers."

Katherine frowned. What could this mean? How did he know Eliza? But before she could ask him to explain, all eyes turned to the door. Johnny sauntered in with his new bride giggling on his arm. Peter Carew clapped him on the back and gave a great belly laugh, soon echoed by the assembled company. Typical Johnny! He wore a jester's cap backwards so that the bells hung in front of his nose, and proceeded to beat Peter over the head with a pig's bladder he carried on a short, painted stick. Everyone found this hilarious. When Katherine looked again, John Pollard was gone. She meant to ask Kat what the strange conversation with the brooding priest might mean, but forgot all about it listening to Johnny's tales.

Their time in the city sped past in a whirlwind tour of the sights of London. First stop was St Paul's, which everyone knew was the greatest church in all the land, with its towering spire that made the little one at St Mary Major in Exeter seem a mere spindle. Nearby stood the school where Cousin Peter had briefly avoided his studies, and where Johnny had laboured for the sake of his Latin. It was a joy to search for new volumes amongst the booksellers' stalls in Paul's churchyard, groaning under the weight of all those words.

Next they ventured further upstream to the magnificent Abbey of Westminster, with the smaller Church of St Margaret nestling in its shadow. They returned past York Place, Wolsey's former trophy house, now part of the royal palace. An icy shiver ran down Katherine's spine. It was so unsettling that she had to shake herself to be rid of the grim sensation – dark and terrifying; a premonition of some evil deed. She shivered, wiped clammy hands on her gown, and was relieved when they moved on.

On another day they browsed the shops crowded along Cheapside, where Katherine bought expensive bolts of cloth, but only admired the wares in Goldsmiths' Row. They peeped into the Guildhall, and Otho checked prices in the cloth market. Everywhere they went, the crowds were so thick that Modbury's May fair seemed a trifling picnic. The deafening noise and hubbub, from the calls of street sellers to the builders' hammering, made her head throb. It was hard to take in the sheer scale of the city, with all its strange buildings crowded and crammed together along its narrow streets. The river, used by any who could afford the fare, was the swiftest thoroughfare in the teeming city. A crush of wherries and boats, barges and lighters bumped and bobbed along. There was no escape from the din.

Otho accompanied Edward on his rounds of the London merchants, leaving Katherine to sit with her hostess. A shrunken figure lying in a splendid bed, too ill to leave her chamber, Anne could not be long for this world. Katherine held her hand and read to her, hoping to ease the lady's pain.

When he returned, Otho was keen to show off his new understanding of their business. "The London merchants ship a lot of kersey to Antwerp," he said, leaning forward in his seat, slender hands planted on his knees, for all the world like a master about to instruct his addle-brained pupil. "They bring back luxury goods: paintings, jewellery, tapestries, and imported fabrics like silk, velvet, satin, taffeta and even sarcenet to be used for linings. All those fancy goods fetch a fine price amongst the newly rich of this city, I can tell you. Oh yes, my dear, the wealthy seek to adorn both their fine

London houses and their new country seats in the latest style. The old nobility like your family will have a hard time keeping up."

Katherine watched the smirk spread across her husband's face. *Pompous idiot!* She kept a fixed smile on her lips, as her fists itched to hit him. Yes, merchants, lawyers and administrators were gaining lands and power alongside those of ancient blood as the monastery lands were distributed. It was indeed a hard task for noble families to keep pace. But she wouldn't let Otho see that he'd hit his mark.

"I am sure I need not trouble my mind with these matters. It is, of course, proper that you should think on such things, not I. But how fascinating it is, dear husband, to consider how each trivial decision on the purchase of some commodity might have such a rippling effect on so many lives," she said in her sweetest tone.

The remark flew right over Otho's head and he continued his lecture. "Edward will venture to Antwerp soon," he said. "I'm sure Uncle John will relish news of the Great Bourse. You couldn't know this, but that's a place where deals are struck, all under one roof. Edward says there are ideas afoot for something like it in London. You should have seen them all, out in the rain in Lombard Street," he added with a snort of laughter. "Antwerp's the place for information! And not just about trade. The agents who travel there to strike deals for their masters are charged to send back regular reports. It's said that Master Cromwell has a whole network of spies amongst those men, and has his finger firmly on the pulse of everything that's happening."

Katherine almost laughed out loud. It was so funny to see Otho come over all pompous and tell her things she knew already. But she said nothing. He was probably relieved to be away from all the fine company at Uncle Gawen's house, where his stammer came back with a vengeance every time he opened his mouth. She'd asked Uncle Gawen if he could arrange for Otho to visit the royal armouries and the gunmakers of London, and Otho had come back much happier. He could hardly get the words out to describe all he had seen, and completely forgot to patronise her.

"Christopher Morris, the Master of the Ordnance, showed me the arsenals and workshops close to the Tower. Then I went to Houndsditch to see Peter Baude's gun foundry. They're making a new sort of cannon, Katherine. The King wants stronger coastal defences and better shipboard weapons. But, Katherine, you should have seen the handheld guns! At the foundry they told me all about a murder with one of those!" Otho grabbed her and held her arm in a vice-like grip. His eyes sparkled, and she listened patiently while he told the tale. "Robert Pakington! Merchant! Member of Parliament! Well-known figure in the Worshipful Company of Mercers! Two years gone, felled in Cheapside with a single shot from a new type of handgun!"

Katherine had seldom seen him so excited.

"That such a weapon can be used at close quarters with such accuracy!" he exclaimed. "I'm sure such firing pieces could be put to use in defence of our Gilbert ships."

"Poor Master Pakington," she cried, throwing up her arms. "To be murdered in such a dreadful fashion in a crowded street! Oh, Otho, it chills me to think of all the others that might perish due to those horrible portable killing machines."

But Otho just smiled.

Katherine was tingling and breathless as she stepped lightly into the barge that would take them to Greenwich. As they passed St Katherine's she picked out the Gilbert flag, arms topped by the squirrel crest, fluttering bravely amongst the spars and masts. They glided past the gloomy walls of the Tower, and Uncle Gawen, who was travelling with them, showed her the Traitors' Gate where so many entered, never to return. A cold shiver ran down her spine and the hairs at the back of her neck stood on end, as if those walls foreshadowed some primal fear deep within her soul.

It was easy to see why the Palace of Placentia was a favourite royal residence. With a facing of red brick, added by the King's father, it stretched along the riverbank, warm and inviting in the spring sunshine. The splendid buildings sat in open parkland, trees and green spaces rising up behind the palace; such a contrast to the dirty, crowded streets of the city. A lump came to Katherine's throat. How she missed the hills of Devon!

"King Henry was born here," said Uncle Gawen as the barge tied up at the steps directly before a wide doorway, "as were both his daughters. He enjoys the chase amongst those ancient oaks, though not so often as he'd like, I warrant. It's not far from the royal shipyards where he can oversee his latest vessels." He pointed to a group of low buildings away to their right, beyond the palace complex. "New forges and armouries, extra stables, and over yonder there's a tiltyard."

Anthony Denny, gaunt-cheeked and clad in lawyer's black, walked through the door to meet them. He greeted Otho with an easy nod of his head, then bent to take Katherine's hand, his deep-set eyes moving quickly over her as though assessing her worth. "You have arrived just in time," he said in a deep voice with the ring of authority. "The King will be here shortly."

They followed him into the King's splendid new banqueting hall, crowded with well-dressed people all hoping to catch a glimpse of the King.

"Wait here with all the others," Anthony advised, before leaving them standing open-mouthed amid the throng.

Otho tried to shrink into the shadows, but Katherine grabbed his arm.

Like a ship parting the waves, King Henry sailed through the crowd with Anthony at his side. You could see he liked Anthony. Both men were laughing. Katherine had expected to be dazzled by the King's magnificent clothes, the rich, jewel-encrusted fabrics all dripping with gold. But nothing had prepared her for the size of the man within. It was not just his enormous bulk. Towering over the crowd, King Henry seemed to fill the space around him to the exclusion of all others, drawing all eyes. Glad that she had heeded advice and donned a rather old-fashioned hood out of deference to Jane Seymour, with chin trembling, Katherine dipped a deep curtsey. The men bowed low beside her. As she rose, she thought the King's piercing eyes seemed to warm a little. A smile flitted briefly around his pinched mouth; a mouth that looked far too small set in that huge moon face. She felt breathless as he looked down at her.

"Why, Anthony, how many flowers like to your dear wife and this fair rose does Champernowne keep hidden away in deepest Devonshire?" he asked, laughing heartily.

Anthony laughed with him and replied that Philip Champernowne did indeed have a bevy of beautiful daughters. Katherine dared to raise her eyes, but King Henry had already moved on to another lady standing behind them: Anne Basset, daughter of that same Lady Lisle who was in debt to Otho's mother, and some distant kin of theirs.

"Some say she's already his mistress," whispered Uncle Gawen, "though he makes a show of mourning his dearest Jane."

Katherine had already heard this from Johnny, who said that some people thought that the King might wed Anne Basset and make her his fourth Queen. As she watched the woman simpering before the King, she remembered a conversation with Kat. Cromwell and others of the Privy Council had other ideas about the next woman to share King Henry's bed. Kat said they were pressing for a marriage alliance with a foreign royal house, but the King wanted reassurance that any bride he took would be comely. He'd dispatched the court painter, Hans Holbein, to capture the likenesses of prospective candidates so that he could judge their charms. Katherine looked again at Anne Bassett, curtseying low before the King and revealing quite a lot over the top of her shift in the process. She envied neither the Princesses nor women like Anne. Not one jot! Any woman who valued the head upon her shoulders, even a foreign Princess, would surely run a mile from this fickle King. For all his glittering court and his magnificent palaces, he cut a sad and lonely figure. As he walked away, she noticed that he was limping heavily. All his fine clothes could not conceal the bandages on his leg.

Joanie looked resplendent in an expensive silk gown, with a gold cross set with five magnificent diamonds at her throat and gold enamelled bracelets gleaming at her wrists. She and Katherine chatted while Otho completed a tour of the new armouries; the highlight of his visit. Later, as the three of them sauntered toward the riverbank, another barge drew in bearing a corpulent figure clad in black robes of the finest quality. Thomas Cromwell was attended by several earnest looking men carrying sheaves of documents. He greeted Joanie pleasantly, bowed to them, and hurried off about his business.

"It seems Cromwell's star is in the ascendant for the time being," Katherine confided as the barge took them back towards the city. "All these affairs of the court, they remind me of a game the boys play in the woodyards behind Galmpton Pool. You know it, Otho? They call it 'see-saw'. They set a plank of wood across a newly felled tree trunk.

One boy sits at one end, the other climbs up onto the opposite end, and up and down they go in turn. Teeter-totter, up and down, until one or other of them falls crashing to the ground. Those that jostle for influence seem just like those boys at see-saw. Thomas Cromwell, he's riding high in King Henry's favour. As he goes up, down go his foes, be it the Duke of Norfolk, Nicholas Carew or the Marquess of Exeter. Up and down, up and down they go. Who knows which of them will be the next to fall from his perch and come down to earth to lose all he has? He might even lose his head!"

Otho blinked, and started to laugh, and Katherine joined him in blessed relief after all the tension of the afternoon. "What a picture! The wiry old Duke of Norfolk at one end and fat Cromwell at the other! Ho, ho, ho! We should not speak of these things, but I can't help laughing," he said, exploding with mirth.

Their laughter set the barge rocking. She hoped the oarsman hadn't been able to hear what they'd said.

After ten hectic days in London they rode north to Joanie and Anthony's new home.

"Your sister's really fallen on her feet in this marriage," said Otho, steering his mount around a large pothole. "He seems set fair to become one of the wealthiest and most influential men at court."

"You're right in that, Otho," Katherine replied, glad that the barriers between them seemed to have come down a little. "Joanie can order whatever she pleases to furnish her new home, as well as new gowns and jewels aplenty. But I don't envy her. I have enjoyed seeing my family, and it has been exciting to be in London and visit the court. But I've no wish to remain."

Otho reached over and squeezed her hand. "I am so pleased to hear you say that, Katherine," he said with a relaxed smile. "I had feared you'd wish to trade places."

She blushed, and fumbled unnecessarily with the reins. There was another place she'd much rather be. But it was not in London as the wife of a courtier. Her dreams were of another life upon the high seas with Master Raleigh. She chose her words carefully. "A courtier's life does seem fraught with danger. London boasts fine houses, but we've also seen the poverty of those who live in its crowded alleys, rife with disease that spreads like wildfire. No, husband, I'll be glad to go home. I do so miss our boy and even that naughty Katie." She forced herself to smile reassuringly at him. She must never admit to herself, even for a second, that she also hoped to see again that Devon man whose ship had come alongside the *Trinity*.

A few days in Joanie's fabulous mansion were all that Otho could manage. Then they moved on to Hunsdon, where Kat and her charge were visiting the elder royal daughter. Kat seemed to be enjoying her promotion to governess to the six-year-old Lady Elizabeth. As the girl worked at her lesson, Katherine noticed how often her eyes flew to Kat's face.

"Poor little maid," Katherine said to Otho as they retired to bed. "Looking to find in Kat the love she's been starved of throughout her short life." She took a deep, pained breath and closed her eyes. An image of Katie wandering in the orchard with her favourite dog at her heel had come unbidden to her mind. Katherine gave herself a shake, before she continued. "To have your mother put to death by your own father just doesn't bear thinking of. Kat's not yet found the man that could put up with her, and at her age she's not likely to have children of her own. It seems she's found just the outlet for all her maternal instincts. But, Otho, that child is really quite formidably clever. Did you see how clearly she could write out all that Latin?"

Otho *had* seen, but it seemed his mind was on other matters. At Gawen's house the sleeping arrangements had been haphazard, with all the guests coming and going. But here they had the privacy of their own bedchamber. Bessie had helped Katherine from her gown and was starting to unlace her kirtle when Otho told the maid to leave them.

Katherine turned away. She'd known this moment must come. In the early days, when he'd first come to her bed, she'd perfected a trick to divorce her mind from her body. While he panted and groaned, fumbled and fondled, and covered her mouth with sloppy kisses, her mind would drift far away. She would rehearse the next day's duties in the still room, plan a new pattern to trim some cuffs, go over the latest news from court, or lose herself in tales of King Arthur's court. Anything to keep her mind busy until she felt his weight shift off her and she could hope for sleep. But could she do it now? The echo of Master Raleigh's laughter reverberated through her still, as a lute string quivers long after the note is plucked. Oh, wicked, wanton woman, to have her mind full of another man when she must be about her wifely duty!

Her laces yielded to Otho's fumbling and the kirtle fell to the floor, forming a scarlet puddle at her feet. She gritted her teeth as he pulled her toward the bed, pressing insistent wet lips into her shoulder.

The next morning they were granted a very brief audience with the Lady Mary. Kat explained that the soberly dressed young woman was not in the best of health. *Her pinched face and sunken cheeks give her away*, thought Katherine. *She must have had a hard life.* Perhaps Queen Jane had been kinder to the royal girls. But with her gone so soon to her grave, who knew what lay in store for either of them, should the King find a new bride?

Katherine and Otho set out for home the next day, taking the journey in stages on hired horses. The roads were busy, with many vagabonds begging by the roadside. Some still had the remnants of their monk's tonsure showing in their unkempt hair. It must be hard to find other work for those turned out from the monasteries without a pension.

There was much to wonder at along the way, but Katherine was now impatient to be home. Glassy tears filled her eyes as she looked again upon the broad River Dart winding its steady way past Greenway Court, and into the faces of her children as she enfolded them in her arms.

EIGHTEEN
1538–1540
KATHERINE

WHEN UNCLE JOHN GREETED THEM WITH A BEAMING SMILE, Katherine turned to Otho and whispered, "He looks sprightly and cheery. His chest's puffed out like a hawk's. I'll warrant that's not just his delight at seeing us again."

Before they could return the greeting, little John came running from the house and barrelled into the old man, nearly knocking him from his feet.

"Off you go, my boy," he laughed, ruffling young John's hair. "We can walk out together later, but first I must greet your parents."

Katie hung back with a long face, kicking her feet in the dust, until Bessie took her hand and she shambled after her brother. Katherine's trunk would not arrive for a few more days, so all the gifts would have to wait.

Uncle John looked from Otho to Katherine and back several times, searching their faces until he seemed satisfied. "Hmm! No doubt you've got much to tell me, but first, let me tell you all my news!" he said with a booming laugh. "While you two have been a-gallivanting, I've been called to serve once more as Justice of the Peace. It's a long time since they've called on my wisdom and experience. But more to the point, I've brought an idea of mine to fruition." He went on to detail the cunning plan he had been hatching with John Rowe. "I'm sure it'll ease my soul through Purgatory, when at last I must meet my Maker. That day, I fear, won't be long in coming."

Katherine opened her mouth to object, to say he would see many more moons come and go, but he put a finger to his lips.

"Hush. No use to pretend, girl. I'm as old as the hills and I haven't led a blameless life. I'll need all the help I can get. Now, you know I've been much afeared that the King will in time lay grasping hands on the wealth of the chantries? I've been puzzling long about how best to secure the welfare of my immortal soul, and now I've found the way. The beauty of my scheme is that prayers will be said for me and mine, but I'll also be helping some poor souls in their time upon the earth. Even better, I've persuaded the Corporation of Exeter to foot the bill long after I'm gone!"

"If this eases your mind, Uncle, then I am delighted," said Katherine, while Otho stood gaping. "But do tell us how it may be."

So he told them how he planned to set up a lazar hospital and have the poor wights say prayers for him and his kin for all eternity. He had found a suitable piece of land not far from the Exeter Road in Newton Bushell. "They will be well housed, with a garden to grow their own food and a chapel to say their prayers," he chirped. "Richard Yarde's been more than happy to join me in the venture. While you were gone, I rode to Bradley to finalise the plans. Oh, oh, I found the Yarde household in some confusion, that's no doubt." And he went on to explain how Richard's son, that same Thomas Yarde who had aided Katherine and her grandmother on their nightmare journey, had recently lost his wife.

"I remember her," snorted Katherine. "Overweening niece of Bishop Veysey!"

"Well, even in death she made sure to underline her supposed rank," old John laughed. "Richard was much affronted when the good Bishop insisted that Elizabeth Yarde must be buried in Sutton Coldfield rather than amongst the Yarde kin in Devon. It cost him more than enough to have her transported there. But it's not all bad news. Thomas has already chosen a second wife. He's to be wed to Joan, the daughter of William Hurst of Exeter, and that suits my plan very well. Hurst served as Mayor of the city but two years since. Now he's allied with the Yardes, he's just the man to secure the support of the Corporation for my lazar-house scheme. It's all in place. Hurst has promoted it, the members of the Corporation are in agreement, and the builders can soon start work on the cottages and a chapel."

Katherine clapped her hands, pleased to hear that her friend Joan was to be wed. "I'll send a basket of gifts to Mistress Joan to wish her well," she announced. "Perhaps a length of cloth, some silk threads from London, and a box or two of my finest quince marmalade."

"How well you have done to achieve this!" she cried, since Otho seemed to have nothing to say.

Her childhood home was filled to bursting when, in early September, Katherine arrived to see Frances marry Roger Budockside. Just like old times, she shared the maidens' chamber with Eliza, who confided that she was expecting a child in the New Year.

Seeing Frances beside her bridegroom at the church door brought back vivid memories of Katherine's own wedding day and the vows she and Otho had exchanged. As they walked back from the church, she noticed that the rosemary bough they had planted had withered. She made another guilty pledge to try to be a good wife, to banish those wicked, unfaithful thoughts of another man.

She had been looking forward to seeing Agnes, perhaps even to seek her counsel. But it soon became clear that Agnes was beyond giving advice. Katherine searched in vain for the comforting contours of the woman who had rocked her on her knee in the gaunt figure she found in the tiny room at the very top of the furthest stair. As Agnes struggled to her feet, Katherine could see how her kirtle hung about her in empty folds, how her face was pinched and drawn, how she clutched at her breast, wincing in pain. She could feel Agnes's bones poking through the coarse woollen cloth as she hugged her close. They sat side by side on the little bed, rocking to and fro, as silent tears flowed unchecked down Katherine's cheeks.

"'Tis nothing, my dear child,'" came the rasping whisper. "It will pass, as all things must. I would have no fuss made at the wedding feast. This is Frances's day of days, just as you had yours."

Distraught, Katherine looked for some way to ease her faithful nurse's last days. Will seemed quite pleased when she persuaded

Johnny to leave him at Modbury. It was clear that he had taken quite a shine to Jenny, the pretty laundry maid.

Johnny's wife complained of the heat and rubbed her aching back all through the wedding feast. Shortly after, she withdrew to the room where many a Champernowne heir had made his first appearance in the world. Katherine joined the women gathered there to support the expectant mother, and in due time a boy was born, named Henry in honour of the King. The proud father was called back to London, leaving his wife sad and forlorn. Katherine noticed how easy it was for Johnny to leave his family in Devon.

Devon was peaceful and calm that autumn. But in London, see-saw, see-saw, up and down went those seeking the ear of the increasingly fickle King. Soon another came crashing down, and his fall sent shock waves through Devon. Katherine heard the news from Father when he called on his way home for Christmas.

"For months I've seen him sailing far too close to the wind. It's dangerous indeed to make an enemy of Thomas Cromwell," he blustered.

Katherine frowned as she watched him fidget in his seat, twist the golden ring on his finger, then leap up to pace around the room.

"That man! He's everywhere! Not only the King's Principal Minister and Chief Secretary, but he holds a string of lucrative posts as long as your arm. Oh yes, his star is climbing high just now!"

"Take a sip of your wine, Father. Be seated and calm yourself," she soothed.

He waved the cup aside, sat down with a thump and took a breath. "They worked together to bring about Anne Boleyn's downfall, but that was just a temporary truce in a long-standing feud. I thought Henry Courtenay might have saved himself after the Northern Uprising. But Cromwell kept on fostering suspicion that he'd plotted to put Mary on the throne. Someone concocted a story that he and the Poles were set on returning the country to the Pope. I think the King panicked. Rumours were rife that the Holy Roman Emperor and the King of France would cement their truce with an invasion to defeat the heretic English. It's not surprising that he saw Papists everywhere. But Courtenay didn't see it. His conservative views were well known.

Gertrude was involved with that Nun of Kent business. To cap it all, he insisted on keeping that Richard Crispin as his chaplain. He made it easy for them. There were plenty of straws in the wind. I've seen how Cromwell can weave them into a case against a man."

"I did hear that the Marquess was taken up. Otho said others were too. Was it Sir Edward Neville? And Henry Pole, Lord Montague? And I heard that Aunt Gertrude and Edward were taken to the Tower. Is that so?" she asked, her voice trailing off as she saw his colour rising.

He was out of his chair again, restless as a cat on a hot bakestone. "They called it the Exeter Conspiracy! Said he planned to raise an army against the King! What nonsense! Why, in these times Henry Courtenay would struggle to raise a dozen men in the West. He's hardly ever here!"

"It's all right, Father. Calm down. It's not good for you to get so agitated. I'm sure no one would think you had anything to do with it," she cried. "The King knows that none of our family want to go back to the ways of the Pope."

"Don't you be so sure. Your mother was named in that wretched Barton nonsense. I thought it might all be turned against us. Oh, Katherine-Kate, I was afraid we'd somehow be implicated and accused. So I went to the Duke of Norfolk. I didn't know what else to do." He paused, sat down again and took a long draught from the cup. "I found the old boy at his London house, eating his supper. 'My Lord,' said I, 'I am come about the Marquess of Exeter, whom you know to be but a distant kinsman of mine. I would make clear to Your Grace – aye, and to any that should question it – that I have only remained familiar with him in any sense at all on account of some long-outstanding bonds. Once they are discharged I will certainly give up my office as Deputy Warden of the Stannaries under him. Aye, as soon as may be, for I would have no further contact with the man.' Do you think I can trust Norfolk in this?"

"Well, I know little of these matters, Father, but I would have thought that you're far too useful down here to get caught up in all the mayhem in London," she answered. "The King has need of you here."

"Well, Courtenay's gone now," he said, scratching at his face and closing his eyes.

Katherine felt suddenly cold. She gasped and her hand flew up to cover her mouth. This she had not heard.

"I was there on Tower Hill on the sixth day of December. I never thought to see that day! What would his mother have thought? She must be spinning in her grave in Tiverton Chapel. His own cousin! All those years so close to the King, when they were children and when they were young men. But it all counted for nought. If he could cut off the head of Anne Boleyn I suppose no one should be surprised that ties of kinship stand as nothing." Father's hands were shaking, and Katherine was shocked to see him looking so frail; shrunken, somehow. "Gertrude and her son are still in the Tower," he went on, lowering his voice. "We must all be careful now. The King's as volatile as a keg of that black powder your husband's so keen on. Between wives, wriggling hard to avoid a diplomatic marriage with a bride he fears might be less comely than some of the lovelies he sees around him at court, he's at his most dangerous. Nicholas Carew is like to be next. Well, we must wait to see who will hold sway in Devon. Whoever gets the spoils from Courtenay's downfall, we must be ready to offer service."

"This is shocking news, Father," she said, giving his hand a squeeze. "But we are safe here in Devon, and you have done all you can. Go and enjoy Christmastide, safe at home with your new grandson. And, Father, will you bring Arthur to visit me next time?"

After the holiday they learned that it was John Russell who came into the bulk of the Courtenay estates, and that set all the local landowners vying to show themselves on the right side.

Towards the end of January, Katherine made her way to Cornwood. The weather was mild for the time of year and she hummed a lilting tune as Dapple picked her way along the lanes. She would always have a fondness for that old house, The Slade, and she was looking forward to the company. As she passed Fardel Manor she couldn't help but think of Walter Raleigh. Try as she might, she could not quite forget him. She chided herself for such thoughts when she was carrying Otho's child. Pregnancy would give her welcome respite from Otho's attentions, which she had found harder to tolerate since her heart had been stirred by another.

After her earlier disappointments, all seemed well and a fine boy named Philip was born to Eliza and her husband on the seventh day of February. William Cole was overjoyed to have his son and heir at last. Eliza was tearful, exhausted, and relieved that she had done her duty, as all wives must. Katherine made no mention of her strange conversation with that handsome priest, Pollard. Whatever it had all been about, she saw no need to upset the new mother.

When she returned to Greenway Court she found her husband in a state. Uncle John had been melancholy since Christmas, always talking of death. He hadn't been to visit the boy for days. The servants were worried.

She didn't even stop to change her costume. They must go at once. They found him slumped by the fireside, gazing empty-eyed at the flames. It was as if John Gilbert had had enough of life; as if, having secured prayers for his soul, he felt he could relinquish his grip on the world of men. He had called for John Ford and Thomas Lynne of Dittisham to act as witnesses to his will.

He spoke in a weak, rasping voice. "I have lived a long and casual life. I wonder that God has allowed me to linger so very long on this earth. My time is near, and my will is sealed."

"Let me fetch my son to cheer you," Katherine offered, her mind skipping forward to think of what would happen if he was right.

Little John chattered and laughed as boys will, but even his precious heir could do nothing to raise the old man's spirits. He took to his bed and they waited for the dread news. But after a week he emerged, looking sad and tired, and called for his horse to be saddled. He braved the sodden lanes for what he declared would be his last visit to his mansion house by the Dart. Once there, he seemed content, resumed his walks with the boy, and spent hours staring at the river. But as the spring buds began to burst, he hugged them all and returned to Compton.

On a warm May morning they found him in his chamber. He had died in his sleep; a peaceful death at the end of a very long life. No one knew for sure how many dawns that old man had seen. His life stretched back to long-forgotten times when Lancaster and York had fought for the Crown. John Gilbert seemed to belong to another age.

Katherine pulled on the ugly black robe Uncle John had decreed all of his family must wear to do him honour at his funeral. She trudged along with the other mourners, following the coffin as it made its stately way through the village. People crowded at the roadside to doff their hats or bow their heads at the passing of the man who had been their overlord for so long. The day was warm and Katherine was growing large. Beads of sweat were forming on her brow and her back ached, so it was a welcome relief to go inside the church and feel the musty air of that hallowed space wrap around her like a cool shroud. She prayed she would bear another boy.

Otho seemed completely nonplussed by his uncle's death, though they could all have seen it coming. When the will was read, he exploded. The *Trinity*, the Gilberts' finest vessel, had been left not to him, but to his cousin Edward. "S-s-so you s-s-see, wife," he said, his stammer more noticeable as he struggled to find a vent for his anger, "I've always said the old m-m-m… m-m-m… man didn't trust me. He's always favoured Edward over m-m-m-m-me."

He stormed off and, from what she could piece together, hot words were spoken. Edward removed himself to a house near the quay in Dartmouth, taking the *Trinity* with him. How Katherine missed his steadying presence during a difficult time!

Otho turned to Penkervell to manage the estate while he indulged his passion for weapons. He spent more than was wise to fit out the Gilbert ships to withstand any attack. He was in the alehouse more often than was good for him. He seemed to be quarrelling with everyone. When the will had been read it had come out that Katherine's father still hadn't paid over all the money agreed for her dowry. Otho was determined he would have it, and caused more bad feeling. Isabel, who still awaited payment of her long-standing debt from Lady Lisle, plagued him with requests for more than the paltry allowance John Gilbert had left her. Otho stood his ground, and, after a heated argument, Isabel took herself off to Tressorrow, one of her homes in Cornwall.

One of the legs that held up the stable platform of little John's life had been suddenly kicked away. He watched at the window and wandered the gardens, searching for his friend. Katherine tried to make more time for the lad, but she had another boy kicking in her belly. Otho could have filled more of the void in John's three-year-old world but, pursued by his own demons, he hardly noticed the change in his son.

She felt the miss of the old man, and listened for his step on the stair. But at least she wouldn't have to conform to his wishes when the next baby came. The next Gilbert boy would be born at Greenway Court. Looking to mend fences with her mother-in-law, she asked if Isabel would be among her gossips for the birth. By mid October, Isabel was with her, writing to Lady Lisle and waiting with her daughter-in-law. This time Katherine was adamant. She would not have the windows covered, nor the room so stifling. So Humphrey was born, without fuss or bother, in a bright room overlooking the River Dart.

Anne of Cleves arrived to be their Queen. Uncle Gawen and Joanie were in the welcome party that brought her from Calais. The Gentlemen Pensioners lined her route through Blackheath on the third day of January. Katherine could just imagine Johnny, Peter and Uncle Gawen in their splendid uniforms.

Toward the end of the month, Johnny called at Greenway Court on his way back to London after a short visit to his wife and son. Father and Arthur crowded into Katherine's snug little parlour with him to hear all about their new Queen.

"Such a magnificent welcome you never did see. One side of the heath was entirely covered with glittering cloth of gold. There were tents and pavilions all along the roadside, with fires to warm her and ladies waiting to greet her with perfumes," said Johnny, waving his arms as if to show them the splendour of it all. "She made her way between those tents, down Shooters Hill, towards the park gate. And there was the King, all dressed in purple, astride a massive horse ablaze with gold and jewels. But, for all that magnificent welcome, word has it," he went on, with a saucy smile, "that the Princess Anne does not appeal at all to our King."

"That could spell danger ahead," Father grunted. "I heard the first meeting between the King and his bride was a complete disaster. He'd have none of her."

"Well, I do hope that the lady will keep her head on her

shoulders," said Katherine. "Now, Johnny! Tell us what she wore!"

Johnny told them about Anne's strange costume, and then turned his attention to the King's plans to improve his sea defences, including those along the River Dart. "He's upgraded Dartmouth Castle again, Otho," he said, and Katherine smiled silent thanks that he had drawn her sullen husband into the conversation. "He's building more gun batteries and a new bulwark to give artillery coverage to the southeast across the Channel into the port."

"Remember, Katherine," Otho said, throwing back his head, "I told you how he must be sure to have firepower covering all angles of attack?"

"Well, I'm sure it makes good military sense," said Johnny evenly. "But Cousin Peter's spitting fire and brimstone. Says the castle's on Carew lands and they shouldn't do anything without his brother's say-so. He's spoiling for a fight. George takes a more relaxed view, but says he may have to build a manor house within those walls to show who has the right of it."

"You must teach me the way of all these matters, for I don't rightly understand them," Arthur laughed.

"Plenty of time for you to learn, boy," growled Father. "It'll fall to Johnny to deal with suchlike when I'm gone, not you."

"Father, please don't speak of such a time. You'll be with us for many more years. Why, I can hardly find one grey hair upon your head!" Katherine exclaimed with a chuckle. "And, Johnny, you sound so full of these defences against the French. I wonder if you hope for war so that you may win your spurs?"

Johnny laughed, but did not deny it.

All too soon the visit was over, and Katherine felt so proud to see Father ride away flanked by his two handsome sons. At the gate, Johnny turned in his saddle and raised an arm in farewell. A chilling tremor ran through her as she waved back to him. She wandered back to the house, feet dragging.

Once inside, she shrank back against the cool stone wall in the hallway, fighting an unusual tingling in her chest, and muttered a prayer. "Please, God, don't let Johnny be led into some hot-headed search for glory, egged on by Cousin Peter. If there be war, oh, please, God, protect him."

It was not war with France she should have feared. It was stories of other conflicts in Eastern Europe, where the Ottoman Sultan had won crushing victories that enticed the lusty gentlemen of the court. They all wanted to go and see for themselves the mysterious, exotic magnificence of the court of the Great Turk. The most fervent in this desire was Cousin Peter. It was not long before he and Johnny were seeking the King's permission to go across the sea.

On a fine May morning Katherine walked with Father in her apple orchard, where the rows of trees covered with pink-tinged blossoms looked like lines of finely dressed dancers about to step a measure. He turned to her, pride and anxiety flashing across his noble face in turn.

"Well, King Henry has quite a fondness for both those boys. At first he refused to let them risk their lives. But you know how persuasive your cousin can be. They wore his resistance down. He's not only granted licence for them to travel, but he's helped fund the expedition; a relief to me, as I could ill afford it. Johnny and Peter set sail for France last month."

"Without even coming down to Devon to say goodbye? What of Johnny's wife left at Modbury, and his son, Henry? I can't believe he could be so heartless," she cried, her voice rising to an angry crescendo as she turned from him to hide her tears.

"There now, Katherine-Kate, he sent letters for Catherine, and the boy will want for nothing with us. Once the decision was made there was no holding those two back. I must say, I'm rather proud of him."

"Well, God send him back safe and sound to us, is all *I* can say," she replied, with a bitter edge in her voice.

"Johnny secured some land for us before he set off. We already had Plympton in the bag, but now he has the promise of land from Totnes Priory as well," Father said with a broad grin. "Oh, this is such a tale, Katherine-Kate! Your brother came upon a line of worthies kneeling before the King to plead their case. Well, Johnny thought he may as well kneel in line with them. When the King found it was his favourite henchman kneeling there, he roared with laughter and agreed there and then that he would bestow those lands on Johnny."

"Just like Johnny," she said, smiling in spite of her anger. "I'm sorry he's gone off with Peter. I've always known he would."

They had only gone a few paces when Father touched her arm and looked hard into her face. "I do sometimes wonder, Katherine-Kate, if you still hold envy in your heart. Am I right? Do you wish that you could go off across the sea to seek your fortune like Johnny?"

It was no use pretending. He knew her too well. "Perhaps you're right, Father. Perhaps I do still dream of such things, though I know where my duty lies," she admitted, as a vision of Walter Raleigh on his ship, sailing a wide sea under starlit skies, came into her mind.

That small voice of envy kept whispering in her ear. She really would have loved to travel; to see with her own eyes the distant places that filled her books. Better still, to do so with the man of her dreams beside her. But no woman could expect that. It was not the way of things.

NINETEEN
1540-1542
KATHERINE

HUMPHREY HAD BEEN BORN IN A TIME OF PLENTY. SPRING HAD come early and the crops flourished in the warm earth under sunlit skies, promising another bumper year. Early in June, Katherine went out with the serving women to pick cherries, the crop so heavy she had enough to make cherry wine.

Otho was away too often, spent too much and drank too much. Katherine didn't see much of him, so was taken by surprise when he rushed into the kitchen garden.

"Looks like my mother can go whistle for any money from Lady Lisle, now," he whooped, making the maids look askance.

Katherine drew him away, sat down on the bench and waited.

"Lord Lisle's in the Tower, suspected of plotting against the King in Calais. Mother's famous kinswoman's held under house arrest over there, so she'll get nothing more. Ha! Your cousin George was in the Tower as well," he crowed, hopping from foot to foot. "Charged with eating meat during Lent, I heard! I'd wager there was more to it. After all, he was over there too, Captain of Ryesbank Castle, wasn't he?"

She glanced at Otho's face and saw his delight at Isabel's predicament replaced by a belligerent scowl. It was like watching a black cloud snuff out the sun.

He dropped onto the bench with a thump and sat stiff as a poker. "Seems he got away with it. I bet the King let him out because he did well in that tournament. Your hoity-toity relations can always creep back into favour."

She could see the bitterness burning in his eyes. *Well*, she thought, pursing her lips, *it's not my fault if my family know how to use their position to advantage. It's not my fault they all get called to serve the King, while you waste your time in the alehouse.* Good for George if he was back in favour! He had left Thomasine in Calais, buried far from home, when he had been charged to accompany Anne of Cleves to London. He deserved some good luck. Of course there was no question of his plotting against the King.

She had flung open all the windows, but still not a breath of wind stirred the air when Father and Arthur arrived on a sultry August day. Otho sat in his shirtsleeves, drinking a cool mug of ale Bessie had just brought from the buttery. Katherine put down her stitching, sending Grandmother Carew's silver thimble skidding across the floor. She bent awkwardly to retrieve it; Humphrey was only ten months old, but she had another child growing within her.

"So what news this time?" she asked as she scraped back a tendril of hair from her brow.

"Well, before you ask, no, we've heard nothing of Johnny. But there is shocking news. Cromwell is dead and gone!"

"Why, how so, Father?" Katherine gasped.

"He went too far in the end, I suppose. Gave his enemies a chance to play the King. He made a big mistake pushing the Cleves marriage. The King didn't take kindly to that at all. Said he'd put his neck in the yoke for a foreign alliance; said she didn't live up to the likeness painted by Holbein; complained that she dressed outlandishly and smelt bad. Gossip has it he already has his eye on another young English girl, Kitty Howard. Dangled in front of his nose at every opportunity by her relations! Pshaw! The King is quite besotted."

"This is all quite beyond my understanding," said Arthur, with a splutter which was silenced by a cold stare from Father.

"The marriage wasn't Cromwell's only problem. He pushed the pace of religious reform too fast. The King still clings to tradition, although he's more than happy to be free of the rule of Rome. Cromwell knew he was in trouble so in April he brought in a new taxation bill to swell the King's coffers. Well, it was a strategy that worked well in the past. The King's always short of funds, so he usually responds to extra cash. It seemed to work again, and Cromwell was raised to be Earl of Essex."

"What?" Otho interrupted, his brow puckering. "I thought you said he was dead?"

"I'm coming to that. Don't you see? Cromwell, the low-born son of a blacksmith, fuller, cloth merchant, brewer, innkeeper or whatever, created Earl of Essex! That put him on a par with the highest lords in the land. It was a step too far for some of his enemies; first among them, the Duke of Norfolk." He paused to let the tension build. "Just as with Anne Boleyn, it all happened suddenly. Cromwell was arrested at a Council meeting. Imagine it – taken to the Tower and stripped of the Order of the Garter! They drew up a great catalogue of his supposed crimes. Even said he'd been plotting to marry the King's daughter, Mary, and accused him of doing it all for personal gain." He snorted. "If every man who acted for personal gain was charged with treason and imprisoned, why, there would be few left at liberty in this land. But Cromwell's time had come. He faced the headsman's axe on the twenty-eighth day of July just passed. The King kept him lingering in the Tower just long enough for him to finalise the annulment of the Cleves marriage so he could marry Kitty Howard. Cromwell was the only one who could pull it off, you see. But to see him fallen! Where will it end? Henry Courtenay, Nicholas Carew… with so many gone, who will be next? No one is safe."

To Katherine's delight, Father said that the former Queen Anne had come out of the ugly business well.

"She has her head intact, an allowance of wealth and lands, and the status of sister to the King."

Katherine wondered privately if Anne of Cleves had been clever enough to engineer her own escape from the old tyrant. *Good for her!*

"It's hard to believe," said Otho, shaking his head. "Uncle John always said Cromwell could fix anything. Sounds like his luck ran out in the end."

"Perhaps I'll look for my chances down here in Devon, Father," said Arthur. "The court sounds far too dangerous, though there may be some comely wenches about the place, I suppose. I'd much rather get the chance to go to war!"

Not another one, thought Katherine.

In December they heard that Cousin George had taken a new wife: Mary Norreys, a well-connected young woman who served the new Queen. That put George right at the centre of things, and Katherine smiled to hear how he'd been at Hampton Court when the King celebrated Christmas with his new Queen. George had swept up lands from a string of smaller religious houses across Devon, and seemed to be sitting pretty. That was sure to set Otho off again. Katherine had had more than enough of his bad temper. She tried to avoid him as much as she could as she waited for the next baby to come.

It was February again; that most depressing of months. Katherine's fourth labour was drawn out over two days, and it was a relief to everyone when another strapping boy, Adrian, was safely delivered.

News filtered through from court. The fall from grace of the young Queen Katherine Howard set the see-saw flying again. People had always said she was no better than she should be, but Katherine could hardly bear to think about what happened to that thoughtless girl, so recently fawned upon by Henry, showered with jewels and fine gowns. At about the time Katherine laboured to bring Adrian into the world, Kitty Howard walked out to meet the headsman.

After Adrian's birth, Katherine felt tired and listless. She spent hours at her chamber window, idly watching the boats go through the steps of their endless dance on the clear waters of the Dart. Perhaps she feigned illness a little longer than was strictly necessary; anything to delay the time when Otho would resume his visits to her chamber. She had given him three likely boys. It was enough.

Months later, Katherine watched as the ship came up the river, heading for the Greenway dock. A broad-shouldered figure with a fashionable bushy beard came into view. That burly frame, those splendid clothes – it must be Peter Carew. But she could see from the slump of his shoulders, the absence of any arrogant swagger, that, if this *was* Peter, something was very wrong.

She hastened to greet him, led him to the parlour and bade him sit by the window. She watched his face as Bessie proffered a mug of ale. A small voice of fear within her was growing louder with every moment. Until that day, she had heard no reports of Peter and Johnny's progress overseas. Now Peter was here, sitting uncomfortably before her. Johnny must be with him. Perhaps he had gone first to Modbury and would come to see her later. That must be the way of it.

"I am come from the court, Mistress Katherine-Kate," he said, startling her with this use of her pet name. "I must go on to Modbury. I took passage this far on that barque tied up at your quay, to get here the sooner."

Peter, the braggart, for once seemed lost for words. His eyes flitted round the room, looking anywhere but at her face. He swilled the wine in his cup, looking into it as though it held a dark secret. At last he raised his eyes.

"I had to give full account to King Henry," he said heavily, but then, with a glimpse of his usual ebullience, he went on. "The King detained me quite a while. Everyone wanted to hear about the wonders of the Turk's court, the manners of Italy, the government of Venice, and all I've seen. Until now I couldn't come to you." His shoulders fell again. He was blustering as usual, but his discomfort was plain to see.

Katherine feared the worst, but could not bring herself to ask; could not yet frame the words. Where was Johnny?

Then Peter told her, with as much gentleness and care as he could, how he and Johnny had fared so well in all their travels, seen such splendours together, been to Constantinople and Hungary, and lots of other places she had never even heard of. How, after a time in Venice, thinking to make their way back to England, they had arrived in Vienna. How they had met with their friend Wingfield. How all three had taken some sudden illness; some bloody flux. How, weakened and frail, he, Peter, had taken horse back to Venice, away from the infectious air of Vienna. How he alone had recovered and made his way back to England.

She battled to close her mind to the true meaning of his words.

But understanding could no longer be denied. Peter was telling her that Johnny was dead, gone, never to return. Her merry, laughing brother; her close companion of those sun-filled childhood days at Modbury; her playmate, who had so charmed the King and everyone he met; who had so loved to ride out with her over the Devon hills; who had been so full of pranks that brought a smile even to the dourest countenance; who had always been sure that he would be a fine soldier and gain glory serving his King. Lost and gone, forever.

The room reeled around her. She felt cold, and then strangely hot and clammy, before everything went black and she fell to the floor.

It must have been Peter who carried her to her chamber and laid her on the bed. He must have called for her women. She was vaguely aware of them fussing around her, but Katherine hardly stirred. She lay still, fighting, fighting, fighting against it. It must be some cruel jest of Peter's.

OTHO

As he sauntered down the path, he had no inkling of it. He was surprised to find Peter Carew pacing up and down in the little parlour, and even more surprised that Peter seemed mightily relieved to see him.

"I came here in such fear that Johnny's favourite sister would take this news badly. So she has. But now I must ride on to Modbury and bring grief to his wife, to his mother and to his father. This is like to fell that tall and gentle man, as a storm brings down mighty oaks."

After sending him on his way, Otho climbed the stair. Katherine was all but insensible.

"The shock of this has been too much for her, Master," said Bessie, clutching a pillow tightly to her breast.

It looked as though the fat maid was right. Otho's wife seemed to have lost her wits completely. She wouldn't even look at him; turned her head away from him. He lay down beside her, tried to hold her, thinking that closeness would bring her comfort, but she pushed him roughly aside.

"Leave me alone; oh, leave me alone." She rejected him as she always did.

Days passed. She hardly spoke; crept about with her face long and set. He had seen her shed no tears. She would not see the children. Stayed in her chamber most of the time. Wouldn't look at him. Didn't even trouble to go down to her new orchard to order the picking of another fine crop. Thank goodness all the servants knew what to do. Where was the woman who had always seemed so strong, so capable, so proud? Where was that clever, noble woman he had married? All that seemed left to him was a hollow shell.

He realised with a jolt that he needed her. What should he do? He ordered his horse saddled and rode off in the direction of the alehouse.

KATHERINE

Katherine sat with Johnny's letters in her lap, her stitching untouched in the basket. She wrapped the letters in a silk cloth, tied the bundle with a yellow ribbon, and placed them reverently back into the coffer.

Bessie's head appeared around the door. "Mistress, come down this instant! There be one here you will surely wish to see," she said, with her hand outstretched.

Katherine's heart lurched painfully. It couldn't be Johnny. For one moment of pure madness she thought it must be Master Raleigh. Who else would she wish to see? But Bessie could not know that, and there was no reason for him to come to Greenway Court. She made to follow, but stopped short just beyond the door, cocking her head to one side to listen. Squeals of joy drifted up the stairs. Was that John laughing? Surely not? The boy was always grumpy these days.

There is a quality in children's happy laughter, their voices lifted in some endless game, that cuts through to the soul. She felt it knocking on the door of her grief and allowed it in. She took a breath, set her foot on the stair, and went down.

Out in the green court, John held a stick outstretched like a sword. Humphrey was struggling with an even longer one, trying to take the on-guard position. Between them stood a man, tall and lean. He stepped back, and at his command the two boys attempted to fence with each other. Humphrey, hampered by his skirts, fell down in a heap, roared and thumped his hands into the grass. John whooped with laughter again and set off. Humphrey struggled to his feet and careered after his brother. "Can't catch me," John called, and they raced around the green.

The man turned.

"Arthur?" Katherine cried. "Is it really you? I didn't know you, grown so manly. What have you been saying to John to bring him to such a merry state? I haven't heard that boy laugh so free for a long time. Just look at them now!"

The boys were rolling over and over in a heap of leaves, their giggles growing more and more shrill. It was infectious. Arthur started to titter, and then, for the first time in weeks, Katherine laughed softly. She laughed and laughed until her sides ached and she could scarcely breathe. Then the tears began to fall, and Arthur called for the children's nurse and guided her inside. He held her, patting her back as she wept.

Much later, he said, "Katherine-Kate, I am sent to bid you come to Modbury with all speed. Our parents have need of you."

They set out the next morning, Dapple skittish after weeks of idleness. Katherine couldn't deny that it felt good to be out, to see the sunlight glinting on the bright tapestry of the Devon woodlands, to feel the gentle breeze on her face. Another tear rolled down her cheek. Johnny would never see the glories of another autumn morn. A bird chattered his alarm: *Wock, wock, wock-a-wock, wock-a-weer*, and suddenly erupted from the bank just in front of them. Dapple shied, and Katherine worked hard to keep her seat.

"One alone brings ill luck " she said.

But Arthur dipped his head and chanted, "Ha-ho, Master Jack Pie. Master Maggot Pie – where's your wife today?"

Miraculously, a second bird swooped over them, a flash of vivid black and white, before it joined the first in wheeling over the broad meadow.

"There!" cried Arthur triumphantly. "Two! That will bring good fortune for sure. Cheer up, sister."

They rode on for a few more yards before he added, "I don't really believe a bird bodes good or ill do you, Katherine-Kate? But happy times and sad times must come to us all. It seems to me that our joys and our sorrows are all wrapped up together. 'Tis those we love the most that cause us the most sorrow. Johnny wouldn't wish you to grieve, you know."

Katherine gave him a long, considered stare and wondered how Arthur had suddenly grown so wise. She pressed Dapple forward, feeling lighter than she had since Peter Carew's awful visit.

Eliza greeted them at the door, holding her hands together in front of her and turning them this way and that as if she were wringing out the laundry. "I'm glad to see you, sister. I don't know how to bring our parents out of this sorrow, and there's more to come. Agnes is very ill."

Father was sitting with his head in his hands by the fireside. He seemed to have aged twenty years. Katherine could no longer tease him that he had so few grey hairs.

"Father, I see you have an ermine's coat upon your head," she said, trying a breezy smile for size. It felt wrong. Instead she took his hand and they sat together in silence, each taking strength from the other. "This is hard to bear," she breathed, squeezing his fingers. "But we will bear it together."

Mother and Catherine, Johnny's wife – or widow, as she must now be called – sat together in the solar, their hands idle. Mother's face was drawn, her eyes red and her famous complexion blotchy.

"Let us walk in the gardens," suggested Katherine. "'Tis a fine autumn day and the air will cheer us."

Outside, as they passed the stone seat, she remarked, "This is where Johnny would always challenge me to race him to the wall. He always won, of course, and I got so very cross!"

"It was hard to be cross with Johnny for long, though, wasn't it?" Johnny's widow Catherine answered with a smile.

"I *do* still feel cross with him for leaving us all so!" Katherine blurted out, her feelings rising to the surface again. She stamped her foot. "Why must he go off with Peter? All for adventure and glory! All for nothing, and now he's gone. Peter should bear the blame."

"Katherine-Kate, if I may call you so, for that is how he always spoke of you," said Catherine. "I miss him more than I can say, but I know that he made his choice freely. It was Johnny's own adventure, not Peter's. Johnny would have gone off somewhere, sometime. It was the destiny of a nature such as his. Even the love I know he bore me could never chain him. He would not have been Johnny if it could. You might as well try to lock a sunbeam in a cage. I count myself lucky to have known his love and borne his son. I'll always miss him. But he would not wish that we waste our own time on earth in grief."

"That's well said," Katherine answered, raising her head as she felt her breathing slow. "You're right, I know. I must shake myself out of this melancholy."

They walked on to the foot of the crumbling wall.

"Oh, Catherine, will you wed again? I'm sure lots of men will be suing for the hand of such a pretty widow."

"No doubt I shall, in time," Catherine answered as her son Henry came flying down the path, his nurse hot on his heels lest he tumble.

"This boy will be the best cure for Mother," said Katherine. "He looks so like Johnny." And she wiped another tear from her eye.

It was as if her old nurse had been holding on, waiting for Katherine to get there. She held Agnes's hand, and talked of well-remembered events and happy times long past. Will Slade, who had married Jenny, brought in his son, but two weeks old. Agnes had no strength to cradle him, though her eyes lit to see the little cherub.

"Will is happy. He has a son. 'Tis all I could ask in this world," she said, smiling through her pain. "Now I must go to meet his father in the next. Hush now. Don't 'ee grieve for me. You were always my dearest girl. Goodnight, my flower."

Agnes had been a widow for years. She had served the family faithfully and well. In this last illness she had borne her pain with fortitude. That night, when all the house was sleeping, gently and quietly, Agnes slipped away.

Bright, staunch, strong Arthur, eighteen years old and vowing to look after his nephew as his own, became Katherine's rock in the bleak months that followed. It was he who told her how Father's spirits had lifted a little when the antiquary, John Leland, visited Modbury.

"He became quite animated, Katherine-Kate," he chuckled. "They talked long into the night about our ancestors; all that business about the King of the Romans, of course! They talked about crops and land and tin mining and sheep and all manner of things. It did Father so much good. He's gone with Leland now to Mohun's Ottery, and then he's going on to Curry Mallet. It's just the stimulus he needed. Mother's improving too; that scamp Henry would make anyone laugh. Our parents have each other too, dear Katherine-Kate."

Love, duty, respect. She hadn't been lucky enough to know all those in her marriage, quite as her parents had in theirs, or as the old couple, Agnes and her husband, had. Katherine's thoughts often turned to the man she had glimpsed on the *Trinity*. She wondered what her life might have been, had she been free to wed at her own choosing.

Another woman would soon be facing the prospect of marrying not as her heart inclined, but as her King demanded. Joanie wrote in the spring to say that her friend Kateryn Parr, had caught the eye of the ageing King, though she had fallen in love with the dashing Thomas Seymour. *How sad! What choice does any woman have?* thought Katherine Gilbert of Greenway Court as she tucked Joanie's letter into her coffer. She must look to her children and to her household. And so she did, as the years passed.

TWENTY
1544
KATHERINE

She often rose early. With Otho away there was much to do. September had slipped into October and the temperature had dropped sharply. It was time to strip the apples from the trees.

As Bessie helped her dress and the sky grew lighter in that chilly dawn, Katherine's thoughts were all of her children. John, almost nine years old, attended well to his lessons, and had a good head for figures, and a sharp wit. In looks he didn't favour Otho's uncle, his long-departed friend, though she often saw in him echoes of the old man's ways. Soon John must leave her and go to some other household, or to study law, or some such. Humphrey was another clever boy, with an imagination that knew no bounds and a confident, questioning mind. Too confident, perhaps; too full of his own ability, with that worrying tendency to cruelty. Only last week she'd had to reprimand him for capturing spiders in the dark recesses of the kitchen and pulling off their legs. The thought of Adrian brought a smile to her face. Such a droll little figure toddling along behind her when she picked the fragrant herbs needed for the kitchen and the stillroom. Her boys were all doing well in their way, and she could be proud of them.

But the same could not be said of Katie. Katherine frowned as

Bessie offered her a headdress. Now turned eleven, Katie was as wilful and difficult as ever, often missing for hours, having gone to some secret place of her own. Her temper had been even worse since Otho had gone to join the King's army in France. The pity of it was that she would be such a pretty girl if she didn't scowl so much.

Katherine glanced from the window and saw that a heavy morning mist was clothing the river in a thick veil of white. She screwed up her eyes and peered out. A dark shape emerged from the ghostly tendrils for an instant, only to be quickly swallowed up in the swirling mist. There it was again; a masthead drawing near the deepwater anchorage down by the Greenway Quay. "Please, dear God, don't let it be the French come to plunder and pillage Devon while King Henry's army is across the sea," she muttered.

With a brisk shake of her head, she dismissed the thought. She would have heard the guns from the batteries in Dartmouth if any foreign vessel had tried to slip into the Dart under cover of darkness. The chain would have been stretched across from Dartmouth Castle to keep them out. No, it was not the French. Nor was it Edward; he'd taken the *Trinity* up to London and beyond, thinking to pick up some business ferrying troops and supplies to Calais for the King's army. The *Charity* and the *George* were both out on charter; the *Hope* laid up for a refit. Intrigued, she took a thick woollen cloak from its hook in the garderobe and ran down the steps, through the courtyard and out along the path. Hoary spiders' webs glinted and sparkled on the clipped hedges as a weak shaft of sunlight broke through the fog. The boatmen's calls echoed eerily in the cold, still air.

She slowed her pace on the wet and slippery path, littered with new-fallen leaves. She could barely make out the outline of the carrack, much less see its flag or the name that must be emblazoned on its prow, as it steadily approached the Dart's bank. Otho had enlarged the gun emplacement on the quay, and the black shape of one of his prized possessions stood stark against the grey stones. The guards were standing straight and tall, ready to challenge those on board the boat.

The mist parted and, from the top of the steps, she saw a tall figure standing at the wheel, his back toward her as he looked to his crew to secure their position at the wharf. Katherine paused to catch her breath and started to descend the steps so that she could hail him and find out his business. On the third step down she stopped abruptly, almost losing her footing. Something about the set of those broad shoulders had set her heart a-racing. And then, as he turned, recognition came so swiftly. A surge of joy pulsed through her body from the top of her head to her feet, to her very fingertips, as she felt his presence. Her eyes sought his. There, standing on the deck before her, was the man she had dreamed of in the darkest hours of many a lonely night.

WALTER

He had the advantage of her. He had known as soon as Champernowne sought him out to convey the Gilbert boy home that, if he agreed to take on the commission, he might see her again.

He liked Arthur Champernowne, who was carving out a fine reputation as a soldier during the Siege of Boulogne. As they waited on the tide in Calais, they had talked of war and trade, of ships and privateering, and of their shared interest in the new ways of religion. By mid September, after the tunnels were dug and English troops could enter the town without fear of French firepower, Boulogne had fallen into King Henry's hands. When the ageing King pocketed his victory and returned to England, he'd left that wily old fellow the Duke of Norfolk to defend his gains on French soil. Norfolk, restored after the fall of his niece Kitty Howard, and his soldiers were on their guard. Emperor Charles was rumoured to have made a separate pact with France, and might strike at any time. Boulogne must be well defended, and Arthur could not be spared for long. Just long enough to bring Otho Gilbert to the port and ask Walter if he'd take him home.

When the call to muster came, Walter had packed his men, together with other Devon boys, into *the Mary Rawle* and sailed for Dover. There they joined the throng waiting to be carried across that scant twenty miles that separated the White Cliffs from Calais. Supplies of arms and shot, food and armour were piled in warehouses all along the docks, awaiting transport to fuel King Henry's war. Sir George Carew was organising the shipping of both men and victuals, seeking out ships to do service, and Walter saw an opportunity. He offered himself and his ship to ferry men, food and arms over to Calais. The high-born would pay a fee to be transported in relative comfort, and Walter was amassing quite a hoard of coin. Sadly, there were also injured or sick men who sought a berth on the return leg. Arthur had paid him well, not only to take Otho Gilbert across to Dover, but to sail all the way to Greenway.

It was not only Champernowne's coin that had induced Walter to forsake his more lucrative cross-Channel trade. It was the thought that he might again meet that beauty revealed but once so long ago that induced him to take on that particular passenger. There had been times on the journey when he'd regretted it. Gilbert's behaviour made Walter think of him as a boy, though he supposed more than thirty years must have passed since the fellow left his mother's womb. He would not be sorry to be rid of Otho's bad-tempered, petulant, haranguing ways. He had wondered what on earth the fool had been doing in France anyway. He could have got an exemption for his men because they were needed to defend the coast around Torbay. The boy need not be there at all. Champernowne had answered that it was bravado and a wish to show how he could use an arquebus that had set Gilbert off on his unnecessary escapade.

Walter had slept little that last night, tossing in his berth, convincing himself that she had long since forgotten him. In the six years since he'd last seen her his life had prospered well. Rents were still coming in from Fardel and Withycombe. His farm and the grazing on Woodbury Common brought a fair, if not generous, living. But ships and trade had become his mainstay, and he wasn't averse to a spot of privateering when French vessels were fair game. The war work – more legitimate, perhaps – had added much to his store, and he had just commissioned another vessel. Walter had ambitions to rival his first wife's family, the Drakes of Exmouth, with his own fleet of ships.

But he had not taken another wife. Most men would have been wed again long before now. But he had shied away from brides who would have brought him much in terms of both wealth and status. The vision of that girl on the *Trinity* still plagued his nights with impossible dreams. He convinced himself it was just a foolish fancy. He schooled himself to act without any show when they met; to greet her with a casual doffing of his cap, just as he would the wife of any passenger.

As he saw the *Mary* secured at her mooring at the Greenway Quay, he turned, and there she stood. His hand rose, ready to sweep her a mocking bow as he had decided. But the look on her shining face stayed his arm midway, and it fell back limply to his side. That lovely face was lit by such delight, such radiance and such wonder that it shone out like a beacon through the morning air. His arms stretched out towards her in a gesture of welcome and warmth he could by no means suppress. His eyes devoured her. The tilt of her chin; the roses in her cheeks; her fine, straight nose; her dark, unfathomable eyes; her curving lips, half parted in amazement, showing just a hint of perfect white teeth. The years had left no mark upon those regular features. Her cloak fell back as she made to take a faltering step, and he could see that she was as slender as he remembered. Only her hair was different: tamed and confined beneath a hood, not flowing in all its glory and profusion down her back. If only he could reach out and release those dark waves that had drifted so often through his dreams! Oh, to bury his face in those lustrous tresses, to hold her close, to drink in the very scent of her!

KATHERINE

How long did they stand there, separated by the quay and the *Mary's* deck, eyes locked, the secrets of their hearts writ so plainly on their faces for all to see? The passing of the minutes had no meaning. She watched him remove his hat, hold it humbly before him and stretch out his arms toward her. Oh, how she longed to fly to those welcoming arms! There were a few more strands of grey in his shaggy curls, but his hair still appeared to her to have its own life as it fell almost to his shoulders. She gazed again on his sun-darkened face and saw that, even in that moment of revelation, a hint of humour lurked in the depths of his twinkling eyes. Katherine acknowledged openly at last what she had sought to deny for so long. This was the man she loved with heart and soul and every fibre of her being.

She had not sought to love him. Rather, to forget him; to bury his memory deep and do her duty. After all, it had been a chance encounter of but a moment. But none can tell where such lightning will strike. Seeing him now, she had no will to resist. No words were spoken. None were needed. Time stood still. She was suspended there, halfway down the cold stone steps, he still on board the *Mary*. She knew in that moment that she would hold no other in her heart, and she saw that it was the same for him. A silent pledge of recognition, of understanding and deepest joy, passed between them.

OTHO

They hadn't noticed him hidden in the shadows of the cabin's gangway, enveloped in a long, hooded cloak. But he had seen it all. Seen her face transformed with radiance as she stared at Raleigh. She had never looked on him, her own husband, like that!

His fists clenched and he felt the blood pulsing in his scar; his stomach burning. A growl rose in his throat, guttural and harsh, torn from the depths of his soul. He could wait no longer. He must put an end to this dumb show between them. Stepping forward, he slammed the cabin door shut, clutched the cloak tightly across his chest, and pulled the hood around his face. Even in his anger he sought to conceal the scar from her. He dreaded the revulsion he would see in her eyes when she beheld it. He was not as she had last seen him, the day she waved him away. *All the dutiful wife and mother to my sons then*, he thought, wincing at the pain in his jaw as he clenched his teeth. *She would pay for this!*

KATHERINE

The noise broke the spell. She didn't recognise Otho shrouded in black.

Walter spoke, his voice trembling with emotion. "Mistress Gilbert, I have brought you a precious cargo all the way from France."

And then she knew. As Otho stomped forward, his cloak caught in the doorway and was pulled back from his face. Katherine started, and nearly fell from the step. She stared, and her hand flew to her throat. The right side of his face was criss-crossed by shining, livid, red and purple scars, all surrounded by discoloured, yellowish skin. The cheekbone was crushed, its shape distorted. The eyelid drooped low across his right eye, which was all but closed, and the skin on the unmarked side of his face stretched tight over the bones, startling and skull-like. A fierce, angry fire glinted menacingly from his good eye, and his mouth was a stern, forbidding line. She stumbled down the last step onto the quay. She could not hide it. Revulsion, loathing and horror must now replace the rapt and joyful countenance she had so recently turned upon Walter Raleigh.

Otho swept down the gangplank. Tearing her eyes from his ravaged face, she noticed his bandaged right hand. She saw how thin and gaunt he was; how, when his cloak parted, his doublet hung loose upon his scrawny frame. Katherine shuddered, which seemed to increase Otho's fury. He stormed across the quay, brushing aside offers of assistance from Walter's crew and his own serving men, and, without a word, stalked up the path towards the house.

Frozen there, she had such a wild and wicked thought. It would take but a moment to cross the stones, walk up that gangplank and be folded in Walter's waiting arms. They could sail away to some place where none should find them. She even made to take a step or two towards the plank. But something held her back. Her shoulders fell. She raised her hands, let them fall, then lifted her chin. She was a Champernowne lady; a woman of noble birth. She could never forget that. All those years as a dutiful daughter, wife and mother could not be set aside, however strong the pull to join her love. She let out her breath in a long, ragged sigh. Whatever had happened to Otho, he was still her husband. She was wedded to him and she owed him all her life and duty. The love – and now she must acknowledge it as such: the breathtaking love she bore for this other man could never find expression while her husband lived. She must follow Otho and make him a good wife.

"Master Raleigh," she said, in a voice so hushed it barely reached him, "I give you thanks for returning my lord to me. Will you come to the house and take refreshment?" It was the offer of any grateful wife but, oh, how much it cost her to say those words!

He answered, his voice low, gruff and faltering, his eyes never leaving hers. "Nay, my dearest heart, I may not tarry. The tide turns within the hour. I must look to my ship and make her ready. I must make all haste to return to the service of my King." He took a breath, and seemed to find his voice. "Your brother Arthur did charge me with bringing Master Gilbert to you. He sends to you, his sister, whom he did name as his dearest Katherine-Kate, his warmest greetings. Katherine-Kate!" He spoke her name again, and she felt it as a soft, lingering caress. He paused, licking his lips, as though to taste her name on his tongue. "'Tis the name Arthur gave when he spoke of you. He fares well in the wars and is a fine young man." Then, dropping his voice even lower, lest the men standing by should hear him, "Katherine-Kate, if this must be farewell, I count myself the most fortunate of men to have seen your dear face again. I shall not forget, and we shall meet again, sweeting, I cannot doubt it."

Another moment, another long parting look passed between them.

"I am so sorry, so very sorry," she whispered. "I must look to my husband." With tears streaming down her cheeks, Katherine stumbled across the quay and up the steps to follow Otho. She turned, looked back and saw Walter standing at the gunwale. She felt a weight in her chest as though her heart was truly breaking. He put up a hand to shade his eyes, straining for one last glimpse of her. They had no choice. The tide would soon be turning and he must go. She saw him raise his arm, and her own hand fluttered hesitantly before she turned back to the path.

She stopped under the shelter of an oak that had escaped the woodsman's axe on the sloping hillside beside the Dart. She wiped the tears from her eyes and tried to still her shaking limbs. She had not looked for this when she had risen that morning with her mind full of her children. For six long years she had fought so hard to conquer those forbidden feelings. For six long years she had done her duty at Otho's bed and board, given him children and graced his household. But all had been swept aside when she saw him again: the man she loved. She could not deny it. She must own it so in her deepest heart. If only she had waited in the house, she would never have seen him. Otho would likely not have had the grace to invite his rescuer inside. But the damage, the exquisite damage, was done. She could never undo that moment.

Leaning back against the trunk of that venerable oak, she pressed the palms of her hands flat upon it; pressed harder and harder, as if she could draw strength from the roots of that mighty tree, as if that strength would set her to rights again. Still trembling, she gathered her scattered wits and walked slowly toward the house.

OTHO

He waited by the door, pacing up and down, his fury growing with every passing moment. Katie's favourite brindle hound slunk, tail wagging, whimpering and subservient, towards him. With a well-aimed boot he sent the animal yelping for cover.

How dare that man look so upon his wife? But worse, how could she – she who had been at his side for so long – show such a radiant face to that blackguard? And then to look with such disgust upon her own husband!

He forgot that Raleigh had been his means of escape from that hellhole, Calais. He forgot that it was Katherine's brother Arthur who had paid his passage after carrying him from that accursed field beyond the town. He forgot that he would likely be dead if Arthur had not seen his wounds well tended. No, all that was as nothing. In that moment, all his shame and disappointment; all the pain, anguish and indignity he had suffered as a bloody flux took hold of his bowels while the army waited in those filthy fields; all the horror he felt every time he saw his ravaged face reflected in the glass, mirrored there on the quay in hers; all was focused in red-hot anger against her.

The blame should fall on her! He had caught her standing there, rapt and radiant, looking into the eyes of another man. That was enough to anger any husband. But it was the face she had turned on him, so full of loathing and disgust, that would haunt him all his days. He curled the fingers of his undamaged hand into a tight fist, clenched them and let them go, then clenched again. He felt the spittle building up at the corners of his mouth, but did not wipe it away. The blood was pulsing in his ears as he paced back and forth before the door. Where was she? Lingering on the quayside with that man, in front of his people? She'd pay for this! He'd show her who was boss!

KATHERINE

She pulled up short and put trembling fingers to her open mouth. Otho was a terrifying sight. The mangled, shiny skin of the jagged scar showed lurid red and purple against his flushed face. She could see the muscles working in his cheek, the knotted veins on his undamaged left hand standing out like ropes. As she took a jerky pace forward, he turned and, without a word, struck out with his good hand, landing a blow on her cheek and mouth that sent her reeling. She fell heavily, tearing her gown and gashing her knee on the step. Shocked to the core, she remained motionless a moment, appalled that he had lashed out at her so. Never in all their years together had he hit her. Trembling and shaking, she hauled herself to her feet. The palms of her hands stung where they had met the gravelly surface of the path to halt her fall. There was blood on her gown.

Otho grabbed her arm; twisted it behind her so hard she yelped in pain. He forced her to walk ahead of him through the doorway and, without losing his grip for a second, shoved her toward the stairs. Pain shot through her shoulder as the muscles tore when he twisted her arm even more.

"Husband, you are hurting me. Pray have a care," she screamed.

"'Tis none but what you deserve," he growled through gritted teeth, and bundled her up the stairs.

Through half-closed eyes she saw someone crouching in the corner of the hall. Katie! Katherine saw a sly, gloating smile spread across the girl's pretty face.

Bessie had been tidying the bed, and was bending to pick up Katherine's discarded shift. With a kick to her generous buttocks, Otho sent her flying across the floor. "Out!" he growled, and Bessie, who saw instantly that there was nothing she could do to protect her mistress, scrambled frantically to quit the room.

Otho kicked the door shut. The loud bang echoed in Katherine's ears as if from a far, far distance. She could do nothing to fight him. She did not try. Her mind emptied; became a space where only fear and loathing registered. He threw her onto the bed, where she lay limp as a rag doll, passive and still, as he started to tear at the front of her gown with his left hand. She felt his weight pressing down on her, smelt his wine-stale breath as he held her down. He rammed his injured arm tight across her neck. She could scarcely draw breath as his forearm crushed her throat. The fabric of the placard at the front of her gown yielded at last and, pins flying everywhere, was ripped clean away to reveal the torn kirtle beneath. Not satisfied with that, he clawed at her shift until her breasts were exposed, digging his nails deep into her flesh. And then he was fumbling with the points of his hose, cursing that he had only one hand to the task.

"Lift your skirt, whore, and get about your business," he snarled. She made no move as he ripped the fabric apart, yanked it aside, and thrust into her, harsh, violent, again and again.

Katherine, frozen, immobile, near unconscious, could not even form the words to pray for her ordeal to end. The smell of him lingered on her after he had gone.

She never knew how long it was before Bessie dared to come to her, bringing water and clean linen cloths to tend her sore and battered body. She had no memory of those tender ministrations that cleaned her gashed knee and the cuts where Otho's nails had dug so deep into her flesh. She never knew how gently Bessie applied healing balm to the bruises on her cheeks, her arms, her breasts and thighs, and dressed her anew in a clean shift. Nor how Bessie stoked the fire high to warm the room, and brought her a calming drink of camomile and herbs, before tucking her under the heavy embroidered covers. A strange and fitful sleep overtook Katherine, in which visions of Walter at the wheel of a great ship were interspersed with terrifying images of raging storms. Death himself was coming for her, wearing the ruined face of her husband.

It was dawn again before she woke and called for Bessie. Her memories came back all too soon. That smell; the smell of him. Would she ever be rid of it? Though she wore a clean shift she felt dirty, spoiled like rotten fruit. No washing would cleanse her. She shifted, and called out as a sharp pain cut through her shoulder like a knife. Emotions flitted feverishly through her mind. Violation, shame, anger, and hatred for the man who until now had never raised a hand to her. From somewhere deep within she summoned the remnants of her pride. She must maintain her position in the household, and she must think of her children. No one must know of the evil thing that had come to pass between them.

"Never speak of this," she whispered as the shaken maid crept in. "Bring me the glass."

Bessie held the little round looking glass and Katherine looked long at the bruise at her temple, already tinged with purple. She considered the dark shadow under her right eye, and the cut by her swollen lip. She examined the bruises on her arms and wrist where he had gripped her. Trying to move her right arm, the one he had twisted behind her, she winced sharply. She took a deep breath and looked steadily at Bessie.

"Put it out that I am taken of a sudden fever and the children must not come near for fear of infection," she said quietly. "I must keep to my chamber until I am fit to be seen again."

It was long afterwards before Bessie told her how that day had ended. Otho had erupted from her chamber still in a rage, kicking the dogs and hurling anything that came to his hand. Mugs and platters, benches and tables crashed across the hall. Bessie made sure the children were locked safely in the nursery with the maidservants, and sent a groom to Compton to fetch Philip Penkervell. By the time his brother arrived, Otho had been into both the cellar and the buttery and, having drunk his fill of wine and French brandy, was slumped in a heap on the settle that stood before the kitchen fire. Katherine never discovered what Penkervell did with him then.

Arthur eventually told her what had happened in France. She remembered Otho's angry reaction when he'd received the notice to muster his men. It had come addressed not to him, but to John Gilbert. Otho took this as proof that no one in the land acknowledged his existence. He had never been called to serve his King as a Justice, a tax collector, or in any office in the county. It seemed he had made so little mark that the authorities hadn't even taken into account that he was now head of the Gilbert family. Stung, he was determined to put on a show. Katherine knew that he had submitted his certificate listing the fighting men he would provide; pointing out that it was he, not his uncle, who would field this fine force. Oh, Otho was very proud that his men were so well equipped; much better armed than those his noble neighbours sent to fight! Five of his archers even had horses and harness, as did three of his bill-men. Later he sent another message, adding a gunner to the list. Few could boast a trained marksman amongst their mustered men, and Otho had one of the latest firearms too. How proud he was!

That pride was his undoing. He had taken advice and, when he sent off his certificate, declared that his mansion house lay near Torbay. The answer came back that his men would be better deployed guarding the coastline. That was more than disappointing when he had kitted them out so well. So Otho decided he would go himself. He persuaded Arthur, against his better judgement, to take him to France. Katherine had waved him off and could not say she was sorry he had gone.

They shipped to France with all the others and lodged in makeshift camps in the fields near Boulogne. Conditions were dreadful. Unrelenting strong winds and driving rain battered the countryside already laid waste by King Henry's soldiers; the local people murdered or chased from the lands; crops ruined; farmhouses, stores and barns plundered for every scrap. By the time Otho arrived, food was reduced to the thinest gruel. The fields became a quagmire. Excrement washed around their feet from the flooded jakes. It was no surprise that so many succumbed to dreadful sickness. Otho went for days without proper food and the weight fell off his already spare body so fast that he was barely recognisable. A bloody flux affected his bowels for three days, and his men were doubtful that he would survive.

But survive he did, and, much thinner, he emerged to join the forces massing in the fields before the town. They did not engage the enemy, and the men quickly became bored and fractious. Rival groups sought every opportunity to pick a quarrel. One morning Otho came across a lordling from the North of the country. In jest, the youth called out, "Hey there, West Country churl!" That hit a raw spot. Otho Gilbert of Compton was no mere serving man. He vowed to show how finely armed was this churl of the West. He set up a target, took the arquebus from the hands of the protesting gunner and prepared to take aim. But as the weapon fired, something went wrong. Instead of sending the projectile hurtling down the barrel toward the target, when the fire struck the gunpowder charge, an explosion ripped through the muzzle and stock.

Arthur had found him lying senseless on the ground with bits of twisted metal and bone protruding from his face. He had carried Otho to a tent and had seen that his wounds were cleaned and dressed. Arthur had Otho watched until he recovered consciousness, and then made sure he was fed and cared for. Seeing the extent of his injuries, as soon as Otho seemed fit enough to travel, Arthur had taken him back to Calais. There they met Raleigh and secured Otho's passage home.

When the musket had exploded, Otho's right hand had shattered, and he'd lost two fingers, along with a lot of blood. A large piece of hot metal had just missed his right eye. It was a miracle that his wounds had escaped infection.

TWENTY-ONE
1544–1545
KATHERINE

It was nearly two months before she saw Otho again. By then she knew that another new life had been started when he had forced himself upon her with such hatred and violence. She was pregnant again. She could never forget that day. She could never forgive him.

But Katherine's duty was, as ever, crystal clear. At the start of the Advent fast, an invitation came from Modbury for the Gilbert family to spend Christmastide there. To refuse might have exposed their estrangement, so she resolved that she and Otho must find a way to keep up appearances for the season.

Since the day of his homecoming Otho had retreated to Compton, leaving Katherine nursing her own wounds at Greenway Court. His temper grew worse. Ever one to dispute with others over landholding rights, if matters did not go his way he now resorted to violent assault. It was only through Penkervell's clever handling that he avoided gaol on several occasions. He took care to avoid Katherine, so she had to surprise him in the hall one morning in December when he came to Greenway Court on some errand or another. As soon as he saw her he turned away, heading for the door. But Katherine stood in his path and spoke.

"This will not do, husband. We must mend our differences, or at least put on some show," she said, fixing her eyes on his. "For the sake of this child I must bear, and for the others in the nursery and schoolroom, we must do better. You must see that?"

His face blanched and he would have pushed her aside, but she stood her ground.

So it was that on Christmas Eve they travelled together back along the road she had first followed as a young bride full of hope. The landscape they rode through was as bleak and wintry as Katherine's heart. At Modbury they sat together at the Christmas board and watched the children enjoy the fun and games on Twelfth Night. It pained Katherine to find her father grown so thin, looking so very old and tired. After Arthur left for the war he had sunk back into melancholy.

"Father, just look at your grandson," she said, thinking it might cheer him. "See there, Henry's having the time of his life with his Gilbert cousins."

But in reply Father could only manage a thin smile. She looked at Mother, who shook her head.

Eliza's boy, Philip, was in the thick of the band of roistering youngsters. Henry, Philip and Humphrey, close in age, were taking full advantage of this rare treat: sweet relief from their studies. John, though he was older than the others, joined in with gusto, but Katie kept herself aloof from the boys and was ever hanging round Otho.

Katherine woke each morning to a vicious churning in her stomach, and rushed to the garderobe to spew up the remnants of last night's dinner. The sickness was more persistent this time, as if the babe she carried was protesting at the means of his coming to be. She felt Eliza watching her.

"Dear Katherine-Kate, is it only the baby that makes you seem so wan and full of care? 'Tis not like you, my sensible sister, to be so sad," Eliza asked with real concern in her voice.

At that, the dam broke and tears streamed down Katherine's cheeks. She stammered and sobbed until the whole sorry story was out: that chance meeting with Walter Raleigh so long ago, the spark that had struck them both, how hard she had tried to feel nothing for him, how she had worked so valiantly to be a good wife, and that moment when the world had stood still as she saw him again.

Her voice shook as she told her sister about Otho's fury and his vile treatment of her. Eliza held her tight until the shuddering sobs began to subside.

"What a strange thing that we, who seemed so different when we were young, should suffer so similar a fate," said Eliza in a calm, soft voice. "Do you remember? I was so frivolous and cared only about my next new gown, while you worked diligently to learn all a housewife should know. Though, if I recall it aright, you forever had your head in a book, and sometimes you went off riding with Johnny on that little grey mare you loved so much. But who would think that both of us would be smitten so?"

Katherine looked up sharply.

"Oh, yes, I too know what it is to be hit by love's lightning bolt," Eliza continued, her eyes fixed on some point far away, like a sailor searching the horizon. "Oh, Katherine-Kate! I met a fine man in London, long ago. Remember that time when you were so ill after riding to Shillingford with Grandmother Carew?"

Katherine remembered it well. Eliza had certainly changed after that trip to London. She was beginning to understand.

"It was my feelings for that young man that made me reluctant to wed William, wicked girl that I was."

"Why, Eliza, dearest sister," exclaimed Katherine, her own grief set aside for a moment, "I *do* remember. You seemed to try and try to put off your wedding day. I couldn't understand it at all. You seemed so changed!"

"Foolish creature that I was, I was hoping against hope that he would somehow escape that closed world of his and come riding down to Devon to claim me. I even threatened to enter a nunnery rather than be wed to William. It was Kat and Uncle George who persuaded me that nothing could come of my infatuation with John Pollard."

Katherine's mouth fell open. "John Pollard?"

"Yes, for I had the folly to fall in love with a priest, a man of God. As you know, I did my duty in the end, and I'm so pleased that I was able to give dear William the son he so desired. He's always been a kind and attentive husband. He deserved better than me. But, Katherine, you say that your true-love, this Walter, remembers you still? I'm sure that by now John has completely forgotten me." Eliza's bright eyes filled with tears as they clung together.

Then Katherine remembered the handsome priest and his earnest inquiries after Mistress Cole, and clapped her hand over her mouth. "Oh, Eliza, I fear I have done you ill," she cried. "For I met that same priest in London, and he inquired most kindly of you. Oh, there was such care, such longing in his smouldering eyes. It seemed to me most odd. But I thought it best to conceal it from you when Philip was born. I am so sorry. He *did* remember you. But surely it must be hopeless? For how can a priest be wed?"

Now it was Eliza's turn to weep. "Well, Uncle George says that stranger things may come to pass. He says there is nought in God's law to prevent a priest living as do other men. It is only the laws of the Church that proclaim that men of the cloth must remain celibate. He says some priests in Europe already marry. It's even whispered that the Archbishop himself has a wife hidden away somewhere. But, all of that means nothing. We are each held fast to a husband not of our choosing, and must continue to serve them well. I am fortunate that William has always treated me with respect and kindness. We must hope that it is but Otho's wounds and jealousy that drove him to treat you so. Perhaps when the baby comes he will be himself again."

As soon as the holiday was over, Otho removed himself to Compton, taking Katie with him. The coldness between his parents had not escaped John. Otho had always been a distant figure for him, so he stayed staunchly loyal at Katherine's side, seeking to help her in any small way he could. The other boys hardly noticed, squabbling and playing happily, as boys will.

The ditches and dykes were certainly full that February. Rough winds and cold, stinging rain continued all through March and April. Unable to tend her gardens, Greenway Court's fine rooms felt like a prison, and Katherine had all but given up hope that spring would ever come. So when the sun at last appeared, one morning at the beginning of May, she was chafing to get out. She bowled into the green court and took a deep breath, inviting in the warm, gentle, river-scented air. Sunlight skipped and danced bravely over the water to be lost in shadow near the verdant banks that kept the Dart in check until it flowed into the boundless sea. Once she had felt her heart fly free as the sea bore her towards that first meeting with her love.

She had a fancy to walk down to the quay, to stand on the very spot where last she saw him. In the cool shade under the trees she stooped to examine a clump of violets, bravely nodding their heads in the light breeze. She picked a delicate purple flower and held it to her nose, drinking in the elusive sweet perfume that would forever remind her of Grandmother Carew. They were very late blooming; testament to the vile winter and the tardy spring. In most years she could have picked her fill by the end of March and put them to use in salves that soothed away headaches. She bent again to pick another. As she straightened up a sudden searing pain ripped across her belly, so strong that she all but cried out. But it passed, and she went on with her walk. Down on the quay it came again; insistent, dragging fiercely down her back. She rested for a few moments before another wave of torment hit her. Then she recognised the pain for what it was, though the baby was not due for two months. She shouted to the guards to help her back to the house. They must send for Mother Shippey without delay.

There was no time to enter her cosy chamber this time. Mother Shippey arrived just in time to guide the tiny head into the world. She made a swift decision, turned to Bessie and said, "This babe is like to die. I must baptise him now, so that he may enter God's kingdom whole and pure." As a midwife she had special licence granted by the Church to allow her to perform the sad task. Never had a child survived more than an hour or two once Mother Shippey had performed the rite. "What name shall I give him, Mistress?" she asked.

But Katherine had drifted away and did not answer. So, unthinking, Mother Shippey named him Otho.

"What shall we do?" Bessie wailed, some hours later. "The baby has come too soon and we have no wet nurse ready."

Katherine stirred and held the tiny bundle close. "There is no need, Bessie. I shall feed this child myself, for that is his only hope of life." She remembered Erasmus's teaching. Feeding her own child was best, and her husband was not in evidence to forbid it. So, with tender patience, Katherine coaxed the child to suck. When the milk came in he struggled to get his little lips fixed at all, so she soaked a clean linen cloth in her milk and squeezed it into his tiny mouth, just as she had seen Dick the shepherd do with orphaned lambs. In time her swelling breasts settled and the baby started to take some nourishment. Katherine focused all her efforts on keeping baby Otho alive.

To everyone's amazement, the child survived, though his life seemed to hang by the merest thread. A week after the baby slipped into the world Eliza arrived, straight from St Budeaux where she had been supporting Frances, whose latest child was also sickly.

"We sisters must stick together and help each other," said Eliza. "I will stay as long as you need me."

They whiled away the hours at their needlework or talking of the changes in religion, of Queen Kateryn, and of all the upheaval that beset the country. As women do, they also talked of more mundane matters like the best recipes for marmalades and sweetmeats, of fashion, and of the achievements of their sons. But most of all they shared their secret feelings and hopes as they watched and waited to see if Katherine's youngest child would live. Wrapped in the cocoon of the confinement chamber, they paid little heed to the disturbing news that had all of Devon in fear: stories of a fleet of French ships gathering on the River Seine.

OTHO

He found it hard to keep still. War was coming! The call to muster could come at any time. He must have his men drilled and ready for action. He'd been with the other local worthies to check the sea defences, to see that the chain at Dartmouth was well placed and to make sure that a supply of shot was ready at the gun batteries. Everyone thought they would attack Portsmouth, but Devon might equally be targeted.

He'd seen the Flemish and Spanish troops pouring in through the Devon ports: more than eight hundred of them, recruited to swell the King's forces to help repel the French. Perhaps he'd follow them to Portsmouth when the time came; see how King Henry deployed them all in battle. Play his part.

He shifted on the bench, wishing he had a cushion or a bit more padding on his skinny frame. He flexed the remaining fingers on his damaged hand. It was still painful but he had learned to manage his sword. He could even raise the arquebus. He was determined to fight this time, determined to prove himself. All the world must see how valiant he was, how fitted to be the rightful heir of the House of Gilbert. He'd show them all. Uncle John should have seen that he was worthy. The cantankerous old fool should have placed his trust in him. Pshaw! Edward still sailed the Trinity!

The boys had joined Katie at Compton, John, it had to be said, with some reluctance. Otho was not well pleased that his mother had also arrived from Cornwall. No doubt she thought Compton the safest place to withstand any attack. He snorted and gave a bitter chuckle. Now the sparks would fly! Katie had been acting for all the world as though she were mistress of the house. She wouldn't like to have Isabel poking her nose in.

His legs felt a bit shaky when he thought about the war. Best be prepared for anything. The lawyer had drawn up his will; listed all the lands he could bestow. It lay on the board before him, ready for his signature. It was the sixteenth day of May. Two weeks since the messenger had come to tell him that he had another son, though none thought he would survive. He hadn't been to Greenway Court. It reminded him too much of that day. He couldn't bear to see her. He spat into the fireplace, as if to rid himself of her. He'd show her that he was every bit as good as her precious relations. He'd thought of cutting her out completely, but her father still lived. There would be trouble if he did that. Let her have her jointure. But she wouldn't have the boys. That would teach her.

They were all ready: Thomas Webbe, the chaplain; various of Otho's servants; and his mother would witness his last testament. Precocious Katie stood beside him, insisting that she be one of the witnesses. Well, why not? At least she had time for him. Otho watched as she added her name, Katherine Gilbert the Younger, at the foot of the parchment.

KATHERINE

The baby clung to life with unexpected determination. On a hot and sticky morning at the end of May, Katherine left him with Bessie, bound for Churston Ferrers for her churching. Summer had come on sudden and strong and the sun beat down on her head as she rode through Galmpton. She noticed women, elderly men and boys out in the fields, toiling to bring in the hay. All the able men had been conscripted to man the sea defences or report to the King. If the oppressive heat continued, the grain harvest would come early. She wondered who would be left to bring it in.

A few days later Father marched into her parlour, grey-faced and breathing heavily. She could see a vein pulsing at his temple, a glimmer of sweat glistening on his brow. She sat him down in his seat in the window while Eliza offered a mug of wine.

"I fear it's come to war, girls," he told them. "The French are harrying shipping in the Channel. Your cousin Peter's already covered himself in glory patrolling the coast in the *Great Venetian*. There are reports of skirmishes near the Channel Islands, and there's been a battle off Newhaven where the English ships met with more than twenty French galleys. I think it was only rough seas that forced the French to retire, so we had a victory of sorts. The waters around the coast of England are perilous in these times." He fiddled with his doublet as if it were chafing him.

The blood drained from Katherine's face and her mouth felt suddenly dry. Walter was somewhere out on those seas in his ship, the *Mary Rawle*.

Father's eyes kept flitting to the door, and then out of the window and down the river. "The King's made it easier for privateers to capture any ship now; French, or any that trade with France," he went on, increasing her alarm with every word. "There's rich spoils to be had. I've just come from Exeter, my dears. John Hull – he's one of the richest merchants there – has gone into partnership with that chap Furseman of Kingswear. They've been out nine times and brought back prizes of grain and Gascon wine, and fish from Newfoundland. And they got a fine ransom for the prisoners they took. Old Hull's coffers will be overflowing."

Katherine could hear the envy in his voice.

"Those rich merchants are the coming men. There's not much of a look-in for the likes of us."

Katherine knew enough of Walter to think that he would take his chances as a privateer. A smile touched her lips as she allowed herself, just for a moment, to imagine him commanding his men as they seized an enemy ship, standing strong and tall as he took the surrender.

Father's eyebrows shot up. "I don't see what you find so amusing," he snapped. "This is serious. All the Carew boys are already at sea. George, Peter and Gawen each have command of one of the King's ships. Charles Brandon is mustering all the King's armies on Southsea Common just above Portsmouth. They called on me to send my men, of course, but Arthur's been recalled from France to drum up more men to work on the fortifucations at Boulogne. He'll lead my men. My fighting days are done." He laid his hand upon his chest. "I worry that our fleet may not prove strong enough to repel them. The King's hiring ships to swell his navy."

Katherine wondered if Walter's ships would be commandeered, and whether he too would be caught up in the battle. She recited a silent prayer for his safety. As Father stood up and paced the room, she admonished herself sternly. A dutiful wife would save her prayers for her husband, who she assumed was busy preparing the coastal defences. She watched Father striding from fireplace to window and back again.

"I must say I'm amazed and furious to find you two here with only the most minimal defence against attack. Is the babe fit to travel yet?" he demanded. "You must go to Compton, Katherine, where you can be better protected. I can't think what that husband of yours has in his mind that he's not seen to this before now. I'll take you back to Cornwood on the way home, Eliza, but I'll not leave until I'm sure that Katherine and the baby are safely on the road."

Katherine saw that he was in earnest. "I do think little Otho might be fit to travel the short distance to Compton. It's high summer, and a hot one, so there's no danger of him taking a chill. I've heard no word of plague or other infections. Indeed, fresh air might do him good. I'll go."

An escort was arranged and Katherine, Bessie and the baby were ready to leave soon after noon.

"Dearest Father," she said, giving him a brave smile as he took her hand. "Take care on your journey back to Modbury, and give my warmest greetings to Mother and young Henry. I shall never forget your kind and loving care of us all."

"I am so proud of you, Katherine-Kate," he said, looking deep into her eyes. "I look around and see what a capable mistress of Gilbert's house you've become. Your children do you credit, too. It's near a miracle that you've kept that last little mite alive. Now, let's get you to safety, my dears."

Katherine's convoy was met halfway by a group of armed men wearing the Gilbert colours. Otho had belatedly remembered his wife and youngest child and sent for them the very same day. She passed under the Compton gatehouse with a sense of dread and hugged her baby close. Even on a bright summer's afternoon the stone walls rose, forbidding and gloomy, towards the sky. Compton was Otho's territory and she never felt completely comfortable there. She prayed that she would not remain imprisoned there for long.

TWENTY-TWO
1545
KATHERINE

OTHO STOOD, HANDS ON HIPS, CONFERRING WITH PENKERVELL. Piles of arms, pikes, staffs, billhooks, leather jerkins and a few hackbutts cluttered the hall, so that Katherine had to pick her way carefully. As she negotiated all the obstacles she saw Isabel and Katie. The girl wore a smug grin as she stood in her mother's place.

Katherine drew herself up and said, in a clear, strong voice, "Husband, I have brought your son here to wait in safety while you serve your King." She showed him the baby. Seeing the wonder in his face as he gazed at the fragile scrap that had come from his ill treatment of her on that autumn day, Katherine felt the first stirring of pity.

He left a few days later, taking his troop of heavily armed men with him. The Compton household settled into an uneasy time of waiting. To Katie's disappointment, Katherine was quick to establish her authority. Accompanied by a puffing and protesting Bessie, she embarked on a whirlwind tour of the storerooms, giving orders for more grain and salted fish to be procured in case they came under attack and must endure a siege. She visited the brewhouse, still room and buttery, checking the shelves. She had fodder stored within the walls in case they had to bring in the milch cows. Chicken coops were set inside the inner court, where the fowl caused havoc as they pecked amongst the neat herb beds. She ordered the still-room women to make more salves and medicines in case they had to tend injured men. The fruit must be picked and preserved as usual. The men left to guard them must be well fed, and they would need to brew plenty of ale.

To her annoyance, Penkervell was still there. Katherine quizzed him about arrangements for getting in the harvest with all the men away. Even he had to acknowledge that she was right, and busied himself to find enough able hands. Isabel and Katie looked on with long faces, unhappy at being sidelined, aware that their own preparations were being shown up as inadequate. Katherine did all of this while still feeding her baby. She didn't care what Otho thought. He had not visited her bedchamber before he left. She hoped he never would again.

Katherine's baby clung to life like a limpet to a rock, his growth slow but steady. His swaddling bands were loosed and his tiny arms flailed in the air. His cries were never quite so lusty and strong as those of her other boys, who had all kicked up a fearful din in the nursery. But he survived. Satisfied that the household was ready to face whatever might befall, Katherine relaxed. She tended her baby and, as the days passed, sat sewing in the warm summer sun that streamed through the solar window. All remained peaceful at Compton. No alarms sounded; no French attack came.

In the last days of July, Otho came back. Katherine's eyes lit up to see Arthur with him, dismounting at the block. But her delight soon faded when he blurted out his mission.

"I must make haste. Father is gravely ill. I'll send word as soon as I get home." He stayed only long enough to eat a hasty meal, leaving Katherine wringing her hands.

It was left to Otho to tell the tale of the Battle of the Solent. As the boys gathered around him, all agog for news, he threw back his bony shoulders and began. "The King had assembled a truly magnificent force. We were all there, at the ready," he said, turning to Katherine. "Your cousin, Sir George Carew, had 3,600 extra mariners, gunners and soldiers pressed for service under him."

"But whatever must that have cost?" Katherine exclaimed.

"I can't even begin to think of that. The King's put the seamen's wage up to six shillings and eight pence a month, and that's without feeding and clothing them, not to mention the cost of the ordnance. Why, this must be the most expensive war ever waged by the English."

The boys were shifting in their seats, wanting to know about the battle, not how much it cost. Typically, it was six-year-old Humphrey who piped up. "But, Father, tell us of the battle, do."

"Well, the French fleet of two hundred ships lay at anchor off the Isle of Wight. King Henry's troops were gathering above Portsmouth harbour. Although the town was heavily defended, I suppose the French saw it as a special prize," said Otho. He went on to explain, for the boys' benefit, that if Henry lost Portsmouth he would lose control of the Channel all the way from the Thames Estuary to Brest in Brittany. "And that, my boys, might open up the way for a full-scale invasion of our land.

"The King himself came to take charge and oversee the battle. He's aged a bit since we saw him in Greenwich, but he's still a terrifying figure in all his splendour. On Saturday the eighteenth day of July, King Henry went to dine on board the *Henry Grace à Dieu*. It's a magnificent ship, my boys. The High Admiral, John Dudley, and your Carew cousins and your Uncle Gawen went on board with him, wife," said Otho, unable to hide the envy in his voice. "The King ordered everyone to their stations, and he gave your cousin George a gold whistle to confirm that he was to be Vice Admiral and have command of the *Mary Rose*."

"How proud George must have been!" Katherine cried, clapping her hands together. "It's a sure sign that he's fully restored in the King's favour. For the King to recognise him as a commander of men would mean a lot to George."

Otho fidgeted in his seat and did not meet her eye. He picked up the tale. "Sunday dawned bright and calm; a perfect day for the French to deploy their rowing galleys. They must have hoped it would tempt the English out into open water, where their larger ships could pick them off. I saw the King himself walking with a group of the Queen's ladies near the castle at Southsea. They all watched the *Mary Rose* move slowly out into the harbour mouth. Katherine, your sister that's wed to Anthony Denny, she was there; and so was your brother John's widow that's now wife to Berkely. And of course George Carew's wife, she was there as well. All talking and laughing with the King." He clearly relished the look of surprise that appeared on his wife's face. "You'd have thought they were all just out to watch a tourney, not a real battle in a real war."

Humphrey's mouth fell open. "So you really saw King Henry and all his ladies, Father?"

"I did indeed. I had to deliver a very important message, and found a vantage point to see everything," Otho said, perhaps over-egging the significance of his role. Later, Katherine heard that in reality his task had been merely to oversee supply lines.

"It all happened so quickly," he went on. "As the *Mary Rose* put about, perhaps to return fire, all on a sudden, she heeled right over."

The boys gasped in unison. You could have heard a pin drop amongst the rushes. They all held their breath, anxious for more.

"It was as if a strong gust of wind had caught her sails. The gun ports all stood open and ready to fire. As she lurched at an angle, they must have filled up with water. She slipped away so very fast," said Otho, shaking his head. "There was nothing anyone could do. The other ships tried to come alongside, even the one commanded by your cousin Peter. But before they could come near, the *Mary Rose* was gone." He paused again, waiting for the import of his story to register in their minds. Seeing the look of disbelief on every face, he repeated, "The ship was lost, with near all souls gone to the bottom of the sea with her; aye, and all the weapons she carried, too."

They sat, open-mouthed, hardly able to believe their ears. Humphrey was jumping up and down, frantic to understand what it meant. "So, Father," he cried, "did the King lose all in the battle? Will the French soon be upon us? Shall I fetch a sword to defend us?"

Meanwhile Katherine was shaking her head vigorously, as if doing so would deny what Otho was saying; somehow make it not so. "But George, he is safe, of course?" she murmured.

"Steady, Humphrey, my boy. The ship went down, with seven hundred or so men aboard her. They could not escape, all readied as they were to fight. Some were in full armour; you can imagine how that would weigh them down. And the scramble nets were spread to keep the enemy off their decks. They must have been trapped beneath. Only a handful were saved. But the French did not win the day. The wind dropped and our Admiral, knowing those waters well, used the tides and currents to position his other ships and keep the Frenchmen out of Portsmouth harbour. They soon retreated to the Isle of Wight, and they say the forces there beat them back quite easily."

Again Katherine asked, a little louder, "But, husband, what of my cousin George?"

Otho turned to her and said gravely, "Katherine, my wife, he is gone. Neither he nor Roger Grenville was seen again. There will be an inquiry as to the cause of the tragedy. The King's given orders that an attempt must be made to bring the ship up again, to salvage anything that's possible. Your cousin Peter saw the whole thing; saw his brother perish and could do nothing. He's hot to lead a recovery, but I fear the *Mary Rose* is gone."

Katherine's shoulders fell. She raised a shaking hand to her throat and closed her eyes, squeezing them tightly to shut out the horror of it. She remembered George's strong arms carrying her from the church in Shillingford all those years ago. She remembered his merry face at his first wedding to the Pollard girl. Oh, like all the Carews, he had got into scrapes. Why, only last year he had been captured in France, but was ransomed and got away unscathed. She caught her breath. Another bleak thought had occurred to her. George's wife, Mary, had been there; had seen her husband lost before her very eyes.

As if following her train of thought, Otho added, "She saw it all, of course: George's wife, or widow as she is now. I saw her fall in a swoon and your sister raise her up and hold her, the King close beside them, giving what comfort he could before they helped her inside. The Queen will keep her at court. I heard that your brother Arthur went and spoke long with her."

That was just like Arthur, Katherine thought. Thank God he was not at the bottom of the sea with his cousin and all those other lost souls.

Otho was back, but most of his men had yet to return. He busied himself ordering what remained of his troop and counting his arms and weapons, while Katherine struggled with her grief.

On the fourth day of August a rider approached Compton as she was walking from the chapel where she had been saying another prayer for Cousin George. As she saw his livery, she stopped in her tracks. Father's, and a black band on his arm. She knew instantly what it meant.

"Mistress Gilbert," the messenger said in a voice thick with emotion. "Sir Philip was struck by an apoplexy some weeks past, but did come back to his right mind, though he could by no means move his left arm or leg. Aye, and he spoke strange. Master Arthur came, and on the first day of August called gentlemen to witness the will. Only two days later another attack came and he was gone. He was the best of masters!"

"I must go at once to Modbury; see him properly laid to rest," she cried.

But the man gave her a letter from Arthur. 'Father would not wish it. You must think first of your boy,' he said.

She accepted Arthur's bidding reluctantly, but could no longer bear to have the walls of Compton pressing down on her. As soon as it seemed certain that the roads were safe she went back to Greenway Court, where she spent hours staring at the oak seat in the parlour window. It was a bitter blow. Father had always been there; a steady, witty, caring man, trying to do his best for his family in changing times. There were so many words left unsaid. She had never truly thanked him for all his love and care, and above all for allowing her, a mere girl, to sample such a wide education. He had introduced her to the world she loved to explore within her books. And he had so loved music. To think she would never again hear his strong voice raised in song!

As if to put the seal on her sorrow, the hot weather that had been so uncomfortable through June and July erupted in August into the most cataclysmic storms. With the able-bodied men yet to return from their posts, the crops were still in the fields. Corn lay flat on the ground, which soon became flooded. It was nigh on impossible to salvage much, as steady rains set in. The threat of invasion was replaced by the threat of hunger, as prices rose higher than anyone could remember. Katherine saw to her tasks mechanically and wearily, trying to eke out her stores against a hard winter to come.

Perhaps it was the shocking news of Father's death, or the loss of the *Mary Rose*. Perhaps she wasn't eating enough. Perhaps feeding the fretful child was taking too much from her slender body and robbing her of sleep. As summer turned to dismal autumn and then bitter winter, Katherine had never before felt so desolate and bone-weary.

Arthur often called and kept her up to date with all the news. All was in hand for Father's Inquisition to be taken at Tiverton in early December. "They'll establish Henry as his rightful heir, and then everything can be passed on as Father wished. The debts are paid and the Champernowne estates are in fine fettle," he said proudly. "The monastery lands we came by have helped."

"Oh, Arthur," Katherine replied, smiling for the first time in ages. "Wouldn't Father be proud to know that his life's work was not in vain?"

"Aye indeed, he and Mother worked hard all their lives to secure our place in the world. What an example they set us," said Arthur with a touch of wonder. "Father left strict instructions that neither I nor his executors, Kat and Uncle George, must meddle with Mother's lands while she lives."

Katherine managed another thin smile, wondering if bossy Kat would be able to keep her fingers out of the pie.

"Father wrote of the most obedient duty and gentleness that Mother has always shown to him. There was such a strong bond between them," Arthur went on. "Mother's distraught to be left so. Thank God for Henry. It's arranged that I'm to oversee his care." He paused and then added, with a twinkle, "And I have high hopes that soon I may also find a true and loving wife." Sitting in that same oak seat in the parlour, he looked just like Father.

"So which of the Queen's ladies has caught your eye, Arthur?" Katherine asked, her smile growing wider as she saw the sparkle in his eyes.

"Keep this close and breathe not a word, dear Katherine-Kate," said he, "but I do hope that Cousin George's widow, Mary, may not need to leave our family for too long."

"That's perfect," she said, planting a kiss on his cheek. "I suppose the King will have to give his approval?" Mary was young and pretty, and very well connected. How wonderful it would be if she brought more than wealth to Arthur. How wonderful if, like Katherine's parents, they found love as well as duty in their life together.

By the time baby Otho celebrated his first birthday, a day she had hardly dared hope to see, Arthur was not the only one caught in the coils of love. On a warm and sultry day with no breath of a breeze, she heard hooves upon the stable yard cobbles and was delighted to see Arthur bearing gifts for the boy. Inside, it was pleasantly cool as Arthur took his place again in the oak chair by the window.

"Katherine-Kate, you'll never guess who's in love?" he said, laughing. "'Tis Cousin Peter, who has set his cap at fair Margaret, the widow of old Tailboys."

Now this was indeed a juicy slice of gossip. "Wasn't she the Margaret Skipworth whose name was once linked to the King?" Katherine asked gleefully.

Arthur confirmed that she was the very same. "What a scandal that was," he chuckled. "Peter might have a hard time persuading her and getting the King on his side, but he's fallen so under her spell, he'll do anything to get her."

"Imagine! Boastful, bragging Peter languishing in love!" she cried.

"Well, let's see if the lady will have him! I heard he fought bravely under Dudley to rid English waters of the French. He and Uncle Gawen were both knighted," said Arthur, taking a draught of cooling ale.

"How Johnny would have loved to have been part of all these alarms and excursions," Katherine said with a sad shake of her head.

"I heard the King's got so fat that they've made a sort of chair contraption that they haul up and down the back stairways at Hampton Court," said Arthur, swiftly moving the conversation away from his long-lost brother.

"I do feel a bit sorry for the King, you know," she said, remembering the limping figure amongst the courtiers at Greenwich. "Good thing he's got Queen Kateryn to care for him."

"I hear a commission's gone out to survey the wealth of the chantries," Arthur went on. "When they got to Mohun's Ottery, they found that Peter had stopped paying a priest to say Masses for his ancestors. Any jewels and plate the chantry chapel held were long gone."

"So Otho's uncle wasn't so wide of the mark," she replied. "How pleased that old man would have been to know that his clever scheme to keep men praying for his soul paid off."

The sound of small feet clattering furiously down the stairs halted any further conversation. Humphrey bounced into the room calling, "Uncle Arthur, Uncle Arthur, come and see how well I can hold a sword!"

"Off you go, Uncle," she trilled, giving his arm a squeeze. "My boys think the world of you and you have such a way with them."

Otho and Katherine had come to an unspoken agreement of civility. He was often away with Penkervell, looking to estate business. He'd taken land upstream at Northhall, part of the Dartington estate now held by the Queen. He had agreement to fell some oaks and float the timber downstream to Galmpton Pool, where he had big plans to build more ships. To his chagrin, Edward Gilbert still sailed the *Trinity*, sometimes testing the line between piracy and privateering. He'd taken a Spanish vessel laden with sugar and alum, but on the King's instructions the Dartmouth harbour master made him restore the cargo. Of Walter, Katherine heard little, though Arthur had once mentioned him and his sons being in similar case to Edward.

Trying to keep the excitement out of her voice, she'd asked, "Is that the man who brought Otho home from France? I did wonder if he's the same that holds Fardel, near Eliza's home?"

"Indeed he is," said Arthur, smiling. "People think that because Raleigh has let out his family properties and rents a farm over near East Budleigh, he's in poor financial straits. But he's much more well-to-do than you might think. Why, he now owns several ships, and knows how to put them to use. And Peter says he's a sound man as far as religion goes, too."

She hoped her face did not betray her special interest in Walter, but her heart lifted to have word of him.

Arthur's wooing of George's widow progressed slowly. In September, more than a year after the *Mary Rose* went down, he was in high spirits. "The King's agreed!" he called, before he was in the door. He grabbed Katherine's hand and danced her round the parlour. "Anthony Denny's persuaded him to write to Mary, in favour of our marriage. I'm off to my wedding, Katherine-Kate!"

"I wish I could come with you to wish you well," she said, breathless after the impromptu jig. "Be sure to bring Mary to meet me soon."

He was away again in no time, the strains of a merry song echoing in the courtyard as he left.

TWENTY-THREE
1547
KATHERINE

KATHERINE PREFERRED GREENWAY COURT, BUT OTHO HAD taken the notion that the Christmas feast should be held at his ancestral home. She went unwillingly, but the children were bouncing with excitement. The plague that had raged through the county since the autumn had not abated, so after the holiday they stayed on at Compton, afraid that the Devon lanes were full of plague carriers.

They heard the rumours. The King was gravely ill. None knew what ailed him. He had died. He had recovered. Otho grew impatient to know the truth. Against Katherine's advice he went to Exeter, where he said he had pressing business to complete. She suspected he was glad to be away from her.

On the thirteenth day of February he was back, in very high spirits, jovial and loud. *Probably drunk*, she thought, as her youngest son cowered behind her. She stepped aside to escape Otho's blundering embrace and instead he lifted the frightened boy clean off the ground and held him close.

"The King is dead, Katherine, and now we shall be ruled by a boy. Or rather, by men set up to rule in his stead. The Seymours are in high place, and your brother-in-law Denny is named for the Council," he laughed, jiggling little Otho in the air.

She was at a loss to know why the King's death caused him such joy. He looked strange. His brow glistened with sweat and his scar showed purple against his flushed cheeks. But she made no comment. Swaying, he made his way to his chamber while Katherine put her little one to bed.

The next morning John Tapleigh, Otho's serving man, raised the alarm. "The master be sick with a fearful fever. Now he's a-shivering; next he's burning up. He's been sick as a dog and he's speaking strange," cried the frightened man.

Katherine's blood ran cold. *Please, God, not the plague.* No, it must be some other ailment he'd picked up amongst the sailors and merchants in Exeter. She stamped her foot hard. She'd told him to keep at home, but he had insisted upon going, when the plague was still rife and all manner of other sickness too. She pulled the covers over her boy, sleeping soundly in his truckle bed.

She ordered medicines and draughts prepared; had the fire stoked high in his chamber; sent him broth; had them put red hangings around the bed. But Otho was soon beyond these ministrations.

February: dim days when the sun never shone. Long nights of persistent rain and biting cold. On that dreary morning her world was dark indeed, though her husband's passing had hardly registered in her mind. She gave no thought to who must be told, nor what arrangements must be made. All that day long she watched her son. She saw the unmistakable flush come to his rounded cheeks; saw him running about, all frenetic energy; saw the beads of sweat upon his dear face. In the dimpsy light of that fearful afternoon she saw him fall into a slumber so troubled and disturbed it had him crying out, murmuring and tossing off the covers one minute, only to be shivering the next. She could give him no comfort. In that fatherly embrace her husband must have passed on whatever foul humours had taken him to meet his God. Thanks be to that same God that Otho had not been near the other boys or Katie. But her youngest boy, born too soon, had little strength to fight. A day passed, another night, and then, as dawn streaked the morning sky, her darling, the one she had so protected and nurtured, the one she had kept from death for so long, lay cold and still.

Penkervell arranged a hasty funeral for his brother, for fear that infection might spread. Otho Gilbert's passing could be properly marked later with a splendid month-mind. Webbe, the chaplain, had been to see Katherine. The funeral would be on the morrow. Her boy must be laid to rest beside the man who had given him to her in such violent fashion and taken him from her through his carelessness.

Her boy could not go to his grave with no flowers to cheer him. Not bothering to put on her cloak, though the wind was chill and it looked like to snow, she went down to the gardens in search of blooms. Mid February; too early for violets or primroses; in this season, few flowers showed their faces. All looked bare and wasted as she walked aimlessly round Compton's orchard. Eventually, lower down by the stream in a sheltered spot, she found a few buds of coltsfoot showing palely yellow. She picked some, added a sprig of rosemary, and took them to the chapel where little Otho lay in a tiny, hastily made coffin. She arranged those few flowers next his cheek, now drained of all that furious colour, and thought he looked like an angel as they closed the lid and took him from her. The priest said he was with his father in Heaven. But what of that? His place was here on the earth, to grow and play and become a man and enjoy all that life might offer.

Days passed. The other children and the servants crept about her, hardly daring to speak. Eliza came and sat with her, holding her hand and trying to tempt her from her sadness.

It was only when the will was read that Katherine showed some spark. Much of the estate was entailed for John, who would be a royal ward until he came of age. She'd expected that. But Otho had given charge of Humphrey and Adrian to the hated Penkervell! Oh, he'd left plenty of lands for her boys to inherit in turn; first Humphrey and his heirs, or, failing them, Adrian. He'd even decreed that Otho would be next in line, so he had really believed that the little scrap in the nursery might survive.

She wrung her hands and paced the room. Oh, he had directed that his wife was to have care of their youngest boy, and left good provision for that and his future. That was of no use now! Worse, Otho had made no provision at all for Katie's future. The girl might go where she pleased at her own election, said his will. Katherine took no interest at all in the jointure left to her, which on the face of it was a fair one. She burned with anger that Otho had devised matters so that, as a widow, she would have hardly any power over the fate of her children. That was a harsh punishment.

The world, of course, kept turning. The see-saw still swung up and down. A new King sat on the throne and would soon go to his coronation. Edward Seymour, Duke of Somerset, the late Queen Jane's brother, moved quickly and established himself as Protector. Had Otho Gilbert's widow the will to listen, she would have heard a lot of talk about the Protector's wife, Anne Seymour; how she would raise herself to be the first lady of the land. But, locked deep in her anger and grief, Katherine didn't care.

She went back to Greenway Court soon after the funeral. Arthur came and tried to shake her from her despair.

"We'll see things move at pace now, Katherine-Kate," he said, sipping wine in Father's chair. "Somerset should be able to push through the changes thwarted by King Henry. Oh, how he did cling so steadfast to the old ways at the end! Cousin Peter secured his dispensation and married Margaret on coronation day. He wore Margaret's glove in his headpiece in the tournament that celebrated the new reign."

The twenty-fourth day of March dawned dull and blustery. Katherine must don a black gown and hooded cloak and go to the Church of St John the Baptist to join the crowd gathered there to do honour to her departed husband.

The church was full to bursting with local notables and neighbours. It was not respect for her husband that brought them through the rutted lanes to Marldon that day. They came for old John Gilbert, or for Otho's namesake and grandfather, or simply out of curiosity. She stifled a bitter little laugh. Some might even be thinking that Otho's widow was young and well connected. Let them think what they liked. She would never again marry against her own will.

She squared her shoulders and took a deep breath. With her veil pulled down, she fell into step with Arthur as they pushed through the gaggle of Otho's serving men crowded near the door. Her heart skipped a beat as they passed a tall man. There was no doubt. She would recognise those broad shoulders, that curling hair anywhere. But she dared not pause. To turn and stare would draw too much attention. As she moved to her allotted space, a tiny butterfly of excitement stirred within her.

She watched as Richard Crispin clambered up into the pulpit. Short and nondescript, he was clad all in black, and a rather outlandish pair of horn-rimmed spectacles sat precariously on his pinched nose. Katherine glanced around the company. All were waiting expectantly for him to extol Otho's virtues. John Rowe, Serjeant-at-Law, John Gilbert's accomplice in so many endeavours, was smiling up at Crispin.

After only a few sentences, Katherine's head went up sharply. This was very strange. The words were all wrong. Crispin launched into a diatribe against Luther's teaching that Scripture was the touchstone of truth. Neither their new King nor his council would have truck with such words. Even John Rowe looked surprised.

Ah, yes, she remembered him now. Crispin was chaplain to her dead kinsman, the Marquess of Exeter. He'd been up to his neck in the to-do about the Nun of Kent, and had been a potent symbol of Henry Courtenay's allegiance to the old ways. So that was why John Rowe, whose Popish views were well known, was smiling. Penkervell must have done this deliberately. Better that he had asked Uncle George, who was Archdeacon of nearby Totnes, and like to rise further under the new rule. He'd have spoken aright.

She glanced at Arthur. His mouth was drawn in a thin, disapproving line. Mutters echoed around the church as others noticed the direction of Crispin's discourse. No one wanted to call him out there and then and disrupt proceedings, but Katherine had no doubt that trouble would follow. A clatter from behind her suggested some had simply walked out. Turning, she caught a glimpse of a pair of broad shoulders in the doorway.

At last it was over. As they left the church, Arthur introduced Philip Nichols, a youthful clergyman obviously cut from very different cloth to Crispin.

"Why did none of the Christian men assembled here challenge his words?" Nichols fumed.

"It was only out of respect for my sister that I did not pull that Papist from the pulpit myself," Arthur hissed. "This is not the time, Nichols, but Crispin must be called to account."

"Sir, I will write to the man and refute his arguments. And rest assured, I will report this day's work to my patron."

"Good man, Nichols," Arthur replied. "My cousin Peter will know exactly what to do. Come, Katherine-Kate."

The hall was packed; the board spread with a fine feast; the best ale tapped and the fire well stoked. She had been exchanging pleasantries with Thomas Yarde when the press of people became too much for her. She mumbled an apology and slipped through the curtains into the screens passage.

The air felt cool and fresh as she crossed the courtyard and climbed the steps to the garden. She found a quiet arbour, where she sat on a rough wooden bench, twisting her fingers in her lap. Visiting the church had brought back memories of her lost son. That was to be expected. But she was shocked by the bubbling excitement that had filled her when she saw Walter. How wicked to be thinking so of another man so soon after the death of her little darling! Her shoulders sagged, and soon the tears started to flow.

WALTER

It hit him like a cannon ball in the guts. As soon as he saw her, shrouded in that ugly veil in the church, he knew he loved her still. Gilbert was dead. She was free. He must speak. Desperately, he tried to find her amongst the hubbub in the hall. Everyone was talking of that fool Crispin. Try as he might, he couldn't reach her through the press. When he saw her go, he was after her in an instant, nearly breaking into a run in his haste to be with her. But as he came through the gate and saw her sitting in the arbour, crying her heart out, he stopped in an agony of indecision. Her slender shoulders were heaving. He could hear the sobs catching in her throat. Perhaps he'd mistaken her. Perhaps she'd truly loved that idiotic Gilbert boy. Perhaps the connection between them had all been his imagining, and she cared not a fig for him.

She looked up and saw him waiting, half hidden, behind the clipped yew. As their eyes met, he had his answer. He covered the few paces that separated them so fast he nearly tripped on the lavender bushes that lined the path.

"Katherine-Kate, my dear one, to see you in tears put me in fear that in your grief you had quite forgotten me. But now I see you do remember me still. Of course, 'tis only fitting that you are sad to lose your husband. Am I come to you too soon?" he asked, turning his hat round and round in his hands. He saw her lovely cheeks flush; a little shiver – surely not of cold? – pass through her.

"Nay, Walter; my husband was lost to me long ago. 'Tis my baby son I grieve for now. That sorrow is raw indeed, for I lost him just a few days after his father. My little darling! He came into the world too soon, so very tiny. I struggled near two years to keep my boy alive. Now he's taken, lost forever, and all because that fool that was my husband would go abroad and bring back some dread disease."

"Forgive me. I did not know of this," he said, still hesitating, though his heart cried out to take her hand, to give her comfort.

"I did not seek my husband's death, for I have always known my duty well. But my tears are not for him. 'Tis my innocent boy that I miss so." She dabbed at her eyes with her sleeve, and then looked full into his face. "But, Walter, you must know that of all people in this world you are the one I would most wish to see this day; the one I have so often longed for."

His heart leaped. He couldn't help grinning. As her tears started to flow again, he opened his arms. She took a pace forward and leaned towards him. He felt her shaking as she rested her head against his chest; tremors that set his whole body in tension. She was clinging to him as though to hold him fast forever. He held her close. All those years of dreaming and longing for this one woman! Dare he hope that she might soon be his? His lips brushed her forehead tenderly, and he let his arms fall. Still holding his hat, he knelt on the cold, wet stones, inwardly cursing the moss that covered every surface in the damp Devon air. He took her hand again, kissing each finger reverently.

"This may not be the time, but you must know. I must speak. Since I saw you that day on the *Trinity*, I have dreamed of you and only you. Now that you are free, will you be my wife, my dearest Katherine-Kate?"

"Oh, Walter, you must know that my heart is yours. It has been the same for me. Since that day I have tried and tried to forget you and do my duty. But I could not. I never dared to dream of this. Could I really be your wife in truth? What would people say if I were to marry again so soon? And I don't know what I might bring you. It will be a time before my husband's affairs are put to rights, and be in no doubt, I'll have to fight with Penkervell for what is mine. Oh, and I have such a parcel of children. I would see all settled for their future."

Still kneeling, he looked up into her eyes. "Good God, woman, I would take you in your shift if that was all you had in the world! I care not for your fortune, whatever it may be," he blustered, making out that he was affronted at her hesitation. His pulse was racing. He could hear his heart thudding loudly in his chest. He ached to reach out, to free her hood and let that splendid mane of hair he had dreamt of so often fall freely. Oh, to bury his face in all that glistening beauty! He smiled, anticipating the wonder of it; a broad, confident grin, his white teeth flashing.

"Katherine-Kate, my own love, you may bring as many children with you as you wish. Aye, and I'll hope that we may soon add to that tally. You may come with or without your lands or your monies. Leave all your fine gowns and jewels behind. I care not. Come live with me and be my love. My home is not so splendid as you have known. But I give you my word: I will love you forever as no man ever loved a woman before. I will share with you my life, my all. Answer me do, dear Katherine-Kate." And then, with another mischievous grin, "Will you keep me kneeling here forever, woman? I'm not so young as I was, you know, these stones are cold and damp and I've been a long time a-waiting. Will you give me my answer?"

The confusion had gone from her face, which now shone with pure joy as she answered him, laughter at last bubbling up within her. "Yes, and yes, and yes, a thousand times, yes!" she cried.

He leapt to his feet and, lifting her from the bench, took her in his arms again. This time his lips found hers hungrily and she returned his kiss, honey-sweet, passionate, yielding and oh, so full of promise.

KATHERINE

She was trembling as, for the first time, he kissed away the tears that lingered around her eyes. She put a hand up to his face and felt the faint stubble on his chin; ran her fingers through his curls; drank in the very essence of him.

All too soon they heard Eliza calling loudly from beyond the gate. They were wanted within. Arthur was looking to take his leave. A knowing grin spread across Eliza's face as she came upon them.

"I see, Master Raleigh, that all is well and my sister shall at last be happy," she said, laughing.

Katherine blushed and giggled. Eliza must have been standing guard to make sure they were not discovered too soon. Walter chuckled. She took his arm and felt as if she were floating on air. It took several minutes to cross the courtyard, for every few paces she stopped and gazed into his eyes, hardly able to believe that at last she was walking beside the man she loved.

There was time for more than one more kiss before Arthur erupted through the door. He stopped in his tracks, pushed back his cap, and scratched his head. "Why, Raleigh, you are a dark horse, sir!" he exclaimed, clapping Walter on the back. "You have wasted little time in wooing the widow, I see. And I can see that your suit is well received!"

"Shush, Arthur," said Katherine, glowing with happiness. "You're a fine one to talk. Why, in no time at all you paid court to George's widow, and look how happily that has come about."

As Arthur spoke with Walter about arrangements for her wedding, she thought how quickly and surely this brother of hers had stepped into Father's shoes as head of the Champernowne clan. Arthur might still be young but she would trust him in anything.

WALTER

He'd have ridden away with her there and then if he could. But there was much to be done. Arthur Champernowne was a good fellow. He'd help Katherine make what arrangements she must. Now he was sure of her, Walter supposed he could wait just a little longer. Soon he would take his lovely bride to his farmhouse at Poer Hayes, near the village of East Budleigh. It was a small place. He had more than enough people about him already, so she need bring few with her; perhaps only the maid called Bessie. He'd seen straight away how carefully, and with what affection, the plump woman with the merry eyes waited on his love's every need.

He sighed. There was much for him to do. He must look to his ships, set all his affairs in order, and tell his boys and Mary that he was set to take a wife. He thought of his new barque, near ready for launching. A bold idea formed in his mind. He would have all in place to welcome her. If all went well they would be wed at midsummer, under blue skies and the summer sun. Some might say it was too soon, but what cared he for wagging tongues? He would not wait a moment longer than was necessary.

PART THREE

THE WOMAN

TWENTY-FOUR
1547
KATHERINE

THE STANDING CROPS WERE TURNING GOLD AS SHE RODE through the Devon countryside to her wedding. She drew her horse to a halt on high ground overlooking a green valley surrounded by low hills, all clad with thick forest of oak and beech. Soon that valley would become as familiar to her as the lanes around Compton and Greenway Court. Squealing gulls competed with the cuckoo's midsummer tune above her vantage point. The lush meadows of the valley bottom gleamed emerald-bright, and fields of ripening wheat stood out like golden patches embroidered on a rippling length of rich green velvet. Beside the sparkling, silvery line of a brook, at the very heart of this glorious picture, was a house. Her new home.

A delicious tingle of anticipation ran down her spine, and she set her heels into the black gelding's sides. Years before she had taken a sad farewell of her old friend Dapple. Katherine missed the bond of love and comradeship she had shared with her first pony, but the gelding was spirited. They soon covered the last mile to the church.

Katie rode beside her, hair hanging down her back, cap set at a precarious angle. Against all predictions the girl had chosen to stay with her mother. Katie had invested such effort to become Otho's spoilt darling, but now he was gone. She could have taken her chance with Penkervell and his frosty wife Joan, or she could have been ruled by her Grandmother Isabel in Cornwall. But she had come with Katherine, though neither her humour nor her rebellious spirit had improved.

A gaily clad party waited to greet them. The two barefoot boys Katherine remembered had transformed into handsome, swarthy young men, as tall as their father. Walter stood beaming beside them, his face glowing, showing no fear of the superstition that seeing his bride so early on their wedding day would bring bad luck. She felt his eager eyes all over her as she dismounted, light as a feather, and Walter announced himself the luckiest man in all England. John Raleigh's grey eyes were warm and welcoming as he took her hand. George, the elder boy, stood aloof with a rakish expression on his fine features. He was certainly a handsome lad, but there was an air of danger and recklessness about him that was completely absent in his brother. *A ladies' man*, Katherine thought warily.

Walter encouraged a timid girl to come forward and make her curtsy. "This is Mary," he said.

Katherine looked into the girl's fair face. Strands of hair, so strikingly blonde it made Eliza's harvest tresses seem dull, escaped wildly from beneath her cap. Pale blue-green eyes that changed colour like a storm-tossed sea fixed shyly upon her new mother. Katie was presented, clearly enjoying the chance to preen before Walter's boys. Katherine noticed that George held Katie's hand a mite longer than was really seemly upon first introduction, and felt a tremor of unease.

All was prepared for the wedding. Walter had arranged that she might rest and change her gown at the farmhouse across the lane. Two serving women hurried to provide ale and food, but Katherine was far too excited to eat. A chamber had been prepared, and there was Bessie taking a new gown as blue as the summer sky from the coffer.

WALTER

Walter waited at the church door, bouncing from foot to foot as he adjusted his cap yet again. It was only right and natural that she would want to rest and change her costume before she came to stand at his side. But now the day had come at last, he could contain his excitement no longer. Soon – oh, so very soon – she would be his!

He drew his eyebrows together in a frown. Would she be happy? After that grand house, Greenway Court, and Modbury's Court House, he feared she'd find his rented farm, cold, draughty and uncomfortable. Poer Hayes, the old house named for the Poer family who used to live there, suited him well. From there he could play the part of country landholder and farmer, grazing cattle up on Woodbury Common. It was handy for his ships. The harbour at Budleigh Haven was now out of commission, filled up with silt as the shingle drifted across the mouth of the Otter. So his ships rode at anchor in the nearby fishing village of Exmouth. The farmstead was far from prying eyes, but close enough for him to be on board his ships at short notice. He liked it well. Oh, how he hoped that Katherine would come to like it just as much! How much longer would it take for her to be ready? It felt like he'd been fidgeting by the door for hours, though he knew it was really only a few minutes. He might as well wait inside, out of the sun.

The hushed church welcomed him in like a trusted friend. There was his bench; he'd spent a sizeable portion of his second wife's dowry on that carved seat. He traced his finger over the carving – the Raleigh arms and the date: 1537. Over the years others had added their own designs to bench ends behind his: the ships that brought wealth to the thriving community; a dragon; a sea monster; tradesmen with their tools. There was even a nod to the half-forgotten beliefs of their forefathers in the startling face of a bearded Wild Man of the Woods with a strange headdress of leaves. It meant a lot to Walter to wed his Katherine in that little church. He hoped she would not take it amiss when she saw the gravestone in the aisle that marked the spot where his first wife lay.

KATHERINE

She wondered if she dared loose her hair. How Walter would love that! But she was no longer a girl. Perhaps it was a step too far. She squeezed Eliza's hand, pleased to have her there. They had so much in common: both married first to the wrong man, and both now widows. William Cole had followed Otho to the grave not long after the month-mind day; taken by some contagion he'd picked up in Plymouth. The shock had rocked Eliza, but she put on a brave face.

"At my first wedding I was but a frightened child, Eliza," said Katherine with a saucy grin. "I know more of the world now. Oh, I'm in haste to wed this man! But do you think he will find me comely? I've borne all those children. I do so want to please him."

"Have no fear," said Eliza, her blue eyes all a-twinkle. "That man worships the very earth beneath your feet. All will be well."

Katherine stepped out in all her finery to become the third Mistress Raleigh, and there he was, grinning at the church door, eyes wide and sparkling. The vows exchanged, the ceremony done, they led the procession down the lane. Family, guests, a gaggle of villagers and a band of sailors from Topsham and Exmouth all walked in step to the musicians' beat. Passing between two yew trees, they came to the white-painted house, where tables were set out on the grass for the feast. Katherine had no memory of what they ate, or what was said, or the dancing, or the laughter, or the throng of people who came to enjoy Walter's largesse. Only Walter beside her seemed real at all. She overheard one sailor saying to another, "He's a fair master, though he be apt at times to bend the rules. I'd follow him anywhere."

WALTER

His face ached from grinning so much. It had gone well, but now he wanted to be alone with her. How soon could they decently retire? He'd have none of that bed-blessing flummery with the priest, who was knocking back a fair amount of his best sherry sack. None of that escorting them to bed. He would have her all to himself.

He could wait no longer. Before the sun was near going down he took her hand, swept her off her feet and carried her over the threshold. Her gown snagged for a moment on the apothecary's rose flowering profusely by the open door. She yanked it free with impatient hands, and her laughter, throaty, warm and husky, shot a delicious shiver through him.

Only when they were up in the chamber and he had kicked the door closed did he set her down. At last, at last, all the long years of waiting were over.

KATHERINE

The sun was already up. She stretched, arching her back like a cat, basking in the warmth of their love. To her surprise, he was already dressed and pulling on his boots.

"What, tired of me so soon, husband?" she asked, stretching out an arm enticingly.

He leaned across the bed and kissed her bare shoulder. "That day will never come, my love. But there are things in this world that wait for no man," said he, with a beaming smile. "Come, wife; not a moment is to be lost."

"What is all this mystery, my dear love? Where should we be but here, together?" she asked, reaching out again to entice him back to bed.

But Walter would only chivvy her to dress. He fumbled and cussed as he tried to lace her kirtle. Bessie had put out her oldest gown.

"I must call Bessie," she said. "This gown is not in the latest style. I would look well for you."

But he stayed her, saying, "Nay, wife; I will be your tiring woman this day, and this gown is most becoming."

The horses were waiting at the door and soon they were riding past the church and on towards the sea, she laughing all the time at his secrecy. As they came through the streets of Exmouth toward the docks, she saw a company gathered there on the quayside: Arthur, Walter's sons, Eliza, and Katie with her hair all unbound and standing far too close to that handsome boy George Raleigh. A cheer went up as they came into view.

"What's all this, Walter?" Katherine asked, thinking that she must speak to her girl about her behaviour.

They dismounted beside a fine new ship, well afloat as the tide was near its fullest. Walter introduced Katherine to the ship's master, who made way for her to step up the gangplank. The crew all stood at attention, each beaming face telling Katherine that they shared Walter's secret. And then she saw the name emblazoned on the ship's side: the *Katherine Raleigh*. With the broadest of smiles, Walter bade her take the standing cup and raise it to port and to starboard, and then to fore and aft. He would have her launch his pride and joy: the new barque he had named for his lady love.

Katherine knew what the ceremony required of her. She raised the cup to the four corners, took a sip, and then poured a libation. The red wine spread quickly around her feet to stain the new boards of the deck. With a grin she hurled the cup over the side, and watched as a sailor swam out to retrieve it. Most of the crew missed the chance to receive the reward Walter had offered for bringing back the cup, for they had never learned to swim. But that one lad had grown up by the sea and had no fear of the waters of Exmouth harbour. He heaved himself out of the water and held the cup high above his head in triumph.

Another cheer went up. "May God bless the *Katherine Raleigh*, and all who sail in her. Hurrah!"

The rest of the party started down the gangplank, and Katherine made to follow.

"Oh no, my lady wife, you shall not go. Come and see what a fine cabin this vessel of mine boasts."

The gangplank was raised and the crew cast off, and the turning tide took them slowly out into the Channel. Inside the cabin she found a coffer with enough simple clothes for several days' wear. Katherine clapped her hands and danced around just for the joy of it. Walter was taking her aboard his new ship on her maiden voyage! Now she understood why he had been so insistent on her choice of gown: it was the one she had worn that day on the *Trinity*. As soon as the roofs of Exmouth faded to a thin line against the sky, he loosed her hair and bade her walk to the bow.

"I would look again on my sea goddess. I have longed to see the vision that has tormented my dreams for so long," he declared as he handed her aloft.

Forgetting all her cares, Katherine felt again the thrill of the waves surging beneath her, and knew her heart had found its true home. The weather was fair, the sails billowed above them and the *Katherine Raleigh* bore them across the sea, as they discovered each other. The crew went about their tasks discreetly through the long and loving hours she spent with Walter on the cabin's narrow bed. He'd had the cramped space decked out with velvet and silk;

a sumptuous welcome for his sea-nymph bride. Simple meals of bread and cheese, wine, oranges and pomegranates he'd hoarded for the voyage appeared at the cabin door uncalled for. Each evening they emerged briefly to stand at the bow, his arm resting lightly across her shoulders, and watch the sun go down as in her dreams of so many tormented nights.

For Katherine the world beyond the cabin door faded, lost all meaning as she revelled in the intensity of their love; an intimacy that stretched beyond ecstasy to their thoughts, hopes and dreams. She yielded to its blessing with pure joy. Oh, those languid hours with her head on his chest, her breathing in step with his! They talked as lovers do. They shared their ideas freely, bound by bonds of respect and care. She could weep with him for Johnny, for her boy, and for Father. She could laugh with him at Peter's lovelorn quest for his Margaret. She could tell him of her dreams of faraway lands and her thirst to know more. She could even tell him how she saw her God. After her brittle relationship with Otho, to find in Walter a man who treated her as an equal in so many ways was pure delight. Such trust was granted to few women in her world.

After several days cruising the Channel they put into the port of Roscoff, with its newly built grey stone houses ranged behind the harbour to secure protection from English raiders. How proud she was as he handed her onto the shore. They stayed two nights in a fine room at the inn, where she marvelled at the food flavoured strongly with onions, and surprised him with her fluent French.

WALTER

By God and all that was holy, it was worth the wait! He was overwhelmed, carried away on a wave of love for this perfect woman! He'd known she wouldn't disappoint him in the marriage bed, but this was beyond his wildest imaginings! He'd found his heart's desire; his other half in all things. He'd been able to talk to Joan, but she had never really stirred his loins. Rather, they'd got their two boys through duty. His lust for Isabella had been snuffed out as soon as he knew how empty her head was. But in Katherine he had it all: beauty that drove him mad with desire; an educated mind that could argue, imagine and debate; nobility; humour and compassion. Best of all, she loved him in return; whole-hearted, undivided care shone from her eyes every time she looked at him. He'd never dreamt to find such a well of contentment; he'd never plumb its depths, however many glorious years they were granted together.

The temptation to just keep sailing on the silver sea, on and on to the far horizon and beyond, was tugging hard. But he wanted to show her off, to tell the world she was his, and his alone. The peace treaty agreed with France the previous year meant it should be safe to bring in his barques and trade in the French port without hindrance. How long that would last now that both England and France had a new King upon the throne he couldn't say. There were already signs the peace would crumble, and who knew what the new French King Henri might do. If he sided with the Scots there would surely be more trouble. But on that summers day, Walter rightly judged that his trade would be welcomed.

How the wealthy merchants of Roscoff, grown fat selling canvas all down the coast, had looked at him in envy to see that he, Walter Raleigh of Fardel, had such a prize on his arm! He chuckled. How she raised that pretty chin; how her eyes shone; how she smiled and laughed and squeezed his arm as they walked between the stone houses of the town. Walked? Why, he was strutting like a peacock! He laughed again, warm and throaty. How she'd gabbled away to the innkeeper in perfect

French. How they'd tested the bed in the inn's best room. He ran his fingers through her hair; traced the line of her collarbone; felt her stretch toward him, unhurried, welcoming.

A knock came. He groaned. He knew they would only be interrupted if it were truly needful. The ship's master stood hesitant, uncertain, pointing to the sky where dark clouds were gathering. They'd been meandering back in the Channel for a couple of days, locked together in the world of their love. Walter let out a reluctant breath, wrenched from the depths of his soul. A storm was brewing and they'd best set course for home.

TWENTY-FIVE
1547–1549
KATHERINE

WALTER REACHED FOR HER HAND AND SHOOK HIS HEAD AS HE gave the order. They set course for Exmouth, to start their life together in earnest.

Bessie met them at the gate, her face stricken. "Mistress, the young mistress is gone. She's nowhere to be found, though we've searched high and low. Master Walter, your son, Master John, has been out all over the county, hoping to have word of her, and not yet had time to tell us what he's found," she cried, her shrill voice growing louder and louder as the words came spilling out so fast she could hardly draw breath.

John Raleigh stood in the doorway. "Father, I do have some news, though it will grieve you to hear it. Over in Withycombe Raleigh I met one who had seen our Miss Katie. Father, it is our George that's taken her!"

Walter exploded, his white teeth flashing. "What foolishness is this?" he demanded. "Are you saying the silly girl has run away with George? Well, where are they, then?"

"None can say. I went to the priest and he told me how George begged him to marry them," replied John, meeting Walter's eye.

Katherine stood ashen-faced, her brows drawn together in an

angry line. She felt the solid ground of her new love shifting onto a quicksand of despair. She wouldn't have it! "That girl! That wicked girl will be the death of me! She's done this in pure spite, seeing me so happy with your father. But, John, surely the simpleton priest cannot have agreed to marry them? The girl's not of an age to be wed without her family's consent. And as for George, I have no time at all for him. He should have known better."

"We must fetch them back," said Walter icily, his face a mask of fury. "Just wait until I get my hands on that boy! He shall be no son of mine hereafter!"

"But no one knows where they may be, Father," said John.

"Walter, dearest, pray do not allow this to spoil the first days of our life together," Katherine pleaded. "'Tis what that minx wants: to see us all at sixes and sevens over her. Let us be patient and wait for more news before we upset our homecoming on her account."

Walter growled and sputtered, but had to agree that they must wait. "So be it," he said, frustration writ large on his handsome face. "George is a rascally knave to take advantage of the stupid girl, but I do see that there's nothing to be done now."

"At least George will get no wealth from the Gilbert estates," said Katherine with a rueful smile. "Otho left no instructions as to Katie's marriage portion. It seems he washed his hands of the wayward child years ago."

They didn't have to wait for long. Only a week had passed when George appeared, shamefaced and shaking, all his bravado and confidence gone. He shifted from foot to foot, twisting his cap in his hands. "Father, I do admit it freely: I was the biggest fool in the land to dally with Katie. But you must understand; you who have been so overtaken by your love for my good stepmother."

Katherine snorted and her lip curled, but he persevered.

"Surely you of all men can see how Katie's wild ways and dashing beauty took me by storm. I was out of my mind with love for her, and she kept teasing me on and on."

"George Raleigh, you're a grown man, and Katie a maid of only fourteen summers," Katherine hissed. She did not pause to consider that by that age she herself had been almost a mother. Oh, she could see that Katie had laid down a challenge to the philandering boy, whose earlier conquests had no doubt been easy and swift. But he was old enough to know better. And under his father's roof, too!

"Katie demanded that I make her my wife, or she'd have none of me."

"Fool!" Walter barked, then shook his head. "George, I'm beyond disappointment."

"But, Father, there was nothing for it. I had to defy all and make her my wife, or she said she'd call me out for a blackguard who had seduced her. So I gave in. Oh, Father, I did want her so!"

Katherine noticed the tears running down the boy's face. She looked at him more carefully, wondering for the first time why Katie wasn't with him.

"So," George continued, the words coming in short gasps as he gulped back his tears, "I found a priest to marry us with no questions asked, and we rode off together."

"What a toil," Katherine said quietly. "What a sorry toil indeed."

"But oh, she was so reckless. She knew no fear," said George, shaking as the words tumbled out. "We rode out along the very tops of the sandstone cliffs that border the sea, over beyond the silted mouth of the Otter and on toward Sidmouth. She laughed at me, and called out that she didn't care that the rain soaked her to her skin."

Katherine could well imagine.

"It was a wild day, and as the storm broke around us, I tried to persuade her not to go so near the edge. I knew it wasn't stable," said George, "but she would have none of it. She called me a craven coward. She went to push her horse forward, though the sensible beast reared up in fear. But, oh… How can I tell it? In a moment both were gone; fallen to the pebble beach and the sea swirling below."

Katherine gasped. A chill silence fell.

"How can you forgive me this? How can I ever forgive myself?" George wailed. "I loved her so, and now she's gone. I called for men to help me and we went to search for her at the foot of the cliff. In the storm, the tide ran high. We had to wait for the waters to retreat. We struggled against the wind and rain, and I dug into the heap of sand and earth with my bare hands, but we could not find her. It was such a fall. She could never have survived it. It must be that the sea's taken her and the horse as well. I don't know where she is." George's shoulders sagged and a ragged, wrenching sob tore from him.

Katherine stepped back and covered her mouth with her hand. It couldn't be true. She felt cold and dizzy as she sat down hard on the settle. Walter stepped forward and she felt his comforting arms around her. She sobbed on his chest. She had never known that child; never been able to calm her wilful ways. Now she was lost forever. She wanted to blame George, but could see no further than her own fault. Later she would admit to another emotion that had fought with her guilt. It was relief. She would no longer have to deal with Katie, the misguided girl who had never been happy.

"Don't cast George out. It won't bring her back," Katherine pleaded later, though how she would ever look George in the eye again, she couldn't say. But they must move on, and Walter needed both his boys.

"Aye, you're right," Walter replied, letting his breath out slowly. "The boy has faced the hardest of lessons. We must hope he's learned it well. Best get him out of the way for a while. He and John can take the *Lion* and the *Mary* down the French coast to bring back a cargo of wine and salt."

After they left, the household at Poer Hayes began to settle. It was not the start to married life Katherine and Walter had hoped for, but it only served to strengthen the bond between them.

"The girl was ever wayward, Katherine-Kate," he coaxed. "Whatever made her so is past undoing. Put her away with all the other memories of your old life. Let us go forward together. There are those still living that have need of us."

So Katherine locked away her grief, looked to her new household and turned her attention to timid, blonde-haired Mary. With gentle praise and kind words she started to draw her out as they sat sewing together. She found the shadowy presence of the girl, who looked like an angel, soothing. They walked together in the gardens, and in time Mary would even join Katherine on visits to her new neighbours.

In the autumn, Humphrey and Adrian came for a short visit. Humphrey was an arrogant lad, well aware of just how clever he was, but Walter soon captured his attention. They spent many an hour down on the quay or on board Walter's ships, where Humphrey plied the sailors with endless questions. Walter also talked to him about his time as a ward of old Vaux; an experience that had clouded his early years.

"My brother John is held as a ward too, and Adrian and I must do as Penkervell bids us," Katherine heard Humphrey announce. "Sir, what use is there in a likely boy like John wasting his time as a ward; a prize for some ageing courtier? There must be other ways for us boys to learn and serve our country?" Well, he was right, of course. But the precocious boy would hold forth his views to anyone. His opinionated ways wouldn't go down well with the Penkervells.

Adrian was happy to follow Katherine about the gardens and orchards. He had a natural eye for planting and seemed to know instinctively where a tree or bush would thrive best. But more than that, he loved to devise arrangements of plants that were pleasing to all the senses. His enthusiasm for the gardens, where they plotted new beds and walks, helped Katherine overcome some of the grief that threatened to darken what should have been her happiest time.

One afternoon, as the leaves were turning, lighting up the hillsides around Poer Hayes with splashes of vivid russet, gold and brown, Arthur came calling. The wind was chill, so they sat by the parlour fire as he shared the latest gossip.

"Joanie's given Denny another boy, and he's consolidating his position under the new order. Groom of the Stool to the young King now!" he said, laughing as he pinched his nose. "I saw Kat. She's in Chelsea with Tom Seymour and his new wife. That fellow was quick off the mark to wed the King's widow, I must say. They've set up a splendid household fit to put both the King's and the Protector's in the shade. Kat's charge is there with them, of course, and Seymour's also taken little Jane Grey as his ward. She's cousin to King Edward, so who knows what game Tom's playing? You can bet it's all to compete for power with his brother, Protector Somerset. Our Kat seems quite besotted with Tom Seymour. Aye, she's near as blinded by his charms, as is his new wife!" Arthur shook his head. "And now my Mary's been called to swell the ranks of ladies serving there. How will I get heirs, if she's always away at that rival court?"

"Well, Anthony Denny doesn't seem to have any problem in that department, even though Joanie's often at the Chelsea house, waiting on her friend," said Katherine, smiling. "Look how quickly the Dennys fill the nursery! Oh, Arthur, I do hope the Dowager Queen finds some happiness with Seymour. Just think how awful it must have been for her, wedded to the King as he grew older and fatter and even more bad-tempered! When I was a maid that was always my greatest fear: that Father would wed me to some ancient fool. Of course, you won't remember how Johnny used to tease me."

Arthur spluttered with laughter at the face she pulled. "Well, surely, Katherine-Kate, Raleigh's not quite so ancient, is he?" he cried, still chuckling. "You're right, though: Joanie brings forth babies like shelling peas. All the faithful ladies still flock to Kateryn Seymour's side as she builds her own court to compete with Somerset's wife. Now there's a difficult woman, that Anne Seymour. Always looks as if she's just sucked on a lemon!"

"But what about Thomas Seymour? I've heard the Admiral's very handsome," Katherine said. "He must have swept that lady right off her feet! I feel easier in my mind about marrying again so soon now I know that she didn't wait the customary two years after the King died; nor even two months, if the gossips are to be believed! But Seymour sounds dangerous to me. Hmmm…" She knit her brows, searching her memory. "Wasn't he out in Vienna as envoy for the King all those years ago when Johnny and Peter were there? I've always thought there was more to that mission of theirs than anyone would ever let on. Posing as merchants to get into the court of the Great Turk, indeed. Spying, more likely!"

"Well, I know nothing of that, but I'll tell you this. Our Kat might be inordinately fond of him, but even she's getting a bit worried about Tom Seymour's intentions with the Lady Elizabeth. He wanted to marry the girl before he took his present wife, and now Kat's hinted that his behaviour towards that maid isn't as it should be. She says he goes a-visiting the girl in her bedchamber every morning, and she not yet fourteen! Right under his wife's nose, too! I did advise Kat to tread carefully in this," said Arthur, raising his eyebrows.

"Yes, who knows where it all may lead? I do hope Kat will pay heed to your wise counsel. Now, where's Walter?" Katherine called, smiling to think of the little imp from the Modbury nursery now giving out advice to the august and formidable Kat.

Arthur spent a lot of time on that visit deep in conversation with Walter. There was much to discuss for those who favoured reform. Peter had published Nichols' paper about Crispin's misspeaking at Otho's month-mind, and it was more than likely that Crispin would soon be thrown into the Tower.

"I wonder what Otho would have thought to cause such controversy, Katherine-Kate," laughed Arthur. "The events at his month-mind have made him quite notorious throughout the land."

"Poor Otho," she said. "To think he only came to notice after his death."

At this, Walter pursed his lips. "Notice usually has to be earned," he snapped, crossing his arms over his chest. "I'm afraid your first husband did little to recommend himself in life. He could have treated you a lot better!"

Walter was quite prickly when it came to Otho. She nodded and smiled to show that she understood. "He did his best, Walter. His start in life was not of the easiest. Perhaps I could have I have helped him more, but we were over young when we wed."

Walter grunted, then continued in a more positive tone. "Good to hear that Peter has it in hand. Crispin and his ilk will get their comeuppance. Your Uncle George is well placed within the new hierarchy, and so is Joanie's Anthony. Better times are coming, Katherine-Kate."

He was right. When Walter's name appeared on the list of Justices of the Peace, she teased him mercilessly. "'Tis a fine thing you've a wife so far above you, to propel you to such heights," she joked.

"Well, I've achieved more than your first husband ever did," he shot back with a laugh.

As they rode through lanes shimmering under a lacy veil of blackthorn blossom, Katherine hummed a lilting melody, and Walter picked up the chorus. Peter had invited them to Mohun's Ottery. It was quite a gathering. Memories of Grandmother Carew came flooding back as she embraced Cousin Cecily, now a stately matron with a brood of children. Katherine turned and, taken unawares, stared at the priest standing beside Uncle George. John Pollard was still a strikingly handsome man, though he had perhaps put on a little weight. Eliza, who had also joined the party, blushed furiously as he led her aside.

"John's a sound fellow, you know. Served in the King's Chapel Royal. Took over the Archdeaconry of Cornwall for a time, back in '43," said Uncle George gently. "Held the fort when Bishop Veysey was dealing with the mess left by Thomas Wynter."

Katherine remembered the story that Wynter was the son of Cardinal Wolsey himself. Heavily in debt, he'd rented out the rights to the archdeaconry to a man named William Bodye, who harvested the Church's wealth for himself and was charged, as the King's agent, to strip away more. The Cornish people hated him.

"I doubt if it's finished in Cornwall," said Uncle George, smiling as Eliza dimpled as Pollard took her hand. "It's a powder keg just waiting for the spark. Pollard is Archdeacon of Barnstaple now. He's all right. It's not his only living, and he's got a fine house in Exeter close to the cathedral. All will be well for Eliza in time."

Rumours were flying that priests would soon be allowed to marry and live with their wives openly. But Katherine still wasn't sure whether she should warn Eliza to stay well clear of the handsome priest or encourage her to take her chance of happiness.

She didn't have long to ponder. The two priests returned to Exeter after only two days.

"Bodye's been killed by a mob on the steps of Helston's church as he tried to remove statues and valuables," announced Peter, his colour rising. "They rang the bells to call for support; declared they'd have the laws of King Henry until his son's of age. Much good will it do them! The Protector must make an example of the ringleaders, or more trouble will follow."

Walter was needed in Exmouth where his boys had just brought in a cargo, but Katherine and Mary stayed on with Eliza and Cecily. Katherine took an immediate liking to Peter's wife, Margaret. *It's easy to see how she might once have caught King Henry's eye,* she thought, as her hostess told them all about Peter's grandiose plans to improve his ancestral home. The finest embroiderers were working on a red-and-white silk tester and hangings for the new chamber by the gatehouse, and sheets edged with gold lace.

"We'll have new hangings for the other chamber too, of black and yellow, I think," said Margaret, who was clearly not sparing her fortune.

Listening to the musicians in the solar was just like the old days, and Katherine relaxed.

"Why, Katherine, you look so well," said Margaret softly. "Fair blossoming, if I may be so bold! It seems to me that Master Raleigh may soon have cause to celebrate. Am I right?"

"Your eyes are sharp," laughed Katherine. "Yes, indeed, I do hope for another baby in due time. We would be honoured if you would stand as godmother."

"But of course, my dear," Margaret replied, and the conversation turned easily to other matters.

Katherine came to love the peace and quiet of the farmstead which lay waiting for her amid the rose-tinted orchards under that Maytime sky. It was a rambling old place, much extended to include a new parlour and kitchen that shared a huge chimney. Next to the kitchen hearth a brushwood oven served for baking their bread. Above the hall, several bedchambers nestled tightly under the eaves, all reached by a rickety oak stair. All Poer Hayes lacked was a brewhouse.

"Walter, my dear," she said, "it's neither wise nor convenient that we must resort to the alewife in Budleigh to keep the household supplied."

His eyes glowed as he promised that she would have one.

In the evenings they sat together on an oak settle before the fire like any country couple, musing on the day's doings and the ways of the world.

"Well, Tom Seymour's attentions to that girl were too much for even his love-blinded wife to stand," Arthur said in shocked tones the next time he called at the farm. "Kat and her charge, Elizabeth, have removed to Joanie and Anthony's place at Cheshunt. Seymour's ambition knows no bounds. I fear he'll pull others down with him, should he fall. Our Kat's overly tolerant of the dashing Admiral,

Katherine-Kate; I do declare, she's half in love with the man herself! Who'd have thought our plump, middle-aged sister would be so foolish? John Ashley should keep her in check."

Soon after Father's death, Kat had found a man who would take her on. John Ashley was a cousin of Anne Boleyn and served her daughter along with Kat.

"Well," said Katherine, "I'm sorry for Seymour's wife. That gentle lady has had a hard time of it, and now it sounds as if her new husband plays fast and loose with her love for him. A woman's lot can be hard to bear."

"The ringleaders of the Helston riots have been put to death to deter others from rebelling against the King's laws," Arthur said, changing the subject. "Times are hard, though. There's still a lot of murmuring."

"Bessie brings back tales from the marketplace of people struggling to make ends meet; of starving children," Katherine replied. "I do fear the countryside's ripe for unrest to fester."

"Aye, wheat's now at four times its price but two years since," said Arthur. "Times are hard indeed for the ordinary people."

"That's as may be, but they will mix it all up with religion," Walter cut in, his frustration clear in his voice. "They're a narrow-minded lot, in truth. Dig their heels in against any change, even when it's good for them. I do wish they'd grasp that the new ways of worship are no threat."

"Walter, they fear the loss of their age-old ceremonies," Katherine interjected patiently, for this was a discussion they often had. "The Church and its festivals have marked out the rhythm of their lives for generations. They find it hard to give them up."

"You might have thought that the townsfolk would be more open to new ideas," Walter blustered. "But a lot of the rich merchants in Exeter still cling to their traditions. And Bishop Veysey's certainly not a champion of reform; he's hardly ever here."

Katherine twisted the posie ring he'd given her on the day they wed round and round on her finger and bit her lip. Perhaps it was just the fears of a silly pregnant woman. But Walter was so outspoken, so fervent in his embrace of reform. One day it might put him in danger.

"Walter, things are moving forward. Best keep on the right side of the Seymours," Arthur warned. "Somerset's bought Berry Pomeroy, so he's a neighbour of sorts."

"Did you see Tom Seymour's lady wife, then?" Katherine asked.

"That I did," he replied with a smile. "I wouldn't be surprised if she soon has a little one in the cradle, though it's taken until her fourth marriage."

He was right. A few weeks later Kateryn Seymour was delivered of a daughter around the time that Katherine entered her confinement above the parlour in the farmhouse at East Budleigh. In that room – not closed and shuttered, but with the windows open to let in the September sun – Katherine's labour was short, and her dark-haired daughter came into the world bawling loudly. They named her Margaret for Peter's wife. Walter was delighted, and Mary doted on her new sister, rocking the cradle and laughing as the baby grasped her finger if she put it near. Kat sent a gift for the baby, and a letter that bore the sad news that the Dowager Queen had not lived long at Sudeley to enjoy being a mother.

"So that's another woman dead while bringing new life into the world, Eliza," Katherine remarked to her sister, who had stayed on after Margaret was born. "Thanks be that I'm hale and hearty, and this rosy-cheeked little maid has such a strong grip on life."

"Yes, indeed, we women have much to bear. But I'm full of hope," Eliza replied, beaming. "Parliament's due to meet soon, Katherine-Kate. Reform is on the cards. The Bishops are talking about a new Book of Common Prayer, and all church services will soon be in English."

After his wife's death, Thomas Seymour really overstepped the mark. The following January he was charged with treason, caught trying to break into the King Edward's apartments at Hampton Court. His brother, Protector Somerset, did nothing to save him, and the following March he went to the scaffold. Kat was held in the Tower under suspicion of abetting the Admiral's attempts to wed the King's sister. But no proof was found against her and in time she was released.

On the streets of Exeter, in Exmouth market and even in the tavern run by the alewife in East Budleigh, voices were raised. They railed against a new poll tax on sheep that would hit the people of Devon hard. Wild rumours ran rife. Walter had to reprimand one of the Poer Hayes serving men for saying that new taxes would soon extend to geese and pigs, upon which many relied for their winter diet and Christmas table. Still the rumour mill ground on.

As they sat at their fireside one March evening, Walter gave an impatient snort. "Zounds! The fools look back at the past and see it painted in a rosy hue, Katherine-Kate. They think they remember a time before the King took the monasteries, when Henry Courtenay was high lord in the West, and all was well. The fools hanker after some dream of a past when the sun shone every day and everyone had plenty of food on the table. Now you and I know that it never was like that."

"But, Walter," she answered, "there are those that feed those dreams with rumour and lies. The Cornish are already seething after that business at Helston. I'm afraid they'll drag our men into rebellion."

"The men of Devon won't be so foolish, dear heart," he said, patting her hand. "They hate change. They'll complain, but I doubt they'll be that stupid."

TWENTY-SIX

1549

KATHERINE

WHIT SUNDAY MORNING: A FINE JUNE DAY; SHAFTS OF SUN
bursting through fluffy clouds that scudded over Hayes Wood
like bundles of new-washed wool ready for the carding. Katherine
stretched lazily, but there was no time to luxuriate in her feather
bed and enjoy another hour with Walter. From this day Archbishop
Cranmer's new prayer book would be used in every church in the land.
Bessie had laid out her best gown and Walter put on a new doublet to
do justice to the occasion. Smartly arrayed, they set out to walk the
short distance to church. Mary tripped along beside Katherine. The
girl was growing more beautiful with every passing day. But however
good a catch she might be, Katherine was determined that she would
not be rushed into marriage. Neither Mary nor her Margaret would
be wed as she had been: too young to know themselves, let alone the
world. A vision of Katie popped into her head. She pursed her lips
and looked hard at George Raleigh, carefree and laughing beside his
more sober brother.

They took their place on Walter's bench and the congregation
crowded in. The priest wore no fine vestments. The words were
simple and clear. As she stood at the head of the line of women to
receive the Communion, Katherine thought that surely this was as

the Lord intended when he said, 'Take, eat in remembrance of me.' Not just for one priest to mysteriously hold the Host aloft, divided from the people by some ornate rood screen. No, it was surely right that everyone could join together in a simple act of faith, not just at Easter or on their deathbed, but as part of their everyday worship.

They stood at the head of two columns, one of men and the other of women, like two lines of dancers at the Twelfth Night revels. She grinned at Walter, thinking that it would take but a step and she could cast off and lead her women round the men. Those less welcoming of change made that same comparison to a Christmas dance, saying that the new way diminished the celebration of the Mass. Even in sleepy East Budleigh there were murmurings and mutterings after the service ended and they spilled out into the sunshine. The gossipmongers were doing their work well.

A few days later Bessie burst in, outraged and trembling. "Mistress, they say in Exmouth market that a farmer – William Hellyons by name; by all accounts he was a fair and honest man – the poor man was run through with a pitchfork on the steps of the church house at Sampford Courtenay! Protesting about the new prayer book and all, they were, and he tried to talk 'em out of their folly when the Justices feared to act," she blubbered, near wheezing in her distress. The news had spread to every part of the county, as if a trail of gunpowder had been lit. "And now Sampford Courtenay has found common cause with the men of Cornwall. They're all marching together towards Crediton. More are joining them as they go. Oh, oh, we'll all be murdered in our beds!"

"Nonsense, Bessie," Walter scolded. "'Tis but resistance to the new ways. Our Devon men will soon calm down. They'll see sense. I'm sure of it."

The story was that Father Harper, the rector at Sampford Courtenay, had held the Whit Sunday service in English as the law required. But the people swarmed out of the church like angry hornets, vowing to return the next day. So, on Whit Monday they demanded that the priest revert to the service they knew. No doubt there were agitators there, stirring up the crowd; disaffected priests and supporters of the old order kindling the fire, telling the assembled masses how courtiers, not content with swallowing whole the riches of their abbeys, would steal away the church treasures the people's own guilds had provided. It was easy to see how people with little to lose might be swayed. So the scene was set. A commotion led to the first bloodshed in the county. William Hellyons was slain and the malcontents enticed more and more to their cause.

As she sat with Margaret upon her knee, Katherine felt a tremor of fear. "Walter, Cornishmen are rallying to the banner of the Five Wounds and the men of Devon are joining them. 'Twill be like the Northern Rising years back."

"Don't fret. Miles Coverdale's on his way to the West Country to persuade the people to calm down. All will be well," he said.

But the King's Council, fully stretched by war with both France and Scotland, misjudged the strength of feeling. It was too late for persuasion, and Miles had little success. A week passed before Walter heard that help was coming.

"Gawen and Peter are on their way now, Katherine-Kate, with orders to persuade everyone to go home. I'm sure they'll soon have it all under control."

But the rebels had dug in near Crediton. On Saturday the twenty-second day of June, Katherine was overseeing the cherry picking when Walter sauntered through the orchard gate, booted and spurred.

"I've had enough of kicking my heels here," he announced.

"No, no, Walter, please don't go. Don't leave us all undefended here," she implored. In her panic she upset the basket, scattering ruby fruit across the grass. Bessie scrambled to pick them up, her face as pale as the new-washed linen drying in the sun.

"Dearest Katherine-Kate, would I leave you here if there were really any danger?" he said, patting her back and brushing his lips over her brow. "I'm quite certain you'll be safe. I doubt much will happen at all. Peter's sure to get them to see sense. If anything does flare up it'll soon be snuffed out. Have no fear, my dear love. I'll only ride to Exeter to find the latest news and be back before you have time to miss me."

She followed him to his waiting horse, still clutching his hand. She nearly pulled off his leather glove in a last desperate attempt to hold him there, but knew it was useless. As she stretched up to receive his kiss she saw the sword at his belt, the short dagger nearly hidden in his boot. He might be all jaunty reassurance, but it looked as though Walter was prepared for anything. He bent from the saddle and stretched out his gloved hand to smooth the wrinkles from her brow. How she loved him!

WALTER

He was in high spirits. It was a fine day and all was quiet. It'd all blow over in a day or two, he was sure of it. But he'd had enough of sitting idly by. In these times a man must answer the call to defend what he believed in. These misguided people must obey the laws of the land and give up their silly superstitions. Peter and Gawen Carew were both strong for reform, and he would support them.

He headed for the bridge at Bishop's Clyst, his thoughts all of Katherine. He was sorry he'd vexed her. What a woman she was! What happiness she'd brought him! He'd find a gift for her in the city. Whistling, he tried to decide what might light up her lovely face.

As he rounded a slight bend in the road his horse shied. He struggled to regain his seat, and then he saw the old woman. No wonder the horse had balked. In her dark clothes, chanting away with her rosary beads, she was enough to frighten anyone. Walter felt his anger rising. She had no business with those Papist fripperies. The horse threw up his head and refused to budge. There was nothing for it. He'd have to get down and lead the animal forward. Fuming, he dismounted and moved towards her.

"These are the old ways, crone," he yelled as he reached out an arm to snatch the beads from her hand. "You must put aside these relics and come to the new learning. You should know, we have laws in this land that require you to set them aside."

The woman's face contorted and she flailed about, trying to regain the rosary. He held it high, just out of her reach, as she capered around him.

"These have been good enough for us Devon folk until now. Who are you to rob me of them?" she shrieked.

He bared his teeth and planted his feet wide apart. "I am Walter Raleigh, hag, and you will desist," he commanded, raising the rosary higher.

She made a desperate grab for the beads and, as he moved to calm the horse, managed to get her fingers on them. She clung on. So did he. The thread broke and the beads scattered into the road. She looked down, her face stricken, then, all on a sudden, picked up her skirts and ran off in the direction of the church.

"Wouldn't have thought that beldame could move so quick," he muttered under his breath as his horse's hooves ground the beads into the dust.

He shrugged, mounted up again and pushed on toward the bridge. He had not gone far when he pulled up and cocked his head to one side. What was that? Drumming? Feet running over the hard-baked road? He wheeled his horse round to see a crowd of youths packed between the lane's high banks, brandishing cudgels and sticks. A few even had knives already drawn. They crowded closer, yelling at him.

"God's blood," he cursed. The old woman must have run to the church and brought them. "Hold hard! What do you here, my boys?"

Other men were advancing with a heavy piece of ordnance he'd seen before in Topsham.

"Good God," he muttered. "They've joined the rebels' cause. They're going to bar the road." His hand flew to his sword hilt, ready to draw and defend himself. But there were so many he changed his mind. Best flee. He set his heels to the frightened beast's flanks and the gelding charged forward into the melee, scattering men and weapons.

Walter struggled to get his horse under control, but after a moment or two was able to spur out of the crush. When he glanced back down the lane, fights seemed to be breaking out. He recognised an Exmouth sailor landing a blow on a skinny lad. His attackers then turned their attention to the mob who had suddenly appeared behind them. Walter pressed his horse onward, round the next bend in the road. Out of sight, he turned off towards the chapel, barely visible amongst the trees. Best hide and wait. He tethered his mount quickly, well hidden behind the walls, and pushed the ancient door aside.

Sitting in the musty darkness, he let his breathing subside. *That was a near thing.* He grinned. Those sailors, men who'd served on his ships and had their share of the spoils when his boys took a prize, must have been following him. They must have seen him leave Poer Hayes as they came up through East Budleigh on some errand of their own and thought to protect him from the mob! Well, they were better informed than he. He'd meant what he said. He'd really believed the East Devon men would have more sense. This was serious. He must get to Exeter and report to Peter.

The sailors must have done their job well, for all remained quiet around his hiding place. Much later, when he thought the road must again be safe, he ventured out.

He found Peter lodged at The Mermaid, trying to determine his next move. Walter told him that the rebels were planning to bar the road to Exeter . "So it's not just at Crediton?" he blustered, pacing around the inn's best chamber like a caged lion. "By God, they're well organised, Walter. When I got to Crediton, I was met by a well-armed force. Trenches, heavy plough chains hung across the road, and men hidden in barns by the highway, ready to loose arrows at us. We couldn't pass the barricades. I don't know how we'd have fared if the barns hadn't caught fire. Dry as tinder, they were, and the blaze scattered the rebels. I gave no order to fire those barns." He stared at Sir Hugh Pollard, who looked as though he'd seen better days. "Did one of your men decide to smoke the rebels from their holes? If so, it worked."

Before Pollard could answer, Walter jumped in. "They'll blame you for burning the barns, Peter. What next?"

"Parlay at Clyst Bridge, I think."

The next morning, they clattered out of the city. As they neared the village, one of Sergeant Prideaux's men suddenly barged across the road, grabbed the reins of Peter's horse and shoved him from the saddle. A shot whistled past but found no mark. Men quickly overcame the marksman, identified as Hammond, a smith from Woodbury.

"Aye, I did raise my weapon and fired straight at you, heretic," he spat as he struggled in the grip of two burly men. "I'd rid the world of you and all your sort."

As they bundled him away, a white-faced Peter gritted his teeth. "Thanks to your man's swift action, Prideaux, no harm's been done. Raise the white flag. We must parlay."

He'd chosen his envoys carefully. Sir Hugh Pollard, Sir Thomas Denys and Thomas Yarde were all well known to the rebels, and Peter hoped that they might be trusted. But after protracted talks they had made no progress. Back at The Mermaid, Peter was in despair.

"I've tried to carry out my orders from Protector Somerset; tried to avoid bloodshed. But it's past that now. Once the men of the West are riled there's no stopping them. No, they'll fight to the last drop of blood, and they've got Arundel at their head. The Protector must send a force to quell them. I'll have to go myself to persuade him. We'll have to trust in the Mayor and the Aldermen of the city to stay loyal while I'm gone."

"I'll lead a party of men out through the East Gate with a great show. That should distract them while you slip away," Walter offered.

Peter's face brightened. "Good man, Raleigh," he said, clapping him on the back.

It was a bold and brave move, and it worked like a dream. But as Peter set his spurs to his horse's flanks to find his way through little-known byways, the rebels fell on Walter and his troop. Outnumbered, hurled to the ground, his sword snatched from his hand, he thought this was it; his end was come. He waited. He thought of Katherine's steadfast eyes. But the blow did not fall. Instead a Cornishman spoke up, his accent so broad it was hard to untangle the words. The gist of it seemed to be that such a fine gentleman as Raleigh might prove useful as a hostage. They bound his arms and led him towards St Sidwell's Church, not far beyond the city walls.

Thrown into the dimly lit space beneath the bell loft, Walter found he was not alone. He recognised Thomas Colyford of Cullompton and John Stowell of Exeter. A couple of others he did not know. Walter looked up at the stone walls of the tower stretching high above him, trying to see a means of escape. Boards had been nailed up to cover the arched opening that led towards the steep steps to the loft above. If they tried to climb up there they would surely fall to their deaths.

The door slammed shut. He heard the key turn in the lock. As Stowell untied the cord that held his hands he muttered, "At least my life's been spared. God willing, Peter has escaped and will bring reinforcements to put a clean end to this business."

At first they disdained to touch the stale bread and thin gruel the guards brought them. But after a few days hunger drove them to fall on the meagre offerings, scrapping like starving dogs. For drink they had but water, which Walter hoped was taken from the clean well he knew lay nearby. The bells were silent. No services marked the passing of the hours. He found a fragment of stone, perhaps fallen when repairs had been made at some long-forgotten time. As the first tiny shaft of light came through the boards of the loft, each day he scratched a mark on the wall with that stone. He watched as the tally grew. Sometimes they heard commotions outside, but had no way of knowing if the city fathers had surrendered. Their rations were just enough to keep body and soul together, but as the days passed they all began to weaken.

Thoughts of Katherine, safe at home and well guarded by his boys, were his only solace. He conjured the memory of her upon *the Trinity* that day, and tears filled his eyes as he vowed that he would survive to see her again.

KATHERINE

Katherine watched the gate between the two yew trees for the return of her man. George, sent out for fresh supplies of ale, met some of the sailors who had come to Walter's aid. They told him how they had seen his father hidden safely in the chapel, but couldn't say if he'd reached the city. The old woman had decried Walter, and the sailors said he was a marked man. Katherine feared for her dear love, but for the first time she also felt real anxiety for those waiting at home. Even their own village might be harbouring rebels.

She gathered the household together in the parlour. "Best not venture out to church next Sunday," she said. "Stay close to the house. John and George, have timber cut and barriers raised. We must protect our home."

They lined up all the billhooks, sickles, scythes, sticks, staffs and staves they could find. They laid out the bows and the supply of arrows Walter kept against the next call to muster. Two hackbutts and some powder and shot stood in readiness. The two boys were well trained and had their armour and swords. If she had to, Katherine knew she would raise a cudgel herself to protect her own. They had enough food, but if matters were not resolved soon she'd have to send out for ale again. How she wished Walter had got the new brewhouse built! Concentrating on practical matters helped still the fear that gripped her. But as she lay alone in their bed, dark dreams troubled her sleep.

When she rose in the morning she had black rings under her eyes. Katherine felt a burning anger against those who had taken her man from her. She directed that anger into terse commands and harsh words, with endless rounds to check that all was well prepared. The boys were in awe of the fierce termagant she'd become.

Goodman Carter, a man well known to her as a steadfast supporter of reform, came to their gate with barrels of fresh ale and what news there was. "Sir Peter wants to avoid bloodshed. He sent envoys – men they would trust – to parlay with the rebel leaders," he said. "Sir Thomas Denys, Thomas Yarde and Sir Hugh Pollard came back after hours of talks with no agreement. The rebels have drawn up their defences by the river. They think to starve Exeter so that they can take it for their own stronghold. Mistress Raleigh, some of the men from our village have joined the rebels, more's the pity. But there's as many that stand fast to the King's laws."

She had the casks filled and set rations for each of them, supplementing the ale with a raid on Walter's best wine. For food they would not want. The cows were safe in the shippen for milk and butter. They had plenty of eggs, and could kill some hens if need be. She had carefully hoarded supplies of salt fish and bacon. In time they might run short of wheat flour, but they had raisins and rice, prunes and a few wizened apples. The animals must still be tended, the cows milked, the butter churned, the baby cared for, and the laundry done. Ordering her people about these daily tasks helped Katherine keep a slim hold on sanity. Of Walter there was no word. As time went on she struggled to keep a calm face before Mary and Margaret. Days of absence became weeks.

Goodman Carter came again. "The Mayor and Aldermen watched them bring their banner of the Five Wounds close to the city gates. But, Mistress Raleigh, God be praised – the city leaders stayed loyal to the King, and the gates remained locked and barred. Exeter's in for a long, hungry time of it."

One morning she found that George was missing and a horse gone from the stables.

"Mother, he wants to offer his sword to fight with the King's forces," John told her.

"Well, how he'll find those forces, I don't know," she snapped. "Let him take his chance. I'll shed no tears for his leaving us."

Bad weather and a lack of labour delayed the haymaking. On the morning of the sixth day of August, Katherine set the serving men to salvage what they could from the meadow and build a rick close by the house. She glanced toward the lane and grabbed a stout staff. A group of men were shuffling towards the village, supporting each other and stumbling along at a snail's pace. As they drew closer, Katherine put down the staff. She could see blood on their tunics and bandages about their heads.

"What can this mean?" she whispered to John.

But John had no more idea than she.

Later that day, Goodman Carter appeared at the gate once more, a broad smile on his face. "There's been a big battle at Clyst Heath. The King's forces have won the day, and the meadows are stained by the blood of those rebels. The men you saw walking through our village, they're the lucky ones. They're wounded, but they can stumble home."

"My thanks for bringing this welcome news, Goodman Carter, and for your kind care of us in these times. You'll be well rewarded when Master Raleigh returns. It can't be long before Lord Russell's troops relieve the city and everyone can get on with their lives again. And I shall have my husband restored to me."

Goodman Carter could not meet her eye.

WALTER

In the tower at St Sidwell's his tally of days had gone past thirty. It was hard to believe that they had been locked up for five weeks. As the shaft of light hit the wall beside him that morning, he rubbed his eyes and stretched his aching legs. His ears pricked up. It was quiet. No voices; no laughter; no feet scraping on flagstones. Silence.

Shaking, he hauled himself to his feet and tiptoed towards the door. The others were awake by now, staring at him. He put a finger to his lips and leaned on the heavy door. It creaked and swung open. He screwed up his eyes, blinked like an owl, and peered into the sunlight flooding through the empty doorway. There was no one there! He beckoned to the others and they stumbled out into the empty church. All the plate, silver cups and rich vestments were unguarded. He would never really understand what made him do it, but in that instant, he and John Stowell saw a chance to make away with those riches. Perhaps it was that they were potent symbols of the rebels' cause. Perhaps it was pure avarice on his part; to gain something from his long incarceration. Concealing his share of the church plate and vestments beneath his cloak, he joined the others rubbing their eyes in the unaccustomed light beyond the door.

Summoning what was left of his strength, Walter shuffled toward the East Gate, his legs so weak that each step brought a stab of pain. Clutching the stolen goods in one hand, he raised the other and pounded on the rough boards. The others joined him, and they all hammered on the gate until their fists ached. But no answer came.

At last, a noise came from beyond the gate. A bloodshot eye peered out through a crack in the timbers. A gruff shout: "Identify yourselves, you ragtag ruffians. I'll not fall for any ruse from you blasted rebels. I'll not open the gate."

"Go to and fetch the Mayor or any of the Aldermen if you don't believe it is I, Walter Raleigh of Poer Hayes. No rebels here. We're all friends of this city, and we've been held for weeks in St Sidwell's tower."

Muffled voices, then feet retreating. Walter peered through the crack in the gate's timbers. He noticed that some of the boards were new; others charred and blackened.

"'Twas them rebels," the ageing gatekeeper replied when Walter quizzed him. "Thought they could burn us out, they did. Set fire to the gate and the flames spread to the houses yonder." With his eye close to the crack between the boards Walter could just make out a solitary chimney stack standing precariously, black against the sky. "Reckoned without us true Exeter folks, they did," the man went on with a toothless grin. "Take more than they to shift us, so it would. Us all ran to beat out the blaze and see 'em off. They rapscallion Cornishmen was all afeared to come inter our city through they flames. Us stood firm behind the blaze. After they turned tail even the priests and the Aldermen carried buckets of water to put it out."

At last the Mayor himself, John Blackaller, came puffing along and cut short the gateman's tale with a whoop. "Master Raleigh, God be praised. I never thought to see you again! The city stood firm. To see you free gives me hope that the danger is past."

Walter ate sparingly of the feast the Mayor had ordered. He knew from long sea voyages that to eat too much too soon after a long period of near starvation could be dangerous. News of the victory at Clyst Bridge had soon reached the city, and the people of Exeter, long deprived of decent rations, rushed out to bring in cattle and slaughtered them for the feast. Many did not follow Walter's example, and so much meat on empty stomachs made them ill. Some even died. After giving a full account of their captivity, Walter and Stowell sent most of the stolen items to be hidden at Stowell's house. But Walter kept hidden in his saddlebag one finely embroidered silk cope.

KATHERINE

Katherine would not let down her guard. The dispersed rebels could still pose a threat to her small empire as they fled to escape the Earl of Bedford's men. So when she saw a lone horseman advancing down the lane, she picked up the nearest weapon to hand. Gripping the sharp billhook, she called for John and stood watching warily at the door. She stared, mouth open, as the horse passed between the yews.

"Is it? Can it really be?" she muttered as she stumbled forward. Then she ran out screaming at the top of her voice, still brandishing the billhook. "Walter, Walter, my dearest husband, can it really be you? Are you returned to me?"

In a moment he was off his horse and had her in his arms. "Katherine-Kate, my only love, I am home at last. Though I am in much fear of my welcome here," he laughed. "I did not look to be met by such a fierce warrior come to slay me afore I'm off my horse." Taking the weapon gently from her grasp, he touched her face, murmuring, "It's over, my dear love. I am home."

As the afternoon sun slanted through the chamber window, they lay together on the feather mattress. At first she had no eyes to see how changed he was, how thin and ravaged. Such was her delight in the miracle that had brought him home to her that she saw none of the changes weeks of starvation had wrought. He was there; that was all that mattered. But later, as she lay in his arms, she traced his razor-sharp cheekbones with her finger and looked deep into his sunken eyes. Resting her head against his chest as he drifted into a satisfied slumber, she found she could feel every rib poking through his skin. But her Walter was whole. He was home. All else could, in time, be remedied.

Later, as he ate, he looked hard at her. "I see new rings around those pretty eyes, my dear," he said, spooning another mouthful from the platter. "Hmm! I think perhaps I see a bit less of you, though nothing to compare with all the weight I've shed. But you're still my own Katherine-Kate. How have you fared here while I was having such a high time in St Sidwell's tower?"

John spoke up, nodding and grinning. "'Tis my good lady mother that has kept us all safe here, Father," he said, the admiration clear in his voice. "She commanded us all; drilled us as though we were her troops in battle. She ran the household as well as any quartermaster. Had us muster our weapons, and kept us all safe and fed through this Commotion Time."

Walter laid a hand on her shoulder. "So the fine lady I wed can turn her hand to fierce action to safeguard her own, can she?" he said, with no hint of mockery. "Fetch me that saddlebag. I have brought a prize for you, my valiant lady." He brought out the embroidered cope, and presented it to her. "I remembered how you spoke with such envy of the fine bed-hangings Margaret will have at Mohun's Ottery," he said, unable to keep the proud ring from his voice. "So I have brought you this. My warrior wife, it will make a fine tester for our bed."

She didn't ask how he'd come by it. She found she really didn't care. She had that cope hemmed and placed over their bed, and made cushions of the remaining fabric. It would forever be a reminder of that dreadful time.

The whole country was in a ferment that summer. If all the insurgents had joined forces, perhaps the outcome would have been different. As it was, none of the uprisings lasted long. Joanie's husband fought with Russell in Norfolk, where, stirred by land enclosures, the people had followed a man named Kett. When Anthony Denny returned to Cheshunt he was very ill having contracted some battlefield contagion. On the tenth day of September he died, leaving Joanie a very wealthy widow with a brood of children to settle in the world. Katherine sent messages of condolence but, with Walter so lately restored to her, was loath to leave him even to support Joanie.

When everything had calmed down, Humphrey and Adrian came for a short visit. George arrived, full of exaggerated tales of his role in the action at Clyst Bridge. The boys hung on his every word, though Mary's lovely face was rigid as she held Margaret on her lap.

"The King's forces were in total disarray," George announced, raising his voice. "The Earl's men were in retreat from Arundel, and there was bloody fighting indeed." He waved an arm theatrically, as though making a sword thrust.

Katherine watched Humphrey's face, alight with fascination,

wrinkled her nose and swallowed hard. He was sure to want to hear all the gory details.

"I was with Grey's band. When we reached Clyst St Mary, the rebels were on the other side of the bridge," George went on. "It wasn't looking good for Lord Russell and his men, so our leader wanted to get across the river as quickly as he could. But the bridge was defended and we could find no way across. Then along came John Yarde of Treasurer's Bere, who knew the lay of the land. He showed Lord Grey how our troops could cross at a shallow point, not by the bridge. We were soon caught up in the action."

That must be Thomas Yarde's brother, thought Katherine, remembering that, like Thomas, he served Bishop Veysey.

"The thatched roofs were all set on fire. A lot of the rebels were put to the sword, but others were taken alive." George turned to Humphrey. "What do you think we did with all the prisoners, then, lad?"

Humphrey fixed blazing eyes on George. "I would have killed them all; hanged 'em from the highest tree!"

"Bloodthirsty little wretch," laughed Walter. "No doubt Grey showed mercy to the stupid fools and sent them home?"

"Father, it was not so. Grey ordered that the prisoners held by the King's troops must be slain."

Mary's face was white as a sheet and she looked like to faint away.

"That's enough, George," Walter growled. "Best we put it all behind us and be thankful that the our King won the day."

So George took Humphrey outside to tell him all about the dispatch of those prisoners; an event that sent shock waves through Devon when it became widely known. Corpses were left to rot in the fields and meadows around Clyst St Mary. For years after, Katherine shuddered as she passed that way, thinking of all the lives lost in the name of religion. Those lucky enough to escape went home chastened. A few of the leaders, including Humphrey Arundel, were taken up and put to death. The King's Council determined to make an example of them to deter any who might think to disobey the laws of the land. Open resistance to the new laws was at an end. The new prayer book was used in every church, and Preacher Coverdale stayed in Devon, hoping to win everyone over.

"Good thing Miles is out and about," said Walter to Arthur, who had called at Poer Hayes when the leaves were just beginning to fall. "Old Veysey's been conspicuous by his absence! I suppose he'd rather be in Sutton Coldfield."

"Aye, people resent that he's diverted so much money from Exeter. He's set up new charities and schools in his home town," Arthur replied.

"His days as Bishop must be numbered. He's eighty-odd if he's a day, and he's been a drag on reform long enough," said Walter, daring to say openly what others had been thinking privately for a long time.

Arthur had played his part in the victory. He'd been in London when Peter appealed to the Council, and with Russell at Mohun's Ottery, which Peter had placed at the Earl's disposal. He'd fought alongside Francis Russell, the Earl's son and a comrade-in-arms from the Siege of Boulogne. "Got my reward, Katherine-Kate," he laughed. "The clapper bells they took out of all the churches so they can never again be used to summon the people to rebellion. The lead will fetch a good price. I went down to Modbury and seized the cross and plate, too. Sold it all to raise money to pay the King's army. Got to keep in with whoever's in charge of the Council, you know. They're all at each other's throats. I don't think Edward Seymour will last much longer. He's stretched the King's forces too far, waging war with both Scotland and France at the same time. He should have dealt with uprisings like our West Country Commotion much more decisively. And on top of that, he's depleted the King's coffers to build up his own splendid estates."

"To please that pushy wife of his," Walter replied. "Be sure to keep yourself well positioned, my boy."

"I've come from Compton, trying to get Penkervell to agree to send Humphrey to school," said Arthur. "The boy's getting more unruly by the day! Eton's the place to sort him out. But Penkervell's digging his heels in about the cost. You know he's pressing a case to take back a portion of your boy's lands? He says that might be enough to pay the fees. It's blackmail of a sort, but it might be the best answer."

Katherine nodded. She knew her brother was right. Last time her second son had visited she'd been quite shocked by his arrogance, and the way he picked on Adrian. "It's kind of you to take this on for me, Arthur," she said. "I'm convinced it will be best for Humphrey. Perhaps he'll also learn some tolerance and humility. Adrian has a different nature. He can wait his turn."

So, in time, Humphrey went to school. Somerset was pitched off the see-saw that autumn, and eventually arrested. Arthur had been wise to find favour with John Dudley, who everyone thought would eventually hold the reins of power. In November, Arthur was knighted. Sir Arthur Champernowne! It had a fine ring!

TWENTY-SEVEN
1550–1554
KATHERINE

ELIZA WAS NOW THE WIFE OF JOHN POLLARD, AND SHE WAS happy. On a fine afternoon she sat with Katherine in the chamber at Poer Hayes, where another baby slept soundly in the cradle.

"'Tis a fine thing to name him for our mother's family," Eliza said, as beams of afternoon sunlight streamed in.

"Well, 'tis more for Cousin Peter, who stood godfather. My Walter does value his friendship so, though I worry that rapscallion will lead another of my menfolk into rash adventures one day," Katherine replied with a little grimace.

"I thought you'd have forgiven our cousin by now," said Eliza.

"That I have, and Margaret's a true friend to us," Katherine replied, peering at the sleeping baby to check he was still breathing.

Eliza smiled. "I used to do that when my Philip was tiny," she said. "They seem so very still, don't they? Carew's a fine, lusty boy; you need have no fears for him."

"Walter dotes on him," Katherine replied, still leaning over the cradle. She could just hear the baby's regular breathing, soft as a lullaby. "Why, Eliza, I've often crept up on him hanging over the cradle, cooing and grinning. How he does laugh when that tiny fist reaches out to grasp his finger! Walter really is inordinately proud of this son who joins his name with that of Peter Carew. Oh, it's clearly pleased my husband mightily!"

As she resumed her seat Katherine upset the work-basket, sending brightly coloured silks spilling across the uneven floorboards, needles dancing and glinting in the sun. "What would Mother say? She always knew I had little stomach for this feminine art," she chuckled, as they scrambled after a fast-unravelling skein of crimson silk thread.

Eliza's sweet, joyful laughter floated down the stairs like birdsong on morning air.

"Oh, Eliza, it's such a joy to see you happy. But are you quite sure all's well, now that you're the wife of a priest, I mean? It does seem so strange. I've always thought of priests as aged men, like that dotard who served at Compton. Of course, John's a fine man, and handsome too. But people question how such men as he may marry. What if aught should change and something should happen to John? Do you fear for the future?"

"I have no fear," declared Eliza. "My John will see me well provided for, should anything happen to him. He's a wealthy man, you know. He can keep me in the manner to which I'm accustomed. He has lands on long leases from the cathedral, and so long as the rents are paid, there'll be plenty to provide my portion. His sister's son, James Moore, stands steward for him, and will assist should the need ever come. But let's not think of that. At last, I can show the world how I do love that man." Eliza, puffed up with pride and excited as a young maid, told Katherine how much she liked living in Pollard's fine house in the city. "There's so much to see and do there, Katherine-Kate. I'm sure you'd like it too, should Walter ever find a place there."

"Ha! I suppose Walter put you up to saying that," Katherine snorted. "Oh, Eliza, you don't fool me! He's hinted before now about a house in Exeter. But I'm so happy at Poer Hayes. I don't want to move." She turned the conversation swiftly back to John Pollard. "But has John now reconciled himself to being a priest, but no longer celibate? You said he came to your marriage tormented by conscience." She remembered the haunted look on the cleric's face as he left Mohun's Ottery the last time she had seen him.

"I can certainly have no complaints in that way," replied Eliza with a saucy smile. "John's been much encouraged that Miles Coverdale has a wife himself, and children too. You know him, don't you, Katherine-Kate? He helped with the English Bible. Uncle George worked with him years ago in Paris."

"I do remember. He's tipped to become Bishop when Veysey goes. Will Uncle George also take a wife?" asked Katherine.

"Yes, as sure as eggs are eggs," replied Eliza with a smile. "He's got his eye on Anne Harvey, Sir Nicholas's daughter. If she can wed a man of the Church, I see nothing wrong in a Champernowne lass doing the same!"

"Well, of course not. They always said Uncle George had a wife years ago in France, but she died. I say good luck to you all. Why should priests not know true happiness, just as other men?"

Veysey was dismissed and, as expected, Coverdale became Bishop of Exeter.

"Now mark this, Katherine-Kate," Walter declared. "Archdeacon John Pollard, was one of those who saw Coverdale safely enthroned. Put his name to the certificate of induction. He's climbing up the cathedral hierarchy, you know. Eliza will be all right. Oh, and you remember that Papist preacher, Crispin? The one that caused such a stir at Gilbert's month-mind? The one the rebels demanded be released from the Tower? Well, I'm not sorry to say, he's dead and gone. Under Coverdale, surely our cathedral will move forward unhindered. Now, tell me: are you content that we remain here at the farm? 'Tis time to renew the lease."

"Oh yes, indeed I am," she replied without hesitation. "I am so happy here. It's a fine place for the children. If the farmstead still suits your purposes, well, then there's nowhere I'd rather be."

A few weeks later, Walter signed a new eighty-year lease for the farm with Richard Duke. With Katherine's complete agreement he included his son John as co-lessee. "I'm getting older, Katherine-Kate. See all these grey hairs in my beard?" he said.

She laughed out loud, giving said beard a tweak and then gave voice to a bawdy chorus. "Aye, 'tis true. You're pushing fifty, old man," she taunted, "and me just a maid with a babe in the cradle!"

"Not so long in the tooth that I can't chase you around this chamber, Mistress Raleigh. Aye, and catch you too," he laughed, as they fell upon the bed.

Later they talked more soberly and Katherine agreed that it was prudent to set things well in train for the future. John Raleigh was a steady boy. If she still needed to live at the farm when the time came, they could trust him not to turn her out. As the eldest son, George would get Fardel and all the other properties. John deserved some security for his future too.

As Walter signed the new lease on the farm, another crashed off the see-saw. Former Protector Edward Seymour was sent to the Tower on a charge of treason. Soon after the Twelfth Night revels, he went to the block.

"We'll see where this leads," said Walter when he heard. "Dudley's strong for reform, but the country's near bankrupt. He'll need to get a grip quickly."

And so he did. The new Protector's first act was to end the costly and controversial wars against France and Scotland.

"Hmm, my boys," Walter told George and John. "We'll have to take more care which ships we approach now, or we'll be in trouble with the Admiralty. Dudley's going to appoint Lord Lieutenants in every county. It'll be John Russell here. He's the most powerful landowner."

But soon the whispers started that Dudley, now styled Duke of Northumberland, was out to advance his own family. According to some reports, he would cast his greedy eyes on the highest prize of all.

On a sultry summer's day, Eliza had come a-visiting. She sat with Katherine in the shady arbour amongst the herb beds, watching Carew toddling along behind Margaret and Mary as they snipped lavender blossoms.

"Did you hear how Walter was called to give account of the church goods he brought out of St Sidwell's?" Katherine asked. "They're drawing up an inventory of all our churches so they can confiscate anything of value for the Crown. What a good thing Peter was appointed one of the commissioners, or Walter might have found himself in trouble. Do you know what Walter told them? He said he would have loved to return that fine churchman's cope, if only it were not already cut up to make a tester for his bed."

"So that's where that embroidered cloth that so proudly adorns your bed came from, Katherine-Kate!" cried Eliza, laughing as chubby-faced Carew upset the girls' basket and put it on his head.

The next day Walter came home from Mohun's Ottery, where he'd been hunting in the park with his friend Peter. The Carews were spending more time in Devon, and Peter was intent on building up his standing in the county. He had served with Arthur and other worthies on various commissions and, like Uncle Gawen, had licence to keep more servants than strictly allowed in the Act of Retainers. Walter said he must have more than forty men in his livery.

"You look quite worn out, husband. Too much carousing into the night with my cousin, no doubt!" she teased as she helped him off with his boots.

"Well, yes, you're not far wide of the mark. I'm afraid I can't keep pace any more. I'm not so used to the high life as Sir Peter! He's hot to take Dartmouth Castle back, you know. I wouldn't go along with him, you'll be pleased to hear. I doubt it'll make him popular down there, and I certainly don't want to fall foul of the Dartmouth worthies."

She thought no more of it, but as autumn mists clung about Hayes Wood, they heard that the running sore of Dartmouth had become too much for Peter to bear.

"Rash as usual," Katherine laughed. "That's Peter all over. Are you telling me he actually stormed the castle?"

"I'm afraid he did, Katherine-Kate," Walter laughed. "Changed all the locks. Caused quite a stir. Told them he couldn't see why the town should benefit from it so freely, when the land has always belonged to his family. But it hasn't won him any friends. They know him pretty well, down there. After all, he sat for Dartmouth in the King's Parliament not long ago. I hope he doesn't need their support any time soon."

You never knew what to believe. The rumours came thick and fast from London in that spring of 1553. An outbreak of the smallpox; the King had caught it and was like to die; no, the King had survived and was sure to rule for many years to come. But, as primroses touched the Devon lanes with yellow, there was no doubt. The young King was very ill. The boy on whom their hopes had rested was dying.

In the middle of May, Arthur brought other sad news. Beautiful, clever Joanie had gone to her grave. Katherine leaned heavily on her brother's arm as they walked toward the house.

"To die in May, the merriest month of all. Arthur, please tell me it's not so," she wailed. "Oh, I do so wish I'd spent more time with Joanie. She invited me so often. Now it's too late, and all that learning has gone with her into the cold earth. What use is it now? All lost and gone."

"Her children are her legacy, dearest wife of mine," said Walter. He took her in his arms and held her against his broad chest. "It is the way of the world."

"Ah, yes! It is the way of things," she snapped, stepping back from his embrace. "To think of those children, alone in the world; orphans with neither mother nor father to guide them."

Carew stood in the doorway, staring at his parents, his face a study of confusion. Katherine swept him up into her arms and, sobbing, held him tightly to her breast.

"Who'll take the throne if King Edward dies?" Walter asked as they sat side by side on the orchard bench, enjoying the last rays of the sun. "King Henry made his two daughters his next heirs, even though he branded both illegitimate. But how would a woman fare on the throne? There's never been such a thing before!"

"'Tis not just the fear of being ruled by a woman that keeps you awake at nights, is it, Walter, my dear?" she said earnestly, letting her needlework fall onto the grass as she turned towards him.

"Well, I have quite a liking for being ruled by one woman in particular, as it happens." He grinned, giving her behind a playful pat as she bent to pick up her stitching. "But you're right. Mary's sure to want to bring us back to the Church of Rome. She never really let go of her mother's religion. The sister would be a better bet."

"Kat says she's very clever," said Katherine. "She'll commit to nothing. But, Walter, dear, how dreadful it would be for either woman to have to rule, with all those ambitious men seeking to direct whom they must marry!"

"We must watch Northumberland. His power has rested on the King. Mayhap he won't want to cede to Mary and her Catholic ways."

They did not have to wait for long.

"Word is that he's married his son Guildford to Jane Grey," Walter announced a few days later after he'd been at Mohun's Ottery, chewing the fat with Peter and his friends. "More than that, there are whispers that he's persuaded King Edward to name the girl his successor."

"But if Northumberland, that John Dudley, does place Jane on the throne he'll be the puppet master, pulling the strings through her and his son. Poor maid!" declared Katherine.

Walter stared into his mug of ale. "Kat told Arthur that Northumberland's alienated people with his overweening arrogance. He might have overreached himself. She says we shouldn't underestimate Mary."

"Kat always said Jane was not worldly-wise, for all her learning."

"That's what Arthur said," Walter confirmed, rubbing his hand round his face. "The consensus at Mohun's Ottery was to declare openly for Mary when the time comes. Then we'll hope her choice of husband will moderate her religious views."

Katherine bristled and rose from the settle.

He smiled. "Well, how can a woman rule alone? There must be heirs to secure the succession."

"Ha! Good husband," laughed Katherine. "So a Queen may sit upon the throne by virtue of her birthright, but she can only do so with a man beside her? A man who will rule her, Queen though she be? Woman's lot was ever a hard one!"

"I can't help the ways of the world, my dear," he chortled. "There's few women free to choose as you did. I'm ever thankful you chose me!" He made a grab for her and chased her up the stairs, and for a while they quite forgot about Kings and Queens and all the problems of the succession.

Men toiled under the summer sun, scythes cutting swathes through the meadows. News came that King Edward was dead. With quite a show at both Dartmouth and Newton Bushell, Peter and Arthur pledged that they would serve Mary as their true Queen. The men of Devon were with them. Even Walter.

But not long after came startling news

"Northumberland has followed through with his plot," shouted John Raleigh, hurling himself from his horse. "I've just come from Exmouth. He's put Jane on the throne. Declared that King Edward signed a device setting her up as his heir before he died."

"What!" Walter shouted as he and Katherine rushed to the door. "I wonder... It's a fair bet that Northumberland put the boy King up to it."

"Well, they say King Edward's signature was clearly written in his own hand, so the Council has supported Jane," said John.

"Well then, we men of Devon will just sit tight and see how this plays out," said Walter.

It wasn't long before they learned that Kat had had the right of it. Mary rallied forces to her banner in East Anglia and rode triumphant into London.

"Those of the Council that declared for Queen Jane changed sides in the blink of an eye," Walter declared. "That girl's nine days of wonder were soon put to an end."

"To think of it," Katherine replied, her sympathies all with Jane. "That unfortunate girl! She never asked to have any of this thrust upon her. Now she's cast into the Tower with her husband. But what about Queen Mary? I'm quite amazed that that worn-out woman I met all those years ago could have done this."

"She led her forces into London as a warrior Queen. It all depends now on the choice of husband," Walter mused. "If only she'd take Edward Courtenay. We'd have a Devon man beside her."

"But what on earth will become of the other Princess?"

"We'll have to wait and see," Walter answered, with a gloomy look.

On a biting cold December day, they rode under the splendid new gateway at Mohun's Ottery.

"Perhaps Peter's copying the palace at Hampton Court," Walter laughed, pointing upwards. "King Henry had his and his wife's initials carved on every possible surface there, though it was a bit of a problem when he changed wives. See Peter's initials carved beside the door? And there are the arms of Carew. I suppose these are for their Mohun ancestors."

"How can Peter afford all of this?" she whispered. "He's got Margaret's fortune, but those old debts to the Crown are still outstanding. Just look at those new chambers, and that gatehouse!"

Margaret greeted them alone. It seemed that Peter was about some mysterious business. He'd come to Exmouth by ship, only to vanish again on horseback; none knew where. The mood amongst the guests was far from festive. Everyone spoke in hushed tones. The men rode out to hunt or pretended to enjoy the usual feasting. The women wore worried frowns as they sat at their stitching. It was hard to make merry when you heard what their new Queen had already done.

"She's overturned many of King Edward's laws. King Henry's Nine Articles are back. All the Popish trappings back in our churches," Walter snarled. "Bells and smells and all!"

"Walter, what will become of Eliza and John?" Katherine asked, twisting the ring on her finger.

"That I don't know. It doesn't look hopeful with Ridley and Latimer in the Tower, and Cranmer taken. Our new Queen won't forgive him his part in ending her mother's marriage."

"Latimer must be over eighty," Katherine said, shaking her head slowly. "How can she be so cruel?"

"Miles Coverdale's been arrested. I think he'll be all right," Walter said, though his bleak look denied it. "The King of Denmark's pleading for his life; offered him exile there. What a pass we've come to! She's gone and brought that old fool Veysey back. She doesn't forget her friends. There might be some hope if she'd agree to marry an Englishman."

"Well, Edward Courtenay's out of the Tower, but it won't have gone down well that he's said he'd prefer Elizabeth. Mary hated Anne Boleyn; she won't take kindly to being compared to Anne's daughter."

"She's listening to her Spanish relations. Showered favours on Courtenay's head at first: made him Earl of Devon and removed the attainder. I did have hopes. But I fear she'll go for the Spaniard."

On the Feast of St John, Arthur joined the party. "I made a detour to Dartmouth," he announced. "The place is alive with rumours that the

Prince of Spain won't be content with marrying Mary. No, they say he'll take the country by force and if we don't resist, the good men of Devon will be murdered in their beds, and their wives and daughters ravished by Spanish soldiers. Word is that Plymouth's already up in arms. But even there, many are loyal to Mary. I'm not sure enough will stand firm if push comes to shove."

Uncle Gawen bristled, and Peter, who had at last returned, had a face like thunder. "We can't be overrun by foreigners," he declared, thumping the table. "Do we want the Spanish Inquisition? Oh, you've all heard of the horrors of the Inquisition, haven't you? This Spanish marriage has to be stopped, whatever the cost."

Peter didn't confine these comments to the friends assembled at his home. He'd already been heard declaring his opposition to the Spanish marriage quite freely in Exeter, and sent servants to sound out friends and neighbours.

"No doubt that'll be reported," Katherine overheard Arthur say to Walter. "Peter's too hot-headed by half! Well, he's not popular, is he? The people think of him as the one who burned the Crediton barns."

Walter made to protest, but Arthur went on.

"Yes, yes, we know that's not fair. But these stories have a habit of sticking. The merchants of Dartmouth certainly can't forgive him the castle business. I'm not so sure he'll gain much support."

Katherine pursed her lips, fuming inwardly. Peter might be nearly forty; he might have grown portly as he enjoyed all that high living since marrying Margaret, but he was the same rash and reckless fool he'd ever been. She'd not have him draw another of her men into danger.

Messengers kept arriving on exhausted horses. Katherine picked up disjointed snippets. Wyatt could raise a force in Kent to put a stop to the marriage. Henry Grey, the Duke of Suffolk, father of the Nine Days Queen, could rally a force. James Croft might bring the men of Herefordshire. The French Ambassador might even be involved.

Margaret confided that Peter had met the conspirators at Suffolk's London house before Christmas. "If the West Country joins he thinks we can prevail," she whispered to Katherine, out of earshot of the others. "Breathe not a word of this, but they plan to take London. They intend to see Edward Courtenay married to the Princess Elizabeth and have her replace Mary as a true Protestant English Queen."

Katherine doubted that the plan would work. All might depend on what the feisty, flame-haired Princess had to say about it. From what Kat said, that clever lady would play her cards closely.

Katherine felt queasy and drained. Her daughter would soon be six and Carew was four. She'd begun to wonder if she was past childbearing. Not so, it seemed. Margaret Carew looked at her questioningly, and she nodded. "I have yet to tell my husband this news, his mind being so full of Spaniards and alarms."

Katherine wasn't sorry when, after Twelfth Night, they said farewell to Margaret and made their way back to Poer Hayes. For once she was pleased that Walter would be off with his sons for a few days, seeking cargoes of dried fish, herring and other goods to trade in Exeter. In recent months he'd left it to the boys to take charge, and they could easily have done it all without him. But he still hankered for the sea, and she encouraged him to go. It might keep him away from the dangerous, fermenting brew of trouble.

Peter had set up post horses all the way from Andover so that Edward Courtenay could come to Devon and rally the county. When the weak-willed Courtenay failed to appear, Peter decided to act without him. While Walter was away, rumours ran high that Peter and Gawen Carew were going to take Exeter Castle by force. Bessie heard from the butcher's boy that Peter's servant had been spotted with a wagonload of armour in the very streets of Exeter. It seemed that Sir Thomas Denys panicked and barred the city gates, and at first it looked as though he was with the rebels. But Denys stood firm for the Queen, and demanded that Peter report to London to give an account of himself. Uncle Gawen had scaled the city walls to make his escape.

"All go in fear of the Spaniards," Bessie said. "Mayhap your uncle did no more than his duty to save us?"

Walter returned to East Budleigh, leaving his boys to guard the cargo. He turned a deaf ear to Katherine's pleading and headed for Exeter.

TWENTY-EIGHT
1554
KATHERINE

SHE WOKE WITH A START. DARKNESS; NOT THE SOFT, HOPEFUL darkness of the hour before dawn, but impenetrable pitch-black that robbed reason and replaced it with a nameless fear. With shaking fingers she fumbled to find the opening in the bed-hangings and pulled them aside. No light; just total, utter darkness, black as jet. In her panic she thought she'd been struck blind as she slept.

Something had dragged her sharply from her slumber. There it was – a steady banging, regular as a drumbeat, on and on. *Bang. Bang. Bang. Bang.* She pushed down an image of soldiers marching through Hayes Wood, coming to murder them all. "Why, 'tis nothing but one of the servants has left the shutters unbarred on the new brewhouse," she said aloud, hoping to draw courage from the sound of her own voice. "That's it; a shutter banging to and fro as this fierce gale rages."

She slipped from the bed and an icy draught nipped at her bare feet. Intent on exploring every nook and cranny, the wind had found a crack under the ill-fitting oak door. She could hear it whistling round the chimney as she felt her way across the room with a hand placed protectively across her belly. Her leg brushed against something, and she jumped back, heart pounding as loud as that drumbeat. She gave a nervous laugh. Whipped away from the wall, the hangings were flapping about like flags in the breeze and had touched her leg like a ghostly hand. She stumbled on towards the faint outline of the window. The rain was pounding on the leaded panes with such force she thought it would shatter the glass, soak the window seat and spoil the embroidered cushions. A storm in Devon at this season could be fierce indeed.

Suddenly the night sky was split by a flash of dazzling light. She gasped, sprang back from the window, and felt the floorboards beneath her feet jump. A mighty crash shook the old house and the timbered walls shuddered and shivered as the pressing darkness closed in again. She tiptoed back towards the comfort of her bed and huddled down under the velvet coverlet. And then she remembered why the bed beside her was empty. It wasn't so unusual for her to sleep with no more than a pillow for company. Their life together was punctuated by Walter's frequent absences, a series of fond farewells and, oh, such joyful reunions. It was almost worth bearing those bittersweet partings for the pleasure of welcoming him home again. She gazed up at the silk cope tester. A thrill of pleasure crept through her as she remembered how he'd carried her to bed when he'd brought it back from St Sidwell's. Oh, what sweet relief that had been, for she had truly believed him to be in mortal danger. But her Walter always landed on his feet. Only a year ago he'd been held in Fleet Prison for over a month on some charge of taking a Scots vessel. But she'd had no real concern. With all his charm and connections, he'd been sure to secure his release. And so he had. She always missed him. She ached for his touch as she sat lonely by the fireside of an evening after the children had gone to bed. But Walter always came home, swaggering up the path to cup her face in his two hands, gaze hungrily into her eyes and whisk her off her feet.

Another blinding flash lit the room. She shuddered. Perhaps it was the storm. Perhaps it was just the strange contrariness of a woman with child. But as she clutched the covers tight around her middle and hugged her arms across her belly, she remembered where he had gone and realised she was trembling. Walter was somewhere on the sea.

Peter's messenger had met him in Exeter, told him the news and set out the plan. Gawen was held at the castle; caught at Bickleigh where he'd sought shelter with his nephew. No word of Arthur beyond that he'd been at Mohun's Ottery; perhaps he'd have the sense to step back from the brink. But there was no stepping back for Peter Carew. He'd failed to answer the summons to London and was set to flee.

The plan was for Walter to sail his barque to Weymouth, making show that it was but a routine voyage to sell his cargo. The local ports were already watched but they gambled that word had not yet reached the Dorset coast. If Peter managed to avoid capture by taking the byways, Walter was to give his friend passage to safety in France. It was a dangerous scheme, but Walter was gone on the next tide in time to make Weymouth by nightfall. *Aye*, she thought, shivering in her bed, *and in time to have left the safety and shelter of that port before this storm hit!* On a night like this, far out in the Channel, what chance would they stand in the *Katherine Raleigh*? She tried to picture him in that well-remembered cabin, safe and secure, snoring in his bunk. But instead she saw flying spars, sails cut adrift, splintering timbers, and icy waters closing over his head.

The long night hours passed, oh so slowly, as she tossed and turned and the storm raged on. She gave up all hope of sleep, pulled on her thick nightgown and wrapped the bedcover round her shoulders. She rekindled the embers of the kitchen fire, and when the logs blazed fierce, heated a poker and mulled a cup of ale.

Bessie found her there, stiff and cramped on the settle, when the house began to stir into morning life. "Come, Mistress, you'll catch a death of cold. Let us get you gowned and ready to see how those fierce winds have left us."

Katherine peeped in on the children, wondering if they had been afraid in the night. The two girls – one so fair, the other so dark – lay close together in their bed, Mary's arms wrapped around her raven-haired half-sister. In the other room Carew snored, so secure of his own self that he would sleep through anything.

"I wonder, Bessie, what character the new life growing within me shall put upon when he or she comes into the world? I pray that Walter comes home safely to see another babe in that cradle," she added, her fingers twisting and untwisting the cloth of the bedcover. She hadn't told him about the baby yet.

The rain had stopped; the wind died down to a whisper. She strapped wooden pattens under her shoes, hitched up her skirts, and picked her way across the slippery cobbles. There was the shutter hanging askew on the brewhouse after its battering. She must have it repaired.

Clutching her cloak tightly across her belly, she leaned on the gate and stared at a scene of quite terrible destruction. In the meadow the majestic oak still stood, stretching a skeletal finger toward the clouds. A livid white scar ran top to bottom; strong boughs ripped right off the once-sturdy trunk lay at odd, twisted angles. The grass was scattered with debris; remnants of the oak's bare branches blown sky-high and flung all across the meadow. She must direct the men to fetch in what they could to be cut and dried for fuel.

She watched the sheep slowly emerging from their hiding place under the hedge, their fleeces still heavy from the night's soaking. Thanks be that they hadn't looked to shelter under those spreading branches. She'd heard the like before, many years ago: a group of rams all struck dead in an instant under another mighty oak on Father's land. The ewes carried new life, just as she did. The lambs would all be playing in this meadow when spring came.

"Please, dear God, let Walter be back here safely by then," she cried, her voice rising to an anguished rant. "Damn the Queen. Damn the cruel Spanish Prince whose coming brings such ill times for the true people of England. Why could she not take an English husband? And damn Peter to Hell for his rash folly." Her hand went again to her growing belly in that involuntary gesture of protection, as she leaned on the gate and sobbed.

A few days later Bessie came back from the market with a tale she hardly dared breathe. "They're saying Peter Carew is drowned in the sea at Weymouth," she murmured when Katherine insisted she tell all she knew. "'Twas as he tried to take ship and flee the country."

Katherine stared at her maid with her mouth drawn into a tight, pinched line. "If that tale be true, Bessie, then what has become of my Walter?" she wailed.

Not long after, her heart had cause to lift. A tall man was advancing down the lane on a horse she recognised as one of their own. But her hopes were soon dashed. The shoulders were too narrow; the hat too well pulled down. It was her stepson, John Raleigh, not her dear Walter, riding between the yews.

John soon put the lie to the story of Peter's watery death. Much later, when she saw Peter's wife again, Katherine learned how that story had started. Margaret too had slept badly on the night of the storm. On waking, she recounted a vivid dream to her serving woman. Well, the maid told the steward, the steward told the brewer, the brewer told the laundry maid, the laundry maid told the cook, and the cook told the tale at the market in Exeter when he went there for provisions. So the story had gone the rounds, growing in the telling as will happen with such gossip, until Peter was most surely gone to his death at the bottom of the sea.

"No, Peter's safe, and the last time I saw him, my father was too. Let me tell you all I know," said John, patting her hand. "My father decided to remove the cargo from the *Katherine* and the *Lion* before we took the tide for Weymouth. But we left some of the barrels of dried fish on the *Mary*. With most of the cargo stowed securely and the warehouses well guarded, we set off, all three ships together, and made headway with a fair wind behind us. As we came near to the Bill of Portland..." He glanced at Katherine and must have seen some confusion in her face. "Ah, yes – well, it's a long finger of land that sticks out to sea. We gave a wide berth to the dangerous shallow reefs and the Shambles sandbank. My father and George stood off out in the Channel, before the headland. As my father had ordered, I took the *Mary* onward into the more sheltered waters of the bay that lies by Weymouth. I tied up at the quay in the harbour, all as though I was come to sell my cargo of dried fish to the highest bidder." John was not well known in those parts and could, at least for a time, get away with posing as just another merchantman. "So they waited in the other two vessels at some distance from the point, ready for the signal that Sir Peter Carew was come."

Warming to his task as storyteller, John told of how he hadn't liked the look of the sky. With some relish and a lot of arm-waving, he relayed how the dark clouds gathered and the rain swept in. "But I must obey my father's instructions," he said. "So I waited for Sir Peter and the others to come. Before darkness fell completely I saw the *Katherine* and the *Lion* seeking shelter on the lee side, though they still kept far out in the bay. There were some on the shore that saw them then but they couldn't make out their colours, being too far off."

Katherine reached over to fill his mug with ale from the jug and realised how dry her own mouth was. She filled a second mug. Perhaps cool ale would quell the churning in her stomach.

"It was late in the night when they reached us. I took up the lantern and gave the signal for my father to approach as close as he dared. We already had a rough swell on the waves and the *Mary* was tossing about like a little cork in a barrel," said John dramatically. "With rain driving hard, every deck was soaked and slippery, Mother, dearest."

Even in her anxiety she suppressed a smile at this, for John was no more than ten years younger than she.

"You would so have laughed to see proud Sir Peter Carew wrapped in a ragged cloak, disguised as a serving man. A servant was staggering under the weight of a gold belt, trying to strut as though he were lord over them all. One of the Killigrews was there, and three others: John Courtenay of Powderham, Andrew Tremayne, and it might have been James Kirkham, but I can't say for sure. We had some pains to launch the jolly boat, for that was the only way to convey them over to the *Katherine*. At last our sailors had it down, tossing on the waves which looked set to fill it in no time. Sir Peter and his party made to cross the deck, ready to be lowered down. Perhaps it was the wet boards that did it," said John, pausing. "Perhaps the sailor holding the ropes slipped. But all on a sudden Sir Peter fell, missed the boat, and was floundering in the sea. Had one of the sailors not acted so quickly our Bessie's story might have been proved true. He could so easily have drowned there and then. But they fished him out, all the while cursing the weight of that old cloak. Then they set to the oars and my father soon sent signal with the lantern that the boat had reached them and his cargo of men was safely stowed. I must suppose that he and George then put about to set their course for France in convoy so that they could put up a stout defence against any challenge. My jolly boat returned, I made sure all was secured aboard the *Mary*, and I saw no more of them."

Katherine bowed her head and closed her eyes. All good news, so far as it went. But who knew how they had weathered the storm, or if they had come safely to the coast of France? She twisted her hands in her lap, then grasped John's hand. "There is nought to do but wait," she murmured. "Wait to know if they be safe or no."

Weeks passed before she had her answer. John sold part of the cargo in Exeter and brought back the latest news of the plotters. As Katherine had hoped, Arthur had pulled back.

"He told Sir Peter he would do nothing that might be construed as against his Queen," said John. "Then Sir Arthur heard Sir Gawen was arrested and decided to throw himself upon the Queen's mercy. 'Tis said he declared to them all that if it was the Queen's true pleasure that she shall marry the Spaniard, then he should be well received," said John, raising his voice. Then, more quietly, "Sir Gawen and Sir Arthur are taken to the Tower in London."

Katherine gave a strangled cry. Arthur, to be taken to the Tower! John said that Wyatt was captured and eventually put to death with some ninety others. Katherine could only pray that her brother was not included in that number.

"It's said Queen Mary appealed to the people," said John. "Stood in the Guildhall as a warrior Queen wedded to her country. Promised not to marry without the will of all her people. It seems she swayed them to her side."

"Well, I'll believe it when I see it," Katherine declared. "I'd lay good odds that she'll be wed to Philip of Spain before this babe bawls his first. But what of Jane Grey?"

"Her father supported the rebellion. Queen Mary knew she could not allow the girl to live. She's been sent to meet the headsman along with her husband, Guildford Dudley," he replied, with a shake of his head.

"I met the Queen long ago," Katherine remarked to Bessie as they sat stitching with the girls. "If I'm any judge of character I'd wager she'd be driven by conscience to be merciful. But she couldn't brook any threat to her rule. She remembers how her mother was treated. All the odds stacked up against Jane Grey. It must have been a hard decision. How odd that a woman has the power to send another to her death. We live in strange times."

A puzzled frown creased Mary's brow as she threaded her needle, but she said nothing.

"Of course they accuse Elizabeth, those that would be rid of her," Katherine continued. Thinking about the Princess kept her mind off Walter. "They got nothing out of Wyatt. There's no proof she was even aware of the plot, though she's arrested and kept in the Bell Tower. I pity the maid! Brought to that dread place, just as her mother was, long ago. She must have seen the scaffold where Jane met her end. Kat's not allowed to go to her. All those men trying to wring some confession from her. How dreadful! But she'll stand firm, I'll be bound."

Bessie put a finger to her lips and motioned towards Margaret, who stared, round-eyed, at her mother, her face ashen.

"Fear not, Margaret. That brave young woman will come through. There's nought for us to fear. But I do wish I knew if Kat's under suspicion. Aye, and there's still no news of Arthur."

March had passed, and they were well into April. The fire burned fierce in the brushwood oven in readiness for the day's baking. Katherine had her back to the door, her hands covered in flour as she took out her frustration on a ball of dough. She glanced over her shoulder. Someone was whistling a merry tune; probably one of the serving men. She turned back and went on pummelling the dough. She didn't see him sauntering up the path; didn't hear as he crept up behind her and put his arms around her waist. Her startled scream soon became a whoop of joy. She turned, and Walter wrapped his arms around her so tightly she nearly lost her breath. They stood locked together, not wanting to let go their hold, lest it prove a dream. Kissing the tears tenderly from her eyes, Walter traced the line of her chin with shaking fingers. He stood back to look at her, and tapped the stomacher that covered the gap at the front of her gown where she'd let out the laces.

"So, what's this, then, Katherine-Kate? Am I come home to find a cuckoo in my nest? You never told me that I was to be a father again. How can this be?"

She stamped her foot and beat on his doublet, leaving a pattern of floury handprints on the worn leather. "How dare you make such a cruel jest?!"

A joyous, infectious torrent of laughter burst from him as he held her again. She couldn't be angry with him for long. Soon they were both snorting and chuckling as though they'd never stop.

When he paused to draw breath he put a hand on her belly again. "I shall be proud to show the world that an old man like me can still put a babe in my wife's belly."

Later he told his story of how they had set off into the teeth of such a storm as he had never known. "Out in the Channel it was so rough that we must turn back again and find shelter in the waters beyond Portland Bill," he explained. "We dared not put into the port for fear that a hue and cry would be raised. So, with Peter and his friends safely housed in the cabin, we somehow rode out that dreadful tempest. Only on the following day, as the wind abated, could we head for France, hoping that we were not followed. We neared safe harbour across the Channel, and one of the Killigrews' boats met us. They thought to land the fugitives further down the coast in Normandy. Peter pressed me to throw in my lot with him. But I replied that there was one at home waiting who would never forgive me if I deserted her. I told him I must return."

He took her hand, but Katherine was not to be fobbed off.

"Why, then, did it take you so long? 'Tis nigh on three whole months you've been gone from me. I've been out of my wits with worry for you!"

He looked uncomfortable as he replied, "Well, at Peter's insistence, I waited a time in safety till all the fuss had passed, just in case they were looking for me. I know you've been anxious, Katherine-Kate, but I feared to send you word lest they find me. And there was never a man so keen to return to his own wife and fireside as I."

She snorted, and laughed. She knew he was dissembling. He could have returned to her sooner. Peter's escape had paved the way for a tide of exiles who could in no way stomach Queen Mary's changes, nor a Spanish Prince on the throne. He'd told her already that he'd found there was money to be earned transporting others across to France.

"Peter's gone first to seek aid from the King of France," Walter continued, without meeting her eyes. "He might offer ships to plunder the Channel Isles or the Scillies, but the French King will be careful not to show his hand too strong. No, I doubt Peter will get any real help from that quarter, so we must bide our time and put up with all these changes. Grit our teeth and pay lip service to the Latin-mumbling priests in their chasubles and copes. Get used to all the candles and incense and all. Better that we sway with the prevailing breeze than allow ourselves to be cut off and trampled underfoot."

"But, Walter, will they come after you for aiding a fugitive?" asked Katherine.

"It'll be more or less forgotten by now," he answered. "The Queen has more sense than to do away with any more West Country men. She knows she needs us and our ships. She may hold your brother a little longer because of his kinship to Kat, but when she and her mistress are released, Arthur will be too. Men like him are too valuable to Queen Mary for her to squander them away for petty vindictiveness."

Eventually Kat's mistress was released, but kept under virtual house arrest at the palace of Woodstock.

"As the lady journeyed there, her ears rang to warm cheers from all the people," said Bessie after a trip to market. "As she passed through the countryside people came out to call out blessings on King Henry's true daughter and to shower her with gifts."

"Ah! So perhaps the Spanish marriage is not so popular," Walter observed. "It'll test the loyalty even of those who favour Rome if he brings his Spanish ways here."

"Thank goodness nothing came out that could threaten my sister," Katherine whispered to Walter, late one evening upon the settle. "But I do wonder how much they were really involved. John Ashley, Kat's husband, he's fled to Padua. Do you think he played some part in Wyatt's attempt?"

"No, Katherine-Kate, I do not," he replied. "More likely he's gone to see Joan Denny's boys safely out of the country so that they can continue their education as directed by their father."

Katherine knew that Anthony Denny had left money and a wealth of advice in his will as to how his children should be brought up. She'd laughed when she'd heard about his instructions. His sons must be educated so that, as he put it, 'the commonwealth would find them profitable members and not burdens as idle as drones in the hive'. "Perhaps you're right. Walter, I do so wish my Gilbert boys could go. Richard Chudleigh's sent Christopher, you know. I suppose John could never get permission? As for the other boys, Penkervell would never stump up the money. Arthur had a hard enough time of it to persuade him to agree to Humphrey going to Eton College. Not that I'd ever trust that man. I can't forget that he had a hand in bringing that odious preacher to Otho's month-mind. No, Penkervell won't shift himself to send my boys across the sea."

"We won't be sending our boy either, Katherine-Kate. Carew can learn well enough from the parson here in the village, and from you and me," said Walter, studying her face. "Margaret's had to part with a sizeable payment to prevent all Peter's goods and chattels being taken, you know. He's lucky to have her. She'll work away, steady and determined, and use her wealth and position to bring Peter back into royal favour in time. A good wife's worth is far above rubies, as I know, my dear."

TWENTY-NINE

1554–1555
KATHERINE

ANOTHER MAY MORNING FOUND HER WALKING BENEATH delicate pink-and-white apple blossom when she saw riders approaching. Despite her increasing girth, Katherine bounded forward through the side gate to greet her visitor.

"Katherine-Kate, will you give me lodging here for a space? I am in sore need," shrieked Eliza as she threw herself from her mount. Her face was ravaged by recently shed tears and her chin trembled as she started to pace up and down the path.

"What's put you in such a state?" cried Katherine.

Walter emerged from the shadow of the doorway and took his sister-in-law by the hand.

"Why, 'tis declared I am a concubine!" Eliza spat the ugly word out, as though to rid her body and mind of its poison. "To think that I, a lady of the ancient Champernowne line, could be called so! Banished from my true husband's fireside!"

"Ah," said Walter. "I had heard that Queen Mary issued an edict that all married priests must be deprived of all their benefices. I'm just surprised it's taken so long to filter down to Exeter. Of course, Veysey's still in Sutton Coldfield. That's probably held things back until now."

Gradually, Eliza sobbed out the whole sorry story. "My John's been told he must set me aside; live completely apart from me," she blubbered, gulping before swallowing hard. "If he does, and he can prove it, then he might be allowed to take up office in the Church again. They're making him choose between the Church and me."

"We women have so frail a hold on happiness, when men can set such laws to upturn us," Katherine muttered bitterly, thinking that Eliza's marriage was no more than a dream of the thinnest tissue.

"Nay, Katherine-Kate, this is ordered not by men, but by Mary, the Queen, a woman just like us. How can she? I am wed within the law and in the sight of God. Damn her to Hell! She's got more care for that Spaniard than for the sisterhood of women." Eliza broke away from Walter's comforting embrace and hurled her gloves onto the grass, a splash of red leather amongst an ocean of green.

"Hmm! At a stroke she's rid of a whole lot of reformist clerics," Walter mused under his breath. "She'll replace them with conservatives who'll follow her law to the letter." He raised his voice. "You're quite right, Eliza. 'Tis a sad pity that that foolish woman's fallen under the spell of her Spanish suitor. Besotted! A one-sided affair if ever I saw one. The Spaniard thinks of her only as the means to power in this land. He wants our men at his disposal to fight his battles. But he's a young man. I wonder how he'll relish taking her as his mate: a woman so wizened and worn out? Mayhap he'd have preferred her comely sister." Walter gave Eliza an understanding nod and took her hand again. "Dear sister, you are welcome to my home. Katherine will be glad of your company before long, I warrant."

"When shall I see him again? My own true husband," Eliza wailed as she followed Katherine through the door. "The cathedral church was thrown into sorry upheaval after Coverdale was snatched from office. None of the Canons, nor the clergy, knew what was going on. Then in January there came a visitation to check their titles and dispensations. There was a loud dispute about what payment they should have; something about getting their emoluments even when they were away from the diocese. Oh, I don't know! Everyone was under suspicion. My John offered to restore all the broken silver and gilt and copes and vestments that had come his way, though he wasn't the only one to have so profited. But it was to no avail. He's been deprived, all on account of me."

Katherine thought that John Pollard should shoulder far more of the blame than her sister, but there was no point in saying so. Eliza missed her man too much to hear anything against him.

Later, as they lay in bed, Walter laid his hand on her belly. "Eliza's welcome to stay for as long as she likes. She'll bear you company until this little one comes. 'Sblood! He's a lusty knave! That was quite a kick! I hope John Pollard's made some provision to secure his estate. Probably set that Moore lad to the task, I should think."

"Eliza says John's gone to London," said Katherine, wriggling as she tried to find a comfortable position. "It'll be a hard thing for her if he's chosen the Church over her. I always had my doubts, but I did so hope she'd find happiness. Oh, Walter, I am so lucky."

Arthur was released at last. He called on the Raleighs as he made his way home. "With luck I'll get to Modbury in time to see my son born," he said, as Eliza hurried to join them. "It's a relief to be out of that place, Katherine-Kate."

"Your Mary must have been waiting so very anxiously for your release," Katherine laughed. "I had thought to go to her, but I'm grown so large and lazy. I'm strangely unwilling to leave my own hearth." It was more than the normal lethargy of pregnancy. She simply couldn't bear to be away from Walter for a moment longer than she had to.

"Well, that's easily solved," said Eliza, with more briskness than she'd shown since her arrival. "I'll go with Arthur now and make up the party. I can be back at Poer Hayes well before your time comes, Katherine-Kate."

"Mother will be glad of some company," said Arthur, as Bessie packed a bag. "She's near blind now, you know, but she's determined to be there when another Champernowne baby's born. Hurry up, Eliza, and let's get going."

Eliza seemed better when she arrived back at Poer Hayes in June.

Arthur had a son. It seemed he harboured no rancour against his uncle for his part in the failed plot, for he named the boy Gawen.

So the summer wore on. Walter went about his business, making as much show as needed of his compliance with the restored ways. With his boys, he continued to profit from a steady stream of refugees seeking to slip away to France. In July it was confirmed. The Queen of England had taken Philip of Spain to husband.

"Oho," said Walter, after letting out a string of curses. "John Russell saw to it that he landed at Southampton. Dared not risk it further west when the Spaniard came to his wedding!"

Katherine pursed her lips and wiped her brow, but said nothing. She had other concerns. Carrying a child through a blisteringly hot summer was not pleasant. Her gown stretched ever tighter and she was forever at the close-stool. The tiny feet dealt blow on blow.

WALTER

He couldn't sleep. Not with what was happening upstairs. No, he'd sit up the whole night long. He shifted on the settle again, got up, walked round the room another time, and sat back down with a thump. Oh yes, he knew she'd gone through this agony many times before. But she wasn't as young now as she liked to make out. What if something went wrong? What if, like his second wife, she never recovered? How could he bear to lose her? No point to any of his endeavours without her by his side; no point to life itself without her. He got up and paced round the room another time.

As the first shafts of light of that early dawn turned the new panes of the parlour windows pink, he must have fallen into a fitful and awkward slumber. He was ripped awake so suddenly he banged his head against the settle's oaken back. As he struggled to come to full waking, he realised what had stirred him, stiff and aching, from his hard resting place. A loud and insistent bawling was coming from the room above. The child was born!

His foot was on the stair in an instant. On the bed lay Katherine, her arms outstretched to take a noisy bundle from Mother Crosse. She looked up as he filled the doorway.

Bessie rushed to shoo him away. "Master Raleigh, 'tis not fitting, you must wait awhile," she cried.

But Katherine's lovely smile lit the chamber like sun on a spring morning. "Let him come near, Bessie. Let him see this fine boy that sings so loud he'll wake the whole parish. More like the whole country, too!"

Grinning, he took a step forward. How could she look so serene and beautiful after hours of torture? She beckoned. In two more strides he was at her side, bending over the baby cradled in her arms. Her fingers touched his, setting him all a-tingle. Together they pulled back the linen cloth wrapped around the child, not yet properly bathed or clad in his swaddling bands. Together they gazed at the small person they had made. Two steady eyes seemed to look straight into Walter's before the rosebud mouth opened wide and another piercing and insistent yell came forth.

"See the boy we have made, husband. He seems a likely fellow," said Katherine. "He has much to say for himself, like his father. Let us name him Walter."

The tingling sensation started again in his head and spread to his chest as he grinned. He felt his heart would burst. "Aye, Katherine-Kate, he's a rare boy. He'll do. Welcome to the world, little Walter Raleigh!"

"I shall call him Walt," said she.

Mother Crosse sat resting in the window seat.

"You had an easy time of it, Mother Crosse," Bessie purred, as pleased as if she'd been the mother herself. "Only had to wait and receive this fine boy. Just listen to him!"

"Aye," the older woman replied, with a toothy grin. "The mother's hale and healthy too, so I'll not need to tarry long." She packed her bag.

Walter fumbled for his purse and paid the midwife's fee, then waited anxiously as the days passed. He'd heard too many stories of women coming through the pains of childbirth only to be snatched away days later. He waited and prayed and ached for Katherine's company.

After two weeks all was well and he began to relax. What a boy! So lusty that he could still hear him squalling halfway down the lane toward the village. There was something very special about this boy; his namesake. He thanked God for his fine son, but even more that his wife had survived unharmed. His proud sea nymph was with him still.

KATHERINE

She was as contented as a lark, humming a gentle lullaby as she cradled the boy. Only three weeks after Walt took his first breath, Walter stormed up the stairs, paying no heed to the convention that she should be left alone until her churching.

"Katherine-Kate, Katherine-Kate, they say the Queen's with child! A Spanish heir will set the dye forever. All hopes for the other daughter, dashed!" he called. He burst into the room, breathing heavily and shaking his head. "Kat's out, but she's had to retire to John Ashley's place. The Lady Elizabeth's still closely guarded at Woodstock; only allowed to have one long-serving steward with her, Thomas Parry, and he's had to find lodgings somewhere in the town. Pshaw, they made out that the palace is too small to accommodate him!"

"Well, as one mother to another, I must wish the Queen well, though 'tis bad news for reform," Katherine replied, as the baby bawled insistently. "Come see your fine boy, husband."

In due time she went to her churching. Baby Walt thrived. The harvest was no more than average. It rained. John Veysey, Bishop of Exeter, breathed his last.

"Can you believe it? Eighty-nine! His going could prove a problem for us here, there's no doubt about it," muttered Walter angrily. "She'll appoint a new broom to sweep away all who do not cleave to her ways."

None of which boded well for the likes of John Pollard, who had so far been able to show that he had put his wife aside while still, Katherine suspected, managing to visit Eliza occasionally.

The following February, as Walt sat contented on her knee, they learned just how far the Queen would go. A fire had been lit in Smithfield. The preacher and translator John Rogers was the first to suffer and die an awful death.

"They've brought back the laws against heresy," said Walter with a worried frown. "Any who won't fully embrace her ways risk being sent to a dreadful end."

Katherine shuddered and remembered her anger at the fate of

Master Benet in Exeter. "How can our Queen put her name to this?" she whispered.

"It's her wish to please her husband that drives her," Walter said grimly. "She's following the example of Spain, with their Inquisition and their auto-da-fé. In Spain they have a quicker death – the fires burn fast and fierce in that dry and dusty land – but in the damp and dirty air of Smithfield at this time of year, a fire takes a long time to kindle and burn." He threw up his hands, and then sank back onto the settle. "God alone knows what those poor souls must endure! Keep your counsel close, dear Katherine-Kate. We must learn to dissemble well in these times."

In April the Queen's sister was released from house arrest at Woodstock, called to attend the expected birth. The rumours flew. A son and heir was already born; the bells rang in London; the bonfires lit, not, this time, to consume those the Queen called heretics, but to celebrate a birth. The rumours proved false.

"God's teeth," said Walter angrily one May morning. "Now she's made the Spaniard her regent should she die in childbed. Mayhap he's a mind to wed her sister if that comes to be! We'll be overrun with foreigners, and never be rid of them."

The tide of refugees continued. Some had permission; some simply slipped away. Even Francis Russell, who had succeeded his father as the foremost landowner in the county, went, apparently with the Queen's consent. Arthur was given leave to go for four months. But Walter would not join the rush to leave the country.

How strange that we have no news of the Queen, thought Katherine. It was a fine summer morning and she carried her basket amongst the herb beds. Stooping to snip some sprigs of thyme, she turned to Bessie, who stood close by. "Surely it's months since the Queen entered her confinement?" she said. "Is there no news in the marketplace? Something must be greatly amiss."

"Aye, Mistress," Bessie replied. "I never did hear of a healthy babe coming from any woman that went with child so long. The Queen thinks she's mistaken the dates. But everyone's wondering if we shall see an heir for England at all."

As they sweltered under August's heat, Katherine set a pan to boil for blanching green apples. She had a mind to make suckets to set aside for their Christmas table. Apples picked well before they ripened brought a bright green colour to the crystallised lozenges that would look pretty beside the dark ruby of quince marmalade.

Walter found her wiping her brow before the fire. "The Queen's confinement chamber's been returned to its former use," he announced with a triumphant chuckle. "Like as not, she never was pregnant at all, though some say she miscarried and was loath to admit it. There's even rumour that a plot to smuggle in a changeling Prince was discovered and thwarted."

"I think she truly believed that she would have a child," mused Katherine. Just for a moment she entertained some sympathy for the Queen. "If so, she must be sorely disappointed now. She must feel the sands of her time draining away, and with no babe at all." But then she remembered the fires of Smithfield and withdrew her kind thoughts sharply.

"That's as may be," said Walter, "but I'm sure that Philip of Spain, unlike his needy, love-struck wife, saw the marriage as one of pure political necessity. He's up and left to fight the French in Flanders. We can breathe more easily. At least for now, no Spanish heir will be foisted upon our land."

In October there came a letter from Kat. Her mistress had at last been allowed to recall her household. 'My Lady is delivered out from the shadow of the axe,' wrote Kat dramatically. 'After this frightening time, she is sad and lonely. I thought it might cheer her to have the company of bright young people; those that might discuss the classics, exploration, or whatever may lighten her spirits.'

Katherine clapped her hands. Kat had permission to arrange for Humphrey to join the household at Hatfield. What an opportunity! It would do him no harm at all to serve Elizabeth, however the die might fall in future. Kat had already sent messengers to Humphrey, who had moved on from Eton to Oxford, and to Penkervell as well. And so it was arranged; a straw of hope in trying times.

Walter was often in Exeter, currying the favour of people like William Hurst. In this he had some work to do. His ardent support for reform and his exploits during the Commotion Time didn't play well with everyone; nor did his known close friendship with Peter Carew bring him many other friends. But Walter was well regarded as a seasoned mariner, and was growing wealthy. He greased a few palms and in time they granted him his wish to become a Freeman of the City. He hoped it would give him an inside track on any deals in the offing.

"Will we go to war, Father?" asked an excited but fearful five-year-old Carew as he tugged at Walter's sleeve. "The butcher's boy says we will. Will you go, Father?"

"I doubt it, son," said Walter, swishing his arms through the air as if delivering a sword thrust to the boy's chest. "I'm too old. But perhaps the French will attack us here, and provoke Queen Mary into joining the war."

Seeing Carew's face drain of colour, Katherine said sharply, "Don't tease the boy so, Walter. No, Carew, your father will not go to war, and we are safe enough here at Poer Hayes."

"Aye, boy," said Walter with a grin, "and your mother will surely defend us if any Frenchmen dare threaten us. Just as she did before you were born, when the rebels were about. I would go trembling in fear of such a fierce warrior!"

Katherine picked up a broom and started to chase him round the parlour, before they both collapsed, laughing, onto the settle. Carew giggled and went to see what sweetmeats he could steal while the kitchen maids' backs were turned.

Later, Walter spoke more seriously about the wars. Charles V, the Holy Roman Emperor, had abdicated in favour of Philip, who seemed determined to protect Spanish interests in the Low Countries at all costs. Everyone watched and waited to see if England would be drawn in.

"Best that I make a show of offering myself and my ships to serve the Queen, Katherine-Kate. We must be careful to keep on the right side in these times of burnings. There are people I can speak to and put myself in a good light."

Just as well he can bring in a steady income from the sea, thought Katherine as the maids set out the paltry apple crop on the shelves.

Looking up at the leaden sky, she cursed under her breath. Her cloak was wet and heavy, and another band of rain was sweeping through the orchard. The fruits promised by a fine spring had been tossed by strong winds and dashed from the branches in September, long before they were ripe enough for picking. It was fortunate that they had taken the green ones so early. The storms and persistent heavy rain had ruined the wheat harvest, too. Prices were shooting up. It took all her skill to manage their stores against the coming winter. Some said famine would come. They blamed the Queen and her marriage for everything from the unrelenting foul weather and disastrous harvest, to the vagabonds on the highways; from the waves of sickness that swept the land, to the debased coinage that wouldn't buy enough bread to feed a family. Everyone, rich and poor alike, was downcast and depressed. The fires continued to burn. Former Bishops Ridley and Latimer suffered cruel deaths in the streets of Oxford. No one at Poer Hayes was surprised when whispered rumours of another uprising reached them, though accounts were garbled and confused.

When he called at Poer Hayes before Christmas, Arthur confessed that he hoped to see the Queen's sister wed to Edward Courtenay. "After all," he said quietly, looking around to make sure they could not be overheard, "Courtenay's of the royal line of York. The Queen is ailing. Elizabeth is like to be next in line. Were she wed to Courtenay, we might hope again!"

Appointed to represent Plympton Earle, Arthur said he'd voted against the government more than once. Katherine's face went white when he said he'd met other reform-supporting Members of Parliament to discuss tactics.

"Have a care, brother," she said as she pressed a box of her green lozenges into his hands to take as a gift for Mary. "Your actions might be misconstrued. Don't take any risks."

As the year turned, details of the plot leaked out. Suspicious eyes turned on the red-haired Princess and all her household.

THIRTY

1556–1557

KATHERINE

APRIL 1556, AND ARCHBISHOP CRANMER, WHOSE PRAYER BOOK had caused the Commotion in the West, the architect of the changes they had so welcomed, was sent to the stake.

"To think that she forced him to witness Ridley and Latimer's agonies last year," said Katherine. She spoke slowly, unable to take in the horror of it.

"It must have gone hard with him," said Walter, shaking his head. "When they put the full force of the Church of Rome to work on him, they say he recanted. I find it hard to believe Cranmer could shift his allegiance so. Perhaps that was just a short time of weakness from a man worn out with care and woe."

"The Queen always saw him as chief architect of her mother's ills," Katherine remarked. "She could never forgive him. Tell me again what you heard."

"Before he took his last steps they let him speak from the pulpit at the university church in Oxford. They expected he would publicly recant; that he would espouse the Church of Rome. God's blood!" Walter exclaimed. "That would have strengthened their hand! But, as the tale is told, he stunned the Queen and her advisers by calling out the Pope as the Antichrist! Took back any recantation of the views that had shaped his whole life. When they tied him to the stake he pushed his right hand, the one that had signed, first into the flames."

Katherine shuddered.

Not long after, as they dodged the April showers, she found Carew and Margaret sitting on the bench beside the apple store, poring over a pamphlet. Walt was brandishing a stout stick, marching up and down and lisping what sounded like "Run the Spaniards through." Oh, how proud the little tyke was of those newly learned words as he strutted about, waving the stick in front of him like a rapier! Katherine couldn't help but smile.

Later, she showed the pamphlet to Walter. It had long been their habit to read together and to discuss the matters of the day before they retired to bed. Lately, Walter often asked her to read aloud to him.

"I do so love to hear your sweet voice shape the words, my love," he would say, though she knew that the truth was that his eyesight was failing and he was too proud to have eyeglasses made.

So it was Katherine who read out the words the children had been so engrossed in; words in support of a plot to remove the Queen.

"'Tis no surprise," Walter said. "I heard in Exeter that the country's flooded with these papers. It's pure propaganda, and though we might hope they succeed we must consign it to the flames. Caution Margaret and Carew that they should not speak of this abroad. Even here in our peaceful haven in Devon, who knows what eyes and ears are set to trap us?"

Eyes and ears were certainly on the alert for seditious material, and Kat had been less careful in destroying it. A copy of the same pamphlet, found in a cabinet at her lodgings, was seized on as proof that she was well aware of the plot, and, by implication, so was her mistress. To Katherine's horror, Kat was again arrested and taken to the Tower for questioning, and then to Fleet Prison.

"How will she survive there?" Katherine wailed. "It's where they put people while they wait to meet their end in the fires. Surely they won't send Kat to the flames?"

"Well, I survived the Fleet, dear heart. Your Uncle Carew has all in hand. I met one of his servants in Exeter yesterday. He says his master will see that Kat comes to no harm."

"How does Uncle George manage to weave a path so surely through all of this?" asked Katherine.

"He is a clever man. Perhaps he takes his text from Nicodemus," Walter chuckled. "Well, your uncle does seem to change his stripes to suit the times."

She bristled at what sounded like criticism, but he cut off her protest.

"Calm down. We all know him for his true colours. But he believes, as I do, that having all of us burned like pigs on a spit will do nothing to help our cause. Having condemned so many, the Queen is as short of seasoned men of the Church as she is of good mariners. Your uncle's time will come again, rest assured of that."

Katherine hoped his words would prove true, since Anne Harvey – or Anne Carew, whichever name they should give her – had two sons to care for.

"Never fear," said Walter. "Your Uncle George knows better than most how to have his cake and eat it too."

Strangely, after a time they stopped questioning the Lady Elizabeth's servants. Her household was simply dismissed, to be replaced by those Queen Mary thought she could better trust. Walter said the word on the streets of Exeter was that the Queen's husband had put a stop to it, saying that Elizabeth's life must be spared at all costs.

"Perhaps the Spaniard has given up all hope that his wife can give him an heir," offered Walter. "He'd be loath to give up his power in England, that's for sure. I wouldn't be at all surprised if Philip of Spain weds again in England."

This provoked a wry comment from Katherine. "Why, how strange that such a staunch Christian, who must know the Scripture so very well, does not take the same view as King Henry about that text in Leviticus! You know, the one about marrying the brother or sister of your dead spouse. But of course, he wouldn't, would he? How these powerful men do argue this way and that to suit their own purposes."

"Well, my dear," said Walter, with a twinkle in his eye, "who can blame him for fancying his chances with the younger, prettier one? She might well give him heirs, and after all, she's a much comelier package. I'll warrant she's as proud and hard to manage as the one I see before me."

Katherine made a grab for him, and they fell about laughing.

Humphrey's short sojourn as companion to the embattled Princess had come to a swift end. He certainly didn't want to return permanently to Devon, so he went back to Oxford to continue his studies, and then divided his time: sometimes there, sometimes with his Aunt Kat, and sometimes around the Inns of Court. Katherine hoped that when John came of age Humphrey might come home. But she was realistic enough to see that he'd probably seek his fortune elsewhere.

Kat emerged unscathed from her captivity after four long months, and returned to her husband's estates. In September the hopes of many Devon men crumbled further when Edward Courtenay died in Venice. The man who had stirred himself so little in plots to make him King while others risked their all was gone; some said by poison. Walter said it was more likely some ague contracted in the lagoons and standing waters around that far-off city.

In the midst of all this, to their amazement, they learned that Peter was back in England. The story came second-hand and garbled. Peter had been in Antwerp with Sir John Cheke. The Sheriff had them seized and blindfolded and their arms tied. They were bundled into a fishing boat bound for England, and then taken directly to the Tower. It all sounded very odd. It didn't sound like Peter at all to walk into a trap.

"How will my cousin escape this time?" asked Katherine plaintively.

"He'll do," said Walter with a thin smile. "Cheke's ill, and likely won't survive. But Peter's well, and Margaret's working hard to secure his release. The Queen will soon see that he's worth more to her alive than as a rotting corpse."

Where had the years gone? How could her first boy, her John, be nearly twenty-one? Leaves crackled under the horses' hooves and mist hung in the air as they approached the Church of St John in the village of Ashton on that November day. John was to be married to Elizabeth Chudleigh.

Richard Chudleigh, father of the bride, stood beside the lychgate, shifting from foot to foot as he twisted a gold chain round his bony fingers. His eyes were fixed on a spot between his feet as Katherine approached on Walter's arm. Her bright smile froze and she struggled not to show the shock she felt at seeing him so changed. She could guess why. All of those stories about his son Christopher, still in hiding across the sea, must have cut such a proud man to the quick. At near seventy, he headed a family of staunch reformers all set firm against Spanish ways. It must have been hard for him to hear his own son accused of giving away the secrets of the latest failed plot. It really didn't matter that neither Katherine nor Walter believed a word of it. They felt sure it had been one of Christopher's men, captured while bearing letters, not Christopher himself who had betrayed the plotters. But for Richard the mere suggestion of the boy's guilt had been enough to bring him to despair. Katherine reached forward, took his hand and looked into his rheumy eyes.

"This is a happy day, Richard: to see my boy joined to such a noble family, and one so strong in honour, in these dark days."

His eyes lightened a fraction as he took the meaning from her carefully chosen words. He led them into the porch where John stood beaming happily, eager to plight his troth.

As they left the church after the short service of thanksgiving, Katherine had to look twice and then once again at the tall lad who walked beside Arthur. Henry Champernowne was so like his father that for a moment she almost believed he really was Johnny. Only after close study did she note that his nose had a slight upward tilt, that his smile was not quite broad enough, that the laughter lines etched about his eyes were not quite so deep. Arthur, who had been an honest steward for his nephew, said Johnny's boy was a likely fellow who excelled as a swordsman but also loved to read and learn. One glance told Katherine that this was indeed so.

As Henry moved off to join the other young people, Arthur turned to Katherine with a knowing grin. "Yes, Katherine-Kate, he's a fine boy. He'll make a fine soldier."

"Oh dear, not another of our boys who'll be lured away by dreams of glory?" she cried.

Arthur flashed her a dazzling smile. "Now, Katherine-Kate, it's only natural. All boys want to win their spurs. Henry's no fool, and he's sound on religion too. He'll do. But it will soon be time for me to hand Modbury into his keeping. He's old enough to be looking for a wife of his own. Mark this: we'll see him wed to Edgecumbe's daughter before a year's out."

"Well, that's wonderful news," she replied. "Edgecumbe's kin to my husband. Mother will be pleased, I'm sure. But where will you and Mary live when Henry's wed?"

"Mother's delighted, of course. And you're right – Mary and I need to give Henry space to come into his own." Arthur straightened, and his chin went up. "I have my eye on a fine estate. I'm sure you know it well, for it is upon the good old River Dart that was backdrop to your life for so long." He teased her for a few more moments before revealing that he meant to have Dartington Hall.

Her mouth fell open. "Now that would be a fine thing! I remember it well. A large estate upstream from Greenway Court, with a grand deer park. Ah, and there's some fine trout fishing on the river. Otho held land there of King Henry's last Queen. It bore wondrous oak trees fit to build fine ships. They used to say there was a rather splendid hall built long ago by a half-brother to a King, but I never saw it. Why, that will come at quite a cost, will it not?"

"Fear not, sister; I am now a man of means, not the little boy who would defend you with my wooden sword," Arthur exclaimed, puffing out his stomach in imitation of his young self. "If all goes to plan we'll soon have everything ready to receive you and Walter as honoured guests."

She laughed, thinking how well Arthur had managed the family finances and his own over the years. He'd made the most of the lands they'd picked up when the monasteries were dissolved. If he could get Dartington she'd be delighted.

After the wedding they heard that, against all the odds, Peter was released. Ironically it was his grandfather's long-standing debts to the Crown that saved him. The Queen was short of funds, and clever Margaret had raised enough to discharge the debts as a condition of her husband's release.

"So Sir Edmund's profligate ways in support of his King were the means to his grandson's salvation with this troublesome Queen," Walter remarked.

"Well, I hope Margaret will keep that errant husband of hers under control now," Katherine chided.

By the following March the Queen had given in to her husband's entreaties to support him with arms.

"That foolish old woman's as excited as a girl that her husband's back at last," complained Walter, who'd hoped that the country would avoid any involvement in the war in the Low Countries. "She couldn't gainsay him. There's reports that the deluded woman even convinced herself that she might still give the Spaniard a son. I suppose she thought the least she could do was support him in war with the French."

"Ah, my husband," Katherine commented. "So once more England is at war with the old enemy. If I'm not mistaken, that'll make French vessels fair game again. I've no doubt you and the boys have thought of that."

They had indeed. Walter's boys were looking to take every chance they could to seize prizes amongst the French fleet.

"You know us well," Walter replied with his old wolfish grin. "Do you know what I think, though? I think if Queen Mary puts out a call to arms we might see some of the men who stood strong against the Spanish marriage volunteer their service to their Queen and country."

"What? Even if they must fight against those who, like them, are against Popish ways? Even if they must fight alongside Philip the Spaniard?"

"'Tis complicated, my dearest," he replied. "But think on this. What better way for the likes of Peter, pardoned at last, to demonstrate strong allegiance and re-establish themselves in the Queen's favour? It may not be for long. She's very thin and looks like an aged crone, though she be but a few years older than you, dear Katherine-Kate. We may have a new Queen soon. Then we shall see which way the world turns."

Katherine looked around to make sure no one stood in the shadows to report Walter's incautious words. "Aha!" she cried. "So self will trump principle and scruples."

"It will serve for now," he replied. "We must all put our hopes on the longer game."

Walter was right. All those who had been languishing in exile rushed to heed the call. Francis Russell went straight from Italy to join the battle with his followers from the West Country. The Dudley boys had received pardons and were falling over themselves to show their loyalty. Peter armed himself and led a troop to swell Lord Pembroke's forces. Arthur left in haste in early July, determined to see some action. Walter said they were all headed for Saint-Quentin, where the Imperial Army had the French under siege. Pembroke's forces arrived too late to play a part in the battle, but were heavily engaged in taking the town, which fell into English hands on the tenth day of August.

In that same week, Katherine and Walter set out for Exeter, where papers must be signed. Her son John was determined to set right what he saw as the wrongs done to his mother. He would exchange the portion left as her jointure for Smallridge, the lands the Raleighs had sold to old John Gilbert long ago. It was a clever idea, guaranteed to please not only his mother, but his stepfather too. How fitting that for the rest of her life she would have the income from those fertile lands a few miles further to the east.

A stay in the city was a rare treat: a chance to visit the haberdashers and glove makers, to choose trimmings and fabric for new gowns in the latest style, to find trinkets for Margaret and Mary and toys for the boys, and to visit John and his wife Elizabeth, who had taken a town house near the cathedral. She was looking forward to catching up with all the latest news. Her eyes were sparkling and her heart was light as they rode in through the city gate. Walter turned to look at her, and she felt a familiar joyous tingle right down to the tips of her fingers.

"You're still the fairest woman I ever set my eyes upon, Katherine-Kate. All the merchants of Exeter will be green with envy when they see me ride into their city with you at my side," he said, his voice warm as a caress. He wore his pride in her on his sleeve for all to see. "'Twas a lucky day indeed when first I spied you on the *Trinity*. My sea-nymph bride!"

"'Twas a lucky day for us both," she answered, her cheeks dimpling as she returned his gaze. He had pushed the rose she had plucked for him into the front of his doublet; a reminder of their wedding day when the apothecary's rose was in full bloom beside the door; a reminder of the heady days of their honeymoon voyage aboard the *Katherine*; a reminder of how much she loved him. She looked into his eyes and saw them alight with yearning, love and pride. His smile broadened to a beaming grin. There was something in Walter's smile that could still set butterflies dancing inside her. Oh, how she was looking forward to a few days' holiday with her love

She took his arm as he steered her through the streets. She could hardly keep from skipping down the broad pavement outside the Guildhall. Walter's booming laugh rang out as he greeted acquaintances, and Katherine blushed as he showered her with compliments. After a short visit to the lawyer, he led her round the shops, encouraging her to spare no expense. Bessie followed behind, her arms soon full of packages, which she carried willingly, excited to see inside those shops. Like her mistress, Bessie was definitely enjoying the rare treat of a day in the city.

Their business complete, they chanced to meet with John Hooker, an important city official whom Walter had known for years. After a few moments' pleasant conversation Hooker invited them to his house, which lay close by the Palace Gate. Bessie was dispatched to convey all their purchases to John's house, just around the corner, and they followed the city recorder into an imposing building of pleasing red stone.

"Why, what a fine house this is, Master Hooker," Katherine said as her gaze flitted round the large parlour with its splendid fireplace and leaded windows.

Walter gave her a quizzical look, as if surprised by her enthusiasm. "Do you think that one day you might forsake the countryside and live within the city walls in a place such as this?" he quipped. "I'm beginning to feel my age, my dear. Perhaps we would be more comfortable in such a house as this as I grow older. I'd still be able to go down to the sea often, and to visit our other properties. Your son and his wife have a place nearby, and you would have the company of other ladies. You've said yourself how much you've enjoyed the shops today. Oh, and I'm sure there would be room for a small garden." He cast a hopeful look at her.

"Walter, my dear, you know that I would live with you here or anywhere and be the happiest woman in the land," she said, artfully giving no answer either way.

"Hmm," he said, turning to their host. "What say you, Master Hooker? Shall I persuade her, do you think?"

"Well, sir," John Hooker replied, with a twinkling smile, "I can say this: it would be a great pleasure to one day welcome you as my neighbours."

Hooker's wife, a bustling dumpling of a woman introduced as Martha, dimpled and nodded but said nothing. Katherine smiled and inclined her head as Hooker invited her to sit. For the first time she studied their host. She judged him to be a few years younger than she was herself. Clad all in the severest black, relieved only by a startlingly white ruff at his throat, he looked every inch a man of letters. She knew something of his history. He was the son of Robert Hooker, a well-respected Mayor of Exeter. An Oxford man, John had served Miles Coverdale briefly and was recognised as a skilled administrator. Appointed Chancellor of the city two years previously, he was now responsible for the city's finances, and had a reputation for dealing fairly with disputes between the guilds. Walter liked him, that was clear, and she knew that Peter Carew thought highly of him too. *Aha*, she thought, *my Walter will listen hard to this man with his long face and piercing, all-seeing eyes.*

As they sipped ale and nibbled honeyed jumble cakes, Hooker told a most distressing tale. They sat, appalled and fascinated by turns, as he recounted the story of a woman who would be sent to her death the next day. Agnes Prest was not a native of Exeter, but came from a village near Launceston in Cornwall.

"She is but a contemptible person," said Hooker, examining his ink-stained fingers studiously as he spoke. "She is a simple woman of no learning whatsoever, condemned to die for speaking out and denying the presence of the sacrament at the altar."

Katherine thought that Hooker, like Walter, had trimmed his sails to the prevailing wind, though in his heart he favoured reform. Although deep down he probably shared Agnes Prest's views, his words seemed to belittle the woman. Was that because she was not of his city, or was it that she was merely a poor, uneducated woman? Katherine's head tilted to one side and she leaned forward.

Hooker also leaned forward and rubbed his hands together. "Not since Benet met his grisly end all those years ago have we seen like."

So even in this city, so far from Smithfield, the air would be defiled by that dreadful smell. Exeter had seen no such barbarous acts since the Queen set out on her mission to destroy any who disagreed with her favoured version of God's truth. But John Hooker told them that, on the morrow, that would change.

"Pray tell us more, Master Hooker," she said, suppressing a shudder.

"Well," Hooker rejoined. "Oh, this is most shocking to tell. This woman, this Agnes, was decried by her own family; even by her own husband. She lived apart from him, but even so, to do that to one you had called wife! What do you think of that?" His patrician face crumpled as he made a show of struggling to understand. "How could any husband do such a thing Mistress Raleigh?" Martha interjected from her seat in the corner. John Hooker's eyebrows shot up, and Martha blushed and looked down at her hands.

Well, King Henry found it easy enough to decry his wives whether they were guilty or not, thought Katherine. She was intrigued to know what had made Agnes Prest, an ordinary woman, leave her hearth and home, but she let it pass. "Shocking indeed! Do go on, Master Hooker," she said with an encouraging little smile.

"The woman was indicted at Launceston and then brought to Exeter. Found guilty by William Stanford, Justice of the Assize, she was then referred to the Bishop for examination. Blackstone – he that's Chancellor to the cathedral now – oh, he did press hard for a burning right from the outset. But she must give account of herself first. Of course, it fell to our new Bishop to interrogate her. Bishop Turbeville is a gentle and courteous gentleman, but, oh, he is so very hot for the Church of Rome! 'Tis as you might well imagine in these times," said Hooker, giving Walter a watery smile.

"And what did the Bishop find, then, as he examined her?" asked Walter, who was by now sitting on the edge of his seat. "I will give you the report of the very words he used as it did come to my ears by those that were present," said Hooker. "Turbeville did say to her, 'Thou, an unlearned person and a woman, wilt thou meddle in such high matters which all the doctors of the world cannot define? Wilt thou talk of so high mysteries?' But the woman would not give o'er, and stated again most clearly her belief that the sacrament was but a sign and figure of Christ's body. Then said Turbeville, 'Keep thy work and meddle in that thou hast to do. 'Tis no woman's matter. If it be so as I have been informed, then thou art worthy to be burned.' You see, the good Bishop would have none of her words."

Katherine was by now bristling with anger. As her chin came up, Walter caught her eye. Seething inwardly, she looked down and studied her hands in her lap. It sounded as though the woman had been condemned not so much because of the belief she stated openly, but because as a woman she had no right to express her views at all. Oh, that was shameful indeed!

"Then the other clerics laughed at her, and the Bishop pressed his advantage, thinking to make fun of her. He asked her mockingly, 'I pray you, in what schools have you been brought up?' Of course the Bishop knew well – they all knew – that she was a woman of no learning. She could by no means read or write," Hooker continued. "Well, 'tis reported, Mistress Raleigh, that Prest spoke up then, saying, 'I have upon Sundays visited the sermons, and there I learned such things as are so fixed in my breast that death shall not dislodge them.' So then Bishop Turbeville, not wishing to allow her any chance to expound more on her views on the mysteries, probed her about her desertion of her husband. 'Who will waste breath on thee? By what chanced it that thou was sent away from thy husband?' the Bishop asked. Then the woman says, 'Oh, it was a choice between him and my heavenly husband.' Well, that was enough to seal her fate. Oh my, we have not seen such doings in Exeter these many years," said John Hooker, his face alight with the thrill of telling the tale.

Katherine was troubled by what she had heard. There must be more to this. She would know more of this woman, Agnes Prest. "Pray tell me, Master Hooker, where is the woman lodged this night?" she asked innocently.

Hooker replied that she was kept in the castle gaol and would be burned the next day, just beyond the city walls.

After they had all expressed their shock and horror, Walter steered the conversation to other matters. As the two men discussed whether a better harvest might bring down the appalling price of wheat and malt, what the possibilities were of the Muscovy Company opening up new trade routes to the north-east, how badly wool was selling in Antwerp, and what prospects Walter might have to be elected to Parliament, Katherine considered the predicament of that poor Cornish woman. But she knew her manners well, and joined the discussion when it turned to books. John Hooker sat up and beamed as they discussed the finer points of a recent volume.

"Mistress Raleigh, I see now where that son of yours, young John Gilbert, came by his accomplishments," he said. "He's a likely lad. Mark me well: he'll become an important man in Devon when he takes charge of the Gilbert affairs. Why, he has already approached me, as recorder of the city and keeper of its finances. He's keen to make sure that the city Corporation fulfils its obligation to that lazar house over in Newton Bushell."

"I am pleased to hear that John takes his responsibilities seriously," she replied.

"His mother must have given him a fine start in the world," Hooker went on, turning to Walter. "Do you know, Raleigh, he's shown a deal of sense already. He's suggested that, since the number of poor wights suffering from that dread affliction in Newton Bushell is so much reduced, the Corporation should instead declare the property beside the Exeter Road to be almshouses for any poor people of that place, not solely for the lazars. And he's insisted that the Corporation should continue to fund those housed there in accordance with the agreement. Why, he's even stipulated that they must in future be known as the Gilbert Almshouses. I can tell you, I was impressed."

"He learned a lot from his great-uncle, Master Hooker," Katherine said with a modest smile.

"Your son and I share an interest in the stars, you know," the city recorder went on. "We exchanged views on the works of the Italian, Copernicus, whose ideas have started quite a revolution in thinking on astronomy. Having met with you this day, 'tis easy to see how your son did come by his quick mind and winning ways."

"He is but the eldest of my brood, sir," she said, inclining her head again to acknowledge his compliment. "I trust, Master Hooker, that you and your wife will soon have occasion to meet my other sons." She turned then to Martha, who had spoken but once, and drew her into conversation about their respective families.

It was only a short distance to her son John's house, where they were to lodge that night. As they rounded the corner and the lofty towers of the cathedral church came into view, Katherine paused and turned to face her husband. Walter's face wore a resigned look. She'd wager he could guess what was coming.

"Walter," she said, pitching her voice low and steady and ignoring the fluttering deep in her chest, "I will visit the Cornish woman. I will bring her what comfort I may. I will hear her side of matters."

"Katherine-Kate," he said heavily, "did you not heed Master Hooker? She has refused all offers of funds, saying she will soon be gone to a place where money has no mastery. She will accept comfort from no one. Her fate is sealed. The woman is determined that she will suffer and die. What can you do for her? There is danger for you and for all of us in this action. Why, you could be taken up for supporting what they now call heresy. We have weathered this storm right well by seeming to bend to the Queen's laws. Don't upset our applecart now."

He looked imploringly at her, but Katherine pressed her lips together and threw back her shoulders.

"Ah," he declared with a wry smile. "I've seen that look before: your jaw set, and your pretty lips drawing into that thin line. 'Tis no use to argue with that look. When your mind's set on something, Katherine-Kate, you can be as stubborn as an ox. I had other plans for our holiday night, you know," he added, looking forlorn.

She fixed unwavering eyes on his and nodded. "As did I, my dear," she replied. "You know how much I've looked forward to our time here together. But, Walter, this changes all. I would visit the woman. I cannot leave it be." Anticipating his next objection, she went on, "John can escort me and gain me entry. He is well regarded in the city. Walter, my dearest love, I *will* see her. I must judge for myself what has driven this woman to such a pass. Her feelings must be strong indeed to face such horror and not be tempted to retract her words. I doubt I shall persuade her to save herself. But it may be that I can offer a few moments of quiet companionship, as one woman with another."

Walter brought her hand to his lips, and his fingers tightened around hers as he looked deep into her eyes. "That fierce pride, that brave spirit of yours, is what makes me love you so," he said with a nod. "I give in, Katherine-Kate. I'll own, I admire you for it. But this must be handled with care."

THIRTY-ONE
1557
KATHERINE

THE RED-TINTED WALLS OF ROUGEMONT CASTLE ROSE, threatening and invincible, on top of a high bank. They crossed the bridge that spanned the deep, refuse-filled ditch with its all-pervading stink of rotting vegetation, and rode on toward the rounded archway beside the square gatehouse tower. In the quiet of that late afternoon the clip-clopping of their horses' hooves echoed loud on the cobblestones. Magnified by the nearby wall, the hooves beat out their metallic rhythm like hammers on an anvil, setting Katherine's nerves on edge. She managed a smile as she looked at the high walls, and wondered how Uncle Gawen had scaled them so nimbly. He must have been over fifty, and he was quite portly! That was when they were all up in arms against the Spanish marriage. *It was that marriage that brought us to this*, she thought, and felt her jaw tighten.

The men guarding the archway stood back, saluted and waved them on when they recognised John. Katherine dismounted and picked her way across the cobbled courtyard surrounded by the halls where Father had sat so often as Justice of the Peace. A better-appointed building that she supposed might be the governor's house faced them. But John led her to another door set deep into the wall away to the right, and banged loudly on the gnarled boards with his gloved fist. After a few moments the door groaned open and they were admitted to a cramped, low-ceilinged chamber. A large man dressed in grease-stained black sat behind a table spread with a muddle of parchments. The head gaoler, no doubt.

After some discussion, he hauled himself from his stool and led them down a passageway lit by a few guttering candles. His rolling gait set his keys all a-jangle, and his rasping breath sounded loud as the ocean. Katherine suppressed a shiver. Behind each of the gloomy, ill-lit doorways sunk deep into the bare stone walls must lie some half-starved prisoner. As they moved on into the very bowels of the fortress, her nose twitched in distaste. A truly vile smell almost made her retch. Perhaps Walter was right after all. Perhaps this was no place for a Champernowne lady.

"Mother? Are you sure?" John asked, laying his hand on her arm.

She raised her chin and pulled back her shoulders. "Yes, John, I will go on."

They stopped before a rough oak door and the fat man pulled back a tiny shutter to peer inside. He shouted to whoever lurked behind the door to stand aside, then turned the key. The door swung back, creaking in protest on its iron hinge. Katherine dipped her head to pass beneath the low lintel and saw a woman seated on a wooden pallet. The woman rose and bobbed a curtsy as Katherine drifted towards her. Her gaze was neither unduly deferent before so grand a lady, nor by any means insolent.

"Now, Mother," said John, "I shall post my man behind the door, and you are but to knock or call out." Katherine could hear the concern in his voice.

"Why, John," she said, her eyes never leaving the woman's face, "I have nothing to fear in this place. All will be well." She turned to John with a smile. He gave her an anxious look, but turned to follow the fat gaoler out of the cell. The door swung shut with a finality that would haunt her to the end of her days. She heard a muffled exchange and then footsteps retreating slowly, until she could hear them no more.

Agnes Prest had a dignity far beyond the simple working woman's clothes she wore. She seemed to command the whole space of that cheerless cell. It was only when she moved forward and crossed the cold stone floor that Katherine realised how very tiny she was. Agnes's head did not reach nearly so high as Katherine's shoulder as she raised her dark eyes to study her unexpected visitor.

The hand the woman extended was rough and calloused from hard work and long hours at the spinning wheel. Her skin was the deep, sun-burnished brown of those that labour long in the fields. Even confined in this dark and dirty place she had tried to maintain herself in cleanliness. Her hand was scrubbed, even the nails, and she must have found a way to wash the linen coif that covered her greying hair, for it looked neat and tidy. Katherine remembered John Hooker's account of how the priests had made fun of this small, determined woman who had never learned to read, and shook her head.

Even in August the cell felt cold as the grave. The only furnishing was the boarded pallet, which bore no mattress, just a tattered blanket of roughly woven wool. There were two pails. One must hold water, for there was a pitcher hanging from the twisted rope handle. The other, pushed into the corner and covered by a cloth, must have another purpose. Perhaps that accounted for the dank smell that seemed to linger in every crevice and cranny. Katherine sat on the unyielding planks of the pallet and motioned the woman to sit beside her. Agnes seemed as unconcerned as if she were just gone to the marketplace to buy bread.

"'Tis good of you to take such trouble to come to me, Mistress. I see by your looks 'tis kindly meant," she said. The words were smothered in the thickest Cornish burr Katherine had ever encountered. She had to listen hard to get the meaning. "But, Mistress, there be nought in comfort you may bring me. I have all I need in my faith in God my Saviour. I shall soon be in a better place than this."

Katherine was so impressed with the sincerity and quiet courage of the simple woman that she called to the man beyond the door, "You may leave me. Tell my son that I will stay and bear my sister company until morning comes."

They sat for a time in silence. Then, at Katherine's patient questioning, Agnes told her story. Like many a woman she had married when only a girl, not at her own choosing, but to suit her father. The husband chosen for her was a brutish, small-minded man who treated her unkindly, though she seemed loath to blame him. She had borne her lot patiently, cooking his food and coming at his beck and call, as any good wife must. She had followed the laws of the Church along with every other soul in her village. She had seen the priest perform the mysteries of the Mass. She had heard the Latin words droning through the brightly decorated church; words she could by no means understand. But then King Edward had ordered that the Word of God be proclaimed in the English tongue.

"Now," said Agnes, "as a woman of Cornwall, that be not my native tongue. But us all do know it well enough; much more 'n Latin, which I know not at all. So now, Mistress, I could listen to the Scriptures, and follow the Word of God in me own heart as never before. Suddenly I saw all things clearly and knew God's purpose."

Katherine learned how Agnes had left her husband when he criticised her for her simple faith. How she had managed to feed herself by spinning and by working in the fields at harvest time. How it was her cruel husband and his family that had brought her to the notice of the authorities.

"But I bear no rancour against them, My Lady. I do but pray that they shall come to know all that is true one day." At last she spoke the words that had condemned her. "Mistress, it came to me that the priest's pantomime of elevating that cup be nothing but a dumb show to fool us ignorant people. For I do believe no Christian soul eats the body of Christ, but spiritually."

As Agnes spoke these shocking words, a bell rang in Katherine's memory. She had heard those very same words before. Her mind went back to the last time she had seen Joanie, who had come on a rare visit to Devon just before the Commotion Time. She had told Katherine of her own narrow escape from charges of heresy when another courageous woman had made a stand. Katherine struggled to remember the name. Anne… ah yes, it was Anne Askew; another woman who had lived apart from her family and been shunned for her beliefs. Anne Askew, a woman with much more learning than the worn and tired little body seated beside Katherine, had come to the same straightforward conclusion. She'd even withstood the rack, so certain was she of her beliefs. Katherine was sure that Joanie had recounted those same words that Agnes now spoke as coming from Anne's lips. She wondered whether the simple Cornish woman sitting so still beside her had somehow heard of Anne, or if she had come to that knowledge herself.

As they spoke further, Katherine was more and more impressed by Agnes's understanding of Scripture. She could not fault her. It must be that she had come to it of herself, in spite of her lack of education. Here, seated beside her, was the living proof that even those with no book learning could come to see the truth. Agnes had no need of the panoply of silver, tapers and embroidered vestments. She had no need of the Latin mumbling priest. She saw that God's Word alone was enough. In that dark and dismal place, Katherine saw it too.

"Oh, how it did irk that la-di-da Bishop and all them so-called Christian men of the Church that I, a simple woman with no learning at all, could tell so much of the Scriptures," Agnes laughed. "But God's truth may come to any soul who has ears to hear, Mistress."

Agnes would not seek mercy, though Katherine tried to persuade her. "My husband says that we must for a time sway before the prevailing wind, keep faith in our hearts, and wait on better times. May you not do likewise, Agnes?" she implored.

"That path is not for me, good Mistress. I will gladly leave this world. My lot has not been a happy one, but I have been granted knowledge of the true way, and that *does* bring me joy. They cannot harm me, Mistress. But for you, the path is different. You've children? Teach them well." Agnes leaned forward to pat Katherine's hand, their roles reversed as the comforted became the comforter. It felt as though she, the grand, proud, well-educated Champernowne lady, was being granted a blessing by this tiny woman who saw so clearly.

Katherine wept often during that long night. Beside her Agnes remained dry-eyed and serene. When they came to take her in the early morning light, she turned and whispered, "Do not follow. There be no need for such as you, with such gentleness, to see what must now come to pass." Then, taking a breath, she declared, "I go to meet my God."

Katherine watched until she could no longer see her walking steadfastly, head held high, as she followed the fat gaoler through the darkness and onwards towards the light.

WALTER

This must be the longest night he'd ever spent. He'd thrown back more sack than was wise and his mouth felt dry as dust. He'd sat up as long as he dared with the young couple. John was a fine boy. A credit to her, and not much of his father in him.

He fretted and fumed, lying alone in the splendid bed at young Gilbert's house. She was so brave, so strong. He understood why she must go. It was a noble deed. But should he have forbidden it? A wry smile crossed his face as he imagined her reaction had he tried.

It was to be at sunrise. He must be there at the gaol to take her home. He plotted the best route through the city. Somehow he must save her from that sickening smell. In the dim early dawn light he craned out of the window, trying to see which way the weathervane on St Mary Major's tower was pointing. He pulled on his clothes and was ready before John knocked at the door.

KATHERINE

Her legs were as weak and wobbly as jelly in the mould. She leant heavily on John's arm, blinking in the sudden sunlight of the August morning. She let John lift her into the saddle. Through the archway she saw Walter waiting to take her home, then almost lost her balance and had to cling to the saddle pommel until she had righted herself. John, for once at a loss for words, bid them a hasty farewell and made his way homewards.

Walter leaned across from his own mount and squeezed her hand. Without a word he led her away from the castle, down into the city and out through the South Gate. He tried to keep her away from Southernhay, that grassy area beyond the city walls where oftentimes the people of Exeter made merry at the fair. But he could not shield her from it all. Katherine could not help but see, high above the rooftops, a thin trail of smoke spiralling up towards the sky. Such a clear blue sky; such a bright, shining day.

"How can the day be so fair, when such dread deeds are done?" she faltered.

After that, she spoke no more until Walter set her down in her own parlour. Bessie brought a cup of ale and he sat beside her. At last she spoke.

"Walter, I have never been so moved by another in all my days on this earth. If God were not with that simple woman, how could she speak those things? I, who can read; I, who am lucky as a woman to have so much learning – Walter, I could not answer her in her simple faith."

Walter said nothing, but held her hand in his, slowly caressing each finger.

They sat so for a long time, then Katherine said, "Agnes has the right of it. The Church propagates its mysteries to hold the people in its grasp."

"In my heart you know that I agree," Walter whispered. "I applaud what you have done. But your show of compassion for that woman may put us in danger. It is enough that we hold our peace and pray."

He took her in his arms, and her proud chin trembled as the tears fell. She felt numb and heavy, weary to the bone, as Walter rocked her slowly back and forth on the settle before the fire.

Later, after he'd coaxed her to eat a little, her anger burned. Her eyes flashed as she cried out against the Spanish marriage that had brought the Queen to such cruelty. She railed against Queen Mary's Church, the Spanish Church. By the time they noticed Walt watching from the shadows, he had heard it all.

Two weeks later Walter told her how, as he passed along Exeter's broad thoroughfare, he had again encountered John Hooker. The city recorder had greeted him warmly and shook his hand. "He said to me, 'Why, Master Raleigh, your courageous wife has shown the way that others would be too fearful to follow. Oh, I was most impressed to meet your lady. You are indeed a lucky fellow, for – my, my – she is a woman of truly noble wit. One to show the world what are true good and godly ways.' You have quite captured Master Hooker, my dear."

She smiled as Walter gave a fair imitation of Hooker's clipped tones.

"Oh, Katherine-Kate, I was proud as could be to hear him praise you so," he went on, grinning from ear to ear.

"What did you say he said of me?" she asked. It was hard to believe anyone would say such things.

"Why, what I've long known, my dearest Katherine-Kate," came the reply. "That you are a woman of noble wit."

THIRTY-TWO
1557
KATHERINE

In the hot summer months the thick farmhouse walls offered a pleasantly cool welcome. But on this October day, as the weather turned, the parlour struck chill and Bessie was kindling the fire. A sudden downpour had driven them from their orchard classroom and they'd run for cover, pell-mell, all clutching their precious books. The unmistakable earthy smell of new rain had followed them into the parlour.

Walt's none-too-clean finger slipped from the line of closely printed text he was following and he looked up. He glanced in Carew's direction, then his piercing blue eyes sought Katherine's boldly, though his brow puckered. "Mother, may I ask a question?"

"Of course, my boy," Katherine replied. She had noticed that for once Walt's mind was not on his lesson.

"Mother, is it so that God hates the Queen so much that he punishes all the people of England because of her?" he asked, his voice rising to a squeak. "Will I be so punished?"

"Why ever would you think such a thing?" she asked. She sat down next to him and put an arm around his shoulder, noticing that his feet no longer dangled above the floor, but reached all the way down to sit squarely on the flagstones.

"Well, Ralph said that we've had bad harvests for two years in a row," Walt babbled. "He said we've had murrains on the cattle and foot rot in the sheep. He said the new sickness is back and it's killed off ever so many people. And another horrid storm's brought all this rain again. Ralph said it's all 'cause of the Queen. He said it's God's punishment on us all, and we're all doomed." The words came out fast and furious, tumbling over each other as he struggled to hold back his tears. Ralph was the miller's son and the boys had been kicking a pig's bladder round the yard with him that morning while the sacks of flour were brought from the mill.

Carew, seated at the end of the board, put the finishing touches to a laboriously produced line of curly 'C's on the page in front of him and set down his quill with calm finality. He seemed much less perturbed about Ralph the miller's son and his dreadful prophecies. "He did say that, Mother, and I said to him it was nonsense, so I did," he said with a gap-toothed grin. One of his front teeth was taking a long time to oust its baby precursor, and a gaping space still showed when he smiled. "I said, 'Surely God would never have sent the Queen's husband such a victory as we saw at Saint-Quentin if he hated her so?'"

Katherine bit her lip. What the miller's boy had spoken was no more than others were saying. Men who cleaved to Popish ways might still support her, but most of the ordinary people had had enough of the prematurely aged Queen, her Spanish husband, and his war. The dreadful new sickness had taken more in the past year, leaving the workforce depleted. Many of those who survived had gone off to fight in the war. There were few left to garner the harvest, which, though it looked better than those of the past two years, would not be abundant. It was no surprise that the miller's boy spoke so. His father depended on each harvest for his livelihood. No one had yet come to challenge Katherine, or to charge her with heresy, but it would be wise to take no chances. The boys should not speak so. That path might lead to danger.

"Carew has the right of this, at least in part," she said. "The war is going well, and some will say that is through God's support for their cause. Now, Walt, some of the Queen's ways are cruel indeed. You've heard me say as much. But it will be for the Queen to answer to God for herself, as we all must one day. It is not for us to speak of her so, nor to listen to gossip." She spoke more sharply than she had intended, and, seeing Walt's face crumple, took his hand and went on more gently. "Nor do I think that God is punishing the people as Ralph said. You have nothing to fear. I can remember other years when people went hungry, or fell to the plague and suchlike diseases. Yes, it's true that the weather has turned foul, that we struggled to get the harvest in, that prices are sky-high, and that the sickness has returned. When times are hard people always look for someone to blame. Then better years come again, they forget, and everyone is happy. So it will be this time, I've no doubt of it."

"So, why *does* it rain so hard, and why *are* so many people sick, Mother?" asked Walt, still looking perplexed.

"Why, those are big questions, my boy!" she said, ruffling his curly hair, so like Walter's. "So long as we study and ask such questions, so our knowledge will grow. One day I believe we'll come to understand what really causes such sickness, whether it be foul humours that come into the body through the skin, or by some other means. This illness is different from those we've known before, but I do believe our best defence is cleanliness."

Walt looked anxiously at his fingers and rubbed them on his shirt.

"And if I could predict the weather, then I'd be the wealthiest woman in the land," she went on with a chuckle. "But, boys, consider this. There are things we know now that were not even thought of years ago. Why, one hundred years ago no one knew that there were those lands across the sea to the west. But Master Cabot sailed there and our fishing boats now trawl the northern waters, and we learn more and more of a New World."

"Humphrey says the Spanish have taken the lands over there and send huge ships of treasure back to Spain," Walt cut in, his face brightening.

"Well, that's as may be, my boy. Humphrey says all sorts of things," she said. "But my point is that new knowledge comes to us all the time. It is through people studying, experimenting and asking questions, and through brave men setting out into the unknown, that our knowledge will grow. Now, the best thing is for you to apply yourselves diligently to your studies, both of you. Learn from what is already known, learn of the ideas of others, but always ask questions, always stretch your understanding. Then you can stand well prepared for what fortune brings. So, Walt, return to Master Aesop's tale, if you will."

They all loved to read, just as she did, and had all learned their letters at her knee, girls and boys alike. Now it was Walt's turn to wrestle with the mysteries of the written word. With Agnes Prest's words ringing in her ears, Katherine had set about the task with renewed vigour. She smiled and ruffled his hair as she listened to him confidently reading aloud. He took to it as a fish does to the sea, and learned at a prodigious rate; just as quick on the uptake as Humphrey had been at the same age. Walt had such a way with him. He could charm the very birds from the trees, should he want to. He was never short of sweetmeats and treats from the kitchens, and he'd got Walter wrapped neatly round his pudgy finger.

She turned to look at the two girls seated together by the window, heads touching over their book. Margaret, near ten years old, was a thoughtful, steady girl, happy in her close friendship with the lovely Mary. Those girls would not suffer as Katherine had: married when she was no more than a child, far too young to be the mother Katie had deserved. She swallowed hard and wiped away a tear, then squared her shoulders. Best not dwell on that girl. Better to give her love to the others and teach them well. All those long hours with Johnny and old Smythe at Modbury had been worthwhile, and she could give the girls an education far beyond the wifely skills and arts. In the Modbury household, education had been sacrosanct, and you only had to hear the praise heaped upon Princess Elizabeth to see that Kat had taken that same approach when bringing up her charge.

Carew had taken up the pen again and was practising his whole name. Versions of 'Caro Ralygh' crowded the page amongst a cloud of swirly scribbles.

"Spend your time wisely when practising this art, Carew," Katherine said. Any sting from the mild reprimand was diminished by the chuckle that followed as she recognised the faces he had drawn. "I would have you boys well able to wield the quill yourselves, to set down your own thoughts clearly. Better that than to yield the power of the pen to a scribe." She had no small regret that she had neglected to practise her writing as a girl. "Now, Mary, shall we have some music, please?"

It rained so hard that afternoon that a puddle of water washed right under the door and a little rivulet streamed towards the foot of the stair. The wind howled so loud in the chimney that they didn't hear Walter's horse. Mary broke off her song mid-chorus and the lute clattered to the floor when the door suddenly sprang open. Walter had to use all his weight to close it behind him. Bessie bustled in to take his dripping cloak and he was across the room in no time, standing before the fire. Katherine helped him out of his doublet, from which steam was already rising, and everyone looked at him expectantly. When Walter came back from one of his visits to London he almost always had some new volume wrapped in oiled cloths and stowed carefully in his saddlebag. He would scour the booksellers' stalls by St Paul's, knowing that Katherine would relish new works just as much as the children. It might be a treatise on shipbuilding; a new herbal, beautifully illustrated to show both familiar and unknown plants; a book of recipes; or perhaps an account of discoveries across the seas. But today they were all disappointed. He had only been as far as the docks in Exmouth, in search of news. He looked at Katherine and shook his head.

"No news, and like as not there's a tempest raging out to sea," he said with a worried frown. "October storms can be fierce in our western approaches." George and John had taken ship in July to trade down the coast of France. "It's high time they were back," he added, as he struggled into a fresh doublet, rubbing his hands up and down the woollen cloth.

The miller's boy was right in one thing. The new sickness seemed to be spreading rapidly again. It spared neither rich nor poor; it cared not if it was winter or autumn, spring or summer. It had decimated a few far-flung villages during the previous summer, but now it was everywhere. This was no rapid affliction that saw off its victims in a few days, like the one that had robbed Katherine of her first husband and baby son. This infection played with sufferers, keeping them hanging on until their wheezing breath was finally snuffed out. First chills and fevers, then aches and weariness, then a hacking cough that would not give o'er till it left them with no breath at all.

The churchyards saw burials aplenty. Katherine's old acquaintance Thomas Yarde was one. He died not knowing if his eldest son, Edward, still lived. Arthur said the Yardes had had no news since the boy went to France in the service of Lord Francis Russell. But the household at Poer Hayes escaped the sickness, perhaps due to Katherine's housewifery which kept them all well fed.

The dreary days were shortening and it was near dark when, on a stormy December evening, a horseman thundered up to their door. A loud, insistent banging followed, and a cry: "Master Raleigh, art thou within, sir?"

Walter, who had been dozing on the settle, sprang up, bounded to the door and opened it a crack. After peering into the darkness, he turned to Katherine. "Why, I know that man. He served with George on the *Katherine Raleigh*. There must be news at last."

Walter's breath came in short gasps as he flung the door right back on its hinges and stepped outside. The sweating horse, flanks heaving and dropping foam upon the cobbles, drooped its head. "Take this exhausted beast to the stables. Be sure to rub him down thoroughly," he shouted to his serving man. He then turned to the rider, who looked near as worn out as the horse, and beckoned him inside.

"I'm come from Master George. He set me ashore at Popery. Come to tell you, sir, that they have a prize of the Portingales. They would know what to do for the best," said the messenger as he rubbed at the back of his neck with one hand, while clutching his cap in the other.

Walter sent Katherine to bring food, so she heard little of what followed. By the time she returned with a jug of ale and a dish of pottage, Walter's mouth was set in a stern line.

"I'll furnish a fresh horse. Return to George with all haste. Be sure to deliver my message clear," he said as he held out a leather pouch bulging with coins. "Take this for thy pains, and for the love of God, man, eat up and be on your way."

Now that they were again at war with France, French vessels

were fair game, but not Portuguese ones. Taking one could land the boys in the Admiralty Court on charges of piracy if they were found out.

They waited for more news. When it came, it was not good. The prize, the *Conception of Viana*, was confiscated. George was arrested and charged with piracy on the high seas by Dr Cooke, the Admiralty judge. Katherine bit her lip. As owner of the *Katherine Raleigh*, and the boys' financial backer, charges would likely be brought against Walter even though he served as Deputy Vice Admiral under Mr Yonge, whose lands in Colyton and Sidbury were not far from Poer Hayes.

Walter sat down sharply. She saw him take his pen in hand and spell out the Vice Admiral's name. "If I offer Yonge a consideration, then he'll soon see George released," he declared, scratching away with the quill. "Once his recommendation reaches William Howard, Lord High Admiral, all will be well."

Katherine watched his face as he struggled to frame the right phrases, and her eyes narrowed. To think, a Deputy Vice Admiral, but he must resort to begging Yonge to aid him! That he must prostrate himself in this way, all on account of that foolish boy! She drew a couple of deep breaths as she tried to hold back the words springing to her lips. It was no good; those words would out. "That stupid boy! It's just typical of George to get us all into such a scrape. Just like him to put your ships in such peril."

Walter was on his feet in an instant, sending the bench flying, clattering, across the room. He took a stride towards her and his face grew purple as he brandished the ink-laden quill as though it were a weapon. "Foolish woman! This trade, that sometimes be called honest privateering, and then at the whim of the Crown becomes an act of piracy, is what sustains us here!" He glowered at her as he spat the words through clenched teeth.

"I know that well enough. Do not forget that my family were men of the sea too. I know the trade," she fired back, head held high though her voice was shaking. A few spots of ink stained the flagstones between them. Her lips trembled as she studied them. The brooding silence grew longer.

Several minutes must have passed before Walter laid down the quill. "The boy was doing my bidding, dear heart. I would have taken the prize myself for sure, had I had charge of the *Katherine*."

She swallowed and hesitated a moment before speaking again, in more controlled tones. "It is not that. It is George himself that angers me. I fear he'll bring you to ruin one day, just as he did Katie. I cannot forgive that boy. That is what made me sound so shrill. But I spoke out of turn. I am sorry."

Walter's face creased into a broad grin. He held out his ink-stained hand to her. A moment passed before, trembling, she took it in her own. "It's rare indeed for my proud beauty to admit she's in the wrong! I know, Katherine-Kate. You still blame George for the loss of that foolish girl and will never forgive him. In truth, he has his faults. He was wrong to ride away with your girl. He is probably wrong now in his dealings with this Portingale. Certainly he's wrong to be found out! That's what's brought us to this pass. But fear not, I shall find a way to make this all come right."

The letter was dispatched, the messenger instructed to ride hard to be sure it was delivered. But either it came too late or the Vice Admiral could do nothing. George was summoned to appear before the Admiralty Court on the thirteenth day of December, and Walter put up the money for his bail.

When John, who had escaped capture, brought the *Katherine* home, Walter ordered that she be made ready to sail again. He was taking no chances. They might try to seize his prized barque to find recompense for the Portuguese merchants, who were by now pressing their case hard. Within days the *Katherine* was gone, captained by John Philips, who had boarded the *Conception* with Walter's sons. She bore away a sizeable portion of the Portuguese cargo, and Philips was charged to run down the French coast until he could find a market for it all.

Walter kept both his boys on the move, with only short, secret visits home. One wintry evening they arrived under cover of darkness. The girls sat close by a candle, trying to read; Carew was picking out a tune on his lute; and Walt played with a little wooden soldier Arthur had whittled for him. As George and John ducked under the lintel, Walt looked up, face aglow with admiration.

"Where's your sword and armour, John?" he cried, jumping from his seat. "Tell us how you took your prize."

"Hush, Walt. We would all like to hear how you captured the *Conception*, my boys," said Walter as he threw another log onto the blaze.

"Oh yes, please, please do tell," Walt piped up, with cheeks flushed with the excitement of being allowed to stay up so late to see his stepbrothers. "Was she full of treasure – gold and jewels and all sorts of fine stuff? Did you put them all to the sword, George? Did you cut them all to ribbons?"

"Quiet, boy," Walter commanded. "Curb your impatience, you little oaf. Let them speak."

So George recounted the story of their adventure. "With the ships well victualled, we'd been down as far as La Rochelle. After finding good trade there, we loaded a cargo of salt to bring back. I was on the *Katherine*, while John had charge of the *Nicholas of Kenton*."

Walter used the *Nicholas* whenever his other vessels were out of commission. Like the *Katherine*, the *Nicholas* was fitted out as a man-of-war, on the face of it to repel any French attack, but in reality to take any prize that came their way.

"We had a fair wind behind us, and as we came into the waters off the Scillies, we sighted the Portingale. She was making heavy weather of it into the gale, and we soon came upon her," said George, puffing out his broad chest. "Father, she did look well laden. I hailed John to see if he thought we might venture to take her."

John scowled. "I said we should be wary," he said, knitting his brows together. "Well, we could capture any Frenchman with impunity, Father, but I feared that to take this one might bring us to trouble. But I was persuaded."

"I own I was full of the thrill of it and eager to take her," George blustered. "John agreed to support me. So we closed in on the quarry. Ha, ha, young Walt – we loosed off some ordnance. *Boom. Boom. Boom.*" George's fist came down on the oak board three times.

Walt was by now bouncing up and down. Katherine pressed her lips together and gave George a disapproving stare. His face coloured, but he pressed on.

"We fired a few broadsides. Not to sink her, but to frighten the crew. That threw them into a state. They knew we were better armed and more nimble to turn about and give fire. With all the smoke billowing around they took fright and set to flee. They came around and made to outrun us before the wind. Well, we know those waters right well," said George, teeth flashing as he grinned at Walt, who was hanging on every word, mouth agape.

Carew set aside his lute, setting the strings jangling, and leaned forward.

John nodded and tried to pick up the story. "We chased them all that day long, and as the skies grew dark we came alongside again."

"Well, my boys, then I donned my armour," George interrupted. He was not going to let his brother have the glory of telling the tale. "I picked fifteen of our men, our best fighting men, all heavily armed with swords and cutlasses, and some with knives held between their teeth! We came alongside the *Conception*, threw over the grappling hooks, and our men swarmed over the scrambling nets. We were on board before the Portingales could put up much of a fight."

"Oh, oh, did you run them through, then?" chirped Walt. "Show me how you used your sword, George. How many did you send to the bottom of the sea?"

That boy has been spending too much time with Humphrey, thought Katherine. Her second son had favoured them with one of his rare visits but a week ago. Walt had been full of Humphrey's tales ever since.

"There was no need to spill their blood, little soldier. They quailed in fear before us. Well, I may have given them cause to shake and quake a bit as we rounded them up. I called out – quite loudly, as I would hazard it – that we would heave them overboard and drown them all!"

John looked uncomfortable, and his eyes flicked towards Katherine. "We did nothing more than lock 'em all up in the hold. Thought to bring 'em home, ship and all. But not before we assessed the value of the cargo. Irish furzes, hides and wax! That was all she was carrying." His words dripped with contempt. "Shame she was leaving Ireland, not running in the other direction." A disdainful glance at George. "Perhaps then she'd have proven a prize more worthy of all this fuss. Not that I'm against taking prizes, Father, as you know well. Far from it! But 'tis better to take 'em when they're heavily laden with exotic spices, silks, porcelain, and suchlike. It's not worth it for Irish hides and wax."

"But then," said George, turning their attention back to himself rather more dramatically than was necessary, "dark clouds came upon the waters and a fearful wind came up. Aye, it came so rough, the waves so high, we feared we'd join our captives at the bottom of the sea! We could do no more than run before that wind. It carried us all the way back to Cork, which place the *Conception* had but lately left. There we put all the Portingales ashore and waited for the storm to die down before we set off again to bring her home."

As they ran for Exmouth, George said, he had captained the captured prize, with the *Katherine* under John's command. The *Nicholas*, with John Philips at the helm, ran alongside to protect them. George told how they had rounded Land's End and passed the Lizard with no more ado. "When we came to Mousehole we saw a Yarmouth ship; one that had surely seen the Portingale in Cork, and knew her well," he continued. "But the master was easily placated with a bale of cloth and persuaded to keep quiet. And so we went on. As we passed Falmouth, another saw us; one that could have caused us more concern. 'Twas the *Anne Galant*, one of the Queen's ships – you know her, Father? But again we were able to persuade her boatswain not to give us up, though this time it cost us two bales of cloth. We put it out that we had taken her off some Frenchmen, though I doubt he believed us."

Hmm, thought Katherine. It was easy to understand John's frustration. They'd had to give up some of the cargo. Walter had not only paid the messenger, but a tidy sum had gone to Vice Admiral Yonge, to no profit. Then he had put up an even larger amount in bail for George's liberty. No wonder John was wondering if it was worth it.

"Well, we came to Popery and set our man ashore to bring you news. But as we came away we were again driven back by the wind into Looe. There, as you know, Father, I was arrested and the Portingale confiscated. 'Twas a good thing we divided the cargo ere we left Cork, and the *Katherine* and the *Nicholas* could bring some cloth and hides home."

Save for the spitting log, the room was silent as they digested George's story.

Walter sat Walt on his knee. "Well now, my little pirate, what do you think of this tale?"

Walt looked into his father's eyes, steady and fearless. "Why, sir, I should like to take a fine prize when I am old enough to captain one of your ships. But I shall take a Spaniard." He jumped down and stamped his feet hard on the flagstones. "I do so hate those Spaniards," he cried.

Walter smiled to see such belligerence in Walt's usually sunny face. "Why do you hate the Spaniards so? My son, what do you have against the men of Spain?" he asked, as the boy stood his ground.

"Well, Mother was weeping when she came home from Exeter last summer. When I asked her why, she said it was on account of the ways of the Spaniards," said Walt, looking over at Katherine to see if he'd spoken well. "I hate them for causing my mother to weep, and for all the bad deeds they do. I'll run 'em all through if I get the chance! And Humphrey says the Spaniards have ships loaded full of gold and jewels that they carry from the new lands across the sea, just waiting for us to take."

At this they all laughed, and Katherine took his hand. "Well now, my brave boy, have a care with those words. Remember our Queen has taken to husband the King of the Spaniards."

To which the boy replied, "Well, Humphrey says the Queen is old. And Humphrey says the Lady Elizabeth is young and beautiful and ever so clever. And Humphrey says—"

At which Katherine interrupted him, saying, "I think we have heard enough of what Humphrey says for one day! 'Tis time you were abed."

When they rose the next morning, George and John had gone.

"What will become of George when he goes before the court? Will John have to appear beside him?" Katherine asked a few days later.

"George will not appear at the court, Katherine-Kate. It grieves me to kiss goodbye to so much good coin for his bail. But I cannot afford to have him arrested again, or a bigger fine imposed in recompense for the Portingales." A wolfish smile lit Walter's face, and his teeth gleamed. "Never fear, my love. I have many strings to my bow; many friends in high places."

THIRTY-THREE
1557–1558
KATHERINE

FEW CAME TO THEIR DOOR THAT CHRISTMASTIDE. THE TWELFTH Night revels were subdued. Everyone went in fear of the sickness. None knew how it spread; none knew whom it might strike next.

In the New Year news came, told to John as he went to Exmouth to check their ships. It was the worst news for England.

"The French King watched his chance for revenge for Saint-Quentin. In December, King Philip sent word to London of an impending attack," John explained. "They decided to send reinforcements under the Earl of Rutland. But with so many laid low by the sickness they struggled to find fit men. It wasn't until the second day of January that Rutland's expedition finally took ship. They were too late. The French attacked across the frozen marshes to the seaward and held the entrance to the harbour and the fort that commands it. After heavy bombardment, Calais was surrendered on the seventh day of January. Calais, our last bastion across the Channel, is lost."

"I know the lie of the land there," said Walter, in a voice that cracked with emotion. "I can see how it would be." He shook his head and his shoulders slumped. "More's the pity the Queen was foolhardy enough to send Englishmen to support her husband's Imperial Army. Oh, I suppose it was bad luck to have so many taken with the sickness. But here's the real fault: all our generals to a man assumed the French wouldn't attack in midwinter. But that's just what they did; took us by surprise. In warfare you must always plan for the unexpected. To think, Calais lost! Whatever would King Henry say to that? His daughter's made a rare mess of it all! Fanatical Catholic ways! Spanish marriage! Pshaw!"

Katherine, not for the first time, felt a grudging pang of sympathy for the sad and ageing Queen, who, according to Kat, was once again convinced that she was with child. No one gave that story much credence. "Well, husband, had she continued to rule on her own as the warrior Queen who swept aside Northumberland and Jane Grey, the country would be in a better place. It was her marriage that was her undoing." But then she remembered Agnes Prest. "I do believe she's had a hard and lonely life. But I can't forgive the cruelty done in her name these last years. I wish we could be done with her Spanish war and her Spanish ways too."

Walt looked up from his book.

"I leave tomorrow for London, sweeting, for I am now a Member of the Queen's Parliament," Walter announced as they sat by the fire.

"Well, well! I never thought to see you a Parliament man, Walter! I doubt you'll like it with all that talk and pontificating, but at least you're not bound for the wars."

"Your brother seems to find advantage in being in the Parliament. So do your Carew relations. I've been put forward for Wareham, being an Admiralty man, of course," he said with a wry laugh.

Katherine knew that the Portuguese merchants were still complaining and would likely take their case to the Privy Council.

"They'll push for payment for the loss of their cargo, though the *Conception* has long since been restored to her owners," Walter went on. "They'll look to place the blame squarely on my shoulders. After all, I own the *Katherine*; I victualled and financed them. My position will be different as a Parliament man. It may serve its purpose."

She looked into his face, and saw his grin. "Fie, husband, I think you enjoy these scrapes," she quipped.

"I will own a thrill of pleasure in finding a way to turn events to our advantage, my dear."

"Spoken like the true pirate you are," she laughed, and hugged him close. She wasn't worried about all this pirating. After all, her own family really had for generations run ships across the sea. They hadn't disdained to take a prize or two when opportunity came their way. Arthur was building up his own fleet and, like all the seafarers of the West, he too knew how to tread the line. England's enemies were fair game, but sometimes honest traders in the wrong place at the wrong time might also be relieved of their cargoes. She saw no ill in it, provided lives were not put at unnecessary risk.

So she waved him off, London-bound, and early in February, Walter presented a writ to the Privy Council, claiming the right of privilege as a burgess of the town of Wareham. That was the last they heard of the *Conception*. Walter came home with a commission to put his ships at the Queen's command to defend the coast.

Eliza had come from Modbury, where Mother remained, infirm and almost blind. They sat in the warm May sunshine beside the open door, listening to the call of a distant cuckoo, sipping a cool mug of small ale Bessie had set down beside them.

"Visit if you can, Katherine-Kate. Go before the year is out; I doubt she'll be here at Christmas. She's spent the last months worrying about all sorts of land arrangements. It's as if she feels she must set her house in order. She kept going on about lands over by Webberton; something she must get done before Arthur went off to fight in France. Henry went with him, you know. He's another soldier in the making, I fear. I visited Frances, too. She's struggling with ill health at St Budeaux. She's already lost four children and is fearful that this sickness might bear off more."

Not for the first time, Katherine gave thanks that she had been blessed with a fine crew of sturdy children.

"Since Cardinal Pole granted him absolution for the sin of taking a widow to wife and he promised that we'd stay apart, my John has picked up a few livings."

"And did you?" asked Katherine with a grin. "Stay apart, I mean?"

"That would be telling, wouldn't it?" Eliza replied with a rather naughty chuckle. "He has high hopes. Uncle George seems to be climbing the Church's greasy pole again. I think he will be able to help."

John Pollard had gone to his nephew, Arthur's friend Sir John Pollard, who had a house in the fashionable district of St Helen's by Bishopsgate. Eliza probably visited him there, or at The Slade, her official residence after he was deprived.

"John took the sickness last springtime," said Eliza, a frown crossing her still-lovely features. "He made his will, with Kat and Uncle George to stand executors. Of course, he dared not name me, but he's assured me that he's left lands to my boy Philip. And he's made ample provision for me with lands he has of the cathedral chapter over at Sidbury, Dawlish and Bradninch. So fear not, I am well looked after. But oh, I'd much rather be at his side."

No more than a week later, Eliza and Katherine were sitting on the bench in the orchard, watching the lambs playing in the meadow, when Katherine's son John came into view. She looked expectantly at him, hoping he might have news. It was high time she had a grandchild.

But John shook his head. He had news of Arthur, who was back from the wars. "He's having a lot of work done at Dartington Hall. It'll be such a fine place, Mother, with the hall repaired and new chambers added. There's good hunting in the park. He says as soon as it's ready, you and Walter must visit him and Mary. Now, here's letters for you, Aunt Eliza." He passed a packet to Eliza, who could hardly wait to tear the away the seals.

After a few moments she looked up, her face a picture of joy and excitement. "May God be praised! He does now seem much restored, though he says he still coughs at times. The Archdeacon of Totnes has not been so fortunate. Katherine, you remember William Fawell, the last prior of St Nicholas? Well, he ended his long life last July, and my John is to be Archdeacon in his stead! Think of it, Katherine-Kate! I'm overjoyed to see him restored to such a position." Eliza's smile grew wide as she clapped her hands together.

"That is happy news. But surely, Eliza, you cannot be happy that you must make such pretence to live apart?" asked Katherine.

"Of course, I would rather it were otherwise. But Totnes is not so far from The Slade. And with the Queen we have now, what choice do we have?" said Eliza with a grin.

Spring brought better weather, but the sickness kept its grip.

Katherine kept the children close to home, even forbidding the boys their visits to the quayside. She dared not visit Mother at Modbury. In August, John sent word that his father-in-law, Richard Chudleigh, was dead. With Christopher still across the sea, John would have to play his part in caring for the family until his return.

"He was the best of men," said Katherine sadly. "We shall be the poorer for his loss."

She worried that Walter must be away so often, but he showed no sign of illness. Unlike the Queen. There were rumours all that summer that she was very ill.

Eliza visited again. "Everyone says the Queen's not been the same since Calais was lost. It was bad enough after the Spaniard left her, but now she's sunk into a deep depression. Constantly worrying about the succession! Some say she still clings to the hope that she's with child. Now that doesn't seem likely, does it?"

"Perhaps, Eliza, she deserves to suffer."

"But she had a sorry time of it as a young girl, didn't she? To be feted as Princess of Wales for so long, then at a stroke declared illegitimate, then to see her mother so shunned... no wonder it turned her."

"Well," said Katherine, "the other princess had no less sorrow in her childhood. Her father had her mother's head cut off! What could be worse than that? I'll never forget that red-haired girl I met on that visit to Hunsdon, how she turned to our Kat for love and affection, though even then she was so clever. No doubt both those royal women wish they'd been born men! Then there would have been so much less trouble."

"Kat says the Queen's still furious with her sister," whispered Eliza. "She refused point-blank to marry the Duke of Savoy last year, though Philip demanded it. Our Kat's taught that one well. She won't be pushed around."

They burst out laughing, thinking of Kat instilling such independence in the feisty woman who might soon be their Queen.

"Well, if not the Lady Elizabeth, then who *will* succeed?" asked Eliza.

"Be careful. Who knows who may be listening?" Katherine cautioned.

On November mornings the mist was sometimes so thick she could barely make out Hayes Wood at all. The air was still and damp on that particular Saturday when she heard hooves drumming in the lane outside. Someone was approaching at speed, full early. Katherine ran to the door to see George leap from his horse, leave the reins trailing, and hurtle past her.

"Father! Father!" he called. "I'm come from Bedford House, Father! Lord Russell sent a messenger straight from London!"

"Well, boy, out with it. Whatever is it that makes you wake us all so rudely?" chafed Walter, struggling into his doublet. Being disturbed so early had not put him in a good temper. "Have the French declared war again? Or has the Queen decided to set us against the Scots, though there be no coin left in her coffers to bear the cost?"

"No, Father, this is much more important than any of those things. The Queen is dead!" cried George.

Carew and Walt had just bundled down the stairs, followed closely by Mary and Margaret. Bessie and the other servants crowded in, just in time to see Walter dance Katherine round the room.

"Get word to the church, George. They must ring out the bells!"

"What, to mark the passing of Queen Mary?" asked Carew.

"No, my son, to tell all that we shall have a new Queen in her stead," said Walter. "Now we shall see a new order. May God be praised."

"Surely this will bring us good fortune, Walter," Katherine cried, her voice warm and joyful. She felt light, free, as if a great weight had lifted from her.

"Oh yes, for certain it will! This is a day to dance in the street, my love." She could feel his excitement as he lifted her clean off her feet and squeezed her tight. He set her down and looked into her eyes as he kept her hands in his. "I have a mind to stand back from the business, Katherine-Kate. I've come to a decision. I'll go to sea no more. I want to spend my time with my own true love."

She looked at him sharply. "You're not ill, Walter?" she asked in mock astonishment.

"No, no, I'm as hale and hearty as any man could be at my great age," said he, with a chuckle. "But my boys can take things forward now. It's their time, you know. I want to give them more responsibility while I look to our brood. I'm afraid I'll be under your feet a lot more."

"So must I say farewell to my pirate husband, then? I'll rather miss him, I think."

"Not so fast, hussy! I thought we might find time for another voyage on the *Katherine Raleigh* soon," he murmured, and kissed her, long and lingering. "A new Queen will bring us back to a better way of worship, as I've always wanted," he continued when at last they drew breath. "I think I'll put my name forward to be warden of our church. They'll want sound heads to manage a reversal of all Queen Mary's changes without stirring up the people again. You were right; Parliament's not for me either. I'm done with it, and with serving in high places. I want to be a simple country squire with my own dear wife and family. Later, perhaps you and I shall retire to a little house in the city and live and love forever." And he took her in his arms again and held her so tight she could barely breathe. "Katherine-Kate, my own love, I am the luckiest man alive," he declared.

WALTER

He felt a wave of peace and contentment wash over him. God was good. A new, Queen sat upon the throne. The future was bright.

He paused at the foot of the stair, lips parted. There she was, framed in the doorway as though captured by Master Holbein, King Henry's painter. He felt breathless just looking at her. After all those years, the magic had never faded. He wanted to hold that picture in his mind until his dying day. She was still his own love; his own Katherine-Kate! He watched her turn to ruffle Walt's hair. She was still as slender and bewitching as the *Trinity* nymph who had captured him. Her head tipped back, and she laughed, warm and soft as summer rain. Her eyes found his. Her love for him shone from those lovely eyes. And, oh, how he loved her! On that glorious, jubilant day, he was the luckiest man alive.

He stepped forward and took her hands, beaming as though his face would split. "Oh, Katherine-Kate, my dearest, dearest love, you lit a fire in my heart that day on the *Trinity;* such a blaze as shall never be put out, shall never grow old, shall never change."

She laughed up at him, and his heart swelled. He noticed Walt watching them with a slow smile spreading across his bright face.

But true Love is a durable fire
In the mind ever burning;
Never sick, never old, never dead,
From itself never turning.

(*Walsinghame* by Sir Walter Raleigh)

PART FOUR
AFTERWORD

EXETER, 1594

KATHERINE

Perhaps it was the moonlight that woke her, stealing silvery soft between the bed-hangings to fall slanting across her pillow. More likely it was the sharp stab of pain in her hip that wrenched her from her restless slumber. In these past months that unwelcome visitor had plagued her both night and day. Twinging tendrils of torture relentlessly explored her back and the length of her leg, cutting and searing, twining and clinging, never letting go. Small wonder that she slept lightly, tossing and turning in the sumptuous bed; the bed that held pride of place in the house close by Exeter's Palace Gate that had been her home for a quarter of a century. Walter had persuaded her at last, and they had enjoyed their quiet twilight years in the red stone house she had come to love. The story of those years belonged to her children, not to her.

She must acknowledge it. She was an old woman. She had seen more than her allotted threescore and ten summers, and been lithe and limber until this last affliction. And God be praised for that mercy. Why, only two years since, she'd ridden to Greenway Court to see the new gardens Adrian had set out for John. But now she struggled to climb the stairs, leaning hard on Mother Cosens and Marie.

She stared at the gleaming threads shimmering on the embroidered tester above her head; the cope from St Sidwell's. Strange that she could call to mind such vivid memories of long ago, while last week's news faded even as it was told. Strange that the faces of the dead seemed as real to her as those of the living. Perhaps it was the way of old people.

A tear slowly traced the curve of her cheek. So many gone on before, and she still soldiering on. She ticked them off on her fingers: Grandmother Carew, Johnny, little Otho, Katie, Joanie, Kat, Eliza, Frances, Peter, Arthur, Agnes, Bessie, Father, Mother. Oh, and Humphrey, her brilliant second boy, lost to the cruel waters of the ocean as he headed home from the New World he had so longed to claim. Arrogant, proud Humphrey, who, as the Queen said, "hath no good hap at sea". Ah yes, Katherine had wept for Humphrey, though she'd not seen much of him in those last years when he was busy petitioning the Queen: an academy for young gentlemen; a passage to the North; money for his voyages.

She breathed a long, heavy sigh. Worst of all, Walter too had left her. They had known the day would come, with him fifteen years older and she so hale and hearty. He had teased her that she'd soon forget him. "The good men of Exeter will line up at your door to wed so pretty a widow ere I am cold in the grave," he'd said, with a shadow of the grin she loved so much.

A fleeting smile touched her lips as she remembered how they had laughed together, until Walter started to cough, his breath so hard-won at the end. His jest wasn't so far off the mark. Two well-heeled merchants, both widowers and late in life, had come a-courting. She snorted. It must have been her lands they craved, or a wish to forge alliance with her boys. She'd soon sent them packing! Made it clear that until her dying day she would remain Katherine Raleigh, proud widow of the finest man in all of Devon – nay, the finest in all England.

She stretched out her arm across the bed and found nought but an empty space. It was more than ten years now. She needed him still; ached to feel his touch, to hear his voice, to see his smile. She went often to the coffer where his clothes were laid away, hoping to catch some faint trace of him still lingering amongst the folded doublets and cloaks. Soon they would be reunited. Soon she would rest beside him in Mary Major's Church. She felt tears stinging her eyes again.

This would not do. She must put aside grief or it would consume her. She must think of those that remained. Four fine sons, a daughter, a stepdaughter, and one of Walter's boys still lived. She had grandchildren aplenty. She should think on them.

She sat up and pulled back the bed-hangings a little further. The moon still shone bright as day, filling the space around her bed with its eerie light. It reminded her of another moonlit room, long ago at Poer Hayes. A boy kneeling at the window, his earnest face glowing with hope and joy. Walt! She remembered it as though it were but yesterday. How she'd climbed the stair, avoiding the third step lest its creaking woke them; Mary's golden hair escaped in a tangle from her nightcap and spread out in all its glory, mingling with Margaret's dark tresses; Carew's snores ringing out as he slept the sleep of the righteous; Walt's bed empty. How she'd found him at the window, eyes fixed on a glowing moon; the harvest moon, or perhaps the hunter's moon, near its fullest. How old was he then? Perhaps seven or eight, but already with that precocious command of words.

"Mother," he'd whispered softly, "she's so beautiful. Surely I could reach out and touch her, if I could but climb so high. If I could fly near her face, I'd be able to see the whole world below me; all the seas and countries laid out just like an enormous chart."

"Wouldn't you be afraid to fall?" she asked.

"Oh, yes, I would be afraid," he answered. "But it would be worth any fall to come close to such splendour and to see such wonders."

She remembered ruffling his hair and taking a volume from the pile of books on the writing desk. Together in the moonlight they had read of how Icarus donned his wings, flew too close to the sun, fell to the ocean and drowned.

"So what do you think, my son?" she asked. "Should Icarus have heeded his father's advice? Would *you* listen? Or would you fly too high, only to fall?"

"Well," he said, "the father, Daedalus, also warned him not to fly too low, lest his wings become waterlogged. So Icarus heeded part of his advice. But he was too caught up in excitement to realise how high he had gone." He paused, his forehead puckering as he wrestled with his thoughts. "I think I would deem it all worth the risk for such a view of the world, and to touch such beauty. Oh, Mother, I do fear I too might be overcome by the thrill of it all." And Katherine remembered how she'd felt a cold chill run down her spine as she hustled the boy to his bed.

Walt had indeed flown high in the world; so very close to his Sovereign Lady Elizabeth, that radiant being he likened in his fine verses to the moon in all her splendour. Bright, handsome, charming Walt! True, he had followed Humphrey's example overmuch, and Katherine had berated him for that. But he had such a way with words; and he was a fine soldier and a dazzling courtier, so tall and elegant, resplendent in his pearl-encrusted doublets and his fine velvet cloaks. Their lovely boy! All his talents grown from those seeds planted long ago as he stood at her knee, when she was still the centre of his small world. Another tear; another heavy sigh. All boys must break free and take their place in their own world. Even their own dear boy. It was the way of things.

She wished Walter had lived to see him so honoured; to see him rise above all others as he basked in the favour of his Queen. Now his fine-feathered wings were clipped. Like Icarus, he'd come crashing down when he gave offence to his jealous mistress. Lying there in the moonlight, Katherine could see it all quite clearly. Poets played the courtly game; courtiers praised her beauty still. But if ever the Queen looked in the glass she must see the sands of her time running clean away. None should be surprised if Kat's former charge, transformed from that lonely child to Gloriana, was jealous. Jealous of what those younger women might have that she could not: love, marriage, children. All fond looks, all fine words in praise of beauty must be for her alone, and woe betide any who cast their gaze elsewhere. Walt had cast more than a gaze in Bess Throckmorton's direction, that was certain, and they'd both paid for it in the Tower. Released but not yet restored to favour, he was kicking his heels at Sherbourne, itching to set off on some voyage of discovery; to bring back riches for the dazzling goddess he longed to serve.

Suddenly the moon was lost behind a cloud, the moonbeams snuffed out. Hauling her aching body from the cosy warmth, Katherine pulled a thick nightgown over her shift. With gritted teeth she hauled herself from the bed to kneel and pray for her youngest son.

Marie found her there when she came in to draw back the hangings. Marie's father had served the Raleighs in Exeter, and before that at the farmhouse out near Budleigh. When faithful Bessie died, Marie had slipped naturally into her place. "Let me help you back to bed," she coaxed. "Rest there this day."

"I will go down, Marie," Katherine said, fixing the maid with a defiant stare.

So when she was dressed they helped her, step by painful step, down to the parlour and sat her by the fire. Later, since it was a bright spring day, she had them take her into the pretty little courtyard. She turned her face up to the sun, thinking how Agnes used to chide her not to let it brown her skin. No matter now; she was as wrinkled as a walnut. She'd just enjoy the warmth. Her eyes closed. She was so very tired.

She opened her eyes again and looked around the walled garden. Foaming blossom festooned the pear trees she had trained along the wall on the shady side, while the cherries deserved their place in the sun. Over in the sunniest corner, where two walls met at right angles, was her favourite tree: an apricot, or apricock, as many called them. She smiled, thinking of dear Walter bringing that little tree from London when first they came to live in Exeter. He'd known that she would miss her orchard, and so, with an introduction from Kat, he'd begged a seedling from the royal gardeners. How she had fussed over that tree through the years, hanging cloths around its branches to shield the delicate early flowers from frost. How she'd enjoyed its luscious bounty.

She hauled herself from her seat and managed somehow to cross the courtyard, thinking to see if any tiny fruits had set amongst the branches. She didn't reach it.

They must have carried her back to bed, for she was staring up at Walter's tester once again. The girl she called granddaughter was peering at her, offering the apothecary's potion. Kitty Hooker; such a pretty girl, so like her mother, Walter's Mary. Katherine's mind rambled over memories of the day Kitty wed John Hooker's son Robert at the Church of St Mary in Wolborough. John Raleigh, grown wealthy from his shipping interests and his wife's money, had put on quite a show for the wedding of a favourite niece. It had been Katherine's first outing in those hollow years after Walter's death. She had visited her friend Joan Yarde, and Joan's example and kind words had been a healing balm in her darkest days. Joan now lay in the cold earth at All Saints, high above the wooded slopes of the Bradley Valley; and steady, reliable John Raleigh lay in St Mary's on the other side of that same valley. So many gone! She gave herself a feeble little shake, and wondered what had set her to thinking such morbid thoughts. Ah yes, it was Kitty Hooker standing by the bedside, asking if she felt better.

How Father would have complimented her on her well-ordered household, with her serving people in their new livery. She had a fancy to eat meat more often. It was expensive in a time of dearth, but what of that? She would not see another summer. She felt Johnny in the sunbeam that touched her face that spring morning, the eighteenth day of April. She felt it. Johnny was not far away. It was time.

"Marie, will you send for my grandson, Arthur Gilbert? I must set down what is needful. My accounts on earth must be settled."

"Nay, Mistress, you seem much better," the maid demurred. "Sir John will be here in a day or two."

"Do as I say. I cannot wait for my dear sons. I know my time is done," Katherine said, in a voice that could not be denied.

He came at once; the best of Humphrey's boys, with more sense in his head than his brothers all together. Certainly more than the eldest boy, another John, who had all Humphrey's arrogance combined with Peter Carew's reckless ways.

"Write my words, Arthur. I would go to my Maker with all my debts honoured. The butcher, the apothecary, and the tailor who made the servants' livery: all must be paid in full. My faithful servants must be well provided for," she said. "I leave the disposal of my soul to God."

Kitty came and stood by the bed, tears streaming down her cheeks.

"Kitty's to have this great bed, and my saddle and cloth."

Marie stood twisting her apron in her hands.

"Marie shall have my clothes. I have no fine jewels to leave. No, it's like that story Johnny and I read with old Smythe, of Cornelia the Roman matron. Like her, I have my dear sons for my jewels. How brightly they do shine."

Just as Grandmother Carew had said all those years ago, her boys were the crowning achievement of Katherine's short time upon the earth. She hadn't seen new worlds or followed all her dreams. But she'd known Walter's love, and she'd set her boys on their exciting path in life; encouraged them to embrace the new and to think beyond the horizon.

When she was satisfied, Arthur called Bolte the merchant and Jerman her servant to bear witness.

"Now, bring me that book, *The Book of Martyrs*. I would read what was written of me."

Marie brought the book, which fell open to the marked page.

"It says that I am Katherine Raleigh, a woman of noble wit and good and godly ways."

"Grandmother," quavered Arthur, tears clouding his blue eyes, "Master Foxe's words hardly do justice to the love and duty you have shown us all."

"That's as may be. I have always wondered, dear boy, whether 'twas my Walter and John Hooker that put Foxe up to it. Too late to ask now," she mused as she rested back on the pillow.

The world was fading. Through the mists she saw a simple serving woman dressed in a coarse woollen kirtle. Agnes Prest!

She had but to follow Agnes towards the light, where Walter waited, hand outstretched. "Come, Katherine Raleigh, my woman of noble wit."

Walt
Westminster, October 1618

His last words. In the pressing gloom he could barely make them out, inscribed in his Bible which lay open beside the guttering candle.

> *But from this earth, this grave, this dust,*
> *My God shall raise me up, I trust.*

His last words, added to that poem written long ago as an exhortation to enjoy love before time's passing takes its toll; before it is too late. Now it stood as an epitaph. Perhaps he even meant it as a declaration of faith. He set the quill down carefully next to his pipe, and flexed his aching fingers.

His last words. His head dropped to his chest and he squeezed his eyes tight shut. After a moment, his chin came up. He must push down that heavy feeling in his chest. Think of Bess. Brave, beautiful, stalwart Bess. He'd put on a fine show when she left him; pressed a remembrance, a writing, into her hand as he embraced her. She'd make it known if they denied him his chance to speak. He would be heard. Oh, yes, he would be heard! He gritted his teeth. Suppressing a shiver, he wrapped the rough blanket more tightly around his shoulders.

Bess! The love of his life; the mother of his boys. Bess would endure. Only Carew, their third boy, born within fortress walls, was left to comfort her. Their first son, snatched away so soon, had left hardly any impression, for all that they gave him such a noble name. But the loss of their second boy had been a bitter blow. That lively, courageous, reckless lad had borne his father's name so proudly. Now he lay far, far away, buried before an altar in the land of his dreams; lost on that last voyage, at the hand of a Spaniard.

He felt tears pricking his eyes, and rubbed his hand across his brow. With an effort, he focused on the inscription in his Bible. Words. Words. Words were the mainstay of his time upon the earth. He'd used words to persuade and to cheer; to sympathise and to defend; to reach agreement and to set out his case in dispute. With words he'd praised and flattered; sought favour and given it; told of his adventures; painted pictures of distant lands and of times long past. A fleeting smile touched his lips.

Some trace of him would remain in his writings long after he was gone.

He leaned back, drew in a deep breath, and closed his eyes. A memory flashed into his mind. He was back in Devon, behind the house where he had been born. It was one of those shining autumn days aflame with vibrant colour; summer's warmth not quite forgotten. He smiled. Oh, the satisfaction of brushing his well-shod feet through the piles of rustling leaves that lingered in corners all around the old house! In his mind he stood again before the apple store with its heavy oak door looming black in the warm stone wall. How old was he? Very young, surely, for his mother's dark gown seemed to stretch, oh, so high, above him. It was a fine gown of silk; he remembered the feel of it when he reached out to her. Oh, the comfort of burying his head in that soft fabric when some trifling fall upset his infant vanity and brought him to tears!

She was crouching down beside him, her face close to his. He could see her calm brown eyes sparkling with humour and love. She selected a large key from the bunch at her girdle and put it in his tiny hand. The memory was so vivid that he could feel its ponderous weight and the cool surface of the curving ironwork as it rested in his palm.

"Do you like apples, my boy?" she asked with a smile.

"Yes, Mother," he replied, stepping closer.

"Well, if you learn to use this key well, you may unlock the store and select a sweet apple from within. But it is no easy task. The key is heavy and you will have to stretch high to reach the lock. Then you must work hard to learn how to turn it."

Trembling, he'd reached for the huge iron padlock. She was right. For one so small it was no easy task. But the thought of that sweet, juicy apple kept him working until he had the key safely in its place.

"Now you must turn it, so," she said, placing her hand over his.

She showed how he must hold the key, feel for its right place in the lock. After what seemed like an age the key suddenly turned under his hand. She removed the padlock and the door swung open.

"You've worked hard, and now you may choose your prize."

He had stretched out his hand and chosen a perfect rosy apple. Now, in his imagination, he tasted the crisp sharpness of that tart English apple, and fancied he caught again the faint scent of lavender that had always clung to his mother's clothes. He remembered the feel of the hard wooden bench, warm from the sun, where they sat.

When he had finished his treat she took something from the folds of her skirts. "Now, my son," she said softly, with a hint of laughter in her voice, "here is a different sort of key that I may give to you."

It was a bundle of parchment leaves sewn together. Each had a strange shape inked upon it under a thin covering of cow's horn.

"How may this be a key, Mother?" he asked, giggling, as his fingers touched the smooth surface of the hornbook.

"Though it looks so different, it is indeed a key," said she. "Just as you had to work hard to open the apple store, so now you must labour to learn the secrets of these shapes. When you have mastered them, and can add them all together, you will find that they can open doors to untold treasures; to tales of long ago, of distant lands beyond your imagining, and of the deeds and thoughts of men. See, here is 'A', that stands for the apple you have eaten with such relish."

Together they traced the shape until he could remember it well. She took a book from the seat and showed him how to find the letter 'A' amongst all the others on its closely printed pages. Then she read to him in her soft, lilting voice with its hint of a Devon burr, until he fell asleep in the warm sunshine.

He came back to reality with a jolt, and shifted in his seat. What a key she gave him that day in the orchard! Books had been his closest companions all his days. Though he'd sailed the wide oceans and seen wonders with his own eyes, it was the treasures in the chest of books he took with him everywhere that always proved his inspiration and his solace. Now there was but one book left to him, his Bible, in which he had written those last lines.

The last of so many words: all those paeans he had written to his gracious Queen, that glittering, clever, imperious lady, gone now; his history of the world, still unfinished; and all his other attempts, some completed to his satisfaction, others mere rough notions in his mind. Had he taken enough time to write about her: that noble, kindly lady whose loving care had so surely started him on his path towards greatness and honour? He scratched his head. He could think of only one passing reference to a mother in all his works:

Our mothers' wombs the tiring-houses be,
Where we are dressed for life's short comedy.

A fine turn of phrase! She had dressed him well for the parts he'd played on the stage of life. In his time he'd known success as a soldier, an adventurer, a courtier and a poet. Would that he had heeded more her gentle advice and performed equally well as a son, a lover, a husband, a brother, a father and a friend. He shook his head again. His mother, that woman of noble wit, had done so much more than costume him to take his place in the world.

He got up stiffly and threw the blanket carelessly across the narrow bed, lay down and stretched, hoping to ease the nagging pain in his joints. All too soon there would be a cure for that; a cure for all his ills.

He must have slept for a time. Turning his tired eyes upwards, he peered into the half-light, searching for the square of light; the one tiny window set high in the cold stone walls. The sky was dark, but the door creaked as it swung open; the priest, come again with a candle.

He chuckled. "What ho, Dean Townson," he called, as cheery as a sunbeam. How surprised the man had been earlier to find him so jauntily fearless in the face of what must follow.

He would have them remember him in all his splendour, so he dressed with care: a fine doublet, an embroidered waistcoat, black taffeta breeches, a ruff-band, and elegant ash-coloured silken stockings, all topped by the black velvet gown Bess had brought for him. He placed the Queen's diamond ring on his finger. He even put on his nightcap, hiding the grey locks that had of late become somewhat unkempt. He snorted. How foolish! He would soon have no need of its warmth. Perhaps he'd give it to some poor soul come to watch the show.

He savoured each mouthful of that last breakfast; kept up a bright show of mirth as he shared a jest with the serving man who brought it. He smoked a last pipe of his favourite tobacco, drawing it deep into his lungs.

The comedy of his days was all but over. He had but one more act to perform; one last speech to deliver.

It was still early in the day when the door swung open again and a low voice said, "Sir, if you please, it is time."

Stooping to pass beneath the stone lintel, Sir Walter Raleigh stepped out into the cold, grey October morning.

Even such is Time, that takes in trust
Our youth, our joys, our all we have,
And pays us but with earth and dust;
Who in the dark and silent grave,
When we have wander'd all our ways,
Shuts up the story of our days.

These words were found after his death on the flyleaf of Sir Walter Raleigh's Bible at the Old Gatehouse near Westminster Abbey, where he had been imprisoned. They are the final verse for a poem he had written many years earlier. In his cell before his execution he had added these two lines:

But from this earth, this grave, this dust,
My God shall raise me up, I trust.

CAST LIST

NOTE: RECORDING OF BAPTISMS, MARRIAGES AND BURIALS WAS introduced in 1538, but record keeping was sporadic and many early registers are lost or damaged. There remains considerable uncertainty about many of the dates shown here.

THE CHAMPERNOWNES

Katherine Champernowne (c 1519 –1594. Our heroine. Wife of (1) Otes (Otho) Gilbert; (2) Walter Raleigh of Fardel.

Sir Philip Champernowne (c. 1479–1545). Father of our heroine. Squire of the Body to King Henry VIII. Sheriff of Devon, 1528. Knighted c. 1529.

Katherine Champernowne, née Carew (c. 1485–c. 1557). Mother of our heroine.

Kat Champernowne (c. 1502–1565). Sister of our heroine. Governess to the Princess Elizabeth and Chief Lady of the Bedchamber to Queen Elizabeth I. Wife of John Ashley (1507–1595).

Joan Champernowne the Elder (c. 1500–?). Sister of our heroine. Maid of honour to Queen Catherine of Aragon. Wife of Robert

Gamage of Coity (1500–1571).

Joan Champernowne the Younger ('Joanie') (c. 1515–1553). Sister of our heroine. Maid of honour or lady-in-waiting to Jane Seymour, Anne of Cleves, Katherine Howard and Kateryn Parr, and possibly to Anne Boleyn. Wife of Sir Anthony Denny (1501–1549), Groom of the Stool to King Henry VIII.

Elizabeth Champernowne ('Eliza') (c. 1513–1574). Sister of our heroine. Wife of (1) William Cole of The Slade, Cornwood (c. 1514–1547); (2) John Pollard (c. 1490–1560), Archdeacon of Barnstaple. Mother of Philip Cole (1539–1596), who sailed with both Humphrey and Walter and fought with Henry Champernowne in France.

John Champernowne ('Johnny') (c. 1515–1541). Brother of our heroine. Served at court. Member of the Gentlemen Pensioners. Husband of Catherine Blount (c. 1518–1558), daughter of William Blount, Lord Mountjoy (c. 1478–1534). Died in Vienna.

Henry Champernowne (1538–1570). Nephew of our heroine. Son of Johnny. Soldier and supporter of the French Huguenots. Husband of Catherine Edgecumbe (c. 1541-c. 1624).

Frances Champernowne (c. 1522–?). Sister of our heroine. Wife of Roger Budockside (c. 1510–1576) of St Budeaux.

Sir Arthur Champernowne (c. 1524–1578). Brother of our heroine. Soldier and politician. Knighted 1549. Sheriff of Devon, 1559. Vice Admiral of the Devon Coasts from 1562. Husband of Mary Norreys (c. 1526–1570), widow of Sir George Carew. The first Champernowne at Dartington Hall, Devon.

John Hunte, rector of Modbury from 1524–1552.

Agnes Slade, nurse and serving woman to our heroine (imagined character).

Will Slade, Agnes's son and Johnny's servant (imagined character).

Bessie, maid to our heroine and niece of Agnes Slade (imagined character).

Thomas Smythe, tutor to our heroine (imagined character).

THE CAREWS

William Carew (1483–1536). Uncle of our heroine.

Katherine Carew, née Huddesfield (c. 1468–c. 1529). Grandmother of our heroine. Widow of Sir Edmund Carew (1464–1513).

Joan Carew née Courtenay (c. 1483–c. 1554). Aunt of our heroine. Daughter of Sir William Courtenay of Powderham (1451-1512).

Sir George Carew (c. 1504–1545). Cousin of our heroine. Soldier and Vice Admiral. Lost on the *Mary Rose*.

Philip Carew (c. 1505–c. 1535). Cousin of our heroine. Soldier, presumed died fighting the Turks.

Sir Peter Carew (c. 1510–1575). Cousin of our heroine. Soldier, adventurer and politician. Sheriff of Devon, 1549. Husband of Margaret Tailboys (née Skipworth) (c. 1521–1583).

Cecily Carew (c. 1512–after 1575). Cousin of our heroine. Wife of Thomas Kirkham (1504–1551).

George Carew (c. 1498–1583). Uncle of our heroine. Priest. Archdeacon of Totnes, Archdeacon of Exeter, Dean of Bristol, Dean of Exeter, Royal Chaplain and Dean of Windsor. Officiated at coronation of Queen Elizabeth I. Husband of Anne Harvey (c.1529–1605).

Sir Gawen Carew (c. 1503–1585). Uncle of our heroine. Courtier, soldier, naval commander, and politician. Husband of (1) Anne Brandon,(c.1485–before 1540), sister of Charles Brandon, (c.1484–1545) Duke of Suffolk and brother-in-law to King Henry VIII; (2) Mary Wotton; (3) Elizabeth Norwich.

THE COURTENAYS

Katherine Plantagenet Courtenay. (1479-1537). Related to our heroine through her marriage to William Courtenay (1475–1511), Earl of Devon. Sister of Elizabeth of York. Countess of Devon.

Henry Courtenay (c. 1498–1538) executed. Son of Katherine Plantagenet Courtenay, Countess of Devon. Marquess of Exeter. Husband of Gertrude Courtenay (née Bount), Marchioness of

Exeter (before 1504–1558), daughter of William Blount, Lord Mountjoy.

THE GILBERTS

Otes (Otho) Gilbert (c. 1513–1547). First husband of our heroine. Son of Thomas Gilbert (c. 1450–1529).

John Gilbert Senior (c. 1448–1539). Uncle of Otho.

Isobel Reynward (?–c. 1562). Mother of Otho. Wife of (1) John Penkervell; (2) Thomas Gilbert.

Joan Gilbert (c. 1510–?before 1547). Sister of Otho. Wife of Richard Prideaux.

Philip Penkervell (c. 1500–1562). Half-brother of Otho.

Katherine Gilbert ('Katie'). Daughter of Katherine Champernowne and Otho Gilbert. Mentioned in her father's will. One source suggests wife of George Raleigh. Fate unknown.

Sir John Gilbert (1536–1596). Son of Katherine Champernowne and Otho Gilbert. Prominent landowner. Knighted 1571. Sheriff of Devon, 1573. Vice Admiral of the Western Coasts. Deputy Lieutenant of Devon. Saw action against the Armada. Husband of Elizabeth Chudleigh.

Sir Humphrey Gilbert (c. 1537 or c.1539–1583). Son of Katherine Champernowne and Otho Gilbert. Soldier, explorer, adventurer and MP. Knighted 1569/70. Husband of Anne Aucher. Lost at sea returning from Newfoundland, which he claimed for Queen Elizabeth I.

Adrian Gilbert (c. 1541–1628). Son of Katherine Champernowne and Otho Gilbert. Chemist, garden designer, politician, and investor in voyages of exploration. Laboratory assistant to Mary Herbert (née Sydney), Countess of Pembroke, for whom he designed gardens at Wilton. Designed gardens for Sir Walter Raleigh at Sherborne. Husband of Elinor Markham,(widow of Andrew Fulford).

Otho Gilbert. Son of Katherine Champernowne and Otho Gilbert. Mentioned in father's will. Assumed died in infancy.

Edward Gilbert (c. 1510–1566). Cousin of Otho. Sea captain.

John Rowe (c. 1478–1544). Serjeant-at-Law. Legal adviser to John Gilbert Senior.

Arthur Gilbert (1577–1597 or 1604). Grandson of our heroine, and witness to her will. Son of Humphrey Gilbert. May have died at Siege of Amiens, 1594, or possibly in 1604

Jane, serving woman to our heroine (imagined character).

THE RALEIGHS

Walter Raleigh Senior (c. 1505–1581). Second husband of our heroine. Privateer, merchant, shipowner, farmer and MP. Husband of (1) Joan Drake; (2) Isabella (?) Darrel; (3) Katherine Champernowne.

George Raleigh (c. 1528–1596). Son of Walter Raleigh Senior and Joan Drake. Privateer and merchant. Listed as a sea captain for the Armada defence fleet (the *Lion*). Husband of Dorothy Snedall. Named his natural son, George Blake, alias Raleigh, as his heir.

John Raleigh (c. 1529–1588). Son of Walter Raleigh Senior and Joan Drake. Privateer and merchant. Listed as a sea captain for the Armada defence fleet. Husband of Anne Fortescue (c 1521–after1596), widow of John Gaverocke of Newton Abbot. Styled himself 'John Raleigh of Forde'.

Mary Raleigh (c. 1536–c. 1615). Daughter of Walter Raleigh Senior and Isabella (?) Darrel. Wife of (1) Hugh Snedall (c.1535–before 1579); (2) John Rouse. Daughter Katherine Sneddall ('Kitty') married Richard Hooker, son of John Hooker.

Margaret Raleigh (c. 1548–?). Daughter of Katherine Champernowne and Walter Raleigh Senior. Wife of (1) Lawrence Radford of Rockbeare and Mount Radford, lawyer, (c. 1551–1590) (2) George Hull of Larkebeare, merchant and landowner c. 1551–?).

Sir Carew Raleigh (c. 1549 or 1550–1626). Son of Katherine Champernowne and Walter Raleigh Senior. Master of horse to John Thynne of Longleat. Soldier, naval commander, and politician. Served on Humphrey Gilbert's first expedition. Knighted 1601. Vice Admiral of Dorset and lieutenant of Portland Castle. Married Dorothy, widow of John Thynne.

Sir Walter Raleigh ('Walt') (c. 1554 or 1552–1618). Son of Katherine Champernowne and Walter Raleigh Senior. Soldier, naval commander, adventurer, courtier, politician and poet. Knighted 1585. Granted royal patent to settle Virginia. Secretly married Bess Throckmorton in 1591. Led expedition to Guiana, 1594. Imprisoned in the Tower from 1603, released by James 1 in 1518 to lead an ill-fated second expedition to Guiana; arrested on his return and executed in October 1618.

Marie Weare, serving woman to our heroine and mentioned in her will. Baptised 1574 at St Mary Major, Exeter. Wife of John Pearson, (they were married in 1599 at St Mary Major, Exeter).

OTHERS

John Pollard, (c. 1490–1560). Priest. Oxford-educated son of Sir Lewis Pollard of King's Nympton, whose large family held many influential positions. Archdeacon of Barnstable, Archdeacon of Cornwall, Member of Chapel Royal, and Archdeacon of Totnes. Deprived 1554. Research that establishes links between John Pollard and Elizabeth (Eliza), the widow of William Cole, will be published in due course.

William Hurst (c.1483–1568). Wealthy Exeter merchant, Alderman, and five times Mayor of Exeter.

Joan Hurst (c. 1516–1591). Daughter of William Hurst. Second wife of Thomas Yarde.

Thomas Yarde of Bradley Manor, Newton Bushell (c. 1490–1557). Steward to John Veysey, Bishop of Exeter (c. 1462–1554).

John Hooker (1527–1601). Constitutionalist, writer, antiquarian and civic administrator. Chamberlain of Exeter from 1555. Legal adviser to Sir Peter Carew.

Agnes Prest (?–1557). Protestant martyr, executed August 1557.

ACKNOWLEDGEMENTS

A WOMAN OF NOBLE WIT HAS BEEN A LONG TIME IN THE MAKING and I'm grateful to the many people and institutions who have helped and encouraged me on my writer's journey. First, thanks are due to the National Trust English Riviera Group and to the late Mr Geoffrey Gilbert of Compton Castle for introducing me to Katherine, Mr Gilbert's 10th Great Grandmother. Also to the Dartington Hall Trust for the history I've absorbed in all the happy hours I've spent leading tours at the home of Katherine's brother Arthur. I am grateful to the Devon Rural Archive at Shilstone, near Modbury, for their help with my research into Katherine's childhood home, and to all the staff of the Devon Archives at South West Heritage Trust who have guided me in my search for secrets of Devon's sixteenth century past. Thanks also to Sandy and Ian Howard for sharing their wonderful research into the early history of Greenway, which has helped me imagine Katherine's home on the River Dart. Special thanks go to my friend, the artist, Daphne Patterson, for her beautiful painting for the front cover, and to my amazing team of test readers (you know who you are), whose suggestions and comments were absolutely invaluable in crafting Katherine's story. I am grateful to everyone at Troubador who have made publishing *A Woman of Noble Wit* a fascinating and enjoyable experience. Finally, a huge thank you to Fiona for keeping me on track, and most of all to David who has been at my side for every step

AUTHOR'S NOTE

Like most women of her time beyond royalty, Katherine Raleigh has left a light footprint on the historical record which, at the distance of more than four hundred years, can, in any case, provide little more than a bare skeleton. At best the record may give us the *when* and *what* and *where,* and that is more detailed for some than for others. It rarely tells us much about the *who,* by which I mean the personalities of the protagonists. Those details, their relationships, their conversations, their inmost dreams and desires, all the flesh upon the bones, must be supplied by creative imagination.

A Woman of Noble Wit is a work of fiction. I have used a wide range of sources for my story of Katherine's life, but the version of her history in *A Woman of Noble Wit* is my own invention. Having said that, my novel is grounded in detailed research into Katherine, her family, and the times in which they lived. Where facts are backed up by reliable source documents I have respected them. But I have found intriguing gaps, and also tantalising clues amongst the dusty documents that do remain to us, which led me to additional storylines. To list all the sources, both primary and secondary, I have consulted would run to many pages. Readers may, however, like to know that:

My title is taken from a description of Katherine's vigil with the Exeter martyr Agnes Prest which was published in the second edition of Foxe's Book of Martyrs in 1570.

The Carew/Poyntz Book of Hours is in the collection of the Fitzwilliam Museum, Cambridge.

Katherine's will was amongst the records lost during a bombing raid on Exeter in 1942. We are fortunate that a nineteenth-century scholar, T. N. Brushfield, left us a transcript of the poignant document that records her last wishes.

Scholars are divided on the exact date of birth of Katherine's most famous sons, Sir Humphrey Gilbert and Sir Walter Raleigh. It suited my narrative to choose the later dates of 1539 and 1554 respectively.

I hope you have enjoyed the life I have imagined for this remarkable woman.

To find out more about me and my writing visit my website where you will find regular blog posts about life in Tudor and Elizabethan England, Devon history, sixteenth century costume, my research, future projects and much more. Sign up for my newsletter to keep in touch.

www.rosemarygriggs.co.uk/.
R.A.G., 2021